Fatal Frost

www.transworldbooks.co.uk

Also by James Henry

First Frost

Fatal Frost

A DS Jack Frost Investigation

JAMES HENRY

BANTAM PRESS

LONDON · TORONTO · SYDNEY · AUCKLAND · JOHANNESBURG

TRANSWORLD PUBLISHERS
61–63 Uxbridge Road, London W5 5SA
A Random House Group Company
www.transworldbooks.co.uk

First published in Great Britain
in 2012 by Bantam Press
an imprint of Transworld Publishers

Written for the Estate of R. D. Wingfield by James Gurbutt
Copyright © The Estate of R. D. Wingfield 2012

James Gurbutt has asserted his right under the Copyright, Designs
and Patents Act 1988 to be identified as the author of this work.

A CIP catalogue record for this book
is available from the British Library.

ISBNs 9780593065389 (hb)
9780593065396 (tpb)

Addresses for Random House Group Ltd companies outside the UK
can be found at: www.randomhouse.co.uk
The Random House Group Ltd Reg. No. 954009

The Random House Group Limited supports the Forest Stewardship
Council (FSC®), the leading international forest-certification organization.
Our books carrying the FSC label are printed on FSC®-certified paper.
FSC is the only forest-certification scheme endorsed by the leading
environmental organizations, including Greenpeace. Our paper-procurement
policy can be found at www.randomhouse.co.uk/environment

Typeset in 11½/14½pt Caslon 540 by
Kestrel Data, Exeter, Devon.
Printed and bound by
CPI Group (UK) Ltd, Croydon, CR0 4YY.

2 4 6 8 10 9 7 5 3 1

Fatal Frost

Prologue

He fought his way through the bracken. The fence was here somewhere – all the houses in the close backed on to these woods. He knew he was in the right vicinity, having taken bearings from the bedroom lights an hour or so ago, but as night crept on and the lights disappeared one by one it became more difficult to navigate through the darkness. He had already made a detour to avoid the mad vagrant who lived in the railway carriage. Last year that crazy tramp had given the police the nod about the bank robbers who'd been stashing their gear in the woods.

Abruptly, the canopy ended and a row of sleeping detached houses came into view, bathed in bluish moonlight. The sky was still clear, after a scorcher of a day.

He was sure the house would be empty. His work often brought him to this close, and this grandiose pile had long been on his radar. He'd noticed on Friday, after showing a property across the road to some clients, movement at number 7, suitcases being packed in the back of an old Audi. The early May bank holiday weekend, a gift! Nevertheless, he was cautious with the torch beam. Though past

2 a.m. it would only take one night-owl to raise the alarm. He opened the back door with the key he'd made an impression of two years ago. That was the genius strategy: leave it as long as possible, then the trail would be cold, and people never changed locks unless . . . unless something like this happened.

He'd memorized the house layout: kitchen leading out into the hall, lounge to the left and . . . He froze suddenly as something warm brushed against his leg. He instantly felt his eyes welling up, which must have been psychosomatic, as his skin had not directly come into contact with the animal's fur itself. He reached into the pocket of the rucksack and pulled out the wire. After the battle with the dog the week before he'd made the noose in advance, which saved him having to fumble and remove his gloves, and avoided the risk of leaving prints.

He wondered about the feline instinct for danger as he easily slipped the wire over the head of the purring animal. An abrupt jolt and a brief but frantic struggle gave way to a sudden stillness as the animal succumbed to its fate. Although still watering, his eyes had now adjusted to the light, and the bright May moonlight allowed him to dispense with his torch. The white obelisk of the tall fridge-freezer stood humming softly in the corner of the kitchen – perfect. He felt a sneeze coming on as he slipped the limp furry body between a loaf of Slimcea and a bottle of Piat d'Or.

Right, first the VCR and maybe the hi-fi – after all it was a Bang & Olufsen. Though he'd have difficulty getting out through the woods, if he got too greedy. Then he'd move on to the major spoils, the real reasons for being here, upstairs in the bedroom.

Monday (1)

Detective Sergeant Jack Frost had been at his desk in Denton's Eagle Lane station since 7.30 a.m. Frost was not a natural early bird, but it being bank holiday Monday, he knew the office would be quiet and he was using the opportunity to tackle the bane of his life – paperwork.

The station ran a skeleton staff on bank holidays. This was one of station commander Superintendent Mullett's many schemes to keep payroll costs down, along with the banning of overtime since January. Mullett's reasoning for these economies was the repair work to the bomb damage sustained by the building last October, which, although barely started, was already predicted to come in at well in excess of the insurance pay-out. How Mullett could subordinate the cost of running the force to the need for fancy furnishings was beyond Frost. He was no less bemused by Mullett's assumption that, like the super himself, most of Denton's villains would be taking a bank holiday break.

So, the super was probably on the golf course, and DI Allen was also nowhere to be seen. So far, only Station Sergeant Bill

9

Wells had appeared, remarking on the fine May weather as Frost passed by the front desk on his way to the Gents, before settling back down to continue mulling over the bank holiday racing fixtures. And Miss Smith, Mullett's secretary, had put in an appearance – she was allowed overtime to meet her boss's ever-growing demand for paperwork and bureaucracy. All was peace and quiet. Apart from a burglary reported an hour ago, which PCs Jordan and Baker could manage, there was nothing doing. Maybe Mullett was right.

All being well, if Frost could tweak his car expenses a fraction, and at least make a start on the crime clear-up stats, he could be out of here by midday and meet Arthur Hanlon in the Cricketers for lunch. Cheer the tubby sod up a bit, and enjoy a spot of sunshine with the rest of Denton.

He was concentrating intently, tongue running along his bottom lip. He carefully changed the '6' into an '8' on the March garage bill. 'Well, if you won't pay me overtime, you stingy moustachioed git, I'll have to shaft you,' Frost said to himself. He took a sip of his coffee and then reached for the stapler, lining up the pages before walloping it down with the palm of his hand. Job done, he thought, and lit a celebratory Rothmans. Now the clear-up stats, although there wasn't quite the same incentive to get those filed.

At 8.15 a.m. Sergeant Wells – who had finished studying the fixtures and was now listening keenly on Johnny Johnson's portable radio to how it was all kicking off in the Falklands – was interrupted by a call. A man out walking his dog had found a dead girl on the outskirts of Denton, near the train track.

Superintendent Stanley Mullett sat inside the Rover in the car park of the Eagle Lane station listening intently. The events in the South Atlantic had him glued to his seat. The Argentine cruiser the *Belgrano* had been torpedoed. It made him proud to be British.

As the news drew to a close and Jimmy Savile was once more given the run of the airwaves, Mullett switched off the radio and smoothed his moustache in the mirror before emerging into the bright May sunshine. Another promisingly warm day, he thought, and very nice it was too. As he locked the car he looked forlornly at the splintered windows of the canteen building. Six months since a terrorist bomb in the nearby Territorial Army base car park had taken half of Eagle Lane with it, the 200lb explosive catching the base's fuel dump as well. Six months, and only now was the boarding coming down and repairs at last taking place.

Six lives had been lost on that day last October. Four civilians, one army regular and one police officer. Mullett hadn't taken to DCI Patterson from the Anti-Terrorist Branch, that much was true, but he'd done a good job. Poor devil had been about to return to London and was caught in the blast as he got in his car.

Despite the bank holiday Mullett had felt obliged to come in. Assistant Chief Constable Winslow's new chap was turning up today. And of course, Denton's new golf club would not open until later in the week, which had an impact on his decision; though not long to go now, he thought as he smiled to himself – the members' private viewing of the new clubhouse was this coming Wednesday. But without his golf, and with Mrs M being away in Dorset, he was admittedly at a bit of a loose end. That reminded him . . . He pulled from his breast pocket the list his wife had left on the kitchen table:

Pick up cleaning.
Key to estate agent.
Filter for aquarium.
Back Thursday! Love Gx

He stroked his moustache thoughtfully again. Clearly all would be in disarray at Eagle Lane, as it always was without him. It would keep them on their toes, him turning up unexpectedly like this. He spotted Wells in heated discussion with contractors outside the still closed rear entrance to the station and shook his head in despair.

The contractors' red Transit was sloppily parked in the disabled bay, next to a Cortina, presumably Frost's. The builders were already running drastically behind schedule and Mullett had stopped any further advances for materials until substantial progress had been made, which was probably why they'd had to show up on a bank holiday Monday. Heaven knows why Winslow had recommended he use this bunch of cowboys.

'Wells!' Mullett called out irritably. 'I say, Wells!' The desk sergeant looked towards him, made a placatory gesture to the tradesmen and hurried over.

'What's going on here?'

'Builders, sir,' the breathless sergeant answered, sweat already forming on his brow. Despite it being only 8.30 in the morning, the sun already had strength.

'I can see that. But what are you doing out here? PC Pooley has been designated responsibility for coordinating building repairs. If you're here, who's on the front desk?'

As Sergeant Wells stuttered an answer Mullett noticed Winslow's 'protégé' from the Met, DS Waters, emerging from a green Vauxhall. He didn't like this one bit. Call him old-fashioned, but Stanley Mullett knew what was what, and this would be problematic, of that he was sure. Not that he was prejudiced, like the bald, bespectacled Assistant Chief Constable. He watched the tall, black officer, casually clad in denims, make his way round to the front of the building.

Wells noticed the super's distraction and gave up on his excuses, clearing his throat before starting again. 'There's an issue over the new back door, sir.'

Mullett looked at him scornfully.

'It has to meet certain criteria – regulations – which go beyond your budget . . .'

'What regulations?' Mullett snapped.

'Health and Safety – it needs to be a fire door, which means the lintel or support has—'

'Safety? Fire regulations? It's a door, Sergeant. A door. The last one was blown to kingdom come. Do these halfwits understand nothing?' He gestured in the direction of two string-vested individuals, idling and drinking tea. 'I don't have time for this nonsense; just deal with it! Oh, and Wells, the "travellers" have returned again. They appear to be setting up camp in the fields off the Bath Road. Get uniform down there to put the wind up them a bit.'

'What, gyppos, sir?'

'Caravans, horses, dogs and unwashed children,' Mullett said with distaste. 'Spotted them on my way in. Just let them know we'll be watching their dirty hides.'

DC Sue Clarke took a seat in the briefing room next to DC Kim Myles, a feisty blonde who'd recently transferred from Rimmington. The windows were open, but the dust still hung in the air. They'd quickly become accustomed to the drilling, hammering and general building-site noise now the renovation work had started, but it was near impossible to ignore the clouds of asbestos, or whatever it was, that clawed at the back of the throat.

Mullett was already in full flow, but Clarke found it hard to drag her mind into focus. She was still dwelling on the weekend and the conversation-stroke-row she'd had with DS Frost.

Anyway, Mullett, who was addressing an audience less than thrilled at his impromptu briefing, was only droning on about staff changes, most of which she'd heard before. DS Frost was to assume a larger role – good for him, but the downside was that this would make it even harder for them to spend time together. She wasn't sure if that would bother Frost. He seemed content with a bunk-up midweek, asking for nothing more. It wasn't as if he was spending the rest of his time with that tart of a wife of his; he wasn't – he was always working. If his modus operandi was more orderly, she fumed to herself, he might spend less time in the CID offices.

Superintendent Mullett continued to bleat on. Something about gypsies, then staffing issues again – DI Allen away on a computer course, DC Hanlon off on compassionate leave, a reminder of her ex-boyfriend Derek Simms's recent promotion to CID. She still found the thought of that mortifying.

Suddenly all thoughts of Simms and even of Jack Frost were swept from her mind at the incongruous sight of a tall, black officer stepping up on to the dais alongside Mullett.

'. . . and although Simms's promotion last month has solved a certain amount of our short-staffing, we are still a senior officer down, so it's extremely fortuitous that we now have DS Waters on loan from Bethnal Green. This is part of a new Home Office initiative called "Ethnic Diversification". I'd like you all to give DS Waters a warm welcome to Denton Police Division.'

There were a couple of half-hearted claps, but Clarke also detected muffled sniggers and murmurs.

'We'll have none of that here!' snapped Mullett. 'Equal opportunities for all is the policy of Denton Division, and you'll be impressed to hear that Detective Waters has received a commendation for his undercover work in the East End.'

'Working at night, was he?' someone quipped.

Clarke inspected DS Waters. He towered over Mullett, who was hardly a shorty, making him 6 foot 4 at least. He stood upright and stoic, but the faintest of smiles was playing along his lips, as if to say, Just you wait. She felt a dig in the ribs and turned to see Kim Myles grinning lasciviously. What on earth?

'Order! I will have order!' Mullett had turned puce. He twatted the little stick he insisted on using at briefings at the incident board like some uppity NCO. 'The next man to even smirk will be on a charge for insubordination. And that goes for any further incidence of this disgraceful behaviour outside this room.' The meeting fell silent. 'Good, I'm glad we have an understanding.' He paused. 'DS Waters will be working with' – Mullett rapidly scoured the room in search of a suitable partner – 'DC Simms.'

Clarke glanced over at Simms, who she could tell was groaning inwardly. PC Baker, his old mate from uniform, patted him on the back, grinning like the moron he was. What an inspired choice, Clarke thought to herself – Simms had only been in CID a month. No chance Mullett would assign Waters to a *woman* – God forbid.

'The pair of you can get straight over to Forest View. Another break-in – the third such instance in less than a month. Forensics and uniform are there now.'

'Do we have anything to go on, sir?' Simms asked. 'A pattern, maybe?'

'Perhaps,' Mullett said.

As far as Clarke was aware, DI Allen had been handling the spate of house break-ins Denton had suffered of late, until he'd buggered off to play computer games, that is.

'In the first case in Forest View, the family dog, a Pekinese, was garrotted with something akin to cheese wire. This time we have a dead cat.'

'Strangled?' Simms asked.

'That's for you to find out.' Mullett paused, as if for effect. 'I want you to give top priority to this case. The victims happen to be friends of mine, and I have given the Hartley-Joneses my personal assurance that we'll find the culprit swiftly. I want this investigation to be the very definition of exemplary policing,' he emphasized pointedly, glaring at Simms. 'Besides, we can't have this class of people . . . *assaulted* in this fashion, in such an exclusive area of Denton. This is not the Southern Housing Estate.'

What a snob, thought Clarke. So much for equality in the eyes of the law.

'Now, moving on. DC Clarke, one for you to follow up. We've had a number of complaints from residents about the Pink Toothbrush, this new sauna and massage parlour on the corner of Foundling Street . . .'

'But that's not in a residential area, sir,' Clarke said half-heartedly, trying to seem interested. Where the hell was Jack, she wondered.

'What about the flats in Baron's Court?' Simms interjected. 'They overlook the car park at the rear.' He turned and gave her a sly smile. 'Folks reckon it might be a knocking shop; soliciting in the car park.'

'People know it goes on,' Clarke said. 'But if there's not a disturbance, why the fuss?'

'Worth checking out,' Simms said with a smirk.

Arsehole, she thought.

Mullett, of course, nodded his approval, smoothing his moustache and adding, 'Get your friend Frost to help. His old adversary Harry Baskin is bankrolling the place.'

Clarke flushed. She hated any reference at the station to her relationship with Frost, although, as it happened, the remark was probably innocent. Catty jokes were hardly the superintendent's style.

Mullett banged his papers on the lectern, signalling the end of the briefing. Chairs scraped back and officers began talking amongst themselves. Clarke watched as Simms approached DS Waters, extending his hand. Kim Myles nudged her again.

'What d'you reckon there, then?' Myles said slyly.

'What do you mean?'

'Bit of all right, him.'

'What, Derek Simms?' Clarke replied absently, noticing

that Frost hadn't done his usual trick of creeping in late at the back of the briefing room. Mullett hadn't even remarked on his absence. Maybe she'd missed something.

'No, stupid . . . the dark feller,' Myles said over her shoulder, as both women made for the door.

'Oh right – yeah, very cute.' The girl's a nympho, she thought. She changed the subject. 'You know DS Frost – did you see him in there?'

'Weren't you listening?' Myles said, lighting a cigarette in the corridor outside the Ladies. 'Dead girl out by the railway track – Frost is out there with Maltby now.'

DC Derek Simms shook the powerful hand offered with all the confidence he could muster. He'd only been in CID a month; having this thrown at him was all he needed. A commended officer from the Met. *Jesus!* And a black one at that. He'd be a laughing stock. The big man grinned amiably, or so it appeared, although Simms wondered whether he was taking the piss, like everyone else seemed to do since his promotion. They left the briefing room together and made for the exit, passing Baker, Simms's ex-beat colleague, in the corridor. Simms caught the surreptitious snigger as Baker disappeared towards the canteen. Idiot, he thought.

'So what brings you to Denton, John?' Simms asked as they entered the car park.

'Home Office initiative – they need a token black man in the provinces.' Simms looked puzzled so Waters continued. 'The powers-that-be want more ethnics in the force, the better to relate to the villains, so they're farming us out in the hope of attracting recruits. Your man Winslow didn't seem too pleased about it. Said there wasn't much call for my type of qualities here in Denton.'

'There's none of your "type" here, that's for sure – you'll

stand out like a sore thumb. As for your qualities, Sarge, I wouldn't know,' Simms said. Waters shrugged as they stood beside Waters' green Vauxhall.

'VX4/90 – nice motor,' Simms commented. 'Pretty pokey, too. Is that standard CID issue in Bethnal Green?'

'Ha. Not standard – guess you could say there is no standard. Drove up this morning.'

'Well, there is here. Would love to go for a spin sometime, if that's OK with you? Better head off in mine for now until you get to know the area.'

'I need to dump my stuff off at Fenwick Street. Know it?'

'Yeah, Plod Park: coppers' housing.' Jesus, he'd be living with the guy, too. 'You'd better do that later, Sarge; we're heading for somewhere a bit more upmarket first.'

Monday (2)

Frost followed the pensioner down the footpath, his dog tugging at the leash as though eager to show off his discovery. This was the man who had reported the body to Desk Sergeant Bill Wells earlier that morning, and far from seeming distressed, there was an air almost of excitement about him. Maltby had yet to arrive, and sirens from an ambulance and area car were still in the distance, so Frost would be first on the scene.

The early-morning sun was refracted in the dew on the tips of the sedge grass.

'Bit overgrown down here,' Frost said, brambles thwacking him in the wake of the dog-walker.

The man turned round and grinned keenly. 'Perfect place to hide a body, eh?'

Frost ignored the comment. 'Who else uses this path?'

'Only me and Nelson this time o' year. 'Orses sometimes, but usually in the winter when it's not so o'ergrown . . . and blackberry-pickers in autumn. Tons of bushes, y'see.'

'Yes, I can see,' said Frost, momentarily losing the pensioner behind one of the aforementioned bushes.

'Here you go,' the man said proudly, the Labrador looking equally pleased as it stood next to the body, wagging its tail enthusiastically.

Before he approached the corpse Frost appraised the location. The clearing in which it lay was covered with grass about 2 feet high, and the path they'd been following cut across it and disappeared over the rise. The railway embankment further off sloped up at a steep gradient to a height of about 15 feet. The body – or all that was visible at this point – lay 6 feet from the path.

'You might have waited!' a wheezing voice said from behind him.

'Ah, Doc, I'd forgotten about you. All that clobber must be slowing you down.'

Frost lit a cigarette as Maltby, sweating visibly, dumped his case and removed his Homburg. He took a handkerchief from his breast pocket as he made his way towards the body.

Frost always tried to get as much as possible from the body's surroundings first before his senses were affronted by the corpse. He walked on past Maltby and the body, continuing up the path towards the railway embankment. He looked both ways before gingerly stepping on to the track – even though the line had been suspended since the report of the body's discovery at 8.15 a.m. Was the victim pushed off a train, he wondered. Or perhaps it was coincidental that the body was within spitting distance from the line – the killer, or killers, may have had no idea they were next to the railway. Or maybe it was suicide, but a bridge or platform would be more usual. Keeping an open mind, he walked along the verge.

The grass surrounding the body showed no sign of having recently been trampled, Maltby's shufflings aside, but judging by the spider's webs glistening in the sunlight, the girl was unlikely to have rolled the 15-or-so feet down the embankment in the last twelve hours or so. From his vantage point, Frost gazed down on Maltby fidgeting around the body and the man and his dog waiting patiently on the footpath, before making his way back down.

'Well, Doc, what have we got?' He peered over Maltby's shoulder at a blonde teenage girl sprawled on her stomach, her head rotated unnaturally through 180 degrees. *The Exorcist* flashed through his mind. There was a trickle of dried blood beneath her nose.

'Ah, there you are, Sergeant,' Maltby said, getting up and dusting his hands. 'I wondered when you might show some interest.'

'Didn't want to cramp your style, Doc. Just checking out the possibilities.' Frost rubbed his jaw thoughtfully, glancing back up at the train track glinting in the bright sunlight.

'Possibilities, eh? Not for her, she's dead, no doubt about that.'

Frost caught a blast of whisky breath. 'You surprise me, Doc. Thought she was out to get an early tan. Time of death?'

'Where are we now? Close to nine thirty? I'd say she's been dead a day or more.' Maltby paused. 'Yes, at least thirty hours, I'd guess,' he repeated, as if to convince himself. 'Broken neck.'

'Did it kill her?'

'It certainly did her no good.' Maltby grimaced. 'You know as well as I do, the pathologists will have the last word.' Frost knew there was no love lost between Drysdale, the county's senior pathologist, and the crabby but dependable Scene of Crime doctor.

'Of course, but you know what a stickler Drysdale is. He'll be prodding around for days before telling me he's found bugger all.'

'If she was pushed off a train, it's possible the fall could have broken her neck.' Maltby took a cigarette from the packet Frost was proffering. 'Of course, she could have had her neck broken elsewhere, and then been dumped here to make it look like something else . . . There's no bruising on her face, in fact there's barely a mark on her that I can see. She could almost be asleep. You need a proper examination.'

'Do you often take a nap with your head in that position?' Frost exclaimed, surprised.

'You know what I mean, Sergeant,' Maltby said, replacing his hat.

Frost moved closer to the body. The girl was wearing jeans and a white T-shirt. No coat, Frost noted. Wait, what was that poking out of the back of her jeans? Frost bent down and delicately retrieved a train ticket. The coarse paper slip was dated Saturday.

Frost turned to the man. 'When did you last walk Nelson?'

'Yesterday afternoon.'

'Yesterday?' Frost said, puzzled, looking from Maltby to the ticket stub in his hand.

'Yes.' The man coughed. 'But that were at the Rec.'

'Here – I meant here.'

'Saturday evening. It were getting dark.'

If she came off a train, then given the time of death, it was probably the last one; they were few and far between on a Saturday night. He could check the times at the station.

Frost turned back to Maltby. 'Thank you, Doc. Well, I guess it's over to Drysdale now.' Two uniform had arrived and were cordoning off the area with tape. 'Time we were off.'

'What about me?' the man with the dog said from the path.

'What about you?' Frost scowled.

'We found, the, er, body. Well, it weren't me – it were Nelson that did it.' He patted the Labrador fondly.

'Of course,' Frost said, stepping over the dead girl. 'Come with me. I'll need a statement from you, and a paw print from Nelson.'

'A paw print?' The man looked worriedly at Frost.

'Yes, a paw print – just to rule him out as a suspect.'

*   *   *

22

Frost decided to make a few preliminary enquiries before returning to Eagle Lane. Pulling up at Denton railway station taxi rank he put in a call to Control to get the line reopened.

The taxi drivers, acknowledging who he was, shot him surly glances; the temporary line suspension was impacting on their business. He entered the ticket office and tapped his ID on the counter glass to attract the clerk who had his back to him.

'Yes?' the aged British Rail retainer said.

'I'd like a timetable, please.'

The man slid one through. 'Passengers would like to know when the line will be reopened.'

'Would they, now. All in good time. Depends on whether people help us out or not, doesn't it?' Frost smiled. 'Any trouble on the last train on Saturday night that you're aware of?'

'How do you mean, trouble?'

'Disturbances? You know, kids messing around, girls jumping off trains – that sort of thing.' Frost squinted at the BR timetable, trying to work it out. Why the hell were these things so difficult to read?

'Ticket office shuts at 4 p.m. Any trouble, you or the Transport Police at Paddington would know before me.'

'So at' – Frost ran his finger along the timetable – 'at 12.45 a.m. no station staff would be on duty.'

'Office shuts at four,' the clerk repeated perfunctorily.

'Yes. You said. But Denton, if I'm reading this right, isn't the last stop. What happens to the train after that?' Frost squinted harder. He could hardly read the print; spectacles were just around the corner for him.

'It was this weekend,' the clerk said. 'Engineering works. The line was shut all the way from Denton to Swansea. Though the London-bound opened this morning . . .'

'But it's a bank holiday weekend?'

'Exactly. An extra day to do the work without upsetting the commuters.'

'Well,' beamed Frost, slapping the timetable on the counter, 'that's a stroke of luck, isn't it!' The clerk stared back deadpan, not sharing his delight. But Frost was cheered by the thought that if Denton was the last stop, any witnesses would have got off here. He thanked the clerk and headed back outside.

The heat soon began to make Frost feel irritable as he patted his mac for his cigarettes, finally taking it off and slinging it over his shoulder. He slipped on the Polaroids Sue had bought him and glanced over at the taxi rank where a bunch of drivers were shooting the breeze. A tall, fair, smartly dressed man was paying the driver of a Cavalier. As Frost ambled over, the cabbie's fare rushed hurriedly past, his briefcase almost clipping the detective's knee.

'Morning, gents. In a hurry, that one. Won't get far this morning, though.' Frost watched the man disappear into the ticket office. 'Light, anybody?'

One of the drivers, a large man with lamb-chop sideburns, held out a box of Swan Vestas.

'Cheers, mate,' Frost said amiably, and as an afterthought added, 'DS Frost, Denton CID.' The group nodded in acknowledgement.

'Farah Fawcett or Cheryl Ladd?' one asked him.

'Excuse me?'

'You know, *Charlie's Angels*. Just finished on the telly. Which one's the coppers' choice, then?'

Frost trawled his mind for anything he knew about the programme. Three women; stunners by common consensus but to his eye a bit on the skinny side; he preferred something more fleshy. One of them divorced the Six Million Dollar man earlier this year, that he did know, the irony being the millions of dollars involved. All right for some.

'Er . . . the one with the big . . .' He gestured. Surely one of them was properly built? They looked at him blankly – clearly the wrong answer. 'Any of you boys working Saturday night?'

They all shook their heads, muttering about the recession and general lack of business.

'So what's all this about, then?' one piped up.

'A dead girl. Found by the train line outside town. It's possible that someone on the last train may have seen something.'

A small, bearded driver in a leather jerkin pointed towards what could best be described as a shed.

''E'll know who was on.'

Frost approached the shed, the domain of the cab controller whose path he'd crossed before. He looked like he'd worked solidly through the entire weekend.

'Saturday night. Any pick-ups from the 12.45?'

'There were three cars working Saturday night,' he said. The man looked weary, his red eyes sunken, heavily tattooed forearms lying lifeless like discoloured slabs of meat on the desk. 'Two were here when the train came in. Charlie took a couple of young girls to Two Bridges, and Bill dropped a punter off at Market Square. You'll have to ask them exactly where.' The man scrawled two names on the back of a newspaper.

'Phone numbers?' Frost prompted.

'Hold on.' He leafed through a filthy address book, huffing as he wrote down a number next to Charlie's name. 'And here's Bill's address. Phone is the call box on Milk Street, though.'

'Cheers, mate.' Milk Street. Southern Housing Estate. Frost knew it well.

'You're welcome.' The controller sighed, stubbing a cigarette out on the largest ashtray Frost had ever seen. 'Don't go knocking them up now, though. They'll be asleep. Both worked last night too. Airport runs.' The phone was ringing, but the man seemed oblivious to it.

'So, three people got off that train?'

'Four.'

'Four?' Frost looked intrigued. 'Who was the fourth?'

'Woman. Saucy-looking. Poked her head in here, then disappeared.'

'What, saw your ugly mug and scarpered, you mean?'

For the first time the cab controller met his eyes. His expression didn't change. He wore the look of the super-tired, one Frost was all too familiar with. 'She wanted to know how long until the next cab. I said none were coming back to base, but I could call one in if she'd like. No trouble for a pretty girl like her. The other car was dropping off in Rimmington. She said, "No, thanks," smiled and left.'

'Thank you. Description?'

'Early twenties. Brunette. Medium height. Tasty.'

'Right, that's it, then,' Frost concluded. 'Four potential witnesses.'

'And, of course, anyone else who walked home,' the controller said sullenly, his gaze now fixed on Frost.

Frost stood on the steps of the controller's hut mulling over their to-some-extent useful conversation. The rank shut at 1 a.m. on Sunday, after meeting the last train. Naturally, some people might walk, if they lived within a reasonable radius, or indeed if they had no cash. He felt certain that the dead girl had been on the train. There was no concrete evidence, but even if it was murder and not suicide, why would someone bother to cart a body out there? The clearing was a good half-mile through all those brambles. Did they do it to fake a suicide? Easier, surely, to heave the body over a railway bridge. So did she jump, or was she pushed? The possibilities whirled through Frost's mind as he opened the Cortina door. He nodded goodbye to the rank drivers.

Chris Everett tried to keep calm as he fumbled in his wallet for the notes for his return ticket to Paddington. The heavy fabric of his suit and the unseasonably warm weather, which was more like July than the start of May, were making him perspire uncomfortably. The ancient clerk was slow to issue the ticket. Come on, he thought – if I miss this train I'll never get there and back in time. The clerk was mumbling something he didn't catch; he only caught the word 'incident' as he snatched up the ticket from under the glass. He hurried downstairs to the platform, and took refuge in the waiting room.

As he'd been paying his taxi fare, he'd overheard the other drivers discussing the approach of a plainclothes policeman; apparently a well-known character, although Everett had missed the name. In his hurry to escape he'd almost collided with him – a scruffy individual in a raincoat and shades. Everett was shaken, but also strangely thrilled by the close encounter. He wondered what brought him to the train station; surely not enquiries into the weekend's burglary at Forest View? Nevertheless, holding a briefcase containing several thousand pounds of stolen jewellery in close proximity to the law had given him an adrenalin rush.

Everett tapped the brown leather case agitatedly. The sooner he offloaded this stuff with his Hatton Garden fence the better. He still had three VCRs at home in the garage; he wasn't really interested in them, but it was hard to resist the latest technology when it was just sitting there. He even swiped a B&O amplifier on Saturday night. Mustn't get too greedy, he thought, glancing around the waiting room. It seemed busy for 11 a.m. He turned to the elderly lady seated next to him, a wicker basket propped on her lap.

'Excuse me. Is there a problem with the trains?'

'They've been suspended all morning,' she sniffed. 'Only just started running again. One just went out; bloody heaving, it was.'

Everett glanced at the indicator board. The next was delayed and wasn't due out for an hour. Bloody hell – he had to be back for a viewing at three. This was hopeless. He'd have to give it a miss today.

Monday (3) _____

DCs Sue Clarke and Kim Myles turned off Market Square on to Foundling Street. It struck Clarke that the empty streets and bright bank holiday sunshine gave Denton an almost picture-postcard look – a far cry from the booze-and-kebab-stained aura of a typical Saturday night. But as Myles brought the Escort to a juddering halt, she realized it was merely a trick of the light.

The Pink Toothbrush was a single-storey building with a tall chimney stack, overshadowed to the west by the four-storey Aster's department store on the corner of Foundling Street. A laundry company had previously occupied the site of the new sauna place, Clarke recalled. Harry Baskin had acquired the premises the previous year. The fascia boasted a gaudy neon sign saying *Sauna and Massage*, which, although switched off, still resonated with the same seedy feel as Baskin's nearby nightclub, the Coconut Grove.

The complaints had come from residents of Baron's Court. Once an opulent Victorian mansion, this relic of the past had stood by while Denton New Town, in all its ugly, slipshod glory, had grown up around it. Now broken up into flats and bedsits, Baron's Court was mainly tenanted by pensioners. The area had certainly seen better days, thought Clarke. Even in the handful of years since she'd left school, the south of Denton had deteriorated visibly. Eventually the listlessness of the swelling unemployed on the Southern Housing Estate had begun to spread north, crime and vandalism flowing with it. The pubs were getting rougher, and Foundling Street now had not one but two sex shops – nothing wrong with that in itself, but was it just a coincidence that complaints about the number of kerb-crawlers had risen dramatically?

The old folk must feel the world is closing in on them, Clarke reflected as she stepped out on to the pavement.

'Looks quiet enough to me,' said Myles, pulling her shoulder-length blonde hair up into a ponytail.

'The complaints came in at eleven at night, not eleven in the morning,' Clarke responded sharply. She noted there were two vehicles in the car park – a mustard Austin Allegro and a white Mercedes convertible.

'Want one?' Myles said, offering a Silk Cut, which Clarke declined as they walked towards the door. Why Mullett allowed her companion to wear skirts that short was a mystery to Clarke. Myles had been at Denton two months now, and was still as brazen as the first day she'd sashayed into Eagle Lane, fluttering her eyelids at DI Allen. Rumour had it that the pair were already an item, now that Allen had split from his wife. Not that she was in any position to make judgements.

Myles rapped on the door. Nothing. The place felt shut. They'd not checked the opening hours.

'Let's try the back,' said Clarke. They walked round the building and there, on the step by the fire door, was a young Chinese girl having a cigarette. She looked up, startled.

'We no open!' she barked.

'Police,' Clarke snapped back. She was struck by the girl's beauty, but also by her age – no more than sixteen, if that.

'We no open!' she repeated, as though not hearing or understanding.

'Dumb Chinky. Where's Harry?' Myles said. Clarke bristled and shot her an admonishing look. 'Well . . . ?'

The girl sat in silence on the step, looking fearful. Why was she so terrified?

Clarke bent down and spoke gently. 'Is Mr Baskin in?'

'Mr Baskin, boss,' the girl replied, momentarily soothed.

'Yes, love – but is he in? Is he here?' Clarke persisted.

'No boss here.'

'Whose is the white Merc out front, then?' Myles interjected impatiently. 'Yours?'

'Well, well, what do we have here?' Baskin bellowed, suddenly looming in the open doorway. 'Hop it, Mai Ling,' he said to the timid girl, who scurried inside.

Clarke squared up. 'We'd like a word with you, Mr Baskin, about your activities on these premises.'

Baskin looked amused. 'Fancy a rub-down? Nice girl like you, we could give you a discount. Or if you're looking for a bit of pin money after hours . . .' He grinned lasciviously, toking on a huge cigar.

'We're given to believe you may be offering more than a rub-down.' Clarke was determined not to be intimidated by the large club owner, who from the fire-door threshold towered over them both.

'I see,' he sniffed, his grin replaced by a sour stare. 'Those moaning old biddies in the flats, was it?'

'It's not important where the accusation came from – and we're not getting heavy, there's no actual evidence . . .'

'You're damn right, there's no evidence,' Baskin growled, on the edge of losing his cool, 'because there's fuck all going on here! Now piss off, and tell those old boots they can piss off too!'

'Mr Baskin, wait . . .' But he'd already slammed the fire door in their faces.

Clarke hammered on it angrily. Baskin hollered back an obscenity, followed by something, too muffled to catch, about Frost. 'Fat bastard,' she hissed.

'That went well,' said Myles.

Clarke shrugged her shoulders, turning away from the door. Baskin's notoriety was such that Eagle Lane would generally pull out the big guns – Jack Frost and DI Allen – to deal with him, and she'd guessed a pair of young female DCs were unlikely to be taken seriously. Sexist pig.

'Without any firm accusations I'm not quite sure what we were meant to achieve . . .' Clarke began, but as they rounded the corner of the building she was stopped in her tracks.

'Oi!' screeched Myles. The Escort door was open and a youth was rummaging around inside. Two more hooded figures on bikes were hovering next to the car, one with his hand on the door.

Clarke and Myles ran at the hoodlums; the two on bikes sped off, the athletic Myles giving chase, but the other was initially trapped inside the car. Galvanized by her lack of success with Baskin, Clarke grabbed the kid by his sweatshirt as he tried to push past her. The pair of them crashed to the ground, Clarke sprawling on her back beneath the snarling boy. She had hold of him firmly, and was just about to read him his rights when a searing pain jolted through her thigh, so severe that she released her grip. The hooded youth scrambled up and legged it, screeching expletives as he went, while Clarke could do nothing but writhe on the tarmac, her thigh pulsing in white-hot agony.

'Jesus, little bastard!' Myles stood above her, trying to catch her breath. 'What a mess. We'd better get you seen to.'

It was Simms's belief that Forest View, for all its leafy desirability, had a basic flaw: the properties on the east side backed on to Denton Woods, and as such were easy targets for burglars. He and Waters pulled up on a vast drive of thick shingle that crunched beneath their shoes as they walked to the door. Well, at least it stops the villains approaching from the front, thought Simms, although clearly that hadn't helped much in this case. The doorbell sounded with elaborate chimes, and a well-dressed, attractive woman in her mid-forties appeared.

'Yes?' she said, surprised.

'Mrs Hartley-Jones? Denton CID.'

She took a step back, regarding them both suspiciously, her look lingering on Waters. 'Can I see some identification?' she asked, frowning.

Simms pulled his badge from inside his leather jacket and then waited uneasily while Waters patted his denims, eventually retrieving his credentials from his back pocket.

The woman peered at the ID. 'You'd better come in,' she said at last.

'Only if it's no trouble,' quipped Simms sarcastically. Spiky tart, he thought. Did she want her sparklers back or not?

'No, no trouble. But we've already had the police in. *They* were in uniform,' she said pointedly. How ironic, Simms thought sourly; to her mind the real police were those in uniform. This time last year *he* was uniform. 'Come this way. Mind those.'

Simms stepped over what appeared to be a pile of large candles. 'Yes, the officers were taking details. Myself and DS Waters are taking charge of the investigation.'

'My husband plays golf with Mr Mullett, you know,' said Mrs Hartley-Jones as she led them down a large, parquet-floored hall. Simms recalled that these were friends of Mullett's, though the concept of the super having mates was a hard one to swallow. They certainly seemed his type, though; he could well imagine Mullett residing in a grand place like this. That's why he's so anxious, Simms thought and smiled to himself – he's worried he'll be next.

'I can only tell you what I told those other chappies. They have a full list of all the valuables that are gone.' She ushered them into the living room. 'Nothing else is missing as far as I can tell. Michael thought his shotgun had been taken but we found it in the boot of the car. And Mr Tibbs has not come back to life,' she added bitterly.

'Mr Tibbs?' Waters asked, halting near the chesterfield.

Mrs Hartley-Jones sighed. 'My sweet angel.'

'The cat,' Simms said.

'Yes, my poor cat. What *are* they going to do with him? One of your better-dressed colleagues took him away in a polythene bag!'

'Yes,' Simms confirmed, 'to ascertain how he . . . er . . . how he passed away.'

'And?'

'We're still waiting.' Simms preferred not to enlighten her about the cheese wire.

'Well, can I have him back when your friends have finished prodding him around? He needs to have a proper burial, underneath the sycamore.'

'Of course,' said Simms uneasily, wondering whether the feline carcass had already been tossed in the incinerator. 'And where was Mr Tibbs discovered, exactly?'

'Don't you people communicate?' Mrs Hartley-Jones said, vexed. 'It's most upsetting, having to go through this again. In the fridge, poor dear.'

'The fridge? Of course, yes, I am sorry. I'm sure there's a note of it somewhere.' Simms made a play of fiddling with his notepad, knowing the pages to be mostly blank. He'd been far too preoccupied with Waters' arrival to pay much attention to the incident report from uniform. Focus, Derek, he told himself, you're CID now. He checked what notes he did have.

'Mind if we look around?' asked Waters. Simms watched him stride across the room and peer into the cavity of the TV cabinet. With his faded denim jacket, afro and flared jeans he certainly looked out of place in this middle-class suburban home. Mrs Hartley-Jones looked quite perturbed as the big man fingered the severed cables that until recently were attached to a VCR.

'Why cut them?' Simms asked.

'Save time. There's a mass of wires: video recorder and all the hi-fi stuff, amp, cassette deck, turntable, speaker cable; he'd be here all night untangling all this stuff at the back of the cabinet. SOCOs come up with anything?'

'No prints – clean as a whistle. So, broadly, it was just the VCR and jewellery that were taken?'

'Yes. And an amplifier, I believe. I don't know much about the hi-fi. I do hope the video recorder was covered by the insurance. It was terribly expensive.'

'Had it long?' enquired Waters.

'A couple of weeks! Michael had only just mastered recording off the television. The instructions for these things are so complicated, don't you find?'

'Can't afford one on a copper's salary, unfortunately,' Simms said. 'And the jewellery – was there anything specific, an antique or heirloom? Those are sometimes easier to recover.'

'My mother's engagement and eternity rings. I took some photos of them some time ago, if that's any use?'

'Yes, please, it all helps.' Simms asked if they could look around further, although he didn't expect to find anything. He thought the woman's manner was vague and disinterested. Apart from concern for the cat she didn't seem to mind that much. They made for the kitchen, where the thief was thought to have entered through the large, latticed rear window. Each of the three main panels was made up of six smaller panes.

One such pane, in the middle of the central panel, had been replaced with a cardboard rectangle.

'Impossible to get a glazier out on bank holiday Monday,' the woman said.

'So,' concluded Simms, 'the thief broke a pane, then reached through and lifted up the lever. Then he climbed in through the window.'

Mrs Hartley-Jones was nodding, but Waters shook his head, sucking air in through his teeth. He reached up and removed the piece of cardboard. 'Mind if I go outside a sec?' he asked. Mrs Hartley-Jones unlocked the back door.

Simms watched, impatient, as Waters stuck his arm through the splintered pane and reached for the nearest latch, at the bottom of the right-hand panel. It was a stretch, but he managed to open the window and stood facing them both from the garden.

'What exactly was the point of that?' Simms asked.

'If I was going to break in, I'd probably have broken the pane right next to the latch, wouldn't you?' He tapped the unbroken section of the window. 'Save reaching through and risk cutting yourself?'

'Good point,' Simms said, annoyed he'd not considered that. 'But it *was* dark.'

'A cat burglar without a torch? C'mon.' Waters then turned to Mrs Hartley-Jones. 'You reported the burglary very early this morning. Is that correct?'

'Yes, correct. We'd been on the South Coast – caravan site – we keep a caravan there and go quite often . . . We didn't get back until late last night.'

'Who was feeding Mr Tibbs? One of the neighbours?' DS Waters asked.

'No, my niece, Samantha.'

'When was the last time she fed him?'

'Well, there's the funny thing. She should have been the first to discover the break-in, on Sunday morning. But when I called my sister that morning, she said that Sam hadn't come home on Saturday night. We rang again in the afternoon. Sam wasn't back, so we decided to come home early, as we were worried about Mr Tibbs. That reminds me, I must call my sister.'

Desk Sergeant Bill Wells glanced at the lobby clock. Only midday and he was starving already. During the refurbishments last year, when the canteen had been closed, the trolley service had been a real bonus. He could conveniently grab a bite whenever Grace trundled by. But the superintendent had not seen fit to redeploy meals-on-wheels while Eagle Lane recovered from bomb damage, and went mental if Wells so much as left his post for a pee.

'Ah, Wells.' Mullett appeared before his eyes, as if the mere thought of the super was enough to make him materialize. 'What's the matter, man, wake up – you're in a daydream. Where's DS Frost?'

'Somewhere by the train line still, maybe – a body—' The phone rang, cutting him off, and he looked at Mullett expectantly.

'Well, answer it then, man,' the super snapped angrily.

Wells picked up the phone. 'It's for you – Mr Winslow.'

Mullett's face fell. 'Give it here. Morning, sir. Yes . . . Yes, he's here. Nice chap. Yes . . . Tall, *yes* . . .'

Wells watched the super intently, guessing the subject of the conversation was DS Waters. There had never been a black officer at Eagle Lane before and the station was buzzing with gossip. Not that Denton was unique in its prejudices. When it came to attitudes towards ethnic minorities, the force's record was dubious at best. Wells clearly remembered the scandal at Hendon when a bloke had been bound and gagged by a bunch of cadets dressed as Ku Klux Klan. Made the headlines. Nasty business.

'Here . . . here!' The super was waving the receiver at him, irritably pulling at his moustache with the other hand. 'Now – where was I?'

'On the way to the Gents, sir?' Wells said hopefully.

Mullett ignored him. 'Get Frost to call me.' He shot Wells a stern look and was gone.

The phone rang again as if to remind Wells of its presence.

'Is that the police?' said a man in angry tones, barely pausing for a reply before firing off his grievance in a voice so shrill with emotion that Wells had no idea what he was saying.

'Calm down, sir. I can barely understand you.'

'My shop has been robbed! Are you deaf? Robbed! At gun point!' The caller had a strong Indian accent.

'Sir, please calm down. Now, can you describe the assailants? How many of them were there?'

'Don't patronize me, you . . . you desk jockey. There were two.'

'And can you describe them, sir?'

'Short!'

Wells waited, but nothing more was offered. 'Any further description to go on? Do you know if they were black or white, for example?'

'They was wearing bloody balaclavas – how the hell would I know? All I know is, they were short. Very short.'

'The fridge?' Frost's voice sounded distant. The line was so dreadful you'd think he was calling from Timbuktu, not a phone box a couple of miles away. Mullett heard the pips go, followed by cursing as Frost struggled to find some change. Then the line went dead.

Mullett drummed his fingers thoughtfully on his polished, spartan desk. 'Yes, the fridge,' he repeated to himself, and pivoted round on his chair.

But his golfing chum's cat was not the main thing on his mind. At the time of Frost's call, Mullett had been reflecting on the morning briefing. If he'd had the presence of mind, he'd have done better to hold DS Waters back and quietly assign him to Frost, but the jeering had flustered him, and his ill-considered act of handing the DS to a rookie like Simms in front of the whole division was one he now regretted. The men had respect for Frost; partnering him with Waters would have reflected far better on the visiting policeman.

The phone flashed again.

'Sorry, sir, ran out of change.'

'Where exactly are you?' Mullett asked, exasperated.

'On my way to the lab, to find out more about this dead girl, the one found this morning . . .' The line crackled.

'Yes, yes, I know which one.' Mullett's secretary, Miss Smith, appeared in his peripheral vision and he waved her away without looking up. 'But what I want to know is, where exactly was the body found?'

'Beg pardon, sir? By the train line.'

'Wells told me it was more or less in Rimmington.'

'Between the two.'

'Well, can't our Rimmington colleagues deal with it?' Mullett was eager to offload the case. Dead girls were not the way he wanted a bank holiday weekend to finish up.

'A Denton resident reported it,' Frost said sharply. 'There's no ID – we'll run the description through Missing Persons; might be local, might not.'

'That's a shame. So was it suicide?' Mullett said hopefully.

'Can't rule it out. I'll find out more when I get to the lab. Sir, while I've got you, about DI Williams's paperwork. I appear to be continuing to handle it, while DI Allen—'

'We can talk about that later,' Mullett interjected quickly as he lit a cigarette. 'You get what you can from Drysdale, then get back here pronto, there's something special I . . .'

The pips went once more, and Mullett was left talking to himself.

No sooner had he replaced the receiver and taken a drag of his cigarette than the phone began flashing angrily at him again. Mullett was about to sound off at Frost for not carrying more than tuppence, but instead it was the doleful voice of Desk Sergeant Wells that greeted his ear.

Clarke clutched Myles's arm as she hobbled through to A&E. Her leg was numb, her hands sticky with congealed blood and she felt light-headed. She couldn't have lost that much in, what, twenty minutes, could she? Her jeans were pretty damp . . .

'Let's stop here a sec.' Myles propped her against a wall, the surface feeling cold against her cheek. Where is he? she thought. Surely Jack must've heard by now? Myles had whacked the blue light on the roof but it had still taken her a fair while to get across town through the bank holiday traffic.

'Did you tell Eagle Lane what happened?' Clarke asked again – meaning Jack Frost does know, doesn't he?

'Yeah, Control are notified. And uniform are all over central Denton. But you can bet those kids are dust by now. Here, flop into this.' Myles pushed a wheelchair towards her. 'We'll get you seen to straightaway.'

Clarke pulled tighter on a makeshift tourniquet – an old scarf they'd found in the boot of the Escort – to stem the bleeding. *Christ*, it hurt.

Frost returned to the car after smoking two cigarettes outside the phone box. 'Something special,' Mullett had said. He didn't like the sound of that at all. Smacked of a stitch-up, if he knew the super. He looked at the names and addresses the cab controller had given him and then at his watch: 12.05. Six hours' sleep would be enough for a taxi driver; more than he ever got, anyway. He'd pay them a call before he headed back to Eagle Lane; the super's special project could wait. The radio was crackling nineteen-to-the-dozen so before setting off for the lab he picked it up.

'Afternoon, Bill. Lot of noise out there. What's up?'

'Sue Clarke, Jack. She's been stabbed.'

Frost held his breath, then said, 'Where?'

'Outside Baskin's sauna place.'

'Not where – I meant, is she badly hurt?' Frost snapped.

'In the leg. Lost a fair bit of blood. But hopefully nothing serious, mate,' Wells crackled. 'Myles took her over to the General. Sorry, I didn't want to panic you – just thought you should know.'

'She all right, though?'

'She's fine – probably.'

'OK, thanks,' Frost said, relieved. 'I'm on my way to see Drysdale.'

'Before you do, Mr Mullett wants you to call in at Singh's the newsagent's, on the Southern Housing Estate.'

'Can't he get his own newspaper?' Flamin' hell, he'd only just got off the phone to the man.

'They've had a robbery – a gang of armed midgets, by all accounts,' Wells explained.

Frost choked on his cigarette. 'Armed midgets? Do me a favour.' He snorted. The first time he and Clarke had been on a date came to mind, when he was recuperating last year, to see a fantasy flick she fancied. 'Maybe they're the *Time Bandits*, though why anyone would want to drop in on Denton in 1982 is beyond me.'

'Straight up. I took the call myself.'

'Surely such a small problem can be handled by uniform.'

'You know the super: anything involving shooters is CID.'

Frost sighed, watching a fox leisurely pad across the road. 'Can't somebody else take this?'

'Everyone else is out.'

'*I'm* out!'

'Sorry, Jack. And Jack, the vicar called again.'

'Again?' Frost exclaimed. 'I only spoke to whatshisname, the church warden, on Saturday.'

'Turner, George Turner.'

'That's him. I said, leave it with me and we'd catch the bugger. Blimey, it's only Monday!'

'He wanted to know how he was going to get the church roof repaired.'

'I don't bleedin' well know: ask the Almighty. Or, better still, ask his punters to dig deeper next Sunday, 'cos that lead'll be halfway to Eastern Europe by now.'

Frost hung up. Poor Sue; he should really get over to Denton General. He'd go after he'd seen the cabbies. On top of that, *and* a dead girl, he was now being lumbered with a 'gang of midgets'; well, he was adamant – somebody else could pick that up. He would do as planned and see Drysdale at the lab. So much for a quiet bank holiday.

Monday (4) ⎯⎯⎯⎯⎯⎯⎯⎯⎯⎯⎯⎯⎯⎯⎯⎯⎯

It was just gone one o'clock when Chris Everett arrived at the Denton branch of Regal Estates. Having abandoned the trains, he'd been out to Mount Pleasant in Rimmington to value a property, a three-storey Victorian terrace. Its owner, an attractive and recently widowed woman, had decided it was time to scale down.

He nodded to Vicky, who was taking down details, phone cradled between neck and shoulder, and she offered up a half-hearted smile. Head office had applauded his initiative to open on bank holiday Monday but the girls had been none too pleased. He headed for his office at the back of the building, passing Sandra at the window, fiddling with the Lettings section. After quietly shutting the door he slid his leather briefcase on to the bare desk, flipping out the *Echo* from inside.

Once again the front page was trumpeting the bravery of a Denton boy off to the Falklands. Every day it was the same – how many more spotty youths could there possibly be left to send? He flicked through the pages impatiently. Nothing – it must be too soon.

He realized that killing the cat in the same way as the dog the previous week was presenting the police with a pattern, but they might not assume it was a local man, as he'd also had forays into Rimmington, including one unpleasant encounter with a Jack Russell. He didn't feel too worried, though; after all, as regional branch manager of a respected chain of estate agents they'd never suspect him in a million years.

There came a rap on the door. He looked up to see Vicky staring through the office window. He gestured at her to enter.

'Afternoon, Chris,' she said. 'Good morning?'

Everett grunted. 'Pair of dithering old time-wasters first thing, then something more promising. I've the details here.'

'Oh right,' she said. Luckily his staff never questioned too deeply his movements or motives – he'd said he'd been valuing property in Rimmington – which made conducting a furtive double life that much easier. She ran through the morning's events. 'Just got another signing over at Baron's Court. Shall I nip down to give it the once-over?'

'Sure, you get over there.'

'That's the third from there in a fortnight,' she added.

Everett nodded approvingly. He realized the likely connection was Baskin's new venture, but he didn't let on; after all, he'd been meaning to give it a try himself, once all the hubbub had died down.

'Good, good. Right, here's the particulars of a nice Victorian place, Mount Pleasant area of Rimmington. Sole agency, owner selling due to bereavement. Very sad considering the two young kids.'

'Oh – I read about that. A famous writer, wasn't he? Had a heart attack?'

'Yes, famous by Rimmington standards, at least.' Everett

laughed nervously, sliding the details over. 'Right, I'll just have a coffee and then I'm off up to town. That meeting at head office has been rescheduled for this afternoon.'

Frost shivered as he entered the lab. No warm spring sun could penetrate this labyrinth of doom.

'Morning, Sergeant. Or is it afternoon?' said Drysdale, pulling on a pair of rubber gloves. 'One loses track of time in here.'

'Just slipped into the p.m., Doc,' Frost replied, wishing he hadn't left his mac in the car.

'If you're here about the young girl, she's only just arrived. I'm about to take a look.' As if on cue his assistant appeared through a set of double doors with a sheet-draped trolley.

'Well, maybe I can give you a hand,' Frost quipped sardonically.

Drysdale raised an eyebrow and moved the trolley to align it with the overhead light. 'Flying solo? Don't you usually have a sidekick – the chubby fellow, or that attractive brunette?'

'The chubby fellow's burying his mother.'

'Oh dear. He ought to take stock of his diet, that one, or he won't be long behind her.' Drysdale had removed the sheet and stepped back to survey the body, hands on hips as an artist appraising a fresh canvas. His assistant pulled out a small trolley of tools from the dark recesses of the lab. 'And the girl?' said the pathologist eventually, looking from the corpse directly at Frost.

'DC Clarke is otherwise engaged.'

Frost moved close to the corpse, his face inches away from Drysdale's, which in the striplighting had taken on a greenish hue.

'A bit of space please, Sergeant.'

While Drysdale examined the girl Frost allowed his mind to wander. He wasn't one to dwell on personal issues, but just lately he'd had more than his fair share. His wife had been unwell, but he'd found his sympathy lacking, believing it was largely an act

– a ploy to stop him leaving her. But as the suffering dragged on and the visits to the doctor continued something had begun to nag at him: what if she really wasn't well? It was nothing, he was sure – she just couldn't face up to the fact their marriage was over.

'Here.' Drysdale's voice brought him thankfully back to the lab. He pointed to a blue-tinged hand. 'Take a look at the fingers.'

'What? Black nail polish? Kids today will do anything to be different.'

'No, under the fingernails. Skin.'

'Sorry.' Frost squinted closer. 'Blasted eyes. Everything starts to pack in when you're pushing forty . . . oh yeah.'

'Apart from that she's not marked.'

'Nothing? No bruising? Nothing at all?'

'Nothing,' Drysdale repeated.

'If someone were forcibly ejected from a moving train one would expect some bruising; finger marks maybe, or signs of a struggle.' Frost was thinking aloud. 'So there's nothing of that sort. But what we do have is a suggestion of self-defence, lashing out, scratching an attacker perhaps? It's a conundrum.'

'A conundrum indeed, for you, anyway,' said Drysdale.

'Yes, quite.' From a tagged tray Frost picked up the poly-thene bag containing the girl's personal effects.

'No ID,' commented Drysdale.

Frost emptied the contents – a purse and hair clips – into the tray regardless. 'What age would you put her at?'

'Fifteen, sixteen.'

Frost nodded. Not old enough for a driving licence, that would explain the lack of ID. He rummaged through a small black purse embellished with a silver star, found near the body by the SOCOs. He made a mental note to check with British Rail; although he had a ticket stub already, he felt sure there must be a bag. All girls had bags.

After some further reflection, he asked, 'Is she, you know . . . ?'

'I'm not there yet,' Drysdale muttered.

A few moments passed. Thoughts intruded again, and this time it was the spectre of Sue Clarke that drifted across his mind. He should have gone to the hospital. The depressing aura of the clinical room and his troubled thoughts combined to make him crave a cigarette. In fact he was desperate. Drysdale loathed smoking, so rather than weasel out for a fag break he decided to make his excuses. 'Right, I'd better go, they have kittens at Eagle Lane if I'm off the radar for more than five minutes.'

'But I've barely begun.'

'Needs must, Doc. Let me know if the autopsy shows up anything interesting.'

'Very well. Toxicology with you by the end of tomorrow.'

'Too kind.'

'My pleasure – oh, before you go. I have something for you.' Drysdale went to the rear of the room and returned with a package.

'What's this?' Frost asked as he took the large Jiffy bag.

'A cat for Detective Simms.'

Frost slung the package in the passenger footwell of the Cortina and lit a cigarette. He was angry with himself. Having sacrificed seeing out the full autopsy he still felt positively unwilling to go and see Clarke. He knew he was avoiding talking to her properly. And it wasn't because she was injured; no, it was the realization that he no longer felt comfortable at work, a place that had always been more home to him than home. It was because of her. Things had got out of hand. He hadn't thought it through.

He was getting a headache, and commanded himself to focus on the job. Maybe it was the heat; the day had already slipped into a scorching afternoon. At least he had the dead girl's train ticket, which could turn out to be useful. Somebody must have seen her leave Denton yesterday morning on a train bound for London.

Having picked up the armed-robbery alert minutes after Wells had first radioed Frost, DC Simms gunned the Cortina through hot, busy streets. Simms desperately wanted this case: armed robbery, that was more his scene, not burgled houses and dead cats. Waters sat in silence next to him.

'Well, Sarge, it's only your first day and already you're experiencing both sides of Denton – from Forest View to this.' They sat at the lights at the bottom of Foundling Street, a vandalized phone box standing like a gatepost at the entrance to the Southern Housing Estate over the canal bridge. 'This is where all the scum and riff-raff live,' he continued. 'It's pretty much a certainty that the Hartley-Joneses' video recorder is sitting in one of these front rooms.'

This place gets worse with every visit, he thought. A chest freezer sat in the garden of a house with boarded-up windows. Sprayed on the wooden boarding were the letters *NF* and a swastika. Simms glanced over at Waters, who sat smoking and taking in the scenery.

'Nice,' he quipped. 'But listen, don't you want to check on your pal first?' They'd picked up Myles and Clarke's distress call from the massage parlour, but Simms had chosen to ignore it.

'Who says she's my pal?' Simms retorted, and then after a pause added, 'It was the wrong side of town for us, anyway. Uniform will have had it covered. Or Frost.'

'Pretty harsh, an officer getting stabbed like that—'

'Well, they weren't in uniform,' Simms said, 'and let's face it, the pair of them hardly look like coppers. Especially Kim. I mean, the skirts she wears – Baskin probably thought she was applying for a job.'

Waters' expression was stony. No sense of humour, thought Simms.

'Right, the newsagent is just on the corner here, I think. Cromwell Road.' Simms parked the car half on the kerb and quickly scanned the street. No sign of Frost's car. Good.

The pair of them entered the shop. 'Newsagent' hardly did it justice; it was crammed from floor to ceiling with everything from household detergent to cat food, alongside the cigarettes and girly mags. Behind the counter was a portly Asian man in a cardigan, shirt and tie. They had barely crossed the threshold when he launched his offensive.

'Where you people bloody been? Robbed – I have been robbed!' He thumped the counter, a cushion of *Denton Echo*es absorbing the thud.

'We got here as soon as we could, sir,' Simms said. 'Is anyone hurt?' Though he knew this was unlikely.

'Nobody bloody hurt,' Mr Singh replied.

Except your pride, Simms thought. 'How much did they get away with?'

'Three of the buggers, there were. Wearing this.' Singh covered his face with his hands, signifying balaclavas. Simms knew this area well from his time in uniform. The post office on the estate was turned over regularly: balaclavas, sawn-offs. Real mean bastards. But never a corner shop.

'Could they have been children?' Waters questioned.

'We're not in the East End now, Sarge,' Simms said authoritatively. 'Kids with shooters? Not in Denton.'

'Did you see the weapon?' Waters asked.

'In pocket, like this.' The newsagent shoved his hand in the cardigan pocket and thrust it forward. Waters raised his eyebrows.

'How much did they get away with?' Simms insisted again.

'Three pounds and fifty-five pence,' said Singh vehemently. 'And many, many cigarettes.'

Simms was incredulous. 'Three quid and a packet of fags? Is that *all*?'

'Money not important.' Singh was indignant.

Simms was visibly deflated. Waters, however, stepped forward decisively, clapping his colleague on the back.

'You're right, sir, it doesn't matter if it's three pounds or thirty grand, we can't have people just wandering in and nabbing stuff when they feel like it, can we? Can you give us any further description?'

Frost had driven past Simms's motor as he turned off Cromwell Road and into Milk Street. He hadn't been down here for ages but little had changed. The street was lined with identical 1930s council houses, pebble-dashed like dirty beaches, and he pulled up outside number 20.

He regarded the car propped up on bricks in the drive, an old Hillman of some kind. Why were there so many cars on bricks in this town? They sat there, raised exultantly all over the estate, cars wheel-less for all eternity.

A big-nosed woman in curlers answered the door.

'Afternoon, madam. I wonder if I might trouble you to call your husband?' Frost said politely.

''Usband? I ain't got no 'usband.' The woman scowled.

'Does one Bill Travers not reside here?'

''E's me brother. And 'e's in bed.'

'No, I'm up,' said a voice from inside the hallway. A grey-haired man in a string vest appeared at the woman's shoulder. The two of them glared at Frost like a pair of heavy-beaked vultures.

'What's up?' said Travers.

'Denton CID,' the detective replied, holding up his badge.

The pair's expressions remained unchanged.

'Mr Travers, you picked up off the final Paddington train on Saturday night?'

'I did – what of it?' Travers growled, scratching his stubbly jaw.

'There was an incident on the train. I'm making some routine enquiries. Do you remember who you picked up?'

'Yeah. A young Chinese feller. Dropped him off at Market Square.'

'Thanks. Don't suppose you noticed how many got off that train?'

'Four. Very lean for a Saturday night – specially as the train went no further. Nah, nothing much. Charlie picked up two pissed birds,' he added, rubbing his belly. 'People ain't got the cash for cabs no more.'

'That would be Charlie Feltham?'

'That's him.' The driver yawned.

'And the woman would have gone with . . .' Frost said, prompting.

'Woman? Didn't see no woman.'

Once in the Cortina, Frost sat back and lit a cigarette. He'd established that the woman got off last, and the two girls were a short way behind the Chinese bloke. According to Travers' account, he'd spent a couple of minutes working out where the Chinaman wanted to go – even went so far as to check he had the cash to pay the fare.

The other driver, Feltham, lived up in North Denton, off Merchant Street. Flipping heck, he was fast growing sick of this driving lark. The radio crackled into life before he could start to miss his mate and stalwart driver, the portly DC Hanlon. He drummed his fingers on the wheel, deciding he would call on Feltham later, and mulling over the choices he was left with. It was Eagle Lane and Hornrim Harry, or Denton General and DC Sue, and he didn't relish either one.

*　　*　　*

50

'That is one worried woman,' Simms said as the mother of Samantha Ellis closed the door on them.

'I agree there,' Waters replied, shaking his head. 'She sussed we were police before we'd said a word – though if she was that worried, why didn't she report it sooner?'

Simms, for all his inexperience, knew why. The pair had called on Mrs Hartley-Jones' niece to discover that, as they'd been told, the girl was indeed missing. The mother was distraught. Samantha was fifteen and a sensible girl, not one in the habit of shirking her duties, let alone vanishing without a word. The arrival of CID had brought the fears she'd been suppressing to the surface; she'd suddenly had to accept that her only daughter might actually be in trouble, as opposed to having run off on a jolly with a boyfriend or her mates. Mrs Ellis had been on the verge of reporting her missing when the pair turned up; she knew she'd been tardy in doing so. Well, it was difficult to know if the police would take the disappearance seriously. After all, Samantha wasn't a child. She was about to start her CSE exams and would soon go on to secretarial college. She was almost a grown woman. Almost, but not quite.

'Here's my theory,' said Simms, opening the car door. 'There was trouble at home, so she robbed her aunt's place and then did a runner.' He paused to allow time for Waters to digest this and then acknowledge his brilliant insight, but instead the Londoner frowned, perplexed.

'Listen,' persisted Simms, 'the circumstances fit: the girl's about to leave school, has a row with her mum and mum's boy-friend, knows auntie's got a few bob – easy. She's got keys to the house, everyone's away, and she knows where the jewels are. And she'll be halfway to Gretna Green with some hippie by now.' He slipped the girl's school photo into his pocket and looked back at the house; the mother, an attractive redhead, was visible behind the net curtains.

'Neat theory,' said Waters. 'Just two little problems. For a start, she just doesn't seem to be that kind of girl – at least not if the mother's to be believed. And secondly, that body found this morning fits her description perfectly.'

Simms took this in and realized Waters was right. He'd foolishly conjured up some Bonnie-and-Clyde-style fantasy when all the time the most likely explanation was staring them in the face. 'I guess we'd better notify Frost, then.'

'Back to Eagle Lane?' Waters asked.

Simms glanced at his watch. Nearly five o'clock. 'The super'll be expecting a progress report. But what do you say we grab a pint first, for Dutch courage?'

'They're not open for another hour.'

Simms turned the ignition. 'You're not in the big city now, Sarge. The Eagle's a coppers' boozer. It's always open.'

'Well, Sergeant Waters, how did you find your first day?'

In an effort to make him feel welcome, Mullett casually slid his pack of Senior Service towards DS Waters, at the same time scrutinizing him closely. These chaps, he mused, can't really make out what they're thinking. Dress sense seems a little awry – denim flares? Why do officers working undercover seem to think it gives them a licence to dress like Al Pacino? Simms was little better, sitting there with slicked-back hair and a scruffy leather jacket like an extra from *Grease*. The lad was barely recognizable from the moon-faced youth in uniform last year.

Waters gave an account of the house break-in and the missing girl.

'So, in all likelihood, it's the same girl.' Mullett grimaced at the sweet teenager smiling up at him from the desk. 'I needn't remind you the Hartley-Joneses are friends of mine – but the matter will now be handed over to Frost' – Mullett picked the photo off his desk – 'and I will be pointing this out to him, too, should he ever turn up. Anything else?' He forced a smile.

'We also took an armed-robbery call on the Southern Housing Estate,' Simms chipped in.

'Is this at the newsagent's? I overheard Wells blathering on some nonsense about it and told him I wanted Frost on this – what's all this about midgets?'

'The shopkeeper was a little overwrought,' suggested Waters. 'It was probably just kids.'

'With a firearm? In Denton? I think it unlikely. We've never had a case of children with guns out here. This isn't the East End, Sergeant.'

'We've never had an armed midget, for that matter,' said Simms, grinning.

'This is not a laughing matter, DC Simms.' Mullett scowled. 'Still, if they are indeed midgets, they should be easy to catch – I can't say I've ever seen one in Denton. The gypsy site, perhaps? No, knives are the weapon of choice for Denton's young delinquents.' He got up from his chair to adjust the blinds and shield the officers' eyes from the evening sun's glare. 'Well, Sergeant Waters – it seems your partner here has shown you many sides of Denton thus far.'

'Thank you, sir,' Simms said, blinking.

'Has anyone checked on DC Clarke?' Mullett asked. Both shook their heads. 'Lives alone, doesn't she? Simms, would you be good enough to check the girl's all right? She discharged herself, but I imagine it must have been quite a shock to the system.' He could see Simms about to protest but cut him short. 'Heavens, man, it'll only take you five minutes.' And with that he slapped both hands on the desk to indicate the end of the debrief. Both men made for the door.

'Oh, Waters,' Mullett called after them. 'Is your accommodation all right?'

'Not checked in yet, sir.'

'It's not the Ritz, I'll grant you, but better than a B&B, one would hope.' The two men nodded and left the superintendent's office.

Mullett leaned back in his chair. The evenings were definitely getting lighter. If things remained this quiet there was every chance he could get a game of golf in one evening after work, in celebration of Wednesday's reopening. His sense of smug contentment barely lasted a moment as he fingered the note left by his wife and realized with a pang that he'd done nothing on it. But it was a bank holiday. Would the dry cleaner's be open? The estate agents were. The Chinese gentlemen worked terribly hard in his experience. He'd give it a try. But first, where on earth was Frost?

'Home, sweet home,' Simms said.

DS Waters followed DC Simms across the threshold of the police quarters in Fenwick Street. Judging from the hall, it was as grotty inside as it appeared to be from the outside – like a neglected council house, only dirtier.

'There are four rooms upstairs. Only myself and Miller are here at the moment. The lounge is in here.'

Waters peered in at a tatty leather sofa that appeared to have seen a lot of action, a huge Grundig TV, and a video recorder almost in the middle of the floor, leads trailing to the Grundig. An assortment of video cassettes was scattered around both.

'Video, eh? But I thought you said . . . ?' Waters was reflecting on this morning's conversation with Mrs Hartley-Jones.

'Yeah, yeah, I know what I said,' Simms said dismissively. 'That one isn't officially ours, if you see what I mean.'

He led on down the hall, along a hessian carpet that could best be described as filthy. 'And down here is where we find mother.'

'Great, I'm starving.'

Sat at a cheap Formica table was a pasty PC in his uniform

shirt sleeves. He was eating beans on toast, washed down with a can of lager, as he leafed through a newspaper.

'Frank Miller, John Waters,' Simms said.

'Wotcha,' Miller said, without looking up.

Simms was a little embarrassed by his colleague's curtness, Waters thought. 'Frank's had a double-shift; he's feeling a bit tetchy,' he improvised by way of explanation. Simms reached into an overhead cupboard in an effort to locate something to eat. 'C'mon Frank, we've a guest,' he said encouragingly.

'There's beer in the fridge,' Miller grunted.

'That's the spirit.' Simms placed several items on the kitchen work surface. 'Well, John, lean times, I'm afraid. Spam and beans OK with you? I think there might be half a packet of Smash kicking around too if we're lucky . . .'

'Any chance we could dine out?'

'At last!'

Although it had gone eight o'clock, Superintendent Mullett was reluctant to go home to an empty house, so decided instead to remain at Eagle Lane to complete a report. It also meant he could wait for Jack Frost, who he had instructed to check in before the close of play. And here the shabby detective finally was, in a tatty short-sleeved shirt that would not have looked out of place on Ronnie Biggs in Rio.

'The girl you found this morning, could this be her?' Mullett passed him the school photo. 'Samantha Ellis. Fifteen years old. Lives with her mother out on Bath Hill. Been missing for two days.'

Frost frowned at the picture. 'Not sure. This one has a nicer smile and bit more colour in her face.'

Why did he affect not to care when Mullett knew damn well he did? Sardonic remarks like this did nothing more than irritate.

'Is it the girl or not?'

Frost turned to go. 'Could be. I'll have to get the family to ID,' he said, his hand on the door handle.

'That's a start, then. I've alerted the lab, they'll be expecting you.'

'Very good of you, sir . . .'

'Wait. Come back, Jack. Sit down. A word if you please, before you go.'

'About the crime clear-up stats . . .' Frost began, slouching in the chair opposite and busying himself with a crumpled cigarette pack.

'No, no.' Mullett waved off the mention of the severely overdue figures. 'Other than the dead girl, what's your caseload like?'

Frost paused.

Mullett could tell he sensed danger. 'In general, how're things going?' he said in a placatory manner. 'What, shall we say, is rumbling along?'

Frost relaxed, and exhaled smoke towards the ceiling. 'There's still the female bank robber on the loose – the driver, Louise Daley. We've had a couple of leads . . .'

'Hang on a minute,' Mullett snapped, the mask of pleasantry instantly dropping. 'Surely you're not wasting time on that? It's hardly a priority.'

'Closure, sir.'

'Closure? That's never been an issue in the past,' Mullett huffed.

Frost was about to object but Mullett raised a hand. 'How many times have we been over this? We nailed three of them, all now inside, one of them in a wheelchair. Forget about it. There's something else, something special you can do for me – for Eagle Lane. Look good on the record sheet.'

Frost said nothing, but sat stoically opposite as though awaiting final judgement.

Mullett steeled himself. 'I want you to pair up with Waters, the chap on loan from the Met,' he began, pausing before adding, 'You know who I'm referring to? Nice chap, was out with Simms today.'

'Heard his name come up on the squawk box. Isn't he the same rank as me? Wouldn't it be more beneficial if you teamed him up with a junior? He's not much use to me; I've got a dead girl to deal with – more routine.'

'I hear what you're saying, Frost. But DS Waters is . . . different.'

'Why, because he's from the Met? We've had them before – bit cocky, but basically the same deal.'

Mullett frowned. 'If I have to spell it out to you, as it seems to have escaped your notice, DS Waters is a *black* officer.'

'Really?' Frost said indifferently. 'I haven't had the pleasure of meeting him. Missed the briefing this morning. Why, is it a problem?'

'Not for me, Sergeant,' Mullett retorted forcefully, 'but some officers are, perhaps, a little less forward-thinking.' His mind went back to the heckling this morning.

'Are you suggesting there's racism in the police force, sir?' Frost's eyebrows shot up his forehead in mock surprise. 'Here, in this day and age? Surely not.'

'I'd like to think it's only on the fringes,' Mullett said, not meeting Frost's eye. 'Nevertheless, to be on the safe side, from here on you're responsible for him.'

'What, like a chaperon?'

'You're the most senior-ranking officer present, therefore it's your duty.' And, Mullett thought, the men respect you, although heaven knows why. 'Besides, DI Allen's away. Simms, Clarke, Myles – they're all under your jurisdiction now. Use them and Waters any way you see fit. Just ensure that this burglary gets cleared up – it's the third in as many weeks.'

'Ah yes – one of your chums, so I gather. The cat in the fridge case, isn't it?' Frost said chirpily.

Mullett got up from behind the desk and paced the office. He ran a finger inside his collar. Before Mrs M disappeared off to visit her sister, he'd been prompted to launder his own shirts as a test run, just in case the need arose while she was away. Too much starch, he now realized. It was irritating the hell out of him, and shortening his patience to a minimum.

'The previous week a dog was also garrotted,' Mullett said stiffly.

'What sort of dog?' Frost asked.

'How the blazes should I know? Does it matter?'

'But how did it fit in the fridge?'

'It wasn't found in the fridge! The dog was dumped on the compost heap. This is all irrelevant – just get on top of it, will you. I know you already have the dead girl by the railway line, but I can't have Simms foul this up. Good lad though he is, he's very green. No arguing – that's an order. Dismissed.'

Frost got to his feet and left the office without a further word. Almost immediately Mullett regretted his harsh tone. Wells had informed him this morning, whilst discussing DC Hanlon's bereavement, that Frost's own mother had died last month. The man, to Mullett's knowledge, had not missed a single day, apart from that of the funeral itself.

He loosened his tie. It was pressing on the scratchy collar and he was tired. But overall the day had not turned out too bad. Winslow, the odious little man, may have actually done him a favour in foisting Waters on Denton. Mullett's gambit to bring him under Frost's jurisdiction was a good one. The situation might well become incendiary if Frost screwed up, and the odds were that, his colleagues' respect notwithstanding, Frost would indeed screw up. And with it lose his chance of promotion, something Winslow had been hassling Mullett to expedite ever since DI Williams's demise.

Yes, Mullett thought to himself, from this perspective he really couldn't lose.

*   *   *

Frost and the WPC stood respectfully at a distance while Mrs Ellis identified her daughter's body. Drysdale solemnly replaced the sheet.

Accompanying her was her long-term boyfriend, Larry; Mrs Ellis was widowed three years ago and Samantha had, apparently, learned to regard him as her dad. Accordingly he seemed just as distraught as any father would be.

Not surprisingly, it hadn't been easy to probe the pair for information prior to leaving for the mortuary, but Frost had tried his best. Mrs Ellis was vague about her daughter's movements in the hours before her death. As she'd already reported, Samantha had gone out on Saturday and had not returned; where she'd been, or who with, the mother didn't know. She was often out at the weekend. It was difficult for Frost to judge whether the girl had been secretive, or whether the mother just wasn't interested in what her daughter got up to. At this stage he didn't really like to push the questioning too far.

From what he had observed at the family home Samantha had been quite an unusual teenager. Her bedroom was devoid of the bright popstar posters that seemed to be the norm for girls of her age; instead it was filled with sombre astrological paraphernalia. Mrs Ellis knew of a diary, but had searched for it in vain when she realized the girl was missing.

Having identified her daughter's corpse, Mrs Ellis was convulsing with grief, and it was all the shell-shocked boyfriend could do to stop her collapsing to the floor. The WPC patted her arm. It was one of the worst parts of the job, observing a family's distress in the cold, grey surroundings of the mortuary. What a god-awful place to kiss your beloved goodbye, Frost thought. He knew there was literally nothing he could say that would make things better, so elected to keep quiet.

The WPC had begun to lead the sobbing Mrs Ellis out of the room, but the boyfriend stayed back and turned to Frost.

'How could this happen in Denton? How could you let

this happen? You're supposed to be responsible for keeping it safe!'

'I'm very sorry, sir, we're doing everything we can. If you'd just like to come this way . . .'

'I'm not leaving until you promise you'll do everything in your power to find her killer. I want every officer in your wretched force to be put on this.'

'Now, we don't yet know if there *was* a killer. It may have been . . . an accident.'

'An *accident*? People don't accidentally fall out of trains! Do you think she was some kind of idiot?'

Frost remained calm; he'd been on the receiving end of such anger many times before. What better way to combat your sense of uselessness than by having a pop at a policeman. He could see this was the man's last great gesture of surrogate fatherhood and was happy to let him have it; it was all part of the job.

'Sir, I realize how difficult this must be for you. If anything comes to mind regarding why Samantha went up to London on Saturday, please do call me.'

'We've already told you! She didn't say! She often went out with friends. It was probably just a shopping trip. Who knows?' He started to move despondently towards the door of the lab.

Frost recalled that there were two drunk girls on the train, picked up by the second cab driver. Could they have been friends of Samantha's? It was worth checking out, although surely they would have reported something if they'd witnessed what had happened. Unless they'd been involved.

'Sir,' Frost called out. 'Could you ask Mrs Ellis again about the diary? It could be crucial.'

Larry nodded as he left the building and emerged into the cool night air.

Monday (5)

Sue Clarke pulled the duvet up close around her neck and took a massive swig of Chardonnay. A small black-and-white portable was perched on the corner of the dressing table, and a heartrending scene from *Brief Encounter* was being played out. She could feel her eyes begin to fill with tears, but not in response to the film, which she'd seen at least a dozen times before and found more comforting than sad. No, if anything, these were tears of self-pity.

When the doorbell had gone earlier that evening she was sure it would be him, and the disappointment must have shown. Derek looked embarrassed and was lost for words. He smiled and mumbled some pleasantries about making sure she was OK, and being worried about her on her own. At least he'd made the effort. She started to wonder if maybe ditching him had been a mistake . . . but just her luck, he was dating Liza Smith, Mullett's secretary, and had been for the last six months or so. Well, you know what they say, the grass is always greener . . .

She gently rubbed her leg, which was smarting again. She

reached over to the bedside table for painkillers and swiftly swallowed two with her wine.

Clarke's romance with Jack Frost had begun last autumn, just after the shoot-out in Denton Woods. That was when she'd first worked with Frost; on the bank-robbery case; and the pair of them had nearly been killed. She knew that a secretive affair with a married man and fellow-officer could hardly be more wrong, and she had no one to blame but herself; she'd made the first move. It was after she'd seen Frost's wife turn up at the hospital; he, the unhappy victim, laid low with appendicitis; she, the sexy, smug victor, complacent in the knowledge that he couldn't bring himself to leave her. The encounter had brought it home to Clarke. She knew the poor devil would never free himself, despite confessing repeatedly that the marriage was over, and the realization spurred her on. She seduced him.

It was eleven o'clock when Frost finally returned home. The house was in virtual darkness. He let himself in the front door and closed it gently. A soft flicker of light escaped from the living room, and he peered through the door to see Mary slumped over, asleep in the ancient recliner – an heirloom of his father's. Some old movie was on the TV; it amazed him that Mary could sleep through the din, as a steam train pulled noisily out of the platform, with a swell of background music. He turned away; he'd had enough of trains and stations for one day. Slipping off his shoes he padded to the kitchen and flicked on the light, the brightness of the blazing fluorescent tube momentarily blinding him. On the kitchen table was a half-empty bottle of Smirnoff with the cap off. No wonder she was sleeping through the racket.

Frost sighed as he poured himself a measure and lit a cigarette. Leaning against the stove and staring through the window at the moon, he reflected on the day's events.

The sound of a creaking floorboard indicated that Mary had

finally roused herself and was heading for bed. He picked up the vodka and made for the lounge. The TV was still on; a woman and her husband were sat in a front room, old-fashioned and yet not too dissimilar from his. He switched it off with a shrug. The pair of them hardly kept abreast of modern trends, apart from Mary and her clothes and music, that was. He turned on the standard lamp and sank into the chair Mary had recently vacated.

Mary and Sue. Sue *or* Mary. Without warning the image of the poor unfortunate teenager he'd seen today on the slab popped into his mind. He blinked, refocused and caught sight of the stack of old 78s that had once belonged to his mother. Getting down on his knees he began to shuffle through: King Oliver, Jelly Roll Morton and Duke Ellington. Frost slipped 'Canal Street Blues' out of its sleeve and flipped up the lid on the turntable. He lifted off a 7-inch of 'Only You' by Yazoo, flopped the weighty disc in its place and moved the switch across from 45 to 78 rpm. As the needle crackled in contact with the vinyl Frost moved back to the recliner and picked up a book he'd been reading the previous night, Oman's *Peninsular War*, Volume V.

He tried to engage with the British resistance at Tarifa, but the jazz and vodka took him before he'd even reached the bottom of the page.

Once he was sure his wife was asleep, Chris Everett slipped out to the garage and retrieved his briefcase from the Rover. He didn't dare keep it in the house; Fiona was always sniffing around, going through his stuff, suspicious old witch. She never ventured into the garage, though. The videos were hidden in the boot of the old MG, which had been off the road for all but a month since he'd bought the blasted thing four years ago.

Back in the kitchen, Everett flipped the case open. He'd laid a shirt on the table and now he placed the jewellery on it gently, piece by piece. Half a dozen necklaces – one pearl, a couple of diamond ones, and the extraordinary emerald one he'd picked up at Rimmington, with its matching brooch and earrings.

Chris Everett, regional manager for Regal Estates, had systematically stored information on every property he had personally valued for the company over the last seven years. His 'hands-on' attitude to the business, and keenness to remain in the field had earned him a succession of promotions throughout his career. Little did the customers or Regal management realize he'd revisit the property a couple of years later with copies of the keys he'd cut whilst they were in his possession.

Of course, he'd always smash a windowpane in order to divert suspicion, but entry with a key was so much quicker and safer than trying to fathom latches and climb through windows. He wrapped the jewellery in the shirt, folded it tightly and placed it in a Bejam carrier bag, and then he made his way quietly through to the living room.

Tuesday (1)

DC Clarke moved stiffly in the breakfast queue in the Eagle Lane canteen, where service had finally resumed. Though she had lost quite a lot of blood, the wound she'd sustained yesterday was largely superficial, and there seemed no reason not to return to work immediately. Better than feeling sorry for yourself in a miserable little flat, she thought; after all it was just a graze by some kid, albeit a bloody one.

Earlier Control had patched through a Missing Person call. Desk Sergeant Bill Wells had taken details from an upset mother. Apparently she'd returned from a weekend break – a very nice trip to the Lakes by all accounts – and her sixteen-year-old son was nowhere to be found. She wasn't too concerned, as he was always sloping off to some burger bar or to the Rec with his friends, returning after dark reeking of cigarettes and cheap aftershave. The worrying thing was that as of this morning he'd still not reappeared, and he should have been at school today. Although she dutifully took the details and accepted the request to follow it up, Clarke had struggled to be sympathetic; the truth was she was still preoccupied with Frost.

She looked across the canteen, and found herself recalling the events of last autumn again, as she had in bed last night. Frost lying prone in Denton Woods, her horror at thinking he'd been shot, and then, as he lay in hospital, the bomb taking out the TA building and damaging the station. Who'd have thought a slovenly, married detective could leave her feeling so exposed. And there he was now, shovelling down a plateful of bacon and eggs and not even bothering to look at her.

Well, she thought, it didn't really matter. Given his blatant lack of concern for her welfare, she'd finally resolved to ditch him, or at least bring matters to a head. She had in her bag a letter she'd written last night, expressing her anger and explaining that unless things changed dramatically, she no longer wanted to see him. She would give it to him today.

She paid at the till and made a beeline for his table before any curious well-wishers could distract her. Noisily she slid her tray across the surface, nudging Frost's breakfast plate.

He gave a start before smiling briefly. 'Morning, love,' he said. 'Good to see service has resumed – Dunkirk spirit and all that – Grace is a marvel. Mind you, it was six months ago, so you'd expect things to start improving by now.'

Typical, she thought. He doesn't even ask how I am! She was all set to admonish him for his lack of concern but was drowned out by the sudden clatter of workmen beyond the serving hatch.

Frost folded the *Sun*. 'I'm a *Times* man myself, but you can't beat the redtops for a bit of chest-beating.' He pointed with his fork to the *GOTCHA!* headline on the paper and gave a wry smile.

'Aren't you going to ask me how I am?' she said incredulously.

He looked up blankly. 'Is there something up?'

'Don't act as if you didn't know – I'll . . . !' She clenched her teeth, barely able to control her anger. 'I was *stabbed* yesterday morning. Stabbed, Jack.'

'Hey, calm down. I thought it was a more of a nick . . . you know, just a flesh wound.'

'Don't tell me to calm down,' she said, her voice rising. 'A flesh wound? Who told you that? I lost a pint of blood! Half a dozen stitches, I needed.'

'Really? But when Bill called me yesterday afternoon, he said you'd . . .' Frost paused, trying to find an expression that wouldn't get him into more trouble. He wisely gave up. 'But you're all right, though? No lasting damage?'

'Didn't it occur to you to find out how I was?' she hissed. 'To find out if I wasn't a little upset by this . . . this *flesh wound*? No. Instead, while I suffered alone in my flat you were at home with her!' Too late she realized that the building work had stopped and that her voice sounded loud above the canteen chatter. She felt suddenly embarrassed.

Frost put down his knife and fork and smiled a pathetic smile. His eyes were on hers, and for a moment they just looked at each other.

'I'm sorry,' he said calmly. 'I didn't finish until late. I had to ID the girl found down by the railway track yesterday morning.'

'What girl?' said Clarke in spite of herself.

'A teenager, Samantha Ellis. She was found with a broken neck about a mile outside Denton. Mullett would like it to be suicide, but I'm not so sure—'

'Jack . . .' interjected Clarke.

'See, Drysdale found skin under the fingernails, which seems to suggest—'

'Jack, please!' she said, insistent. He stopped mid-sentence. 'What are we going to do?'

Frost raised his eyebrows in puzzlement.

'You said we'd be living together.'

'No need to rush things.'

'What do you mean, *rush* – you said it would be by Christmas! New Year at the latest. Look at us, it's now May, and you're still playing the happily married man!' She felt like a tired record, the grooves blurring from overuse.

'Mary's ill,' he said gravely.

'What do you mean, *ill*? How ill? You always say that. She's been ill since I've known you.'

'Always been a pain, I'll grant you that.' He suddenly looked tired, rubbing his eyes with the back of his hand and sighing. 'I don't know. She's out of sorts.'

'Out of sorts? C'mon Jack, don't be obtuse. Had enough of you, more like.'

He wiped his mouth with a napkin. 'I don't know, Sue,' he said firmly, meeting her stare. 'Really. And now is not the time.'

'It's never the time.' She sat down wearily opposite Frost.

'Aye aye, what's this, lovers' tiff?' said Derek Simms, grinning down at them inanely. 'Mind if we join you?'

'Actually, yes, piss off,' Clarke snapped. After last night she'd briefly felt favourably disposed towards Derek Simms, but as usual he revealed himself to be a total arse in front of his mates at the station.

'Touchy,' Simms said. 'And after I looked in on you last night, too.'

Clarke glanced at Frost: no reaction.

Waters loomed up behind Simms, holding a tray. 'Hey, how's that leg?'

'Sore.'

'I'll bet.'

Waters' appearance seemed to jolt Simms into suddenly adopting a more professional air. Clarke felt he wore it like an ill-fitting suit – awkwardly and without grace. 'John, you've met Detective Constable Sue Clarke. And this is Detective Sergeant Frost.'

Frost raised a hand in a nonchalant wave. 'Welcome to Denton, son. It's a hoot.'

Clarke moved over to allow the big man room next to her.

'Heard a lot about you, Sergeant Frost,' Waters said.

'All lies, and please, call me Jack.' Frost glanced cursorily at the new member of CID. 'I could say the same about you. I've been meaning to catch up with you since you arrived, but there's been rather a lot on. So, what do you make of it so far?'

Clarke switched off. No doubt it would all be blokish banter from here on, which left her cold at the best of times. She pushed away her untouched breakfast. 'Sorry to run, but I've got to go out with Myles.'

'You girls off to do a bit of shopping?' Frost quipped, and the others laughed. God, she loathed him at times. Wincing as her stitches tugged, she gloomily left the table.

Frost observed Clarke's painful exit. Cracking curves, that girl. Wounded leg or no, he still fancied the pants off her. And she had certainly been a pleasant contrast to these two ugly Herberts. He lit a cigarette and took a final swig of tea before switching his attention to the large policeman opposite him.

Frost felt genuinely sorry for the burly black detective sergeant, who might as well have been wearing a sandwich board saying, 'Look at me, I'm different!' so out of place did he seem in this parochial police canteen. It didn't help that there'd been riots in Brixton only last year, causing racial tension everywhere, even in places like Denton where minorities were as rare as hen's teeth. The police seemed to think it gave them licence to be rude to absolutely anyone not obviously Caucasian, from a Pakistani shopkeeper to the staff in Denton's Chinese takeaway. Frost, however, would have none of it and had made it clear how dire the consequences would be for anyone he caught behaving inappropriately.

'You must have upset someone mightily to get assigned here, pal.'

Waters was about to respond, but Simms cut in. 'Did the super give you the school photo?'

'Been missing two days. We visited her old dear last night, up on Bath Hill,' Waters added.

The vision of the pretty blonde flashed in front of him once again, a far cry from the pasty corpse he'd seen in Drysdale's morgue last night.

'It's her,' he replied flatly.

'The mother confirmed she'd not been seen since Saturday. She was meant to stop in to feed her aunt's cat, but she clearly never turned up or she would've got a nasty surprise. By all accounts a nice girl; seems odd she'd leave on the spur of the moment, without so much as a toothbrush,' Simms continued.

'Why did nobody report it earlier?' Frost asked; he hadn't felt it appropriate to quiz the mother last night.

Simms shrugged. 'I guess they figured she was old enough to look after herself. She's nearly sixteen, after all.'

'Yes, well, they figured wrong.' He turned to Sergeant Waters. 'Sorry we've not had time for a proper talk. I'll be back in a couple of hours to give you a spot of direction.'

'That's OK, no rush – Mr Mullett has assigned me to Detective Simms here.'

'Has he indeed?' Frost glanced across at Simms, who had his knife wedged up the neck of an HP Sauce bottle. Even the super could go back on a bad decision once in a while. 'Well, he's had a change of mind.' Simms froze in surprise, the bottle held aloft. 'Seems that as of last night he wants *me* to hold your hand, for a while at least. I'll be back for you about midday.'

As he got up to leave he realized what Simms had been referring to in mentioning the cat and the nasty surprise that would have greeted the girl. 'This place that was done over on Saturday night – any progress?'

'Nothing yet,' Simms said.

Frost lit a cigarette, his fifth of the day. 'Hmm, a burglar with a violent dislike for animals. Perhaps he's allergic to them, like me.'

Tuesday (2)

Simms led the way to the CID offices.

Frost had now moved into Bert Williams's old office, and Simms had reluctantly inherited his shabby chair and rickety desk. Arthur Hanlon's absence meant that the desk opposite was also free, so Waters had a base for the time being. The office itself was filthy. It wasn't entirely Frost's fault – the dust-caked windows and mould on the ceiling could hardly be pinned on him – but he was infamous for being pathologically untidy. The floor was considered an extension of his desk, and scruffy piles of paper spilled across the carpet, dotted with greasy crumbs and cigarette ash. Clearly, taking his detritus with him when he moved had been too much of an effort, so he'd simply left it behind, and for Simms it was a point of principle not to clear up after Frost.

'Sorry about the mess,' he muttered.

'Don't worry, I've seen worse.' Waters shrugged.

Simms went to raise the blinds in order to open the window and let some air in. He'd not been in the office properly since

Friday, and the full extent of the musty waste offended even him, although he'd managed to put up with it for a month. Perhaps it was another uncomfortable example of how Waters' presence threw a less than flattering perspective on things. Despite his placid demeanour, Simms was convinced the taciturn officer was judging him, and he sensed he may not be coming out of it too well.

'I know I'm only a guest here,' Waters said, 'an unwelcome one at that, but might I make a suggestion on the burglary case?'

'Fire away,' said Simms.

'Maybe we should check again the method of the break-in on both of the recent cases. Apart from the dead animals, we may find other similarities.'

'Already on it,' Simms said, waving the file at the DS. 'And no problem with making suggestions – we need all the help we can get.' The path of least resistance – perhaps it was the best way forward. Waters was smart, and Simms could learn a lot from the more experienced man. There seemed little point trying to fight it. Besides, anything he came up with, Simms could take the credit for once the bloke returned to East London. Not that he'd have the man's company for long, now Frost was in the frame. Simms wasn't sure how he felt about that – should he feel slighted?

'Maybe Frost has something too. This warm weather we've been having causes animals to moult; plays havoc with allergies.'

'Yeah, maybe. Christ knows it's been hot.' Simms reached over the desk to whack on the fan, and opened the burglary file.

'What's Frost like to work with?' Waters asked, intent on reminding Simms of Frost's babysitter role, or so it seemed.

Simms paused to consider a suitable response. 'Well, some would say he was unorthodox,' he said, eventually. 'Unconventional. The super certainly thinks so,' he added ambiguously, preferring not to indicate whether he agreed with Super-intendent Mullett or not.

Bill Wells watched a very forlorn-looking Clarke leave the building with that Kim Myles from Rimmington Division. Wells didn't really know Myles, who was a recent recruit to Denton, but already he didn't like the way she carried on, teasing the young lads in uniform and sashaying around the station in her short skirts. He didn't think it appropriate, she being a detective and all.

He watched Myles hold the door for Clarke. She wasn't limping, she just looked sort of depressed.

'These young women.' The superintendent had appeared beside him at the front desk, tutting. 'This would never have happened even five or six years ago.'

'How do you mean, sir?' Wells asked.

'Equality for women in the police force, especially in CID, has certain ramifications.' Mullett shook his head wistfully.

'But, sir, it wasn't a dangerous situation – it was a routine enquiry. No one could have expected—'

But before he could make his point Mullett turned and cut him off. 'Don't get me wrong now, Sergeant. As far as progress and the modernization of the police force goes I'm the biggest supporter there is.'

'Of course, sir. Take DS Waters . . .' Bringing a black officer to Denton seemed to Wells's mind about as 'modern' as you could get.

'What do you mean, "take DS Waters"?' Mullett's brow furrowed, his beady eyes staring intently at Wells, who wished, not for the first time, that he would remember to think before he spoke. 'DS Waters is on secondment from the Metropolitan Police as part of a new programme. It's certainly not my doing, and a pretty ridiculous idea, if you ask me.'

'Yes, sir,' Wells said, fiddling with his Biro. He didn't get the super at all sometimes.

'And talking of progress, I see a skip has appeared outside, but why on earth has it been left in the senior-rank parking bays?'

'A skip?'

'Yes, Wells, you know what a skip is, don't you? I've just seen its arrival from my office window. Why have you allowed it to be left in such a position?'

'PC Pooley is coordinating . . .' Wells began sheepishly, aware of how undignified his grassing-up sounded.

'That boy's hopeless, and anyway, he's off sick. It was you I saw chatting with the tradesmen yesterday . . .'

The phone trilled and Wells grabbed it as quickly as possible, cutting the superintendent off mid-flow. 'Denton Police. Yes, wait one moment, please. It's Mrs Mullett, sir.'

His angry demeanour unchanging, Mullett told Wells to put the call through to Miss Smith, before turning on his heels and marching off down the corridor. Wells cursed his bad luck at being caught in the car park yesterday talking to the builders. A few words exchanged about a fire exit, and suddenly he was responsible for the entire renovation! With any luck, come tomorrow Pooley would be back to take some of the flak.

He glanced at the lobby clock above the notice board. It was only ten o'clock. Still a long way to go, he thought, grudgingly.

Tuesday (3) _____

'Truants among fifth years in early May?' The headmaster looked bemused. 'You surprise me, Detective.'

Clarke felt the colour rise in her cheeks. It was a daft idea. Superintendent Mullett had insisted they visit local schools and get a list of truanting kids, since both she and Myles had judged her assaulter to be about sixteen. She only hoped the old fool sitting in front of them didn't recognize her. It had been a good few years since she'd left Denton Comprehensive, though the head was still wearing the same moth-eaten black gown he'd worn years ago. She remembered him careering around the playground like Batman, terrorizing the first years.

'The older ones will have left already on turning sixteen; they've been dribbling out since Easter. Some return for revision classes – the more conscientious, those sitting GCEs.'

'Anyone expelled? Or particularly aggressive?' Myles asked, making the best of the situation. They'd purposely not told the school the exact reason for the visit – not that Mullett had any concern or fear on Clarke's behalf – but he didn't want it getting out that a Denton officer had been stabbed.

The head shamelessly gave the female officer the once-over with his eyes. 'Let me have a word with the heads of year, Detective . . . ?'

'Myles.'

'Detective Myles,' he repeated, a sly grin on his dried purple lips.

Dirty old toad, Clarke thought.

Myles pulled out of the school's staff car park just as the bell went for mid-morning break, and like wasps from a nest that's been poked with a stick swarms of children flew out of the building's doors. You couldn't blame them; it was certainly a lovely day.

'Well, that was a pretty pointless exercise,' she said, lighting a Silk Cut and winding down the window.

'I agree,' Clarke said resignedly. 'This time of year the entire country's fifteen- and sixteen-year-olds are anywhere but in the classroom. They're either revising for or sitting CSEs and O levels . . .'

'Or neither – hanging around street corners, nicking stuff out of Woolies and stabbing policewomen in car parks,' Myles said.

Outside the gates were a bunch of lads, ties at half mast, shirts hanging out, laughing and teasing one another as they passed around cigarettes. 'Look at them, the little sods.' Myles grimaced. One of them blew her a kiss. 'Enjoy it now, kiddo – it won't be so much fun when you're one of the three million.'

'The super wants leads, but I can't see how we'll get anything, short of me hoiking up my skirt in assembly and calling out for someone to come forward.'

Myles tried to remain positive. 'We might pick up something, you never know. So, where to next?'

'Mayflower Comp, I guess. Jesus, that place makes this one look like Eton – what a dump. My brother went there.'

'So did I, if you don't mind!' said Myles briskly.

I bet, thought Clarke.

'Right,' Frost said, starting the car. 'We're off to see one Harry Baskin. He owns a seedy nightclub called the Coconut Grove, and is no stranger to visits from the Old Bill. His latest venture was a hostile acquisition of the huge Chinese laundry in the middle of town . . .'

'Ah, I heard about it yesterday morning,' Waters chipped in. 'Closed the laundry down and turned it into a sauna, didn't he?'

'Correct. Fair enough, really; the place was on the verge of going bust, yet another victim of the bleedin' recession. When times are tough it's surprising how quickly people learn how to iron their own shirts. So, Harry offers the laundry proprietor a deal – ship out to smaller premises, a new dry cleaner's in London Street, with a few select staff, leaving him with a prime spot in town. Not a bad deal for Mr Wang. Trouble was, that leaves half the original staff on the street. Fortunately for them, kind old Uncle Harry offers to take them under his wing.'

'Very generous of him,' Waters replied knowingly.

'Of course it is. Who are we to suggest he then gets them to skivvy for him around the clock while he pays them bugger all? I reckon that young Chinese lad – you know, one of the ones who got a cab from the station after the last train had arrived – could very well be on his payroll . . . Harry being Harry, he made sure he got the younger, fitter staff and left the oldsters to run Wang's new set-up.' Frost paused for a moment. 'Harry's not a bad lad, though. Just overreaches his natural capabilities once in a while, and that's when we need to slap his wrist. Nothing in the league of the East End villains you must be used to. I bet you couldn't believe your bad luck, getting sent down here!'

'I didn't get sent,' said Waters quietly.

'No?' said Frost, surprised.

Waters stretched uncomfortably in the car. 'I volunteered to come here.'

'Blimey! Nobody's ever done it that way before. What on earth possessed you?' Frost looked out on to Market Square, which they were passing, as if to confirm his view.

'Needed to get out of town for a bit – you know, a change is as good as a rest, that sort of thing.'

'Well yeah, but really, Denton? Surely two weeks in Marbella would've done the trick . . .'

'I needed more than a fortnight on the Costa del Sol.' He sighed. 'I'm going through a divorce. Bit messy, to be honest.'

'Sorry to hear that, pal.'

'It's cool. It's just that until we get the settlement sorted I'm out on my ear. I'd been sleeping on mates' couches for the last two months. So, when the Chief Constable came to the nick at Bethnal Green looking for possible candidates, my hand shot up; not that I think the "initiative" is a good thing for the black man, hell no, it sucks big time, but I felt I'd put people out enough and it would do me some good to get away from all that crap for a while. Know what I mean?'

'Sure, sure, well, we'd better try and make your stay a pleasant one, eh?' Frost smiled. 'And here we are at Harry's.'

Frost had returned to the station to collect Waters as promised, in order to appease Mullett. He'd slipped out to see his colleague and friend Arthur Hanlon, though he hadn't felt obliged to reveal this to anyone at Eagle Lane. The unmarried Hanlon had been close to his mother and her death had devastated him. Frost, having recently lost his own mother, was sympathetic up to a point, but to his mind a hasty return to work was the best medicine for bereavement. True, his own mother's death had been a relief, coming as it did at the end of a protracted and painful illness. This was not the case for Mrs H, who apart from a brief stint last year in Denton General had seemed in the rudest of health before being struck by a heart attack. He wondered how Hanlon would cope with his grief in the months to come; as for Frost, the ongoing process of dealing with his mother's estate had caused him more difficulties than the actual event of her death. He did not think himself cold-hearted, but was disappointed to discover that playing his mother's jazz collection – a fond childhood memory – had proven little more than an irritant to his adult self. He couldn't concentrate on his reading with the big-band stuff, and the lighter, softer melodies sent him to sleep. In a last-ditch attempt to connect with her memory he was in the process of making up cassettes to play in the car. He didn't hold out much hope.

Meanwhile, he'd left Simms with instructions to liaise with British Rail to find out if anything had been left on the train Samantha Ellis might have been on, and also to check out the second cab driver, Charlie Feltham, to try to identify those two drunk girls he'd picked up that Saturday night.

Now Frost and Waters made their way across the pot-holed forecourt towards the tatty entrance of Coconut Grove.

Frost had seen and heard little of Harry since last autumn. There'd not been any trouble at the club, and to all intents and purposes Baskin had been keeping his nose clean. Now the sauna had opened it was clear what he'd been up to these past six months.

The club door was opened by a stern-looking heavy with a crewcut, but upon seeing Frost he simply nodded and stood to one side. This was a well-established ritual.

'Frost! What a nice surprise. What brings you here at this time of day?' Baskin greeted them from the corridor, seemingly about to enter his office. 'The club isn't actually open, but why let that stop you? I'm sure you're up for a party whatever the time of day.'

'Not me, Harry, you know that.'

Baskin laughed a deep, gravelly laugh. 'I would say you're all the same, but you, Jack, are one of a kind, I'll grant you that.'

The two detectives followed Baskin into his den and sat down in a pair of large leather chairs, and Frost began his usual search for a light. Baskin slid a large Ronson lighter across the desk in his direction, eyeing Waters with obvious curiosity.

'So, what's up? Surely it's not about my new place in town? A couple of your girls have already been sniffing around. There's nothing to get worked up about; it ain't a bloody brothel.'

Frost exhaled and said nothing, thinking back to the events of last year.

Baskin misinterpreted his silence as disbelief. 'Come on – if I was interested in that sort of thing I'd run it from here, wouldn't I? Not set up in the middle of town next door to bloody Aster's.' His eyes were flicking nervously between the two policemen.

'Harry,' said Frost, reaching across and squeezing Waters' forearm firmly, 'I'd like to introduce Detective Sergeant Waters from the Met Vice Squad.'

'Bloody hell, Jack, that's a bit heavy!' Baskin exclaimed.

'Nothing for you to worry about, Harry.' Frost smiled. 'It's just a fact-finding mission; you know, information exchange, that sort of thing.'

Baskin raised his eyebrows and muttered, 'Fact finding,' as he weighed up the possible implications. Still looking uneasy, he twisted open a cigar case that resembled a torpedo and silently offered one to Waters.

'Don't mind if I do. These look like quality.'

'Cuban.' Baskin nodded, relief washing over his features. Frost knew his reasoning; if the man could appreciate a good cigar, then he couldn't be all bad.

'Romeo and Juliet, Churchill's favourite,' said Frost, stubbing out the Rothmans which appeared like a child's sweet cigarette in comparison.

'Really?' said Baskin with genuine interest. 'Well, I never. Great man. Great man.'

'I wouldn't get carried away. I imagine that's all you've got in common – though you could probably match his post-war waist-line. Listen, I'm not interested in your sauna place, Harry. I'm sure there's nothing going on there apart from the odd Sunday-school lesson.'

'Knew you'd see it that way, Jack.'

'No, *I'm* not interested in that,' Frost said, taking a sip of the single malt Baskin had just poured, 'though the super has other ideas. You know how it is with him, mixing in powerful circles, playing golf with important people. The manager of the bank next to Aster's, for example. He doesn't want anything unsightly within teeing-off distance of Market Square. The super takes these things very personally.'

'Well, you tell him, Jack, I've taken that on board and I'll see him right.' Baskin paused for second. 'So, if you're not here about that, then what are you here about?'

'A Chinese lad got a taxi from the station to Market Square on Saturday night. I'm guessing he works for you.'

Baskin looked momentarily stumped. 'What makes you say that?'

'The sauna, it used to be a Chinese laundry. We believe you "inherited" a number of the staff . . .'

'Maybe.' Baskin shrugged non-committally. 'But I don't have a monopoly on employing Chinamen. There's that Chinky opposite the Cricketers, for starters.'

'Granted, but you've certainly got a number on your payroll – Clarke and Myles were speaking to one young girl only yesterday, just before Clarke got stabbed in your car park.' Frost reached for another cigarette.

'Now wait a minute,' Baskin said hastily, 'that has absolutely nothing to do with me.'

'Did I say it did?' Frost replied quickly. 'However, you know the press – if that hack Sandy Lane gets hold of it, it certainly won't do your business any good. I can see the headlines now: "Copper Stabbed in Massage Parlour Car Park". *Copper*. If the plod aren't safe, then who is?'

Baskin's face was hardening but Frost continued to push.

'Something tells me he works for you. I don't care what he was doing in London, or what he does for you, I'm only interested in what he might have seen on the train on Saturday night.' Frost noticed Baskin's features relaxing as soon as he realized that he and his operations were not under scrutiny. He didn't give a toss about his employees, that much was certain.

'I see, I see. I think Mark's the lad you're after,' he said finally. 'He went up to the West End on Saturday to Chinatown to see his grandma. But I couldn't tell you where he is now.'

'Mark?' Frost said, surprised. 'Doesn't sound very Chinese to me.'

'So what?' Baskin smiled. 'Not prejudiced, are you, Mr Frost?'

'He doesn't seem all that bad,' Waters said as they got in the car. Compared with some exchanges he'd witnessed, he felt the one between Frost and the corpulent gangster had practically verged on the friendly. The Cortina juddered, jolting him in the back. '*Jesus*,' he muttered under his breath.

'Sticky gearbox,' Frost grumbled. 'Do you have to smoke that thing in here?'

Waters wound down the window rapidly; cigar smoke and the smell of hot vinyl that had filled the car was gradually replaced with fresh air. 'Why did you say I was with the Vice Squad?'

'It beats saying you're part of some poncey government experiment, or whatever it is. Besides, Harry has been shunting more porn videos than you can shake a stick at. Doesn't hurt to make him sweat a bit.'

'OK, fair enough. Where to now?'

'We need to try and find this Mark, so we'll swing by the

new dry cleaner's on London Street where the other refugees from the laundry are. If we get no joy there, we'll head over to the Chinese restaurant. We'll just have to hope the boy hasn't gone far.'

'Sounds reasonable to me. The grand tour of Denton Central continues, then.'

'Yep, and the great thing is we can grab a bite at the same time. Ever had Chinese takeaway for lunch? I wonder if it tastes as good without half a dozen pints of IPA.'

Waters thought the prospect nauseating, especially in the current heatwave. 'A little hot for that, isn't it?'

Frost looked at him in genuine puzzlement. 'Talking of which, grab me that sunhat and shades out of the glove box. Pounding the streets in the midday sun doesn't really agree with me.'

Waters passed over the shades and crumpled panama and then relaxed in the passenger seat, toking on the Cuban cigar. He was glad to have explained his personal predicament to Jack Frost. He'd instinctively struck him as genuine and dependable – a good bloke to have on side. On the others the jury was still out.

Derek Simms was in a jubilant mood. He'd been pivotal in ID-ing the dead girl by the train line – an impressive piece of detective work, he thought. He'd also managed to establish that a bag had been found by a cleaner in an empty train carriage on Sunday. The guard had agreed to bring it back on an incoming train, so Simms was on his way to pick it up.

He arrived at the station ahead of the 2.45 to Paddington, on the off-chance he'd catch Feltham, the second taxi driver that Frost had identified. The cab controller said he was on an airport run and would be back any time now.

The photo of Samantha Ellis lay on the passenger seat. Simms had showed it to the station clerk, who remembered her buying a ticket at around 10 a.m. on Saturday. The man checked off the ticket sales that day, day-returns mostly, all purchased around the same time. Given it was a bank holiday weekend there was a fair bit of through traffic.

Christ, it was hot. His back began to sweat against the plastic Cortina seat. He chucked the *Auto Trader* to one side and got out to stretch his legs, wandering over to the kiosk next to the photo booth. He was thirsty as hell.

'Can of Coke and a pack of Bensons, please, mate.'

'That'll be eighty-six pence, please, guv.'

Simms pulled a pound note out of his wallet.

'Nasty business, that girl,' the vendor said.

Simms looked at the man who had handed him his change: flat cap, denim jacket, late fifties. 'What do you know about it?'

The man shrugged his shoulders. Just then Simms heard the train pull in. He quickly made his way down the stairs and on to the London-bound platform, a dribble of alighting passengers greeting him on his descent. The guard was waving from his van a couple of carriages down. Did he really look that much like a copper? He jogged along the platform and the man handed down a sequinned bag. It looked like a teenage girl's, all right. Result. Now all he needed to do was speak to that taxi driver.

Tuesday (4)

'He no here!'

Frost's seemingly innocuous request to speak to Mark appeared to have sent the owner of the Chinese takeaway, the Jade Rabbit, into something of a rage. He gesticulated angrily, banging a large serving spoon on the counter, causing an array of soy-sauce bottles to vibrate.

Waters watched from near the doorway as Frost, still dressed in a panama hat and Polaroids, proceeded to wind him up.

'Yes, he bloody well is!' Frost shouted back. 'Your brother from the dry cleaner's down the road just told us he's living here!'

'He no here – you go, I call police!'

'I am the flamin' police!'

The small, moustachioed owner looked defiantly at the sweaty, middle-aged detective without recognition. If he did know, he wasn't letting on.

'Listen, I know all about the laundry your brother's family ran, I know it was bought out by Baskin and they had to downsize. But I'm afraid to say I've just been down to see them, and bailiffs have locked the place up. Understand? Bailiffs?'

The man retained his silent, inscrutable stare.

'The place has gone bust, so Mark is staying with you. Your bleedin' brother just told me that!' Frustrated, Frost felt for cigarettes, snatching off the hat and shades. The owner's face was suddenly alight with recognition.

'Flost! Mr Flost!'

'He thought you were undercover!' Waters laughed. 'Those dodgy shades and that straw hat – more appropriate on the Riviera.'

Frost responded by jetting a plume of smoke in his direction.

Suddenly, the door of the takeaway opened and in walked a Chinese youth of around twenty, a large scratch adorning his left cheek. He clocked Frost and Waters and immediately turned on his heel, dashing out of the restaurant with Frost launching after him. Twelve stone of detective in full swing caught Waters' little toe through the thin canvas of his Green Flash trainers, causing him to cry out and stagger back. It took him a moment to regain his balance. He limped out of the takeaway just in time to see Frost at full pelt down the middle of Queen Street, ignoring the traffic at the upcoming junction. A car sped out from the left and was forced to swerve wildly around him, horn blaring as it mounted a traffic island and Frost collided with the boot. When Waters arrived at the scene Frost was bent over double, wheezing as if oxygen was going out of fashion.

'You all right?' exclaimed Waters.

'Of course I'm all right! Nearly had the little blighter.'

'Yeah, I'm sure you did. He had a head start, though; gave him the edge.'

'Something like that,' Frost puffed. 'Think I've got a stitch. Anyway, where were you? Big lad like you, thought you'd nab him easily . . .'

'Bit of foot trouble.' Waters smiled at Frost. He did like this unconventional guy who seemed on the verge of a coronary. 'He probably won't get far. Anyway, we should see what this character, his uncle, has to say about Mark's activities on Saturday.'

'Oi, you!' The driver of the stricken Volvo, a bearded, balding man in a polo neck, had climbed out of his car and was shaking a fist at Frost. 'What the fuck do you think you're doing in the middle of the road! You're lucky I didn't kill you!'

DC Clarke pushed aside a Tupperware of cottage cheese and picked up a pen. She was following up on the case of the missing boy. Sixteen-year-old Tom Hardy, a conscientious boy just starting his O level exams, had vanished into thin air, which according to his mother was not like him at all.

'So, Mrs Hardy,' Clarke said, mustering her patience. 'Let me get this straight. You and your husband went away for the weekend, leaving Tom on his own—'

'No, he wasn't on his own – his sister Emily was at home.'

Clarke took down the particulars. The similarities with the Ellis case were not lost on her. It seemed that as kids reached a certain age the parents wilfully abdicated their responsibilities, and their offspring were taking advantage of the situation and exercising their new-found freedoms, sometimes with dire consequences.

'OK, Mrs Hardy, we'll be over. Is your daughter at home?' She thought that the girl in all likelihood would be the last to have seen her brother.

'She's at school sitting exams. I don't want her getting distressed over this.'

Desk Sergeant Bill Wells didn't need to look at the lobby clock to know it had gone 2 p.m. He could tell by the early-afternoon lull. He couldn't wait for the shift to end. All that nonsense this morning about the skip had got him pretty peeved. On the upside, he'd had a recent result on the gee-gees and planned to take the wife for a slap-up meal down the Denton Tandoori on his next day off.

Yes, he thought, between two and three was often the quietest part of the day, as though the villains had an afternoon nap, a bit like half-day closing on Wednesday, or a siesta perhaps. He had hoped to have Johnny Johnson's portable to listen to the races – he felt another flutter coming on – but with Mullett around, fat chance. He daren't risk riling him further, especially as he'd failed to do anything about the bloody skip. He hadn't been able to contact Pooley; he lived in a flat on London Street without a phone.

Suddenly the tranquillity of the afternoon was shattered. An almighty commotion erupted just outside the door, and PCs Baker and Jordan burst through, wrestling a large, red-faced man between them.

'I ain't done nothing! I'm telling you – geroff!' Once he was inside the door the two PCs released the man, who shook himself and tugged down his blue sweatshirt, which had been practically pulled over his head. Wells immediately recognized Steve 'Mugger' Moore, a petty felon, as his nickname suggested.

As a younger man Moore had been a roofer, and had worked on some major projects for the New Town development in the late sixties. Then one night in the Cricketers – it must've been some time in the early seventies – he'd drunkenly tried to lift a toilet up and launch it out of the window in the style of *One Flew over the Cuckoo's Nest*. Wells had been a gawking onlooker, too drunk and meek to put a stop to it. Mugger totally shagged his back and from that point onwards never worked again. He'd turned to drink and Lord knows what else, and here he was now resisting arrest and arguing the odds about some petty crime.

'Bill, tell 'em I ain't done nothing, promise.'

Wells raised his hands in a gesture of helplessness. His

wife was still friends with Moore's missus – they played darts together at the Cricketers.

'Caught him red-handed in the pawnbrokers up on Merchant Street,' said Jordan, hair still on end after the tussle. Merchant Street, a side road in North Denton, was one of those streets full of untaxed cars, betting shops and pubs. It also had not one, but two pawnbrokers. 'Trying to have it away with a carriage clock. What use that would be to him, I've no idea.'

'I was just looking at it, honest.'

'But can you even tell the time, Stevie old chap? That's the 64,000-dollar question.'

At that point a heavily perspiring Frost appeared in the lobby, Waters in his wake. 'Bleedin' hot one out there today!'

'Ah, Jack, about time. The super—'

'Spare me, Bill,' Frost interrupted. 'I know he's anxious to see me, it must be at least an hour since we last spoke.' He smiled broadly at Jordan and Baker. 'We're very close, you know.' The pair looked blankly at each other.

Suddenly, Moore made a break for it and charged off down the corridor.

'Blimey, must be caught short,' Frost said.

'Think so?' said Baker, unsure what to do.

'No, not really.' Frost rolled his eyes. 'I think he's probably about as keen to see me as I am to see the super.'

Wells watched the blank expressions on Baker's and Jordan's faces, who after a moment's hesitation pelted after Moore. Fortunately for them, the hapless felon had quickly been confused by the warren of similar-looking corridors and re-emerged through the swing doors at just that point, running straight into the arms of his would-be captors.

'Think you're right, it's the sight of you, Mr Frost, that's put him on edge,' PC Baker said.

Frost grabbed Wells's glass of water and took a huge gulp. 'I have that effect on people, I'm afraid, son. But Mr Moore here is used to being on edge. In his day, Stevie-boy was on the edge of every roof on the Southern Housing Estate. But now he's found religion, haven't you, mate?'

Moore looked ready to burst with pent-up hatred. 'I dunno what you're talking about.'

'Yes, you do. I've had the vicar on the horn about his bleeding roof,' Frost said. 'Been nicking his lead, haven't you, you naughty boy.'

Simms sat in Frost's office waiting for the DS to put in an appearance. The office was dreadfully cluttered, with paper spilling everywhere. Instead of clearing Williams's yellowing paperwork, of which there was plenty, Frost had simply plonked his own mess on top of the existing piles.

Whilst he'd been in uniform, Simms had loathed the grubby detective, not least because of Sue Clarke's adoration and her subsequent affair. Now he'd been promoted, he recognized the need to tolerate Frost as a necessary evil in order to get on, and at least give the impression of having some regard for him. But in reality, he still disliked him. It astonished Simms how Frost would wilfully rub Mullett up the wrong way – not that Simms had any great love for Mullett, but he *was* the gaffer, and Simms respected him as such. He couldn't summon up such respect for Frost, but with DI Allen absent and Frost in charge of CID, he'd have to put up with him for now, at least.

Like a bad penny, the man himself appeared in the doorway. 'Right, what you got? Anything?'

'The taxi driver, Feltham, I finally caught up with him down by the station. He remembered dropping both girls off in the Two Bridges area. He gave me rough addresses.'

'So, posh, were they?' Frost asked. Two Bridges was a hamlet towards Rimmington. Simms, though unfamiliar with it, knew it to be well-heeled.

'He didn't say.'

'Age?'

'Teens. He wasn't specific. It was dark, I guess.'

'The other driver I spoke to reckoned they were drunk. Did your guy confirm this?'

'He didn't say.'

'What was he, a mute?' Frost stared at Simms directly.

'Sorry.' The DC fidgeted uncomfortably in his chair. With barely any effort the old git had made him feel inadequate. 'I did run out to Two Bridges and I tried some houses, but there was nobody home.'

'Late or early teens?'

'He didn't . . .' A glare from Frost prevented him finishing the sentence.

'Well, if they're early teens, then they're probably still at school. My guess would be St Mary's, the private place out that way. If they're late teens, then where they are is anybody's guess – St Tropez, perhaps?' Frost rolled up his sleeves, perspiration patches visible under his arms. His forehead was beaded with sweat. Christ, it was only May, what would he be like in July? Frost offered Simms a Rothmans, which he declined. 'Yes, my hunch is it's very unlikely these two knew our poor Samantha Ellis, a mere Denton Comp girl.'

'Shall I go back?' Simms said. 'To Two Bridges, I mean.'

Frost took a seat in Bert Williams's old, moth-eaten chair. 'If you think you have the correct addresses, give St Mary's a call. That will soon answer that.'

'Right you are.'

'I know the headmistress,' Frost mused, a twinkle in his eye. 'She's got a soft spot for me. If it turns out our girls do go there, I'll follow it up later.'

Smug bastard, Simms thought. The woman must be blind, and not the only one, either. What on earth did they see in him?

'DS Waters is in with Hornrim Harry, being given an

induction. Let me know when he's finished his talking-to. Decent bloke, that Waters.'

'Yeah, he's all right for a . . .' Simms checked himself, not knowing where Frost stood with the coloureds.

'For a *what*?' Frost said. 'A black bloke? All the same to me, whatever the colour.'

The subject prompted Simms to remember something that he'd previously given little thought to. 'My kid brother, David, is at Hendon. He says there's a couple black fellers in training there. Apparently they get a hell of a time. They tied this one chap up and gave him a right pasting.'

'Well, if anything like that goes on here, I want to know about it, you hear?'

Simms nodded.

'Oh, I nearly forgot – any joy from British Rail on the lost-property front?'

'Yes, they found a girl's sequinned bag at the depot,' Simms said hastily, pulling out his note pad. 'Smoking carriage at the front.'

'Anything in it?'

'A paperback book, ten Silk Cut, a pair of sunglasses, a sun-hat and a Sony Walkman.'

'A what?'

'A portable cassette player – you know, with headphones.' From Frost's expression it was obvious that he didn't. 'Like those Dictaphones they dished out last month, but for listening to music.'

Frost rubbed his damp brow and lit another cigarette. This time Simms took one.

'So, let's assume the bag's hers. Fingerprints on the Walkman and so on will confirm that. Was all the stuff – the book and cassette recorder – inside the bag when it was found by the cleaner?'

Simms nodded; he hadn't heard any different.

'You're sure?'

'Yeah, why?'

'If you're travelling alone, you'd be reading maybe, or your Walkman would be out. So, if those items had been found outside the bag, we could deduce she'd been taken by surprise. But they weren't.'

'In that case,' said Simms, 'it seems more likely she jumped.'

'Unless, of course, someone put them back in the bag to give that impression—'

'Not disturbing anything, am I?' DS Waters appeared in the doorway.

'Come in, John,' Frost said amiably. Simms moved his seat across to allow the man into the cramped office.

'Jack, Superintendent Mullett would like a word.'

'If only it was simply one word it wouldn't be so bad, but it never is.' Just then the phone rang. 'Saved by the bell.' Frost rooted around his untidy desk, finally pulling at the cord to coax out the beige handset. 'Yeah, all right.' He covered the mouthpiece, mouthing the name 'Baskin'. 'All right. No, I won't. All right. Course. Ta.' He replaced the receiver. 'It seems Mark Fong failed to turn up for his shift at the Pink Toothbrush.'

Frost was addressing Waters; Simms was out of the loop.

'Who?' Simms asked.

'Chinese kid. We think he was on Samantha Ellis's train on Saturday night. He's living at the Jade Rabbit but he works on the side for Baskin, doing odds and sods at his new place.'

'What, the one Mullett was banging on about, the massage parlour? Where Sue got jabbed?' Simms asked.

'That's the one. DS Waters and I bumped into Mark Fong outside his uncle's takeaway place. But he seemed in a bit of a hurry, and didn't want to stop for a chat.'

'Jack nearly caused a pile-up pegging it down Queen Street after him.' Waters laughed. He pulled off a tinny from a four-pack of lager and offered it around. 'Still cold.'

'Let me guess,' Simms said as he pulled off the ring. 'He got away?'

'It was close. Of course he would never have outrun me if a Volvo hadn't got in the way.' They all sniggered. 'Where did you get these beers? Hornrim Harry give them to you?'

'Picked them up after our jog, while you were grilling the guy in the takeaway.'

'Nice one. Well' – Frost gulped – 'Uncle Fong confirmed Harry's story that junior was up in town on Saturday seeing his sick grandma.'

'Why would he hare off, then?' Simms asked.

'Exactly. I've got the granny's address in here, somewhere in Chinatown. But even if it checks out, it doesn't rule out him chucking pretty girls off trains on his way home.' Frost searched his pockets. 'Here,' he said, handing a crumpled piece of paper to Simms. 'Meanwhile, I'd better go and see our beloved leader.'

Frost downed the lager, belched loudly, kneed the empty can towards the bin and missed.

After he'd left, Simms squinted at the tatty piece of paper torn from a notebook. 'I can't figure out how he ever made sergeant with handwriting like this.'

'Here, give it to me,' said Waters, placing his lager can precariously on a pile on the unkempt desk. 'I know someone in that manor, Soho, who can check it out for us. Chuck us that phone.'

'Right,' said Mullett, 'this has got to be quick. I've been waiting for you all day.'

Mullett's agitation wasn't due solely to Frost's elusiveness; there was still his wife's list of chores to contend with, which he'd yet to make a start on. It was imperative he got away in time to call in at the dry cleaner's, but he was hardly about to share this information with Frost; indeed, he had never discussed his wife with anyone at Eagle Lane. Likewise, he certainly had no interest in what any of his underlings got up to in their private life.

Frost took a seat. 'I'm all ears,' he said, with his typical air of irreverence.

Mullett felt his eye begin to twitch. 'What's happening about Baskin's sauna place?'

Frost frowned in puzzlement.

'After-hours shenanigans – the soliciting allegations?' Mullett persisted. 'It's only a matter of time before we get serious complaints.'

'Well, I've nothing to report.'

'Nothing to report full stop, or nothing to report because you've done nothing?'

'If there was any such stuff going on I rather doubt it would occur on a Monday night . . .'

'I want that place under surveillance!' the superintendent snapped. 'And stop rocking back and forth on that chair – it's not a toy.' Frost abruptly halted. 'Come on, we can't have this sort of thing going on in the centre of town. I don't care so much about that seedy club of his, but even you must agree that this completely lowers the tone.'

'But there's no evidence of anything "going on",' said Frost seriously. 'What are we basing this on – a gripe from an old biddy who may or may not have seen something?'

'A detective was stabbed on the premises.'

'That's got nothing to do with it!'

'I don't care, I want that place watched – tonight, understood?' Mullett waited for Frost's acknowledgement, which came in the form of a slight tilt of the head, before continuing. 'The attack on DC Clarke – of course, I accept it could be unrelated, but in any case, it's extremely important we get it resolved, without further ado. I can't have police officers getting stabbed. So what are you doing about it? I've already ordered Myles and Clarke to skim around the schools to get a list of the truants, but more than likely it's one of the riff-raff on the estate.'

'Might not be.'

'And lean on Baskin, Frost, make sure he knows it's in his interest to help resolve this.' Mullett paused, before asking hopefully, 'Now then, this girl, are we any further? Could it have been suicide?'

'More likely murder,' Frost replied.

'Are you sure?' Mullett grew vexed.

'As sure as I can be at this stage.' Frost scratched the back of his head vigorously in a way that reminded Mullett of an animal dealing with an unwelcome tick. He flinched at the thought of his unkempt detective's poor personal hygiene. 'I don't get why you're so eager for a suicide verdict, Super. We've had two this year already. It hardly does the Denton Tourist Board any good, does it – come to Denton and top yourself . . .'

'Neither does murder, Frost. For goodness' sake. The parents IDed her, didn't they?'

'Yes. Samantha Ellis. Fifteen-year-old Denton resident.'

Mullett reached for the Senior Service and offered them to Frost, who took one, tapping it on the desk before lighting it. 'Any suspects?'

'Yes, as it happens, there is one.'

'Already? May I ask who? Come on, don't hold back – this is' – Mullett smiled tightly – 'shall we say, unusual for you to make a break in a case . . .'

Frost stared at him, unmoved.

'. . . so early on,' Mullett finished.

'As it happens, I've just come back from seeing Harry Baskin. He's . . . helping us with our enquiries.'

'Listen, Frost, I want you in the office more. I can't have all this . . .' Mullett waved his hand airily. 'Coming and going alone, all this vagueness.'

'I've no idea what you mean, sir.'

'Come, come, you've been skulking around on your own like Williams used to do. Nobody has a clue where you are. Operating on your own. It's not good.'

'Hanlon is off on compassionate leave.'

'Well, continue to keep an eye on Waters until he returns. Simms is proving too much of a hothead. And I want somebody brought in for the assault on Clarke.'

'What, as a priority over the Ellis case?'

'Yes. As I said, we can't have officers being stabbed in broad daylight. Just bring somebody in.' He almost said *anybody*; it was what he was thinking. He looked at his watch. 'Right, I must be off . . .'

'Ah, the golf course beckons.' Frost was an obstinate sod who clearly enjoyed winding him up.

'If you must know, Denton Golf Club has been shut for the best part of the year. The completion of the new grounds overran.' Mullett stroked his moustache. 'Not surprising, as it's the same shabby lot that are sorting this place out. But, happily, there's an inspection of the new clubhouse tomorrow morning for a select few, ready for the official opening on Friday. Denton now boasts a premium eighteen-hole course.'

'Smashing.'

'It may mean nothing to you, but it signals a move up for the town. You wouldn't understand. What's that you have there?' Mullett peered at a crumpled sheaf of paperwork Frost had slid across the desk.

'Expenses.'

'I haven't got time for this now. Leave it with Miss Smith and I'll look at it tomorrow morning.'

Tuesday (5)

'Right, you're driving,' Simms said as he and Waters strode out of the station and across the car park, the late-afternoon sun-shine hitting them full on. 'Only way you'll get to know your way around.'

'Sure thing, but not in this rust bucket,' quipped Waters, thumping the vinyl roof of the Cortina.

'Fine with me, we can go in your Vauxhall, then. Just let me grab my shades.'

Waters was beginning to feel more at ease. Confessing to Frost that he'd volunteered for secondment to Denton had made him feel less like an alien and more like someone others might identify with.

Frost himself looked as if he had his fair share of problems; he seemed on the verge of exhaustion, and whilst Waters guessed his age at mid-forties he wouldn't be surprised if he was in fact younger. Whatever his true age, Waters felt far more empathy with Frost than with the young, naive DC he'd been saddled with again this afternoon.

Simms and Waters were off towards Two Bridges to inter-view the girls who'd been on Samantha's train. Frost's hunch that they attended St Mary's private school had proved sound, and thanks to the addresses Simms had garnered from Feltham they now had two names, plus a bit of family background. As suspected, both girls were squarely in the well-off bracket.

They inched through the centre of Denton past graffiti-daubed walls and bus shelters invariably urging 'wogs' and 'Pakis' to 'go home'.

So far the locals had seemed pretty wary of him, Waters reflected. It was as though Shaft had walked out of the TV set on to their plush carpet without wiping his feet. In awe, but slightly affronted at the same time, and too polite to comment.

As they finally hit open road and Waters punched through the gearbox, Simms gave him the lowdown on Two Bridges.

'It's not really a village. More of a hamlet.'

'What, long and slender, like the cigar?' Waters grinned at his own bad joke.

'Not a million miles off. There's one narrow street neatly top and tailed by . . .'

'A bridge at either end?'

'You win the cuddly toy.'

Waters had pegged Denton as a classic 1960s new-town project where the majority of the town was purpose-built, destined to soak up London overspill. Prior to that it had probably been a quiet village community minding its own business. It surprised him how quickly the urban gave way to the rural. The day was drawing to a close and the sun hung low across the fields, reminding his East End sentiments of a TV commercial for chocolates.

'Up here on the left, behind this boozer.'

Waters swung down a cobbled lane that ran past the leafy

beer garden of the Fox, and pulled up behind a white Saab. A bank of pastel-coloured cottages greeted them, their façades adorned with hollyhocks and clematis like something his ex would coo over on the box – a scene from a gentle TV period drama. On the opposite side of the road, a huge willow hung mournfully over a pond on a small, neat green, flanked by pristine high-end motors.

'Nice,' he said, reaching back to grab his denim jacket; the temperature still dropped after sunset. 'So what's the background?'

'Gail Burleigh is the name of the girl. Father Max is a lawyer, a partner in his firm. The wife is a lady of leisure. Little Gail is the apple of their eye. According to Mrs Burleigh she's the perfect student, predicted straight As in her O levels. And once she's spun through those, she's expected straight back in the autumn for A levels.'

The Burleighs clearly took the visit from the police very seriously. They'd secreted Gail upstairs in order to have their say first. The father was keen to convey that they were both au fait with their daughter's movements in every particular. She'd been to a gallery on Saturday. Yes, they'd read in the *Echo* that a girl had been found by the railway track, but no, Gail did not know a Samantha Ellis, and of course they were sure, she would have said if she'd known her. Compared with what he was used to when interviewing families, Waters found the air of control and protection almost stifling.

'Can we have a word with her, then?' Simms urged. 'I assure you we're not intending to unsettle Gail.'

'Good,' said her mother with a piercing look. 'She's taking her O levels in under a month and we don't want her studies upset.'

'No exams right now?' Waters asked.

'You mean CSEs?' replied Max Burleigh scornfully, removing his pipe. 'No, Gail isn't sitting *those*.' It was difficult to take him seriously, sitting there in his antique leather chair with his pipe and cravat.

'Well, we won't detain her any longer than necessary,' reiterated Simms. As if on cue Gail herself peered coyly round the living-room door.

She had long, dark curly hair and looked far more womanly than Waters had expected. Simms asked her to come in and looked expectantly at the parents, but they were clearly not in any hurry to leave, and one look at Mrs Burleigh's anxious face told them it was fruitless to ask. 'Of course, you may sit in while we ask a few questions, but I insist you let Gail answer for herself,' Simms said firmly.

Gail perched on the edge of the settee. On closer inspection she was more typical of a girl of her age, heavily made up but in an over-plastered way that gave away her immaturity. Her kohl-rimmed brown eyes were mischievous and lively. Bet she runs rings round her dullard parents, Waters thought.

'So, Gail,' opened Simms, flicking out his notepad. Mrs Burleigh visibly stiffened at this formal gesture but Gail remained unmoved. 'I understand you went up to London for an art exhibition on Saturday. Can you tell me what it was you saw?'

'Titian,' was the soft reply.

'He's her favourite Italian,' the mother chipped in. Simms shot her a glance so sharp she looked shocked and her gaze fell to the floor. Well done, mate, Waters thought.

'And after that?' Gail turned her head and stared into the fireplace, avoiding everyone's gaze. 'I assume the gallery would have shut by, what, six? And yet you got the last train home.'

'We went to see a band,' she replied quietly. 'At the Shepherd's Bush Empire.'

Waters noticed this was news to her mother. 'Who was it?' he said with a wry smile.

'Culture Club.'

'Ah, the gender-benders . . .'

'The *what?*' Mrs Burleigh almost screeched.

'Nothing you'd know about, *Mother*,' spat Gail petulantly.

Waters sniggered inwardly at the horror on Mrs Burleigh's face – she was clearly not as au fait with her daughter's movements as she thought – but he didn't want to alienate Gail so he attempted to draw her in. 'Cool band – a little too much war paint for me but some good tunes.'

'A bunch of woofters, aren't they?' was Simms's helpful response.

'It's just an image thing,' said Gail in irritation. She caught Waters' eye and gave him a coy little smile.

'So let's get this straight,' said Simms, attempting to regain some direction. 'You and—'

'Sarah.'

'You and Sarah went to London for the day to see some pictures, followed by some pop music. Samantha Ellis also went to London that day. Did you see her?'

Gail maintained that she hadn't, and that she and Sarah didn't know Samantha Ellis. Simms chose not to press her on this; they went to different schools and lived in different areas, so it seemed fair enough. The fact they'd caught the same trains that day could easily be a coincidence; the majority of Saturday's day-trippers had departed on the 10.15, the ticket clerk had confirmed as much, and teenagers were notorious for hanging around until the very last train of the night.

He made to wrap things up. He'd been easy on the girl in order to gain her trust, but he'd left one important question to last. 'Gail, thanks for that. One final thing – had you been drinking alcohol?'

Her calm evaporated instantly and once again her mother was quick to intervene.

'Certainly not! Gail is a model pupil. That sort of thing is of no interest to a child who's working towards a Duke of Edinburgh award!'

'Duke of Edinburgh, eh?' Simms said, clearly without the faintest idea what this was.

'Yes,' said Mrs Burleigh haughtily. 'And Gail is still very active in the Girl Guides.'

'Oh, Mother, I've not been in ages.'

'Nonsense! You were away camping with them only recently!'

'Oh, Mother, stop it, you're embarrassing me!'

Mrs Burleigh shrugged. 'Girls these days; they try and grow up so quickly.'

Simms thought the mother naive and a pain; the girl took advantage of the woman's apparent ignorance of her behaviour, making his questioning arduous. He decided to call it a night. They could always come back if necessary.

'What did you make of that, then?' Simms asked Waters as they climbed back into the Vauxhall.

He shrugged. 'Not a lot to go on. I guess we'll have to see if Sarah Ferguson's story matches.' He paused. 'I've seen a few disturbing things in my time, but schoolgirls chucking each other off trains doesn't seem likely to me.'

'Hey, just a sec,' Simms said, 'she's coming over.'

Gail Burleigh was furtively making her way towards them across the cobbled lane. Waters rolled down the window. 'What is it, love?'

She tentatively looked both ways before bowing her head to the window. Waters could detect cigarette smoke.

'I *had* been drinking that night,' she said, then added in a strangely affected fashion, 'I wanted to tell the truth, but couldn't, you know, let on to the, you know, the folks . . .'

'We understand, love,' Simms said, leaning across. 'Thanks for letting us know. Mum's the word.' The girl scurried back to the dark of the terrace. 'Not such a model pupil after all.' He smirked.

'Maybe holding your booze is part of the Duke of Edinburgh

award?' Waters suggested as he turned the key in the Vauxhall's ignition.

'Imagine that, the whole bloody lot of them pissed.' Simms lit a cigarette. 'Talking of which, I'm feeling quite parched myself.' He gestured towards the Fox which had just come into view. 'Might as well grab a pint.'

'It's not quite six yet. Will it be open?'

'These country boozers are a law unto themselves. But, before we go in, I just wanted to ask you a question . . . You're not one of *them*, are you?'

'One of *what*?'

'You know, a poof?' Simms looked at him with one eyebrow raised.

'Eh? Because I said I liked Culture Club? I was just trying to relate to the kid. Try it sometime – you might find you win them over.'

'Yeah, yeah, very smooth,' Simms said. 'Well, that's a relief, anyway. Working with the only black policeman within a 100-mile radius is one thing, but being stuck with a *gay* black policeman would really be pushing it.'

'C'mon, pretty boy, we're in the '80s, anything goes.' Waters jigged his hands in the air light-heartedly.

'Maybe on your beat, matey,' grimaced Simms, pushing open the heavy wooden door of the pub, 'but not in Denton. These old codgers would bag you as soon as look at you.'

Chris Everett was surprised to see the shabby Bedford van as he pulled up on his newly shingled drive. Tradesmen at this hour? He checked his watch – ten past six, definitely late in the day for workmen. The back of the van was open and he peered inside to see an assortment of poles and brushes. Shock pulsed through him like a lightning bolt – shit, no, it couldn't be! Bloody Fiona, it was May, dammit! Why the fuck was she calling out a chimney sweep in May? The fire wouldn't be used until the autumn, that was why he'd picked the chimney as a hiding place.

He raced through the hall and reception room and into the lounge. Sure enough, there were dust sheets all over the Wilton and cleaning rods and brushes mingling among the hearthside ornaments.

'All right there, boss,' said a chirpy little man, stepping out of the large inglenook fireplace.

'Where is my wife?' Everett said sharply.

'Just run your girls off to ballet.'

Of course, he thought. But why the hell was this guy here? Everett looked on, paralysed with panic as the man started fitting pipes and brushes together.

'You look like you've seen a ghost!' the sweep said. 'Maybe you have. Old house like this. I bet there've been a few happenings . . .' He detached the hood of the wood burner.

Everett felt perspiration break out on his top lip. 'Look, what exactly are you doing here? We have the chimney swept every October – not in the middle of May, for God's sake!'

'Pigeons,' the man said bluntly, grimacing as he grappled with something up the chimney.

Why hadn't Fiona mentioned this to him? Admittedly, he was seldom there during the day. And pretty elusive in the evenings, too, it was fair to say.

'Been making a hell of a noise.' The sweep began to poke the brush through the vent.

'Stop!' As he said it, Everett felt stupid. 'You can't, we've got people coming. Guests will be arriving any minute.'

'Won't be five minutes,' the sweep said. 'Hello, what's this? Something's in the way.'

Everett stood helpless as the sweep pulled the plastic bag out into the fireplace. Before he had a chance to think what to do, the man had the contents on the hearth.

'Bloomin' Nora!' he exclaimed. 'You've only got the crown jewels hiding up there!'

In desperation Everett made his move. He reached above the horse brasses and pulled his grandfather's salmon gaff off the brickwork chimney breast. The 'gaff' or poacher's hook was made of steel and brass and resembled an extendable butcher's hook, only much sharper. The poacher needed only the deftest of light touches to pierce the fish's flesh and take grip.

Everett didn't hesitate. He wasn't about to let some out-of-season chimney sweep probing for pigeons destroy his life. He came at the man from behind while he was crouched over the booty, and with one swift movement pulled back his head and sunk the gaff effortlessly into his neck, piercing the jugular. The stunned sweep gurgled and twitched for barely a minute, his dust sheets conveniently soaking up the gush of blood. Once he was sure the man had stopped moving, Everett glanced at his watch – he had about ten minutes before Fiona got back from dropping the twins off at ballet class.

Superintendent Mullett hurried down London Street towards the dry cleaner's – passing, he noticed gloomily, firmly shut shop fronts – to finally pick up his shirts. He was dismayed to find it padlocked and not a flicker of life from within. He rattled the front door and then saw the notice. It wasn't as simple as bank-holiday trading hours. Bailiffs had taken possession of the premises due to non-payment of rent, and the business had gone bust. Mullett's mind took a second to compute. He squinted through the window and could actually see his shirts neatly ranged on a clothing rail – a dozen in all, along with a spare uniform.

There was no telephone number on the notice. He stood back from the store in bewilderment.

*   *   *

'Ah, there you are,' Frost said, looking up to see a tired DC Clarke standing in the doorway. He reached across the desk and switched off the noisy fan; the office was cooling as the day drew to a close.

'Yes, I heard you were looking for me.'

'I was. How's your day been?'

Frost's smile was met with a grimace. 'Bloody terrible. My leg really hurts. Also, it's . . .' she sat down opposite, clearly in pain, fighting back the tears. 'It's humiliating.'

Frost squirmed in his chair. He hated this, but he knew he should make the effort to show sympathy. 'I know,' he soothed.

'No, you bloody well don't know!' Clarke was convulsed in sobs. 'Mullett has had me searching for my own attacker. First it was the schools, which was bad enough, then the estates, and then on Market Square, questioning every little oik who goes by. It's really demeaning, Jack. The word's out. I'm a laughing stock.'

'What do you mean, the word's out?' Frost knew what a dim view Mullett would take of this attack being public knowledge. He certainly wouldn't have notified the papers.

'Word on the street, I expect. Probably the schools. A bunch of blasted kids down Milk Street were jeering at us, on the Southern Housing Estate. Myles and I were down there to check out some kid on parole. We stopped at a newsagent to pick up some cigarettes, and there must've been a dozen of them laughing at us.'

'Are you sure they know? I'd be surprised if the schools would let it leak. The press don't know – I'd have heard by now . . .'

'They know, Jack. And then there's uniform.'

Frost loosened his tie further, and pulled out a bottle of Black Label from the desk drawer. 'Here, this'll take the edge off.' He emptied the cold coffee into the bin before pouring whisky into the cup. 'Don't worry about uniform – enough of them have been caught out in far more compromising circumstances.'

'Well, if they have to know about this one, why can't it be handed to them to follow up on? Got any aspirin I can take with this?'

Frost rummaged around in the drawers and pulled out a crumpled pack of pills. He tossed them over.

'Anyway, are you coming over tonight?'

Fair enough she should ask. Tuesday night was the one he usually spent with her while Mary was at bingo. But this week he just didn't want to. He was finding the whole thing too suffocating.

'Later . . . I've got to do these crime stats for Allen. He's skiving off on some computer course . . . a waste of time, don't you think?'

'Whatever, Jack. I'm too tired to argue with you now. Why did you want me, anyway?'

He felt it was a loaded question. 'I just wanted to see how you are, and see if I could help track down the bastard who did this to you.'

'Really? If I didn't know better, I would have said Mullett had been breathing down your neck to sort this out. But I don't actually care. I'm going home.' Clarke got up stiffly and left.

'See you later,' Frost called out half-heartedly, topping up his own coffee mug with Black Label and lighting a cigarette. He pushed the crime stats out of the way and looked at the file on recent juvenile offenders Webster had dropped off. Most were familiar – a right bunch of stinkers. He'd go through those tomorrow. Only then did he notice the envelope marked JACK, his name underlined in ballpoint pen. Though in capitals, he thought he recognized the handwriting as Clarke's. The sharp underlining indicated the contents had been written in haste, or anger. Frost sighed remorsefully and shoved it to one side; he had more pressing worries to contend with.

He picked up the phone and dialled his home number. It rang and rang; no answer. He checked his watch – it was just past 7.30. Mary may well have left already for bingo with the girls. Perhaps it was a sign that everything was all right – she was definitely out of sorts, as he'd said truthfully to Clarke. Not a word this morning. Something was up. He realized he should have called earlier, but the meeting with Mullett and Clarke's appearance in his office had distracted him. And if there was a problem, then surely she would've called him? He got up to refill the kettle, thought better of it, grabbed his car keys off the desk and made for the door.

On his way out through reception, he passed Desk Sergeant Bill Wells, into the last half-hour of his shift. 'Evening, Bill.'

'You off somewhere, Jack?' said Wells.

'Home.' Frost smiled weakly.

'Home?' Wells checked the wall clock behind. 'Unlike you to be leaving this early. There's nothing up, is there?' Before he could answer Simms and Waters came through the double doors.

'Ah, men, what news?' Frost asked with gusto, glad of the distraction.

'Nothing much,' Simms replied. 'We went back to Two Bridges to interview Gail Burleigh, one of the girls from the train. She had little to say and her parents are both posh wallies.'

'Jolly good,' Frost said, deflated. 'That's what I like to see – good, unbiased detective work.'

Frost rang his own front-door bell, something he was unaccustomed to doing, seldom being back before Mary was in bed. Last night had been an exception of sorts. He looked around the close. It was strange being home before dark. Out of habit he'd stopped at the corner shop for a dried-out sandwich and a couple of tins, but it was still only just before eight.

He was struck by the pleasant May evening. Blackbirds chattered melodically, and the cherry blossom in the garden was in the last throes of its pink splendour. Strangely, Frost had no recollection of previously noticing it in bloom. He'd planted the sapling when they'd first moved in fifteen years ago, that much he remembered, but afterwards he wasn't sure he'd even given it a second glance.

As expected, the bell remained unanswered so he took out his key. The second he opened the door the neighbour's cat rubbed around his legs and shot into the house. It drove him spare that Mary fed the brute; she knew he hated cats. Maybe that was why she did it.

The house was dark and silent, but for some reason he still felt compelled to check for signs of life. In the living room his records and cassettes remained scattered on the floor as he'd left them the previous evening. The kitchen was tidy but empty, apart from the cat, who sat expectantly in front of the fridge.

'Think you might have a bit of a wait, pal.' Frost sighed, slumping into a kitchen chair.

Suddenly the phone rang.

'Jack?' It was Desk Sergeant Bill Wells.

'Still there, old son?'

'It's not quite eight yet; I'm counting off the minutes.'

It was a novelty for Frost to be called at home by Bill Wells; he was seldom there in the hours Wells manned the desk, and was far more accustomed to the voice of Night Sergeant Johnny Johnson on the other end of the line. It wasn't unusual to be woken in the middle of the night by such calls.

'What's up?'

'It's the super, Jack. He rang to ask who's watching Baskin's sauna tonight.'

'Flamin' hell, Bill!'

'Look, don't shoot the messenger! Sorry, but he was insistent. He's waiting for me to call him back, and he said he'd left it with you. So, who's gonna watch it?'

'Me.'

'What, from home? Shall I tell him you're using binoculars?'

Frost sighed again. There was no way around it; he'd have to go himself. With Hanlon off, Williams dead and Allen on that stupid computer course, Denton CID was reduced to a pack of inexperienced kids. He didn't want Simms near Baskin – he was too green and hot-headed, with none of the razor-sharp instincts needed to deal with a seasoned gangster. The girls were a risk, too; they had it in for Harry, maybe not undeservedly, but he didn't want them throwing the book at him just because they saw crumpet hanging around his premises.

No, he could handle it quite comfortably.

Tuesday (6)

Frost sat in the car on the corner of Foundling Street enjoying Kung Po beef, special fried rice and a tinny.

After Wells's call, he'd left home straightaway and stopped for a couple of pints in the Bull, across the road from his current position, just to get the lie of the land. It had been too early to be watching the massage parlour; any lewd goings-on surely took place much later. He then drove north on to Queen Street and stopped in at the Jade Rabbit to try and smooth things over. His apologies were graciously accepted and returned in equal measure with the offer of a free dinner, which was gratefully received. It was in their interest to promote goodwill; Frost was something of a regular there, but also they were clearly still on edge with regard to the errant nephew. If they'd previously been protecting him, it seemed they'd now decided on a different tack; the proprietor raised the topic before Frost had even mentioned it. He claimed to be outraged that the boy was in trouble, and that he would urge him to present himself to the police should he reappear. Frost was dismissive; the lad was on Baskin's payroll, ergo he would do whatever Harry wished, regardless of the urgings of his uncle.

Now, at close to ten, while slurping from a tin of Harp, Frost noticed some interesting activity. A black Ford Granada pulled up, and two men in penguin suits emerged from the rear and made their way towards the parlour, the smaller of the two swaying noticeably. The man seemed vaguely familiar, despite being fifty yards off and visible only from the back. The door to the Pink Toothbrush was opened before the men had reached the threshold, and they both staggered in. The Granada remained in situ. Frost was just deciphering the registration, an X plate, new last year, when the lights were killed and the exhaust extinguished.

The Kung Po had filled him up and was the only thing he'd eaten since breakfast. He felt strangely content alone in his car. His elusive, possibly ill wife and his wounded, upset girlfriend were far away in another world. He released the ring pull on another can of Harp.

The next thing he knew, it was 3 a.m. and a flashlight was being tapped remorselessly on the windscreen. He was just coming to when it moved round and blazed through the driver's-side window, startling him fully awake. He wound down the window.

'Evening, Officer.' He smiled.

'Sergeant Frost?' said a uniform in surprise.

'That's me. Oh, blast,' Frost said, looking past the officer towards the Pink Toothbrush; the lights were out and the Granada gone.

Frost turned the ignition key, causing the constable to step back. 'The going-over I got in there must have been so good I dozed off!' he called after him, smiling lamely. Kung Po and lager moved deep within his insides, necessitating an unsettling belch. He fished for a cigarette and reached for the final can of Harp to wash away the after-taste before pulling away.

Wednesday (1)

Simms had woken early in spite of, or perhaps because of, the previous night's heavy booze intake, and getting up had been a monumental struggle. As he and DS Waters left their police quarters on Fenwick Street, the searing brightness of the early-morning sun made his head pound. The booze had afforded them both a poor night's sleep, and in Simms's case a powerful hangover was kicking in.

Neither he nor Waters had meant to get quite so blasted. On the way out of Two Bridges they'd had several pints in the Fox before checking in at Eagle Lane, albeit briefly, then had decided on a Chinese takeaway and some tins from the Unwins next door. It would have all been fine had it ended there, but upon arrival at Fenwick Street they'd found Miller slumped in the lounge watching confiscated video nasties on the mis-appropriated Betamax video recorder. It was just too easy to crack open a bottle of Scotch – also confiscated – and settle down for an early-hours session of *Driller Killer* and *Deep Throat*. Now, of course, Simms felt like he'd actually starred in a video nasty.

He slipped a cassette of Queen's *The Game* into the car ste-reo, in the hope it'd perk him up a bit. But the opening thud of 'Another One Bites the Dust', usually a spirit-lifter, merely served to make his headache worse.

'Got a new album out this month,' he said to Waters, who looked equally pained in the passenger seat. 'A mate's getting me a bootleg tonight.'

'So you like them, do you?' Waters asked.

'Queen? You bet.'

'Just wondered, since you disapproved mightily of Culture Club yesterday evening . . .'

'Eh? Yeah, too right. A pansy in make-up – got no time for that. This is rock, mate.' And he turned up the volume despite his throbbing head.

Eagle Lane wasn't far from the police billet, but for Simms, perspiring heavily and feeling shaky, the journey was taking an eternity. To begin with, they'd been stuck behind a rubbish truck, its progress excruciatingly slow. The jollity of the binmen just beyond the Cortina's bonnet, laughing as they emptied the clanging steel cylinders into the jaws of the truck, grated annoyingly. The collections had all been delayed a day because of the bank holiday.

'About time too,' Simms grumbled. 'The whole of Denton pongs, especially in this weather. We still have to clear up the filth, bank holiday or not. I don't see why that lot should be an exception.'

The lorry finally indicated left. Simms impatiently put his foot down.

'Jesus – watch it!' Waters shouted and the car screeched to a halt. A paperboy on a BMX had hopped off the kerb and into the path of the accelerating car. Simms stopped just in time. The boy, wearing a blue-hooded tracksuit top, acknowledged his good fortune by spinning round and giving them the finger.

'Cheeky sod!' Waters wound down the window as Simms

116

drew up to the boy at the traffic lights. 'Oi, you, if you didn't have that hood up you might . . .' But the boy had begun to pedal off, paying no attention to Waters.

'Oi!' Simms shouted, leaning across his colleague. The boy finally turned and scowled. He was fair-haired and wearing a pair of earphones.

'No wonder he's behaving like a muppet. He can't see or hear with that get-up on.' Simms shook his head in disbelief. 'That reminds me. The Ellis girl had a Walkman on the train with her.'

'Oh yeah? What was she listening to?'

'Listening to?' Simms replied, bemused.

'On the tape? Might be worth a listen.'

'Mmm, good idea. Remind me when we get in, if we get there in one piece, that is.'

Superintendent Stanley Mullett brought the Rover to a halt in the car park of Denton Golf Club. The quality of the vehicles around him spoke volumes. There were two Jags, several Rovers and even a Rolls, which must belong to the mayor. The very cream of Denton was here today.

He got out and sniffed the morning air. It was 8.15, and an extravagant breakfast awaited him in the clubhouse before the mayor officially opened the new course to the members. Yes, Denton at last had an eighteen-hole course, an expansion funded by a local investment committee and designed to attract big business. In addition to today's opening, there would also be a charity match on Friday afternoon, followed by a gala dinner, the whole thing intended as a lavish corporate schmoozing event. Mullett couldn't quite see how a retired boxer and one of the Two Ronnies appearing at a golf-club jolly would promote investment in Denton, but his was not to reason why. He was simply delighted to be on the guest list.

All was right with the world today, he thought. A chinwag

with a couple of notables and then tee-off at nine; how civilized. He straightened his Windsor knot, smoothed his V-neck and checked his plus-fours. Fortunately, none of these items had been at the dry cleaner's – he knew better than to let that lot loose on the merino or herringbone tweed.

He flopped on his hat, pinged open the boot and pulled out his clubs. What a fantastic morning! He even found himself humming as he strolled across the gravel and into the new club-house.

'Stanley, old chap, good to see you.' It was Hudson, the portly manager of Bennington's Bank, who met him at reception, a glass of champagne in hand. Of all the people who could have greeted his entry, Hudson was probably his least favourite. 'Come and grab yourself a glass of fizz.'

'Morning, Hudson.' Mullett smiled tightly. 'Bit early in the day for me.' Or for anyone apart from alcoholics – it wasn't even 9 a.m. – but clearly not for you, you corpulent windbag.

'Nonsense – wouldn't be a champagne breakfast without it, would it?' The bank manager looked distinctly flushed already.

'I guess not.'

Hudson led him up a small flight of stairs and into the main club room, where a dozen or so members loitered expectantly. Mullett found himself rather disappointed with the decor. It seemed gauche and resembled an airport lounge; not exactly how he'd pictured an elite golf club. The only thing that gave a clue to the building's function were the photographs transferred from the previous clubhouse – shots of members, of holes-in-one and of minor celebs shaking the incumbent club secretary's hand, all of which looked totally incongruous in the new surroundings. Hudson led him on through to the main attraction – an entire plate-glass wall looking out on to the fairway.

'Impressive, eh?' said Hudson, as if he were personally responsible for this majestic glass showpiece. And to a degree he was. Bennington's had bank-rolled the improvements on a loan with repayment terms that Mullett suspected were more than lenient. There was nobody more suitable to the role of club treasurer – especially given the bank manager's handicap. Hudson was a truly awful golfer – a blindfolded monkey with a spade could get round the course more quickly.

'Yes indeed,' said Mullett, accepting a flute of champagne from a girl dressed for a cabaret, 'it certainly is.' At that point a burly fellow broke away from the cluster standing in front of the plate-glass window and made his way over.

'Hello there, squire,' said the man in a coarse East London accent, nodding to Hudson, who smiled in acknowledgement. They exchanged a few pleasantries before Hudson made off to join the party at the window. Mullett squinted at this rotund cockney with sideburns and cigar but couldn't place him.

The man clocked the divisional commander's confusion. 'You don't recognize me, do you?' he said, puffing on his cigar.

Mullett reflected briefly on how he'd much rather be talking to the mayor, or even to Assistant Chief Constable Winslow, and surreptitiously scanned the group at the window to see if they were there.

'Have my lads sorted your nick out yet?'

Heaven help him, it was Baskin, Denton's leading 'entrepreneur', small-time hood and owner of the building firm – why else would a type like him be in this sort of club.

'Not quite,' Mullett replied, with a strained smile, feigning ignorance. 'A very good job you've done here . . . Mister?'

'Baskin. Harry Baskin.'

Mullett's smile tightened. 'Yes, of course. I've been wanting to speak to you. One of my officers was stabbed on one of your premises on Monday morning.'

'Yes, what a shame. If only she'd come round after twelve it could all have been avoided.'

'I'm sorry – what do you mean?' Mullett couldn't stand the smug gangster. He felt his hackles rising, but knew his temper would have to be controlled if he didn't want to create a scene in front of Denton's finest.

Baskin was clearly aware of this and was milking it. 'We weren't open, you see. There's no security when the premises are shut. So I can't be held responsible, can I? Any luck in catching the little buggers?'

Mullett was about to respond when he was suddenly distracted by some excitement at the window. Hudson beckoned him over.

'Excuse me, it appears that I'm required,' Mullett said. He made his way over. The tackily dressed girls had been topping him up with the cheap champagne and he already felt light-headed.

'Look!' Hudson exclaimed. Running across the second-hole green was a man who Mullett assumed was the groundsman, in a state of agitation.

'Shouldn't he be on a small tractor, or something?' someone said. The man's run across the course had clearly taken its toll, and he seemed to be on the verge of collapse as he approached the clubhouse. He looked up at the window and began gesticulating wildly.

'I guess we should discover what's up with the poor fellow,' said a tall, distinguished-looking man with a close-cropped beard and a pink cravat. Mullett recognized him as Sir Keith Neal, the MP for Denton and Rimmington.

A small group led by Sir Keith made their way down on to the green. Mullett was one of the party; his instincts were telling him, through the fuzz of the champagne, that something was very wrong indeed.

'Superintendent! Here, please,' said Sir Keith. The huddle parted so Mullett could approach the stout, dark-haired workman in a flat cap, who was panting heavily. 'Give the fellow space!'

'D-dead,' the man stammered, alarm in his eyes. 'Dead boy.'

120

'Where?' demanded Mullett, assuming an air of authority. All eyes were now on him.

'Ninth hole,' the man spluttered. 'I was ch-checking the course for moles . . .'

'Let's take a buggy. Myself, Sir Keith and . . .'

'Knowles,' said the traumatized groundsman.

'Mr Knowles will point the way.'

The buggy trundled across the impressive grounds. It wasn't long before Mullett could make out something lying close to the ninth hole, stark white against the green, and as they drew closer it became apparent that it was indeed a body. Mullett jumped off first and strode towards it. He felt his insides churn.

The boy was naked, lying prone in a star shape.

The body was cut open from groin to neck.

Mark Fong sat looking terrified in Interview Room 1. Frost had requested that DC Myles sit in, in an effort to calm the boy's nerves. He could do with something of that sort himself. It was gone 10 a.m. and although the caffeine and nicotine had reduced the usual midweek befuddlement, which had been compounded by spending half the night in the Cortina, it was the worry of Mary not coming home last night that he couldn't shake off. She'd gone off before, usually to her mother's, but this time he felt it was different. He'd get to it once he had Fong sorted out.

The lad's appearance at the station had been something of a surprise. Frost supposed at first that his uncle had coerced him into handing himself in voluntarily, but it seemed unlikely; the kid was shaking like a leaf. In which case, probably Baskin had had one of his thugs drop him off. Frost disliked Baskin's gesture; the crook doubtless felt he was doing the DS a favour, but it bothered Frost that Baskin thought nothing of dumping some poor expendable sod in the mire.

'Mark, can you tell me why you were on the last train back to Denton on Saturday night?'

'I visit family.'

'Yes, I know, Mr Baskin and your uncle said as much.'

'Huh?' The boy frowned, his features creasing, though the inch-long scratch on the left cheek was still visible.

'Your *uncle* said . . . Never mind. Why did you come back so late? I mean, the last train – if your grandmother was sick, surely she'd be asleep.' Frost observed Myles placing her hands to the side of her head in a sleep gesture. He rolled his eyes. Fong's English might not be great, but it ought to be better than his uncle's, and Frost was sure he understood.

'Family. In Chinatown.'

'Yes, but why so late back?' Frost persisted.

'Eat. In Chinatown. With family. In Chinatown.'

'Do you remember who else was in the carriage with you? Did you see any young girls?'

'On the train, how many people?' Myles asked.

'Carriage empty.'

'Which carriage?' Frost asked. The boy looked blank, but behind the eyes there was fear. 'Smoke?' The detective offered him a Rothmans. He shook his head vigorously.

'How d'you get that scratch on your face?' Myles asked, running her forefinger down her cheek.

'Cat,' Fong said quickly.

'He understood that, all right. OK, will you please excuse me for a minute.' Frost got up and made for the door, at which point the boy began to jabber in earnest, obviously realizing he was in it up to his neck. Myles leaned forward across the desk, trying to catch what he was saying. 'DC Myles, will you come with me, please?'

Frost closed the interview room door behind them. He was thinking back to what Simms had said about the Ellis girl's bag, assuming it was hers. It was found in the front carriage. A smoker's car. Fong clearly didn't smoke, and the station exit at Denton was midway down the platform. Fong had been first off the train. The two girls had not been right behind him as they left the station. He was beginning to think he was barking up the wrong tree. But if Mark Fong had seen and done nothing, and the scratch on the side of his face really was from a cat, then why had he run?

'What's up?' said DC Myles.

'Something's not quite right. When he did a runner from the takeaway, I was convinced he was our boy, especially given the scratch. But now I'm not so sure.'

'Well, perhaps you're right. But as you left, he admitted noticing three girls at Paddington.'

Frost's eyes widened. 'Really? *Three?*' Could this be evidence that Samantha and the pair from Two Bridges had known each other? 'Did he see them catch the train together?'

'Yeah, but I don't think they're our girls. Weren't they all drunk?'

'The taxi driver said the girls from Two Bridges were pissed, but Samantha Ellis's toxicology tests found no trace of alcohol.'

'Well, he thought they all looked pretty sober.' Myles opened the door, ready to step back inside. 'He seems to understand more if you talk to him slowly,' she whispered.

'It seems odd that his English is worse than his uncle's who was an immigrant,' muttered Frost. Then suddenly it dawned on him. 'Mark' hadn't been born here, as Frost had assumed. He was here illegally, without a passport or visa. No wonder he did a runner on coming face to face with CID.

Frost re-entered the interview room. 'Mr Fong, can I see some identification, please?'

Panic spread across the boy's face.

'All right. Where were you born?'

'Denton!' Fong replied too quickly, and then realized his mistake.

'We can soon check that out.' Frost turned to Myles and said, 'Kim, be a darling and check with Denton General for Mr Fong's records.'

The boy started gibbering wildly.

'Relax, son. Kim, stay put.' Frost waited for calm, then proceeded. 'I don't give a monkey's whether or not you're here legally . . . All I care about is what you saw on that last train out of London on Saturday night. Did you see this girl get on the train at Paddington?' Frost slid Samantha Ellis's school photo across the desk.

'Three girls.' Fong held up three fingers, in case there should be any doubt.

'Yes, but did you see this one?' Fong shook his head. Frost felt a pang of frustration. 'Well, can you give me a description of the ones you did see?' Fong looked at him blankly. 'What did they look like?' Frost said patiently.

'Back only.'

'Eh?'

'You were behind them on the platform?' Myles interjected. 'You didn't see their faces, yes?'

Fong nodded vigorously.

'Were these girls swaying . . . you know, drunk?'

The boy frowned until Frost got up and staggered for effect.

He shook his head. 'No. Straight.'

'Did you see any other girls board the train, you know, teenagers?'

'Lots.'

'Hmm,' Frost mused. 'I'm not sure he's really seen anything at all. He's just saying what he thinks we want to hear.'

Just then a uniform appeared around the corner of the door. It was Pooley, looking even paler than usual.

'Yes, son, what is it?'

'Mr Mullett would like everybody in the briefing room. It's urgent.'

'Urgent? Of course it is. Any more details than that?' Frost sighed, blowing out a match in a cloud of smoke.

'The super found something nasty on the golf course.' The thin constable grinned.

'Did he, indeed? Underclasses invading the fairway, are they?' Frost quipped. 'Get a WPC stationed in here. I don't want this lad going anywhere.'

Wednesday (2)

DC Sue Clarke waited for the chatter in the briefing room to die down and the remaining officers to be seated. Having taken the Missing Person call yesterday, she now found herself centre stage, with a visibly shaken Superintendent Mullett to her left. He looked all the more out of place, dressed as he still was in his golfing outfit.

The station was buzzing over the discovery. For 11 a.m. on a midweek morning, there seemed to be an awful lot of uniform present and few CID. Simms and Waters were out on a robbery call, a smash and grab at Sparklers, the jeweller's on Merchant Street.

Clarke took a deep breath before addressing the room. 'We believe the boy is Tom Hardy. His mother filed a Missing Person report on Tuesday morning.' She pointed to a school photograph. 'His parents have been notified, and I'll be on my way to collect them for formal identification, as soon as we're finished here.' She paused. 'Angela Hardy, the mother, last saw her son alive on Friday morning.'

Clarke kept her attention on her colleagues as PC Jordan pinned the scene-of-crime photos to the incident board. Gasps of horror filled the room.

'Why wait until Tuesday, for heaven's sake?' Mullett enquired of Clarke, pulling tensely at his moustache.

'They'd been away for a long weekend,' Clarke replied. 'They got back Monday night, and didn't think anything of it until Tuesday.'

'What sort of person would do this?' Mullett thundered. Clarke almost felt he was angry at her for taking the call yesterday, as though this outcome could have been foreseen at that stage. She saw him wince at the sight of the grisly photographs pinned to the board. 'This is most extraordinary . . .'

'We know that the boy has been dead since the weekend. The SOCOs put the likely time of death as Saturday, or possibly earlier,' she continued. 'We also know that the boy was not killed on the green – this is clear from the lack of blood on the ground. And though dead for several days, the body was not placed on the green until possibly as recently as last night – this would explain why the groundsman only discovered it this morning . . .'

'How do we know that?' a uniform at the back asked.

'The grass underneath the body had not discoloured due to lack of sunlight,' Clarke replied.

Frost moved forward to take a closer look. 'The killer's method itself is clearly significant,' he suggested.

'Of course it's *significant*!' Mullett snapped. 'Somebody has certainly gone to a great deal of trouble to carry out this act. It's not every day you come across a body ripped apart from head to foot, I can tell you. I *don't* want this getting out until we have some idea of what we're dealing with.'

'Too late,' said Desk Sergeant Bill Wells timidly. 'Sandy Lane has already been on the blower.'

'Well, don't say anything more,' barked Mullett, sucking

in his cheeks. Clarke could see he had to maintain authority, given his personal involvement.

Frost shrugged and said, 'I bet one of your golfing chums has already spilled the beans.'

'Nevertheless, let's manage the situation carefully. We can't disguise the brutality of the crime, but we can cloak the details of when we suspect the murder took place. That will not have got out, and at least gives us something to deflect any lunatics claiming responsibility.'

Clarke stepped to one side. Now that Mullett was in full flow and the usual battle of wills between himself and Frost had started, she felt surplus to requirements. She predicted that as usual the briefing would descend into a string of re-criminations.

'I want this case to be given top priority,' insisted Mullett.

'Along with everything else,' Frost retorted.

'But by your own admission, you're solving cases by the minute. The Ellis case, for instance. You said you had a sus-pect.'

'That avenue of enquiry could prove to be a dead end.'

'Yesterday, you were confident of a breakthrough. My fault for listening to you, I suppose. I should have known better than to believe a case might actually be resolved, especially so soon.'

Frost chose to ignore him. 'DC Clarke, you say it's possible the boy has been dead since Saturday? Samantha Ellis may have committed suicide on Saturday night.'

'Oh come, come,' Mullett sighed. 'You really are fumbling around in the dark. The girl kills the lad, in an exceptionally brutal fashion, and then throws herself off a train that evening in a fit of remorse? Even for you that's ridiculous!'

'Similar age,' Frost said. 'It's possible they knew each other.'

'Knowing someone doesn't necessarily mean . . .' Clarke began, her sentence trailing off after a withering look from Frost.

'They attended the same school, Denton Comp,' someone from uniform chipped in. 'Maybe they were even in the same year?'

'Check it out,' Mullett said to Clarke, ushering her to sit down. She imagined he was keen to regain control over Frost in front of such a large contingent of uniform. 'Right, Frost, while we're at it, following on from your dead end on the Ellis girl, what else have you got to report? Presumably there were other people on the train on Saturday night?'

'Two teenage girls. They caught a taxi to Two Bridges. Jolly hockey sticks, and all that. Both are pupils at St Mary's.'

'Tom Hardy's sister Emily is at St Mary's,' Clarke said to herself as much as to anyone else, recalling the conversation yesterday with the boy's mother.

'Well, get on to it,' said Mullett. He turned back to Frost. 'Have you let your suspect go, now that he appears not to be a suspect?'

'Not sure he has anywhere *to* go.' Frost frowned. 'His uncle's probably disowned him, and the dry cleaner's where he lives has just gone bust.'

'He's related to those chaps, is he?' Mullett mused. 'I think I might have a word with him myself, then.'

Frost returned to his office and shut the door behind him. He needed a moment to take stock of the situation. He lit a cigarette and sat down behind the desk, fingers rubbing his temples. Where the hell was Mary? Could he put out an APB on his own wife? He could try calling her mother. Yes, he would call his mother-in-law, just as soon as he'd got to grips with what was on his desk.

DI Allen was away until the following Monday. Mullett had saddled him and Webster with the task of computerizing CID records, hence Allen's crash course. Huh, computers, I'd like to see them tackle this mess, Frost thought. For once he was not remotely envious of Allen, though his lengthy non-appearance had effectively left the bulk of the CID casework for Frost to juggle alone.

Simms was fielding the burglaries, plus this new raid on the jeweller's. There was also the corner-shop armed robbery on the Southern Housing Estate. Frost had a hunch it was kids acting up – possibly the same bunch that had attacked Clarke and Myles.

Clarke would field the Tom Hardy case; she'd taken the original call. Myles would be her partner. They were on their way now to the parents, a task that Frost didn't envy. Clarke, he knew, was hardly on top form. Partly it was his fault – she probably wasn't too happy that he'd failed to turn up at her place last night – and partly it was due to the assault, which, although leaving only a superficial wound, had shaken her up. Frost realized that Mullett had ceased to mention it. Tom Hardy's sliced-open body on the ninth hole had eclipsed all concern about a minor injury sustained by a woman officer in a car park.

Mullett *was* still muttering about gypsies though, by all accounts. Frost didn't buy it; he couldn't see them going on a killing spree the same weekend they turned up.

Then, of course, there was the Ellis case, his alone, which as of this morning was going nowhere fast. Finally there was Baskin and the sauna. This would have to slide for the minute; after all, he'd spent the best part of last night in the car, fruitlessly watching the flaming place (though admittedly he had dozed off at some point . . .). Surely even Mullett would let him off that, given there were two dead bodies on the slab.

The phone went and Frost irritably fished it out from beneath a mound of paperwork. It was Drysdale.

'Morning, Doc. I was just thinking about you.'

'Frost. Two things. Firstly, the girl, Samantha Ellis. The fifteen-year-old.'

'I'm listening.'

'She was pregnant.'

Frost watched a fly make its way round the rim of a Coke can. 'I see. How far gone?'

'Not long – twelve weeks.'

It was still another life, Frost thought. 'Thanks for that, Doc. Anything else?'

'Yes. It's regarding the boy they've just brought in, Tom Hardy. You'd better come down here and take a look.'

'I'm a bit pushed for time at the moment. Can't you tell me now, over the phone? The suspense is killing me.'

'I really think it best if you come down and see for yourself. DC Clarke is on her way with the parents, and I'd prefer they didn't see what I have to show you, so this afternoon? Only if it's convenient.'

'Of course, Doc.' He saw the fly enter the Coke can and dropped his cigarette-end in after it, giving it a good shake.

'Jolly good. Oh, and Frost . . .'

'Yes?'

'Did you give DC Simms the cat back? Your desk sergeant has been pestering me for its return. The owner's keen to give it a proper burial.'

Frost blinked and bit his lip as realization dawned; he'd been wondering what that pong was in the motor. He looked up to see the aforementioned Simms in the doorway, gesticulating for him to come through.

'Yes, Doc.' Frost hung up and scratched his head anxiously. The week was turning chaotic, and he was starting to feel the squeeze. He missed DC Hanlon. Waters could prove to be an asset but he didn't know Denton, and there wasn't time to give him a proper guided tour; Frost needed people thinking on their feet. He should have encouraged Hanlon to come back sooner. Sad though the demise of Mother Hanlon was, an entire week off work was pushing it. He drained his coffee and went to see Simms next door, taking his pocket diary with him.

'What you got?' he asked.

'Details on the smash and grab.' Simms's feet were up on a desk and he was smoking lethargically. Waters was sipping a coffee, propped up against the filing cabinet next to the fan, which whirred away softly. Frost raised his eyebrows on seeing his Hawaiian shirt.

Simms took another drag and exhaled. 'It happened first thing this morning, as the store was about to open. Quite clever, actually; kid comes off his BMX right under the feller's nose as he's laying out the gems in the window. Rides straight into a lamp post. He's on the ground not moving, so the bloke charges out, thinking he's badly hurt, bends over to check – and the next thing he knows, there's a knife at his neck and two kids are cleaning out his window.'

'Did he get a butcher's at the kid's face?' Frost asked.

'No, not a peep. He was in a tracksuit top with a hood, lying face down. The guy reaches down and touches him on the shoulder, and when the kid springs up he sees he's wearing a balaclava.'

'Witnesses?'

'Nothing. An empty side street, the bloke pushed into a shop doorway, the whole thing's over in seconds. Nobody saw a thing.'

Frost paced the length of the grimy CID office. He snatched Waters' coffee and took a huge gulp, nodded in appreciation and lit himself a Rothmans.

'Right, here's what we do. Simms, get back to the news-agent's, grill the man again about the robbery there – they were wearing balaclavas too, right? And go over Clarke's attack with her once more. These three have got to be linked. Now, where are you up to with the girls from the train?' He looked at the pair expectantly.

'We've talked to one yesterday, Burleigh. Ferguson, the other one, we still need to speak to,' said Waters. 'According to her mother, she's in all day today; exam study leave, or something.'

'OK. Well, you and me, Waters, we'll head out to Two Bridges. Nice morning for a run out to the country.'

'What about Tom Hardy?' Simms asked.

'Myles and Clarke are escorting the parents to the mortuary now, then will check in with uniform, who are combing the surrounding area where the body was found – Denton Woods principally. Drysdale just called; for some reason it's imperative we see the body, so Waters and I will take a dekko after the parents have said their goodbyes – and after we've seen Ferguson.' Frost scratched his brow. 'It's all getting hectic, I know. We'll regroup here later today.'

The two detectives nodded in agreement.

'OK. Let's get out of here before Hornrim Harry appears, full of bright ideas, as per usual.'

Frost picked up his diary lying open on a desk, on the page bearing his mother-in-law's phone number, and slipped it into his back pocket.

'She'll have to wait,' he said to himself, shaking his head as he stubbed out his cigarette.

It was around midday when Waters and Frost pulled up at the well-heeled Ferguson residence. Sarah Ferguson seemed fidgety. Waters felt sure something was up. When he and Simms had phoned from the pub last night to apologize to the Fergusons for not calling round, they'd spoken to Sarah's mother, who had talked of being concerned about her eldest daughter. Whether the girl was edgy because she was nervous in dealing with the police – natural enough for a girl of her age – or whether she feared what her mother might have told them, he wasn't yet sure.

'So, when we spoke to your mother last night she intimated you may know, sorry, may have known, Samantha Ellis. Is that right?' he asked the girl, as they sat at the counter of a slick modern kitchen with designer lights.

'No, I don't think so.' She chewed on her nails as if she hadn't eaten in a week. She was lying.

'What do you mean, you don't think so? Either you did or you didn't,' Frost insisted, rummaging for his notepad. 'She said it was through some out-of-school activity. What would that be . . . hockey?'

'I dare say I may have played against her, if she played for her school,' Sarah Ferguson replied. The girl was attractive, like her friend Gail, but troubled by acne that no amount of foundation could hide.

'Your mother was familiar with the name, which suggests to me something more than that,' continued Waters.

'It's just a name to her – you could have said Sally James, and Mum would agree she was in my biology class.'

'Listen, love,' said Frost. 'We're not suggesting you pushed her off the train, for heaven's sake, we just want to know the facts. It may seem like nothing to you, but something you know or saw could make all the difference to us. We need to establish whether you knew who she was; if you didn't, then she could have been sitting next to you and you'd have been none the wiser. See what I mean?'

Waters sat poised, notebook at the ready.

The girl nodded.

'So, did you know her or not?'

'No.'

'And Gail Burleigh?'

'I was with Gail all day Saturday.'

'No, I mean, would Gail have known Samantha Ellis?'

'How would I know?' she suddenly snapped. 'Why don't you ask *her*?'

'Returning to Saturday night,' Frost said wearily, 'whereabouts did you sit? Which carriage on the train?'

134

'Can't remember, sorry. Somewhere in the middle?'

'How many people were in your carriage?'

'Can't remember, really. It wasn't packed.'

'Your memory seems a little hazy.'

The girl ran her hands through her hair and eventually said in a whisper, 'We'd been drinking.'

'Really? What?'

'Cinzano. We met these lads at the concert. They bought us a bottle.'

'Cinzano?'

'Yeah. The stuff Joan Collins has chucked over her on the telly.'

'Of course. Well, if you do remember anything, give me a call on this number.' Frost handed over a business card. 'We'll leave you in peace, then. Exams to revise for?'

'They're not until June,' she replied.

'Well, good luck,' said Waters, noticing a sly sparkle in the girl's green eyes.

'She's lying,' Waters said as he opened the door of the Vauxhall.

'Maybe,' Frost replied, pulling out his Polaroids. 'Going to be another scorcher, I bet.'

He was, to Waters' mind, dressed peculiarly, his shirt made of some sort of cheesecloth. Strangely, Waters had found working with Simms easier. Frost's 'forced chaperon detail' was a distraction. He liked him, but because he liked him he couldn't focus on the case.

'Now, what would a fifteen-year-old girl with her whole life in front of her have to lie about?' Frost asked as they pulled away.

Waters shrugged. 'I dunno, just a hunch.'

'Hunches don't go down too well at Eagle Lane.'

The Londoner waited, but the older man didn't elaborate; he was too busy fumbling for matches.

'All this,' Waters said, gesturing at the sumptuous period homes as he turned the car on to the main road, 'it's sort of not real.'

'How do you mean?' Frost asked, winding down the window. 'It looks real enough to me. Those motors on the driveways are certainly real.'

'Don't get me wrong.' Waters looked across to Frost. 'I know this is your manor. I've been here, what, a couple of days, and the people in Denton seem pretty normal, but in this place . . .'

'Two Bridges?'

'Yeah, and the one I went to first, where the rich guys got robbed – Hartley somebody or other. They all just seem so weird. It's like they're detached from reality. And the parents seem to have no idea what's going on with any of their kids.'

'Not sure I'm with you.'

'I'm not sure I'm explaining it too well, but there just seems to be some sort of disconnect between the adults and their kids.'

'Come on, you've only spoken to a couple of people. Bit of a rash judgement, don't you think?'

'I dunno, there's this atmosphere of . . . coldness. It's not what I'm used to.'

'I'm guessing there's not the same high density of mock Tudor beams and long drives in Bethnal Green?'

'There certainly ain't! No room to swing a cat in most of the houses, not to mention the high rises down near Columbia Road.' Waters paused. 'Are you taking the piss?'

'No way, son, but you seem to be saying it's down to the money. Whoa there, you want to swing a left,' Frost said suddenly, 'for our appointment with Dr Death.'

Clarke and Myles pulled into the car park of the Bird in Hand. After breaking the news to Tom Hardy's parents they needed to take the edge off. Telling anyone about a death was bad enough; informing parents of the death of a child – let alone one ripped apart like this one – was the worst. Thank God Drysdale had been careful to conceal from the parents the full extent of the boy's wounds. Clarke had noticed how Frost loathed these IDs and tried to wriggle out of them whenever possible, although it was fair enough this time. It wasn't his call.

'Two Bloody Marys, please, landlord,' Myles ordered.

The Bird in Hand, off the Rimmington Road, was a cavernous place Clarke had only been to once. Originally a coaching inn, it was now used mainly by farmhands. By the look of them, one or two had been in here since last night. Clarke rubbed her leg, which seemed to stiffen every time she got out of the car.

They took their drinks to a nook beside a bank of mute flashing fruit machines.

'I wouldn't want to do that every day.' Myles grimaced, pulling her blonde hair out of its ponytail and running her fingers through it.

Clarke nursed her vodka in silence.

'C'mon. It's done now,' coaxed Myles, slapping her partner on the thigh. Clarke winced in pain. 'Sorry!' Myles gasped.

Clarke grasped her glass and drained half of it. 'That was, possibly – actually, no possibly about it, definitely – the worst thing I've ever had to do in my whole career.'

'I'd agree with you on that, love.'

Clarke glanced up as a sunburnt young man in a vest and red neckerchief plonked a pint of what looked like cider on the fruit machine in front of them.

'Drysdale was bit odd, don't you think? Seemed keen to get rid of us. Said DS Frost and Waters were on their way over. Do you think we should have waited?'

'Nah, we'll find out what the score is as and when. And there's no need to be formal with me, love.' Myles smiled a broad smile. 'You and Frost – everyone knows.'

'Knows *what*?' said Clarke defensively.

'You know, no need to be coy. You got a thing going.'

'What of it?' she snapped.

'Hey, I don't mind. He's not my type. Just trying to loosen you up a bit, after the morning we've had,' she said. 'Now DS Waters – I wouldn't mind a bit of that.'

'So you said.' Clarke looked up from her drink. 'Look, I'm sorry, you're right. I should chill out a bit.'

'Good girl. Now, knock that back and I'll get another one in.'

The vodka was beginning to have an effect on Clarke, and for the first time that week she felt the tension loosen. She pulled from her bag a pack of Silk Cut and lit one. The pub was practically empty, besides the H. E. Bates type at the fruit machine, and Myles was back quickly.

'Doubles.'

'Is that wise? We ought to check in with uniform at Denton Woods as soon as . . .' Though she wasn't of a mind to turn it down. This morning and Jack Frost had collectively finished her off. She eyed the man at the fruit machine. Maybe she should have a fling with someone her own age; that's what Frost was always telling her. Yeah, maybe she would – see how that went down.

'Forget that – weather's due to break this afternoon. Thunderstorm on its way. The woods will be a quagmire by the time we get there. Sometimes it helps to get a bit numb. Hello, anyone at home?'

'Sorry, drifted off. Things on my mind.'

'Problem shared is a problem halved.'

Clarke drank thirstily. She didn't know this woman, didn't even particularly like her – thought her a bit of a tart, if she was being perfectly honest – but did it really matter? She seemed a willing ear. 'Since you ask' – she exhaled – 'it's Jack Frost.'

The vodka had opened the floodgates and months of frustration came out: the false promises, the forgetfulness, the selfishness, all in the name of the job. 'Even on my birthday, he was following up a lead on a bank robber who got away, who nobody even cares about any more.'

'But, love, you knew he was like that from the start. You can't expect him to change. Men never do.'

'I guess so.' Clarke shook her head and drained the glass.

'Cheer up, love. Live a little.' Myles smiled, her cheeks beginning to glow. She leaned forward conspiratorially. 'I left a note for DS Waters at the front desk this morning, asking him to meet me tonight in the Eagle.'

'You never!' Clarke was shocked. She thought briefly about her own note to Jack, which had so far had zero response. 'Isn't that a bit forward? And the Eagle is a police pub! It's practically on the doorstep of the station. Everyone will know.'

'What of it?' challenged Myles, shooting Silk Cut smoke towards the ceiling. 'It's only a drink. What else would he be doing this evening? Watching porn with Simms and Miller? I reckon it'll be a laugh.'

The pathology lab, with its familiar cold, grey atmosphere, was of course impervious to the brilliant May sunshine outside its concrete skin. Frost knew this well enough, but yet again found himself shivering in the corridor on his way to meet Drysdale.

'Should have put a jacket on,' he mumbled to Waters.

'Afternoon, gentlemen,' Drysdale greeted them while pulling on a pair of rubber gloves. 'You two look like you've just got back from the Costa del Sol.'

'Afternoon, Doc,' said Frost, removing his shades. 'It's called sunshine to those in the world of the living.'

'As long as it's not fashion,' the pathologist said drily. 'I don't believe we've had the pleasure,' he muttered to Waters, though he didn't wait for a response, moving off to adjust the overhead light.

'Come closer,' he said, 'you'll see nothing from there. Prepare yourselves.'

Frost took a tentative step forward as Drysdale removed the sheet. He craned his neck but couldn't work out what he was meant to be looking at.

'Come here, man, you're being coy. Here.'

'Jesus H. Christ,' muttered Waters. Though he'd seen the scene-of-crime photos earlier that morning, the sight of the body was way more visceral than he had expected.

The pathologist explained to Frost that the fifteen-year-old boy on the slab in front of him had had most of his internal organs and his entire genitalia removed. Drysdale, in all his years of practice, had never come across anything quite like it, he went on to say. He'd only ever read about such cases in textbooks, cases like the Jack the Ripper murders.

'But the Ripper murdered women – prostitutes. Not teenage boys,' Waters pointed out.

'Quite. Also, the removal of the organs in the Ripper victims was done with medical precision. The killer knew what he was doing. But here, the operation has been rather sloppy.' Drysdale leaned into the corpse. 'If you look here – the severing . . .'

'I'll take your word for it,' Frost said. 'Any clue to the exact cause of death?'

'Not as yet. However, the victim was not bound as one might expect—'

'What, he just let whoever it was slice him open, then?' Frost said incredulously.

'If you'll just let me finish, Detective – there's no chafing or bind marks, but there are pressure marks, more evident at the wrists.'

'And the ankles?'

'No.'

'If he were wearing jeans, say, could that prevent chafing?' Waters enquired.

'Possibly.'

140

'Well, can you hazard a guess at a cause of death?' Frost persisted.

'At this stage I'm inclined to think death was caused by these wounds.' He pointed at what remained of the boy's abdomen.

'*Wounds?* Wounds is a bit of an understatement, Doc. DC Clarke suffered a wound getting jabbed with a knife on Monday . . .'

'A turn of phrase, Sergeant.'

'So,' cut in Waters, 'are you saying the victim was alive when this happened?'

'It is possible. Probable, in fact. I would need the toxicology report to confirm lack of poison in the bloodstream, but on the face of it, yes, he was alive when sliced open – though not for long. There's no sign of a blow to the head, for instance.'

'I see.' Frost paced the lab, his hands behind his back. He was freezing.

'He's been dead some time. Since the weekend, I'd say. May I ask how and where the body was found?'

'It was left on the golf course.'

'Hmm,' the pathologist mused.

'Hmm, *what?*' Frost said. 'C'mon, Doc, don't come over all mysterious on us.'

'Well, there are very few traces of soil or grass, only those from the body resting on the green, one suspects. No fibres. The body is clean.' He peered down and pointed with tweezers at a spot on the forehead. 'Nothing except this.'

'What?' Frost said. They both moved forward.

'You're in the light, come this side,' Drysdale said. 'Look.' He very delicately lifted what appeared to be a small white pebble from the dead boy's forehead.

'What's that?' Waters asked.

'We'd need to run tests,' said Drysdale, 'but on the face of it, it looks like wax.'

'Wax?' Frost repeated, scratching his chin. 'Strange.'

'How was the body found?' asked Drysdale.

'I've told you – on the golf course.'

'Yes, but in what position?'

'Damn, left the snaps in the car,' Frost said, irritated.

'He was laid out in a star shape, according to Mr Mullett,' Waters replied.

'In other words, a pentagram.' Drysdale paused in thought, then looked directly at Frost. 'I'm no expert, but perhaps the boy's death was part of some sort of ritual?'

'What do you make of that, then?' Frost asked Waters. They pulled away from the lab and headed for Eagle Lane. The weather had changed ominously; dark-grey clouds were looming over Denton.

'Grisly.'

The radio was crackling and spitting, irritating the hell out of Frost. He heard Superintendent Mullett's name mentioned.

'Here, we need something to lighten our mood.' Frost leaned over and clicked off the radio. He fumbled with a cassette. 'Do you mind? Been carrying this around all week.'

'Should you do that while on duty? Turn off the radio?'

'Put it this way, last time I turned off the radio I nearly got blown up. It can't get any worse than that.'

'Whatever you say, man,' Waters said, bemused.

'There we go.' Frost sank back as the music filled the Vauxhall.

'Count Basie?' Waters said, surprised. 'How old are you? Anyway, back to the case. This idea of Drysdale's, pagan rites or whatever, I don't see it somehow. I mean, it's not Halloween or anything.'

'It does seem far-fetched, I'll grant you. Many things've turned up in Denton Woods over the years, but witches or satanists is pushing it,' Frost said. They sat at a junction on the Rimmington Road, the Vauxhall purring heavily while waiting for the lights to change. Frost observed them taking down the May Day bunting from the pub on the crossroads. On a blackboard a colourful chalk drawing advertised Morris Men. 'When did Drysdale reckon the kid was killed?'

'He didn't say specifically; sometime over the weekend.'

'The bank holiday weekend. May Day is, I'm sure, some sort of pagan deal. Originally, before the developers moved in, Denton was a small market town, very rural. We tend to forget.' Frost had an envelope with copies of the crime-scene photographs in his lap. He took out one picture and studied it.

'What you driving at?' Waters asked. 'You worried you're gonna get lynched and burned alive like Edward Woodward in *The Wicker Man*?'

'Just a thought, though I wouldn't say no to the bird who cast the spell or whatever . . . What was it Drysdale said about the lad's position – was it a pentangle?'

'Pentagram,' Waters corrected.

'Pentagram,' Frost repeated slowly.

'So you agree with Drysdale that there might be witches out there?'

'Who knows? We've got bugger all else to go on.'

Wednesday (3) _____

'Witchcraft? Are you sure?' Superintendent Mullett looked from Frost to Waters, vexed. There was a clatter of china as Miss Smith entered with his afternoon tea.

'Thank you, Miss Smith, that will be all. I'm not to be disturbed.' His secretary smiled uncertainly at him and left the room.

'Of course I'm not sure,' Frost said, pacing the office, a plume of smoke in his wake, 'but you said yourself the manner of death was significant.'

'I know what I said, but still, witchcraft? This is the 1980s. The computer age. Not the Middle Ages.'

'Sir, the body was only discovered this morning; it's very early days. This is just an idea.'

'Ideas have no place in Denton CID. Procedure, Frost. Hard evidence. We can't have talk of witches and goblins.'

'Goblins?'

'You know what I mean. We can't have you propounding ridiculous theories. If anything like this gets out, we're really done for.' Mullett frowned. 'Now will you please sit down, before you wear a hole in the carpet!' Mullett had never seen Frost like this, accustomed as he was to the detective slouching in a chair. This pacing about the office was irritating and unsettling. Waters sat quietly to one side, offering nothing up. Mullett's eye was caught by the flashing red light of his new, multi-line phone.

'The press,' Mullett continued, 'have been on the phone constantly. We're going to have to say something.'

'We?' Frost retorted, lighting a further cigarette off the butt of the one just finished. 'It's you who's at the forefront, sir, having discovered the body . . .'

Mullett was sure the smug reprobate was smirking. But Frost was interrupted by a rap on the door, followed by Miss Smith entering the office.

'I thought I said I wasn't to be disturbed!' he snapped.

'It's Mr Winslow, sir,' she said apologetically, 'on line one.'

'Put him though, then,' Mullett said sharply.

'He's there, sir,' she said, pointing at the phone, 'flashing in red.'

Mullett snapped up the receiver, saying to Frost as he did so, 'Here, give me one of those cigarettes.' He pressed the flashing red button.

'Afternoon, sir.'

'Stanley, what the blazes is going on? I've had the *Denton Echo* pestering my people all morning.'

'About what, sir?'

'Whether I thought the sinking of the *Belgrano* was the turning point in the war – what the hell do you think? This boy ripped apart on the golf course, you imbecile!' the Assistant Chief Constable barked down the line.

'With all due respect, sir, the body was only discovered this morning.' Mullett looked at Frost, conscious he was repeating what the DS had said, but Frost feigned not to be listening, and was staring out of the window. 'We're still assessing matters. It's not an unusual occurrence for us to hold back a day, even if the situation is . . . is bizarre.'

'Of course, under usual circumstances the discovery of a body in a most "bizarre" state would accord us a day or so's grace . . .' The Assistant Chief Constable paused; Mullett could hear him take a breath. 'But these aren't usual circumstances, are they? You, a superintendent of the County police force, discovered a body in full view of every town dignitary between here and Reading! You can't just sit back and do nothing. I thank my lucky stars I had emergency root-canal treatment this morning and couldn't make it. I never thought I'd hear myself say that!'

'Root canal? Sorry to hear that, sir – very painful,' Mullett said carefully.

'Not as painful as life will be for you if you don't get on top of this. Who's heading the investigation?'

Mullett was silent for a second.

'Jim Allen?' Winslow prompted.

'DI Allen is on a computer course. At Hendon. At your request, sir,' Mullett added.

'Well, what of it? Who's running this?' Winslow hissed irritably.

'DS Frost,' said Mullett softly, regarding Frost as he spoke, who was still standing at the window, looking like a refugee from the sixties, in what could well be a shirt from Oxfam.

'He can hold the fort for now, but get Allen back pronto. And how's our coloured friend doing?'

Mullett cringed at the reference, staring fixedly at Frost in an effort to avoid the eye of the large, inscrutable officer he was now required to talk about. 'DS Waters is fitting in rather well. It's useful to have a different . . . perspective.' He found himself grinning inanely.

'Good, good. You can never tell with those chaps. I'll let you get on with it, then – and call a press conference.'

146

'*Today?* Isn't that rather rash? We've nothing to go on.'

'Superintendent, that is not the point. Control of the situation is what counts here. You'll think of something. Keep me posted. Good day.' The line went dead.

Mullett replaced the receiver heavily in its cradle, noticing he'd dropped ash over the desk throughout the conversation.

Frost pivoted round. 'All well at Gestapo HQ?'

'That's an inappropriate remark, Sergeant. It seems Mr Winslow would like a press conference.'

'Would he, now. I'd best be off, then – to give you time to prepare.'

'Ah, wait a minute.' Mullett shifted awkwardly in his grand leather chair. Winslow and Frost had a point – his being there when the body was found somehow put the onus on him to apprehend the murderer. The situation was potentially sticky. If he could somehow shift responsibility on to Frost . . . 'Jack, come here.'

Frost halted at the door.

'Sit down a minute. Since DI Williams's demise, we've been a detective inspector down.'

Frost sat stoically in front of the superintendent, saying nothing.

'I think it's time to raise your profile,' Mullett weaselled, not entirely convinced this was the right tack, but proceeding anyway. 'If you tidy yourself up a bit and are seen to be taking command of this situation . . .'

Frost raised his eyebrows. 'I can dress myself, sir.'

'Of course you can, but with a little more effort, and perhaps an occasional shave, it could be you in front of the press and TV cameras instead of me.'

Frost rubbed his bristly jaw. 'I don't know about that, sir. After all, you're so good at it.'

'Well, yes, Jack, but I can't be seen to be hogging the limelight all the time. Wouldn't you agree, DS Waters?'

'I don't think it's really my place to say, sir,' Waters replied, raising the palms of his hands defensively.

'We can swap if you insist.' Frost looked earnest. 'But right now I'm required urgently at the lab; the pathologist wants to see me ASAP.' He paused. 'He's found something in the remains.'

'The remains?' Mullett scratched nervously at his moustache. 'You mean, the body?'

'Call it what you like, sir, it's not a very nice sight, however you describe it – as you would know. We've been there once today already, but since then Drysdale has opened it up . . .'

'Maybe it's best you remain in the field for now,' Mullett conceded, but waving a manicured finger he added, 'Think on, though – for the future.'

'If that's all, sir, I must dash, if I may. Need the loo.'

'Yes, yes.' Mullett waved him off dismissively. On second thoughts, it would clearly be unwise to unleash Frost on the press. He'd only say something uncouth, or at best incomprehensible. He, Superintendent Mullett, was the one most suited to dealing with the media. He should stop feeling so uncomfortable about this case. After all, it wasn't as if he'd murdered the boy himself.

Chris Everett had slept like a baby on Tuesday night, and this afternoon he felt he could take on the world. He'd covered his tracks so well that Fiona had not suspected a thing. The unfortunate sweep had conveniently laid out his own shroud, making it easy for Everett to bundle the body swiftly into the back of his own van before Fiona and kids made it back from ballet. He'd backed the MG out of the garage and just about squeezed the van in its place.

Originally he had intended to get shot of the van and body at dawn, but had surprised himself by oversleeping. This presented him with a problem, as the longer the van stayed in the garage, the more likely Fiona was to stumble upon it.

Nevertheless, he kept calm. He'd taken the kids to school and then dropped her off for a coffee morning, after which she had a hair appointment. He had time. He'd left the Regal office on the pretext of a valuation and had come home to dispose of the evidence. He would, of course, have preferred not to do it in daylight as witnesses could be a risk, but fortunately the well-to-do neighbours were all out at work, the women included; Fiona was the only idler. So he figured he was safe there. The big question was, where? The woods? Too exposed in the daytime, and how would he get back? Come to think of it, how would he get back from anywhere? Sipping his coffee, he looked out of the window at the darkening sky. The weather was about to break in a major way. What he needed was somehow to lose himself in a crowd . . .

Frost hurried out, heading for the Gents. Mullett must think I was born yesterday, he thought; mind you, I don't blame him – facing the press will be pretty gruelling after such a discovery. Frost rubbed his hands gleefully, imagining Sandy Lane's probing questions: *And what exactly was the superintendent of Denton Police doing on a golf course first thing in the morning in the middle of the week when there's a host of unsolved crimes?*

His thoughts were interrupted by Waters, walking briskly behind him. 'What was all that about?'

'I needed a wee – what's to get?' Frost said, agitated.

'No – all the stuff about *remains*? We've just come from the lab . . .'

'I had to say something, didn't I – otherwise he'd have had me in front of the cameras, and we don't want that, do we?'

'No, I guess not.'

'No, indeed. And by the way, we need to let Mark Fong go; no need for Myles to check his records. Lad claimed he was born at Denton General, which I very much doubt. You can sign the release.'

'Shall I run some stuff through the Police National Computer?' Waters said. 'Check him out?'

Frost grimaced. 'Computer checks? On the *what*? Don't start using that sort of language with me!' He paused. 'It's like you've caught Mullett's progress bug just by being in his lair. No, just let the boy go.'

'Without checking any ID?'

'Doubt he's got any. Here illegally, I expect. Life's grim enough for him without us making it any tougher. Harry Baskin probably keeps him locked in a cellar with a bunch of false promises for company . . . Anyway, must dash.'

'Where?'

'For a wee. I told you!' Frost dived into the Gents, but poked his head back out of the door with an afterthought. 'When you've let Fong go, give young Derek Simms a hand, and I'll be back to hold yours as per the super's instructions in an hour or so – all right?' And then he was gone.

Bill Wells sidled up to Frost in the urinal stalls.

'Afternoon, Jack.'

'Bill.'

'What gives?'

'Mr Mullett has come over all camera-shy' – Frost coughed – 'about a press conference for the murdered boy.'

'Not like him.'

'Not like him at all,' agreed Frost. 'Reckons he doesn't want all the limelight.'

Bill Wells shook himself, musing, 'Maybe he's feeling a bit off colour?'

'He was born off colour. Righto, I'll be off, then. If anyone asks, tell them I'll be back in a couple of hours.'

'Who would anyone be, Jack?' Wells asked, washing his hands.

'*Anyone*. DC Clarke for one, and Hornrim Harry for another.'

'Right you are, mate. And should it matter you'll be . . . ?'

'Seeking a bit of help from the Almighty,' Frost said, which was half true. He checked himself in the mirror – something he seldom did – and flattened his sandy-brown hair. The mother-in-law had a dim view of him at the best of times; he may as well look presentable.

Waters was bemused by the set-up at Eagle Lane. Super-intendent Mullett and DS Jack Frost did not strike him as an ideal pairing, though he assumed they must work things through, or they'd presumably already have parted company. Mullett, he knew, was relatively new to Denton and had inherited the likes of Frost, but as Divisional Superintendent he wielded a great deal of power. Though Waters was unfamiliar with County politics, it appeared that Assistant Chief Constable Winslow left Denton to manage itself.

He wondered what a stickler like Mullett would think of Frost's nonchalance about Fong. Admittedly the Met's approach to illegal immigrants was flexible; it depended on the individual's value as, say, a key to the criminal underworld, and was tempered by the prevailing political climate. Frost, on the other hand, genuinely seemed to have the boy's interests at heart. Or perhaps he couldn't face the paperwork; judging from the state of his office, that could well be the case.

Waters signed the release for Fong and headed for the lobby.

'Sergeant Wells,' he addressed the likeable desk sergeant, 'I need to get hold of Simms – could you patch him through for me, please?'

'One second. I'll see if Control can locate him.'

Waters thanked him. He leaned back against the front desk and took in the lobby decor for the first time. The walls were magnolia, and the highly polished floor was flanked with a variety of house plants. If it wasn't for the noticeboard, it could well have been the foyer of a rest home.

'Simms is en route to Milk Street to interview the Asian newsagent.'

'Still? He left ages ago. No matter . . . I may as well wait for my chaperon to reappear. Any idea where he's gone? Left without a word.'

'Jack? He's gone to church for an hour or so.'

'Yeah, right.' Waters made for the door, thinking that he may as well get some air. 'He certainly struck me as the religious type.'

'Oh, Sergeant!' Wells called out. 'I almost forgot. A young lady left this for you.' He passed him a small blue envelope.

Wednesday (4)

Derek Simms sat inside the unmarked Cortina, waiting for the deluge to relent before he made a dash for the newsagent's over the road. His senses heightened by a frisky half-hour with Lisa Smith – Mullett had no idea what was under his very nose – he played the cassette from Samantha Ellis's Walkman one more time, but the hammering of the rain on the roof of the car made it practically impossible to hear. In any case, it seemed to be nothing but gibberish; was it singing? He ejected it and studied it – a standard Maxwell C90. Ordinary enough. There was no indication of what was on it. He tried the other side. Pop music blared out and he hastily turned the volume down. The song was 'I Don't Like Mondays' by that talentless Irish band. It had come out a couple of years ago, and he remembered a fuss because some kid in the States had topped themselves, allegedly because of the song. Not surprising, it sounded awful; the bloke couldn't sing for toffee. Perhaps Samantha Ellis felt she'd had enough of him as well? He'd mention it to Frost. But if the song played OK it must mean the cassette wasn't faulty, so someone must be able to decipher the nonsense on the other side.

He ejected it and slipped it back inside the girl's bag lying on the passenger seat, next to the Walkman and the paperback.

The rain wasn't going to ease up; he'd have to make a dash for it. Curse this bloody newsagent! Why should he care about a poxy paper shop anyway? Nearly running that paperboy over this morning had clearly been a bad omen.

He was suddenly struck by a thought. The boys who had robbed the jeweller's were on BMXs too – perhaps a paperboy, or boys, were responsible? According to the owner they were wearing hooded tops, much like the lad this morning. It couldn't have been the same one doing the robbery of course, the timing was out. But perhaps there was a gang of them? Maybe some of them worked for this character, Mr Singh, or used to; maybe he'd upset one or two of them and they'd decided to rob him in revenge, and then perhaps got a taste for it?

He decided there and then that he and Waters should take it upon themselves to tour the local newsagents and enquire after disgruntled ex-employees. And Singh's was the perfect place to start, given that he'd been held up himself. He reached over for his leather jacket and opened the car door.

Frost pulled the long chain on the vicarage bell. A dog yapped in response. It was a while since he'd been out here. He mulled over when the last time might have been. Bert Williams's funeral perhaps, last October? Father Lowe was a good man. He'd been in Denton donkey's years. Married him and Mary, way back when.

'William?' The octogenarian man of the cloth appeared in the doorway. 'Come in, quickly, out of the rain.'

'Afternoon, Father.' Frost nodded, wincing at the use of his Christian name. 'Might I have a word?'

The reverend stepped back, allowing Frost into the musty

cottage that smelt of dogs and old books. 'Tea, perhaps?'

'I don't think I'll be troubling you that long, Father Lowe,' Frost said, perching on the chintz sofa. A grandfather clock ticked solemnly in the background. It could be 1882 and nobody'd tell the difference, Frost thought.

'Always in a hurry, William. Now the church roof . . .' The old man smiled kindly in the stern way old people did, betraying their anxiety.

'Ah yes. The roof.' Frost forced a smile in response. 'All sorted. We have the naughty man already.'

'I don't care about the rascal who did it. The bloody roof is leaking.' He reached for a pack of Woodbines on a small pile of books, itself precariously balanced on a small round wooden table. 'A rain shower at a funeral often helps to add to the solemnity of the occasion' – Lowe puffed whimsically on the cigarette – 'however, the bereaved expect the experience at the graveside, as their beloved is lowered into the ground . . . not in the actual church, hammering down nineteen to the dozen on the bloody casket.'

'Yes, Reverend, I agree. Most . . . disturbing.' Frost had forgotten how spirited the old fellow was. 'But we're on it, and the felon who nicked your lead will be putting it back.'

'Will he?' Lowe's grey brow concertinaed. 'I do hope so. These carryings-on in the South Atlantic have boosted the congregation numbers. The Church should be a place of comfort . . .'

'Yes, yes,' Frost sighed. 'A good war does seem to boost the Lord's takings.'

'Be that as it may,' Father Lowe countered, 'we can't have it raining on holy communion.'

'Quite,' Frost said. 'Now, important as the church roof is, that's not what brings me here. I need to talk to you about another matter. Do you remember a couple of years back, there was . . . graffiti in the churchyard?'

'Desecration,' Lowe said gravely.

'Desecration, that's what I mean,' Frost said, apologetically. 'It turned out to be an escaped patient from the loony bin outside Rimmington, but before he was caught, you mentioned something to me about occult happenings in Denton . . .'

'I remember – yes.' Lowe scratched his silver head thoughtfully. 'Years and years ago, in the early sixties. Why do you ask?'

'There's been a brutal murder. A young lad ripped open, organs removed. Very nasty business. We're working on the theory that there could be an occult connection. The manner in which the body was found . . .'

But the Father waved him quiet before he could continue. 'No, no, that was just a bunch of silly schoolgirls playing pranks. Teenagers pretending to be witches, that sort of thing. Hardly heretical. Nothing of this nature. How awful. I heard it reported on the wireless. What is the world coming to?' Father Lowe shook his head woefully, stood up and reached for the sherry decanter. 'What does Mary have to say about it?'

Frost took the proffered schooner, full to the brim. 'Mary? My wife? What do you mean?'

'Yes, your wife, Mary, she was one of the girls involved – before you arrived on the scene, I would hazard.' Lowe moved a small dog that Frost hadn't noticed off a deep-green armchair, sinking into it. 'She would have been only fifteen or sixteen at the time.'

'Well, that accounts for a lot. Perhaps she cast a spell on me to get me up the aisle,' Frost said to himself, plonking himself down into the other free armchair. 'No, Father, she's never mentioned it. What happened?'

'As I said, not much. A concerned mother – one of my parishioners – discovered her daughter trying to tattoo herself with a pair of compasses and a bottle of Quink.'

'Painful.'

'Yes. Seems it was some sort of pagan symbol. She dragged

the child to the hospital, brand-new as it was then, fearing blood poisoning. The sight of the star on her wrist sparked gossip that she was a witch. Of course, people wouldn't bat an eyelid today, but back then Denton was different from how it is now . . . people were very superstitious.'

Frost got out his notebook. 'I don't suppose you remember her name?'

'It's too late for that, I'm afraid.' Lowe shook his head solemnly.

'What, you mean . . . Did the blood poisoning get her?' Frost reached for the decanter and topped them both up.

'Hanged herself in Denton Woods. Couldn't handle the stigma. Her parents weren't much help.' He got up and downed the refill. 'Young girls are difficult to deal with at that age. Hormones all over the place, I gather . . .'

'I'll bear that in mind next time I ask one if she's a witch. Anyway, in my experience, they don't get any easier as they get older.' Frost allowed a silence to envelop them, punctuated only by the ticking of the grandfather clock. He thought again about what Lowe had just told him. It was puzzling. 'Surely a tattoo is just a tattoo – no matter what it represents. And to hang one-self? Did she have a troubled background?'

Lowe scratched his head. 'The girl was a pupil at St Mary's, which was strict in those days, and she'd already been caught up in some to-do at the school involving local boys. There were rumours that the girls involved had formed, for want of a better word, a *coven*, to exact revenge for the punishment they received. Seemed a bit far-fetched to me. As I say, talk to Mary.'

'I will, Father.'

'What was it called?' Father Lowe muttered to himself.

'I'm sorry, Father?'

'It had a name . . . this coven,' he said abstractedly. 'There was some connection to St Jude's . . .'

'What, here? The church?'

'My memory's not what it was, I'm afraid. Talk to Mary,' he repeated.

Eventually Father Lowe rose from his chair. 'You must excuse me,' he said, 'I have evensong to prepare for.'

'Of course. Thank you for your time.' Frost almost reached over to help the old man up, so weak did he seem. 'It may not be schoolgirls I'm after, but as you say, people were much more superstitious once, and we're only talking twenty years ago – hardly the Middle Ages. You've been a big help, Father, thank you. I know this isn't really your field . . .'

Father Lowe moved to the bookcase and scanned the crowded shelves until he found what he was after. 'Here,' he said, passing Frost a shabby hardback.

'*A Brief History of the Pagan Calendar* by Professor Leo Hollis. Unusual choice of book for a man in your position to have on his shelves.' Frost blew the dust off the slender volume. 'Do you keep it to swot up occasionally? Know thine enemy, that sort of thing?'

'Nothing so mysterious, or exciting,' Lowe said. 'Leo was a theology student at Cambridge with me.'

'Thanks. Mind if I take a look?'

'Not at all – keep it. Hope it's of some use – or perhaps not. Let's pray you're barking up the wrong tree.'

'Quite.'

Frost made his way down the hallway and shivered involuntarily. Something about the vicarage unsettled him. It was the place itself, as opposed to the good Father, who was a kind, trustworthy man. Lowe opened the door. The small dog fussed around his feet like a hairy rat. Frost held out his hand and Lowe took it firmly in both of his, saying, 'Look after Mary, William.' His pale-grey eyes let on more than was said. Frost nodded, shook hands and made his way down the rambling garden path, wondering what on earth his wife had been up to twenty years ago.

'Where are Myles and Clarke, for goodness' sake?' Mullett demanded.

'You're not the only one wanting to know that,' Bill Wells replied.

A camera crew struggled through the door en route to the Incident Room.

'Outside!' Mullett barked. 'The press conference will be held *outside*, in *front* of the station.' He followed up with an ingratiating smile. 'If you please.'

He turned angrily to Wells. 'I distinctly told that buffoon Pooley to keep them outside the building. There's a big enough mess as it is in here without that media rabble trampling about. It's only a drop of rain, not a plague of locusts.'

Mullett straightened his tie. Wells knew that for all the super's whingeing he loved the camera. And regardless of what Frost had said, Mullett could never pass up an opportunity to appear on the box, even where events as delicate as these were involved. The conference was at four o'clock; in ten minutes' time.

'Wells, Wells! Wake up.' Mullett was slapping his uniform cap restlessly against his thigh. 'Who else wants Clarke and Myles?'

'Tom Hardy's parents.'

'But they were with the parents this morning. Clarke said . . .'

'Yes, sir, but the daughter, Tom's sister, has disappeared now.'

'Disappeared? What do you mean *disappeared*? You're telling me this five minutes before I go on air to report on her dead brother?'

'"Disappeared" might be the wrong word. When the area car took Mrs Hardy to the school, to collect the girl at lunchtime . . .'

'At lunchtime! It's four o'clock in the afternoon.'

'If you'll let me finish, sir,' Wells said forcefully, struggling not to be distracted by the hubbub of press swirling around. The hapless Pooley had appeared and was attempting to direct

159

them. 'They assumed she must have gone to a hockey match in Rimmington, so they sat it out at St Mary's rather than cause a scene.'

'And?'

'She wasn't on the bus when it got back to the school.'

'I see. So, if "disappeared" is the wrong word, what would you say instead?'

'They thought she might be—'

'Superintendent, sir?' Pooley interrupted, clutching an umbrella. 'Might we line you up? The press are waiting.'

'I'll deal with you later, Wells.' Mullett glared at him before storming off, flinging on his cap as he reached the revolving door.

As the room cleared, Wells considered the theories of the missing girl's whereabouts. She might be with friends, or revising for exams perhaps? That was what the school had said.

Though, on reflection, Wells very much doubted it.

Chris Everett had waited until early evening and for the downpour to abate before leaving the house again. He'd called his Hatton Garden contact, who'd agreed to meet him in London at eight. Fiona thought he was seeing Julian, an old schoolfriend now living on the South Coast, London being a midway point between them. After meeting Ahmed, he'd sit it out in some dismal pub near Edgware Road for an appropriate length of time before skulking off home half cut to create the pretence of having had a great time.

Yes, the rain was abating. He smiled to himself; a little over an hour ago, Everett had brazenly driven both van and sweep into Denton town centre. His own daring thrilled him – moving a corpse in broad daylight, in the corpse's own van – but what better cover than a deluge of biblical proportions?

The deceased's disappearance, whether it had yet been reported, was unlikely to grab much attention, as it would simply be eclipsed by the mutilated teenager found on the golf course.

Everett had caught the evening news before he departed for London. A pompous policeman, cowering beneath an umbrella, had given a garbled statement regarding the unfortunate boy, who in his words had been 'brutally eviscerated'. Apparently this senior policeman discovered the body himself.

He hurried down Primrose Drive and on to Rose Avenue. Dusk was still some way off but the street lights were beginning to flicker pink. Dark, ominous thunderclouds continued to clog the sky, giving the impression it was later than it was; it had only just gone six thirty. He clutched the briefcase nervously. He'd get a cab from Market Square.

Everett recapped the last twenty-four hours as he made his way along the pavement. The sweep's death was unfortunate, and a far cry from the original rules he'd set himself three years ago when he'd first embarked on his house-breaking career. Yes, murder was in a different league, but it prevented the boredom setting in, and boredom was the biggest crime of all. Absorbed in his reverie of self-admiration, Everett failed to see the bunch of hostile-looking teenagers lurking against a large, overgrown privet hedge, until one stepped into his path.

'Gi's yer case, mate.' The boy's voice was hoarse – on the cusp of breaking – and urgent. His features were obscured by a tracksuit hood.

'I'll do no such thing. Out of my way, you little tyke.' Everett made to move but another figure stepped out to block him. As Everett swung the case at the second child's head he felt a searing jab in his lower back. In shock he released his grip.

The next thing he knew he was sprawled on the pavement, his case gone and his nostrils filled with dirt. He'd been stabbed, of that much he was certain. He tentatively reached behind him, feeling the dampness of blood through the pinstripe; it wasn't deep, more of a sting. Suddenly he felt something wet tentatively sniffing at his cheek; he jerked, sending excruciating pain through his body.

'Gripper, no! Jesus Christ! No!' was the last thing he heard before the dog urinated in his ear. God, he'd prefer to be hanged than suffer this ignominy! He staggered to his feet and booted the puny Jack Russell into the shrubbery. Things had gone badly wrong, but he was damned if he'd hang around to . . .

'Excuse me, sir?' Across the road was a lean young man in jeans and leather jacket. His appearance suggested someone low on the social scale – a window cleaner, perhaps – but the manner of his address and his bearing set alarm bells off in Everett's muddled brain. 'Are you all right?'

After his interesting discussion with Father Lowe, Frost decided he wanted to check with Records and see if he could pull out anything on the sixties witchcraft incident, before visiting his mother-in-law. If Mary was there, depending on how things went, he could ask her what she recalled of the events herself. He would play that one by ear, though. To be honest, he'd be lucky if that viper of a mother-in-law let him across the threshold.

Good timing, Frost thought, as he crossed the car park and saw the BBC van pulling out, I've missed the media circus and the super's TV appearance.

''Ello, 'ello,' he said, running into four uniform loitering in the station reception area. 'Autograph hunters from across the county, hoping for a glimpse of the famed TV superintendent?'

'Not exactly,' one of them replied.

'So what's going on then, Bill?' he said as the young officers made way to allow him through to the front desk.

'Ah, Jack, a bit of a to-do.'

'Don't tell me – the super went on camera with his flies open?' Frost grinned.

'Not likely. No, it's serious. Tom Hardy's sister has gone missing.'

'You're kidding? Damn.' Frost's face fell. 'What do we know?'

'Nothing. Mullett has just briefed uniform here.' Wells indicated the officers, now leaving the building. 'To cap it all, though, after escorting the Hardys to identify their son's body, Clarke and Myles went to the boozer and had one too many, so when news came in about the sister they were nowhere to be found. Well, you can imagine the super's reaction.'

'Flamin' hell, I can at that. He'll be having kittens.'

'You're not wrong. They're both in there now.'

'This is not acceptable. Two *women* police officers,' Mullett said, emphasizing the word that he clearly felt to be the most important in that sentence.

DCs Clarke and Myles stood stiffly to attention as Superintendent Mullett then let fly.

Clarke felt her bottom lip begin to tremble. She drew it in and bit down hard; she was going to hold it together even if it killed her. To rein in her emotions she focused on her dislike of the superintendent, and when that wore off, she thought about the lad she'd met in the pub with whom she'd exchanged phone numbers.

'I will not have drunks on my force. Do I make myself clear?' They both nodded vigorously. 'You're both bloody lucky not to have been suspended without pay, especially you, Clarke. Thanks to your leg wound we were able to explain why you stumbled into that cameraman – without it that would've been your lot.'

Although it was almost dark outside the superintendent moved to adjust his venetian blinds aggressively as if they were somehow responsible for the appalling conduct of the two CID officers.

'Myles, you're dismissed,' Mullett barked.

They both shuffled off towards the office door.

'Not you, Clarke, sit down.' He paced behind the expansive desk, polishing his glasses as he did so. 'How is your leg?'

The concern in the question caught her off guard. Only a minute earlier he'd been biting her head off.

'OK. A bit stiff. The stitches itch like hell.' She rubbed her thigh as if a mere mention of the wound had provoked an irritation.

'Good, good.' He said distractedly. 'Cigarette?'

She took one. She knew they were too strong for her but Mullett had never offered her so much as a light before.

'It's really important that we apprehend those little hooligans who did this to you.' He pivoted back and forth on the enormous leather chair. The motion struck Clarke as creepy; he reminded her of a Bond villain, minus the charisma of course, and you wouldn't catch Blofeld in those awful hornrim spectacles. 'I mean, we can't have this sort of thing going on . . .'

She nodded.

'Tell me, I forgot to ask yesterday, did they steal anything from the car? Any personal effects? Jewellery, for instance?'

'I don't carry around much in the way of . . . personal effects. When at work, I mean. I think we took them by surprise; I'm sure they would have stolen something if given half the chance . . .'

'Yes, my thoughts exactly.' Mullett leaned forward. 'Well, er, Susan, now the attack is behind you, and you're feeling less distressed, maybe something will come to mind? A face, a description? Anything, eh? Well, that's it, make yourself useful and get on down to Denton Woods before it gets dark – I've just had the sergeant on site moaning there's no one from CID accompanying the search.'

Clarke got up to leave, feeling slightly nauseous. *Susan?* Only her mother called her that. What a creep. As she left Mullett's office she felt sure she was going to throw up; whether it was booze, the shock of the bollocking or the super's saccharine smile she couldn't be sure. She bolted for the Ladies as fast as she could.

Wednesday (5)

It was getting late. The three of them, Frost, Waters and Simms, sat in the Incident Room, beneath the stark light of two naked bulbs dangling forlornly at each end of the room. Frost got up and studied the large cork board that hung on the wall.

One half of the board was devoted to Samantha Ellis, the girl discovered by the railway track on Monday morning. The other half now contained both Hardy children, with the scene-of-crime photos of the boy spilling over on to those of Ellis. The most recent addition was Emily Hardy's school photo. The exact time of the girl's disappearance remained vague; the report from uniform was sketchy. In truth nobody up to now had given her a moment's thought. All attention had been on the other two.

Frost was beginning to feel the pressure mounting. Tension tweaked down his neck and along his shoulder muscles. The situation was growing serious; he needed a result, and quick. A girl was missing; she could be the next body. He refocused on her photo. That uniform, he'd seen it somewhere else; at the

Ferguson house earlier today – school photo on the mantelpiece. So, she attended St Mary's, the same as the two girls from the train on Saturday night. A coincidence, no doubt; there were only four secondary schools in Denton, but nevertheless he made a mental note to make further checks on those two girls.

He moved from the board to the easel, where the various assaults and muggings were mounting up on a daily basis. The day had been topped and tailed by a jeweller's being robbed and a man being stabbed on his way home from work. Simms was filling in the details on the latter incident.

'OK,' Frost said, 'run that by me again. This guy, Everett, was on his way home from work and was jabbed with what, a penknife? They took his briefcase but he doesn't want the police to take action.'

'That's about the sum of it.' Simms yawned, rocking back on his chair. 'He said he was embarrassed to have been done by a bunch of kids, and the briefcase had sod all in it apart from his lunch box.'

'I don't care if he had the Crown Jewels in it,' Frost said wearily. 'These little bastards are more than likely the ones who stabbed Sue Clarke. Not to mention done the jeweller's and probably the newsagent's.'

'Sure, sure,' Simms said, calmly lighting a cigarette. 'He didn't say he wouldn't help, he just wasn't bothered on his own account.'

'Daring little geezers, aren't they,' said Waters, sipping a beer.

'Simms, you went back to Mr Singh today. Did it open up anything new?'

'I thought it might have been a disgruntled paperboy.'

'And?'

'Mr Singh didn't think so.'

'Well, what does he think?'

'He's still insisting they were armed.'

'But he didn't see the gun,' Waters put in.

'He didn't see the gun,' Frost echoed. 'Did they even have a gun? I doubt it. C'mon, we don't have time to waste on this, it really is kids' stuff. Did he say anything sensible?' Frost was beginning to get annoyed.

'He . . . er.' Simms was looking at Waters. 'He thought it might be race-related.'

'Oh, cobblers!' Frost slapped the wall, exasperated, causing the incident board to tremble. 'Drag in Mr Singh and take him through the photos of possibles, see what Clarke and Myles have come up with . . . Honestly, this is a waste of everybody's time. Right, now, on to the serious stuff. Let's start with Samantha Ellis.'

Frost sat down and stretched, cigarette in hand. Waters and Simms were watching him intently. What did he have to say? Initially he was convinced she must have been murdered, but enquiries had led nowhere. Perhaps, as Mullett hoped, she really had committed suicide.

He rubbed his eyes wearily. 'Right, the Ellis girl; we have absolutely nothing to go on. Two girls, Ferguson and Burleigh, the same age as our girl and on the same train from London, who you'd think must have seen something, claim to remember nothing about the trip home because they were too drunk. Convenient, but not beyond the realms of possibility. But them aside, this train did not just stop at Denton – there were a number of stops up the line. What I don't get is why there have been no witnesses. The posters are definitely up?' Frost directed the question to Simms.

'Up and down the line,' Simms confirmed, 'and all over Paddington Station.'

'Somebody *must* have seen something!' Frost exclaimed as Clarke appeared in the doorway looking tired and miserable. 'If not at the station, then surely on the train itself.'

'I'm not sure they would,' Simms said. 'I went back to British Rail to confirm a few details – the length of the train, the number of carriages – to try to corroborate where the passengers who got off at Denton had sat. I asked the guard again to confirm where the bag was found. He said it was in a smoker, yes, at the front, but not an "open" coach.'

'What does that mean?' Frost huffed, rooting around for the bottle of Black Label. 'I'm not familiar with train lingo.'

'It means she was on a closed-compartment-style coach' – Simms flicked through his notebook – 'with just the doors on either side. All the compartments are separate, and there's nothing in them apart from two big long seats the width of the train, seating six each, and the overhead luggage rack.'

'So, if there was a struggle in one compartment, it would be quite possible that nobody saw a thing,' Waters said.

'Or she could have been alone and decided to top herself,' Frost countered, scratching his head.

'I don't buy that,' Waters said. 'Why? No note. Bright future ahead of her, by all accounts. Besides, there are easier ways to go. No, those girls are hiding something. After we'd interviewed Burleigh she rushed out to tell us they'd been drinking – why? To cover something up. It was a calculated action.'

'Maybe,' Frost agreed. 'It's odd, I admit – but you have to be careful with minors, especially with this lot. Social Services could come down on us like a ton of bricks. The lack of witnesses still seems crazy, though. We're asking if anyone saw a fifteen-year-old girl; we know there were at least three on the train, possibly another, and yet we haven't had a single report.'

'Different passengers,' said Waters. 'Your posters are seen by commuters – those punters wouldn't go near a train station at the weekend. Meanwhile, the casual day-trippers are none the wiser.'

'OK.' Frost yawned. 'We know there was nobody at Denton when the train got in, but what about the London end? Those big stations are open twenty-four hours a day. Was there a guard, a ticket inspector, anyone?'

'Er, yeah, there was a ticket inspector,' Simms said, 'but apparently he had a couple of days off once his shift had finished.'

'Well, go rouse him from his slumbers, or whatever it is British Rail employees do to recharge their batteries. Anything further on the girl's bag?'

'I've got it here,' Simms said. 'The only prints we could lift were on the Walkman, and they were hers.' Simms tossed the bag to Frost.

'What about the tape?'

'I've dropped it off at Denton Hi-Fi,' Simms replied. 'Got a mate there who can hopefully make out what the gibberish on the B-side is.'

'Good move.' Frost slumped down in a chair and had a look inside the bag, pulling out a paperback. *'Rosemary's Baby.'* He turned it over in his hand. 'Not the sort of thing I'd want my teenage daughter to be reading.'

'The movie scared the shit out of me.' Waters grimaced. 'You remember it – the Polanski one about satanists? Mia Farrow gives birth to the devil. Nasty.'

'Which brings us on to body number two,' Frost said, shooting a glance at Clarke who was stifling a yawn. 'What's new on that?'

'Forensics are furious,' she answered. 'The grass could have told them a lot.'

'The grass?' Simms snorted.

'The grass,' Clarke repeated. 'Had the manicured ninth hole not been trampled by a squadron of berks in plus-fours, they might possibly have a clue as to how the body arrived there.'

'What on earth are you on about?' Simms said, his forehead creased, confused.

Clarke shrugged.

Frost tried to ignore the dark creases under her puffy eyes. He noticed a whiff of alcohol. 'Let's not dwell on what we don't have,' he said diplomatically, but added with a glint in his eye, 'It's a pity a competent officer wasn't on the scene.' How ironic. If Mullett knew remotely what he was doing and thought less about the spectacle, there'd be undisturbed evidence. A clue in the dew. He smiled at his own joke.

'What's so funny?' Clarke snapped.

'Nothing, nothing,' Frost replied quickly. God, he felt tired. 'Is there anything Forensics can tell us?'

'It's likely the body came from the woods, as opposed to being carted across the green.'

'What – he was killed in the woods?' Frost said, as the phone rang.

'I didn't say that, did I?' Clarke rejoined. The more she spoke the more the tension increased palpably. Frost could cut it with a knife. It didn't help that it was growing late and the week had already seemed long; although in fact it was only Wednesday. The phone continued to ring. 'The new golf club itself is locked at night, and the perimeter is either chicken wire or a hedgerow. Or Denton Woods.'

'I see.' Frost felt for his cigarette packet. Empty – the second pack today. 'Hold on,' he said and picked up the phone angrily. 'Yes?' It was Night Sergeant Johnny Johnson. He had Samantha Ellis's mother on the phone.

'I'm busy,' Frost said. He knew he couldn't delay talking to the mother much longer, but in truth he just hadn't had the time.

'She says it's important. It's to do with Mr Mullett on the television.'

'Tell her I'll call her back.' He put the phone down and scribbled 'Ellis' on a spare piece of blotting paper. 'Right, where were we? Access to the golf club.'

'Mmm.' Clarke sighed. 'Uniform combed the woods all day today. Found nothing apart from some bivouacs left over from some camp, probably Scouts.'

'Bivouacs?' asked Waters. 'What are they?'

'Tents, shelters, made out of fern and bracken. Green shit,' Simms offered helpfully. 'You know, Boy Scout stuff.'

'Where are you off to?' Frost enquired gruffly, seeing Waters reach for his jacket.

'It's nine o'clock. I'm . . . going to meet a friend.'

'Blimey, you don't waste much time. Go on then, bugger off. I want a full report in the morning. Be here by eight; we're off to the posh girls' school, St Mary's. You'll give them a fright, all right.'

As Waters left the room, Frost turned back to Clarke. 'Right, so, bivouacs? So were there kids camped out over the bank holiday weekend?'

'Haven't had time to get on to it yet,' Clarke replied, brow creasing.

'What have you been doing all day, then?' Frost snapped in jest, but before he knew it his remark had released the flood-gates. Clarke's shoulders convulsed as she broke down in sobs in the chair opposite.

Frost exchanged an awkward look with Simms.

'All right, Derek, son,' Frost said, suddenly feeling very tired, 'that'll do for tonight. Well done. We'd better get down to the woods tomorrow morning – not that I doubt the thoroughness of our colleagues, but just to be sure. Get an Ordnance Survey map and plot the entrances and exits – I doubt uniform will have squared that off. Check out the movements of the Girl Guides and Scouts over the last week and interview those in charge. Take Kim Myles, she strikes me as one who's no stranger to leaping around the toadstool.'

DC Simms picked up his leather jacket, nodded goodbye and left quietly.

'Give me a cigarette,' Clarke muttered, sniffing, her auburn hair hiding her eyes. Frost chucked her an unopened pack.

'What's up?' Frost asked reluctantly.

'Nothing,' she said, regaining her composure in an instant. 'Mullett threatened to suspend me.'

'Did he?' Frost said, unmoved. 'He may want to, but he can't afford to.'

'Don't you want to know why?' Clarke said with a sneer. 'Not that it matters; we were on first-name terms by the time we parted company.'

'I know why,' he said, topping up his mug with Black Label. 'You and Kim Myles got rat-arsed then stumbled into Mullett's TV appearance.'

'Aren't you in the least bit concerned?' she asked.

'It's nothing,' Frost said. 'Mullett was bad-tempered. When he goes on telly the rule is nothing can stick to him directly; it was, to say the least, a nuisance that he personally stumbled across a body. Nowhere to hide. I wish I'd been there to see him squirm.'

'But I'm talking about why.' Clarke pulled out a tissue and blew her nose violently.

'Why what?'

'*Why* I was drunk on duty.'

'It's nothing to be ashamed of, darling, most of us are.' He smiled.

'Rubbish. You can't take anything about me seriously. Mullett took it seriously. Getting pissed on duty may be the norm for everyone, but not for me. It's your fault.'

'My fault? How in blazes is it my fault?' Frost got up and paced the room, which was starting to feel cold. The heating had been off since the end of April. He stared long and hard at Emily Hardy's angelic school photo pinned on the board – he hadn't really looked at it before.

'Let me finish up here,' he said, reaching for Father Lowe's pagan book, 'and I'll drive you home.'

172

'It's all right, Jack,' Clarke said, regaining her composure a second time. 'I, too, am going to meet a friend.'

She stood up and strode out of the office.

'Hook up with Simms and Myles in the morning!' he called after her. Whether she heard him or not he didn't know.

DC Clarke stood trembling with anger, alone in the main CID office. She reached inside her handbag, which lay on her desk, and pulled out a crumpled pack of Silk Cut. On the white section of the packet was a phone number. She hadn't wanted Frost to see it, but on reflection maybe she should have let him – it would serve him right.

She lit another cigarette and inhaled deeply, staring out into the darkness through the window. Actually, I'm not angry at all, she thought, I feel terrific; hell, I got stabbed on Monday, so what's to lose.

Clarke picked up the receiver and dialled the local four-digit number. The phone rang four, five times before someone answered.

'Danny?' Clarke felt a tingle of excitement rush through her.

'Knew you'd call,' said a smooth male voice. 'Bad afternoon?'

Alone again and in his own office, Frost picked up *A Brief History of the Pagan Calendar*, the book Father Lowe had given him earlier in the day. With everybody out of the way he finally felt able to focus clearly.

He leafed through the pages until he found May. 'The month of May has been named after the Greek Goddess of Fertility, Maia. Maia is the chief of the Greek Seven Sisters and mother to Hermes, the God of . . .'

Boring.

'May is the month of the appearance on Earth of the mother Goddess, or Lady Wicca . . .'

He skipped the intro and moved on to the calendar itself.

May 1, or Mayday, is one of the most important of the eight pagan festivals. The festival of Beltane, the first day of Summer, celebrates the life force in all its incarnations, plant, animal and man, and harmony between one and all. Traditionally, homage to the Sun God takes the form of unbridled sexuality and promiscuity . . .

Frost scanned further down. No mention of ripping open teenage boys. It seemed to him the whole thing, thinly veiled in mysticism, was just an excuse to shag anyone you felt like, ostensibly because the sun had come out. He could find nothing on sacrifice, but plenty on maypoles.

He yawned. He knew he should get over to the in-laws. Just to reassure himself that Mary was safe. He wouldn't insist she come home, of course. Could something be up – had she rumbled Sue? Would she care, he wondered, not for the first time that day. He glanced at his watch – he could make Rimmington before ten if he put his foot down.

He closed Hollis's *Pagan Calendar*. On the front were three scantily clad women striking peculiar poses. Witches in Denton? No chance.

As he put the book down he spotted a new manilla file on the desk, headed HARDY, T. He hadn't noticed it earlier. Inside were the fruits of uniform's door-to-door this afternoon, an attempt at tracing the boy's movements before his disappearance was reported.

Tom Hardy. Date of birth: March 1, 1966. Barely made it past the age of consent, Frost thought. Or had much of a crack at the numerous O levels he was down for; and there were indeed many. He was a bright lad.

Within the file was his school record. Not missed a day all year. Captain of Denton Comprehensive's football team, too. His form teacher confirmed he had been in school on the Friday despite the lack of compulsory lessons during exam time.

The Hardys' neighbours had stated that they'd seen the boy return home after football practice on Friday afternoon. His parents had already gone away for the bank holiday weekend. After that there were no other local sightings, so no indication of when he next left the house, or what he was wearing. They hadn't had time to interview his sister, Emily, before her disappearance.

Frost was struck by the parallel with the Ellis case – hands-off parenting. It seemed that once the kids were on the brink of leaving school, the parents couldn't wait to shrug off the burden of responsibility. Tom Hardy was just sixteen, so maybe he was old enough to be left on his own for a short while. But his younger sister, at fourteen, was not.

Frost had had enough for now. He picked up his keys, switching off the desk lamp.

'Thanks for asking me out,' Waters said, smiling. A couple of beers in the fug of the Eagle had relaxed him nicely, but he knew it was getting late.

'Well, I bet you wouldn't have got round to it,' Kim Myles teased, the gin bringing a flush to her cheeks.

'Probably not,' he admitted. 'Anyway, I'd better be going. Got my orders for tomorrow morning.'

Myles looked at her watch. 'They've not rung time yet!' Her blue eyes flashed at him. 'All right, you need your beauty sleep. I've got to trawl about in the woods tomorrow, apparently – with Derek Simms.' She gave a look of distaste. 'But will you walk me home? 'Snot far.'

'No problem,' Waters agreed.

'Just nipping to the loo. I won't be a sec.' The girl hopped up excitedly.

Waters liked Kim Myles. She was bubbly, lively, flirtatious and undoubtedly dangerous. Why else would she have asked him on a date – a black cop from the Met, and the newest face at Eagle Lane? Each factor on its own was enough to upset those of a sensitive nature; it was bound to go down badly with the average provincial plod. In defiance of which she'd brought him to the firm's drinking hole. Why? She could only be after trouble. Trying to wind up an ex maybe?

He scoured the bunch up at the bar. The Eagle was within spitting distance of the Denton nick, at the corner of Eagle Lane and Queen Street, and had an odd mix of clientele: off-duty coppers consorting with obvious villains. Both groups had shot glances of disgust in their direction throughout the evening, as much at the girl as at him. He could handle being the only black face in a sea of white, especially with a cute blonde on his arm – the only problem was, could they?

'Hiya. Ready?' Kim Myles stood glowing in front of him. No doubt about it, she was a stunner. He smiled – he'd be pissed off too if he was the local whitey clocking him trundling off with this choice bit of stuff. He downed his beer and picked up his cigarettes.

The clear night sky had induced a temperature drop, reminding them they were only just out of April. Myles took the opportunity to link arms. Waters wasn't about to resist the warmth of the girl against his denim jacket.

'So what do you make of it – Denton?' she asked.

'It's good.' He smiled broadly in the darkness.

'Care to elaborate?'

'It's a novel experience. There's some crazy shit going on. All this talk of witches.' He half laughed. 'You know it's different from what I'm used to.'

'Yeah, I'll bet. But don't you think they're a bunch of odd-balls? Mullett, Frost – the lot of them?' she persisted, stopping to light a cigarette. Waters was loath to be drawn into giving opinions on his new colleagues. Myles had spilled the beans on Frost and Clarke; he'd guessed as much but didn't care, he was more concerned about Mullett hauling the two women over the coals for being pissed when their morning had been spent identifying Tom Hardy's body.

'They're all right – good guys.'

Waters deflected Myles's questions – which he quickly surmised were a roundabout way of uncovering what he felt about her. Before he knew it, they'd arrived at her block of flats off Queen Street.

'This is me,' she said, looking up at him, eyes glinting beneath the orange street light. 'Coffee?'

He shook his head and was about to say, 'Better not', but before he could speak she'd grabbed his jacket and pulled him down. He felt her hot mouth on his. The hardness of her kiss took him by surprise, but she quickly released him.

'Maybe next time,' she said, making off up the path towards the entrance of her building, swaying slightly and searching her handbag for keys as she did so.

Waters felt pleased with himself. He'd behaved well and acted gallantly – the only problem being he had no idea where he was. Myles had disappeared inside her block without giving him a chance to ask for directions. Oh well, they hadn't come that far and he had the number of the police house written down on him somewhere. There'd be a phone box.

He lit a cigarette and walked back the way he'd come. Perhaps because of the booze, or perhaps because his mind was on the shapely Kim Myles, now presumably undressing, Waters failed to notice his attackers.

One grabbed him from behind in a headlock, while another kneed him in the groin and pummelled his ribs. He went down on to the concrete; but just before a boot connected with his skull and he lost consciousness, he knew he recognized that aftershave.

*   *   *

'She doesn't want to see you.' Frost had expected it. Beryl Simpson could give one of Baskin's bouncers a run for his money.

'Come on, Beryl, don't be like that,' Frost pleaded. 'I'm still her husband.'

'Only when it suits you.'

'What does that mean?' His patience was wearing thin. 'I do care, deeply, regardless of what you think. I want her to come home.'

'All you care about is that bloody police force. Come back tomorrow, it's late.' Beryl Simpson tried to close the front door, but Frost had slipped his foot inside. The woman sighed heavily and stepped back and Frost found himself in the opulent hallway.

Frost couldn't remember the last time he'd entered the Simpson residence. He'd been *persona non grata* for many years. Precisely which spat had finally barred him from visiting he couldn't recall – they'd been so many.

He made a show of wiping his feet, to make himself appear like less of an intruder. The surroundings immediately reminded him of how desperately beneath her station Mary had married: the chandeliers in the grand hall, the Stubbs on the back wall – *The Horse* was Simpson senior's pride and joy – the antique furniture. Frost hoped the old boy was at home, he at least could sometimes be an ally, though he was seldom in Rimmington, preferring to linger at his club in London.

'Mary's in the drawing room.'

Frost walked slowly behind his mother-in-law across the polished floor. What a snob she is, he thought, despising the pious old sow. She'd always loathed him even before things went wrong; to her eyes he was common – a scruffy, working-class oik. And he hated her with equal passion – a mother who'd insisted on sending her daughter to board at St Mary's when the school was less than five miles away.

Curled up on the enormous milk-white sofa, his diminutive wife was asleep in front of the colour television. He was struck by how placid she looked, almost impossible to reconcile with the saucy little firebrand that made his life hell at home. Even when she fell asleep in front of their own TV, like the other night when he'd got in late, she didn't look half so peaceful and relaxed. Perhaps I really am the villain of the piece, he thought, and the life I've given her has made her turn out the way she has. He took a step forward. Underneath the standard lamp he could see she'd been neglecting herself: her roots were growing through and the perm was now loosening its grip on her red-dyed hair. Her pale skin was almost translucent in the soft glow of the television set. She fidgeted and wrinkled her small snub nose. His heart went out to her.

'She's all right,' the mother said quietly behind him. 'Let her sleep.'

Frost swallowed. His throat was thick. One thing about Mary, she could look like an angel. Pity it was only when she was asleep.

Why was she suddenly so tired though? It was unlike her – and the other night too, asleep in the chair. He followed his mother-in-law through to the expansive kitchen which opened on to a conservatory. There were rubber plants and wicker chairs everywhere. He didn't recall the conservatory from the last time he'd visited. Had it really been that long, or was he just unobservant?

'Drink?' she offered with a resigned half-smile, holding up a bottle of Scotch.

'Don't mind if do. Straight,' Frost said.

She placed two glasses on the pristine counter. In the harsh light of the artfully placed chrome spotlights Frost took in the red-rimmed eyes and the creases beneath the foundation. Had she been crying? Or maybe she was just tired. In her day, Frost thought, Beryl Simpson would have been a cracker, with the same almond eyes and snub nose as her daughter.

Reaching out to her as best he could he began to speak. 'Look . . .'

Mrs Simpson shook her head, mouthing 'no'. Despite a chink of light the shutters remained down; she didn't want to hear anything he had to say. Instead she removed a bag of ice from a built-in freezer and poured a healthy measure of Scotch into the cut-glass tumbler. He could never charm the old bruiser. He was itching for a cigarette, but knew the Simpson household was one place where smoking was strictly forbidden. He realized he'd get nowhere until he had Mary to himself, whenever that might be. And what then?

He decided to change his tack. 'I saw old Father Lowe today.'

'Father Lowe?' A flicker of interest passed across the tired eyes. Beryl Simpson poured herself an equal measure and left the bottle uncapped. 'Why?'

'Oh, nothing much. Someone's been nicking the lead off the church roof.' Frost mustered a smile. 'A roofer, naturally enough . . . or he was.'

'Some things never change,' Beryl Simpson said, pulling up a kitchen chair, 'they've been stealing lead off that church since before the war.'

'The good father asked after you,' he lied.

'Did he?' she replied. 'Well, it was only the other day I was at St Jude's – after Easter . . .'

'We talked about Mary, mostly,' he fabricated, confident that she was too preoccupied to question his veracity, 'about when she was a teenager.'

'A teenager?' Beryl Simpson's pencilled eyebrows moved upwards to meet a raft of forehead creases.

'Said she was a smashing kid,' Frost gabbled on, shifting uncomfortably against the kitchen work surface – he'd have killed for a cigarette – 'but got mixed up in some sort of a teenage cult.'

Mrs Simpson said nothing.

Frost continued, 'Yes, a bunch of girls messing around with witchcraft. I can't imagine it got that far, myself. Though for one girl it ended tragically . . .'

Beryl Simpson moved to the bag of ice on the counter that now sat in a growing pool of water and banged it to loosen the cubes with a ferocity that made Frost jump. Slowly and methodically she fixed herself a refill.

'Tell me . . . William,' she said slowly, turning to face him with a look filled with malice. 'Or is it "Jack"? . . . Tell me honestly that you're not here on business. This evening. Now.'

Frost felt his throat seize up.

'Yes,' she said spitefully, 'here you are – good old "Jack" Frost from Denton CID – asking questions about my daughter, your wife. Not about how . . . how she is . . . or your sham of a marriage, but obscure questions about what she got up to twenty years ago. A witch! Have you no shame?'

Frost reached for his cigarettes and moved towards the door, but the vision in the doorway stopped him dead.

'The School of the Five Bells,' Mary Frost said.

Thursday (1) _____

Frost pulled up behind a panda car. He was clearly the late-comer to the scene; Maltby's old Hillman was already there, next to an ambulance.

Frost had waited nearly an hour for DS Waters at Eagle Lane, but at ten to nine had given up. He should have arranged to pick him up at Fenwick Street. He'd telephoned but there was no reply. Cheeky sod has overslept, Frost thought – up all night humping, no doubt. He tried to smile but found it only brought him close to tears – if it wasn't for the hangover from last night's bottle of Black Label keeping him together he felt sure he'd crack.

Is Mary all right? The thought he was trying to ignore kept piercing his consciousness, making him shudder every time. As a distraction, he tried to focus on what she'd said about the teenage 'witches', or the School of the Five Bells, as she had re-ferred to them, but the tired look of Beryl Simpson resurfaced in his mind, pushing everything else out of the way.

On reflection he thought his mother-in-law looked drained.

Was something up? No, she was probably going through 'the change'. He should have insisted Mary came home. If anyone's really knackered, it's me, he thought.

Frost gripped the steering wheel and took several deep breaths. 'Right, son. Keep it together,' he said to himself, lighting a cigarette before getting out of the car.

The area was cordoned off and police tape flickered in the early-morning breeze. The white van, complete with its macabre cargo, stood in the middle of the Pink Toothbrush car park, front and rear doors open. So, he thought, here's where it's all happening this week; Clarke being stabbed, his own late-night vigil after the soliciting accusations, and now this. Harry Baskin was giving a statement to PC Jordan, gesticulating angrily with his cigar. He caught Frost's eye but the detective decided he could wait.

He did a reconnoitre of the scene. As indicated by the earlier complaints about soliciting, the car park was overlooked by the flats at Baron's Court. Uniform would carry out a door-to-door, though he bet when it came to something this important those nosy bleeders wouldn't have seen a thing.

Frost wandered over to the crime scene, a white Bedford van. The dishevelled Maltby emerged from the rear, and two Forensics officers in boiler suits exchanged remarks with him before climbing in. Frost glanced inside briefly, taking in the poles and brushes – a chimney sweep's van, as the caller, Harry Baskin, had explained down the phone to a half-asleep Sergeant Johnny Johnson at seven o'clock this morning.

'Ah, Sergeant Frost. Good morning to you,' Maltby said.

'Doc,' Frost nodded. 'The sun's out, so it can't all be bad.'

'Yes, it seems the fine weather has returned after yesterday's deluge.' The crumpled doctor looked around him appreciatively. Frost peered into the van cabin before being ushered away by Harding, the senior Forensics officer; the cab had yet to be dusted for prints.

'What have we got, then?' Frost asked Maltby, lighting a cigarette.

'Male, mid sixties.'

'Dead?'

'Very.'

'Not here to try out Harry's new massage parlour, then?'

'It would take more than a rub-down from one of the ladies to bring *him* back.' Maltby sniffed. 'Been dead at least a full day – thirty-six hours or so.'

Frost moved to the front of the van and noticed the windscreen wipers were stuck in mid-sweep. The only rain in the last week had been yesterday afternoon. 'You sure about that?'

'That's as accurate an approximation as I can give in the field,' Maltby said, removing his gloves. 'Rigor has passed. The corpse is softening.'

'That's good enough for me, Doc. Garrotted, wasn't he?'

'No, stabbed through the throat, though by what it's hard to say. I'm satisfied that it didn't happen in the van; there would have been a tremendous amount of blood, much more than is in there, so I would hazard he was murdered elsewhere and dumped here.'

Frost looked in the back again and waved at one of the Forensics men.

'Fancy a video cassette player?' he muttered, seeing half a dozen assorted machines stacked in the back.

'Not in the slightest – I don't own a television set.'

'Wise move,' Frost said, taking in the severed leads poking out of the VCRs. Was the man a thief on the side, he wondered? He stepped back to allow the Forensics officer out. 'All filth and corruption, Mrs Whitehouse would have us believe.'

'I wouldn't know about that,' Maltby muttered. 'Anyway, as I say, the man's been dead at least twenty-four hours, killed by a wound to the neck.'

Frost clambered into the back of the Bedford and opened the

dust sheet to reveal a dead man in overalls, mouth wide open, guppy-like. Extraordinary: a dead chimney sweep found with half a dozen stolen VCRs in a massage-parlour car park. He scratched his head thoughtfully.

'Don't suppose there was an appointment book helpfully left behind?' Frost called out to Harding who he could see through the open doors removing his rubber gloves. The Forensics officer shook his head. Frost thought that would be too good to be true. They'd have to find some other way to trace the sweep's movements.

'Frost? Where are you?' a voice called from beyond the police tape.

'Here.' Frost climbed out of the van.

'This ain't good.'

Frost turned to face a worried-looking Harry Baskin. 'Morning, Harry. You look troubled.' A Chinese girl hovered behind the gangster like a diminutive shadow.

'Somebody's got it in for me,' Baskin rasped, toking deeply on his cigar, gold-ringed knuckles glinting in the May sun. 'First the bird getting cut on Monday, now this . . .' He flicked ash dismissively in the direction of the van.

'Popular bloke like you, Harry?' Frost said. 'Can't see it myself.'

'Don't get smart. Someone's trying to shag up my new business. Palmer, I reckon – always had it in for me.'

Martin 'Pumpy' Palmer – Frost knew him, a wide-boy wheeler-dealer from Rimmington. 'The Pump? Not his style. No, I doubt it, not unless the pair of you are trying to muscle in on the chimney-sweep business.'

Baskin shrugged.

'A sweep with a side line in VCRs,' Frost added.

'He could have the whole of Rumbelows in there for all I care. I want him shifted, pronto. How long are your lot going to be here? We open at eleven.'

'Keep your hair on, they'll be done soon,' Frost said, watching Forensics lift the body from the van. Baskin's Chinese companion looked nervously down as Frost made eye contact with her. She was slight, but very cute. Must pay the parlour a call, he thought – if he ever had time, that is.

'I thought it was strictly a nocturnal establishment?' Frost enquired.

'Thursdays, Fridays and Saturdays we open at eleven, for Denton's ladies of leisure who want a bit of pampering, and all that.'

'What does a "pampering" involve?' His gaze still lingered on the girl.

'Nails.'

'Nails?'

'Yeah, you know, fingers and toes.'

'Oh.' He was pretty sure the drunks he saw on Tuesday night weren't after a manicure. Still, he didn't have time for that now.

'Good.' Baskin coughed, looking at Forensics packing up. 'Let me know if I can assist with your enquiries in any way. Any way at all.' He grinned. 'I try to look after you coppers where I can.'

'A pillar of the community you are, Harry. My super-intendent was saying so only the other day.'

'Mullett?' Baskin raised a bushy eyebrow. 'Queer one, him. Saw him at the golf club yesterday. Horrible business, that. Got your hands full at the moment, 'aven't you? I'd best let you get on then.' He made to leave.

'We let your lad go, Mark Fong,' Frost said.

'Wondered where he'd got to,' Baskin said. 'His uncle must have pressed him to come forward. Any use to you?'

'Nope,' Frost said. 'I don't know what sort of deal you've struck with him, but I'll be watching out for that lad.'

'If he doesn't like it, he knows the alternative – the first slow boat back to China.'

Baskin clearly couldn't give two hoots about the welfare of his staff, and Frost was determined to be true to his word and keep an eye on them. Of more pressing concern to the gangster was why a murdered man had been left in his car park. And a good question it was, Frost thought. Why here?

'Harry, one final thing,' Frost called out. Baskin stopped and faced him. 'I'm sure you've already given PC Jordan a statement, but bear with me a sec. The body was wrapped in dust sheets in the back of a Transit van, in an empty car park, left some time in the last twenty-four hours. When did you first notice it? What prompted you to break into it?'

'Bastard was in my space. Couldn't park in it this morning when I arrived.'

'Of course, fair enough.'

'And I didn't break in – it was unlocked.' Baskin turned his back and made for the old laundry, the girl scurrying along behind him.

'Morning, guv.' PC Jordan had appeared at Frost's side as Baskin and the Chinese girl disappeared inside the building.

'Morning, son. So, the van was open, then?'

'Yes, and keys were in the ignition. Pardon me, sir, but on a different subject, I've just had a message from Control. DS Waters' motor was done over last night. Tyres slashed – he had to walk to the nick, and he left the keys at the garage next door.'

'Flamin' hell. I wondered where he was this morning.'

'Also, Mr Mullett would like an update on the burglaries.'

'*Burglaries?* Sod his posh mates' cut glass – I've got two dead kids and Dick Van Dyke here to deal with.'

Frost looked at his watch – 10 a.m. This new body had really thrown him off course. That was the job, though, and he knew it. And now he'd have to go to the lab yet again, on top of everything else.

St Mary's School for Girls was out towards Rimmington. Right, he thought, I'd better get my skates on. School first, see my old mate the headmistress, then stop and see Drysdale about the sweep, then I've got the Hardys arriving at the station, and Mullett wants an update this afternoon. In between all that he had to type up the Ellis report. Before he even started he'd have to get back to the station to pick up Waters because his car had been vandalized. What next? Flaming hell, this week was getting complicated, all right.

Simms had arrived at his desk at just gone eight thirty. He'd left Waters to lie in – he knew John had been out on the tiles, not that the nightlife here had that much to offer, as far as Derek Simms was concerned.

He rubbed his stubbly chin thoughtfully and considered the stacks of files on the desk in front of him, and which pile to tackle first. If he could crack these bloody muggings he'd score points with Mullett and could then get on with something more meaty. There was plenty to go around, and Simms wanted a piece of it.

Still, first things first. There was literally daylight robbery occurring on the streets of Denton, and it needed to be sorted. But was he any closer to a breakthrough? Would a disgruntled paperboy hold up his own employer? No, it was just too obvious. He scratched his head and reached for his cigarettes. He didn't have much time; Clarke had just called to say that Frost had also assigned her to the woods expedition, and that she'd meet him in an hour. She was stopping first at the bookshop on Market Square to buy an Ordnance Survey map, as per the DS's instructions. She sounded stroppy as hell. Whatever it was he had once seen in her, that seemed a distant memory now. Frost was welcome to the moody cow. She nearly bit his head off when he asked if she'd checked out the Scout leaders about their troop movements last weekend as Frost had asked. Myles was going to take her own car and meet them there.

He sighed at all the files on his desk. On the left were files of all known juvenile offenders from the last eighteen months; and to his right were Clarke and Myles's list of kids expelled in the current school year and their personal files. Simms drew heavily on the stale Rothmans he'd found – one left behind by Frost – and frowned; the tedious task of cross-referencing lay before him.

Maybe he could just grab a gyppo off the Bath Road site and have done with it? The thieving baskets were always nicking stuff, so who would argue? Mullett would certainly back him and Frost had other things on his mind.

'Morning,' Waters said flatly, and the sight of him caused Simms to almost choke on his cigarette in shock.

'Bloody hell, what happened to you!' Waters' right eye was badly swollen.

'Tripped over,' he said dismissively, lighting up a JPS.

'Come off it,' Simms said. 'A shiner like that. Someone's given you a pasting.'

Waters shrugged. 'Any word from Frost? I was supposed to meet him here at eight. Had a spot of car trouble.'

Simms looked at the wall clock. It was gone nine. The police accommodation was little more than a five-minute walk away. 'What – did you push it to a garage, or something?'

Waters waved off answering.

'What happened?' Simms insisted, determined to elicit some proper answers. There was clearly something very wrong. 'OK, let me guess. You were out with a bird last night. A white bird.'

Waters winced in pain as he gradually lowered himself into his chair.

'Denton isn't exactly the cosmopolitan melting-pot you're used to. The only place people see a face like yours is on *The Black and White Minstrel Show* and on marmalade jars.'

'And on *Love Thy Neighbour*,' Waters added wryly.

'Yeah, exactly. It's fine so long as it's on the other side of the TV screen. Hope she was worth it. Are you OK?'

'It's not that bad. This' – he pointed to his eye – 'was from the kerb—'

'Time to sit around and chat, have we?' Superintendent Mullett suddenly loomed before them, his uniform as impeccable as ever. Just looking at him made Simms feel he needed a bath.

Simms reached to pick up the phone, thinking now would be an appropriate time to wheel the mugging victims in to trawl through the photo files. 'Excuse me, sir, urgent call to make,' he said, flicking hurriedly through his notepad as he tried to find the estate agent's phone number, leaving Waters to chew the fat with Mullett.

Thursday (2)

Chris Everett was at his wits' end, and hadn't slept a wink on Wednesday night. After his initial feelings of outrage at having been mugged by a bunch of kids – the jab with the knife was nothing, barely a scratch – panic swiftly ensued. Clearly, given what was in the briefcase, he needed to completely detach himself from the crime, and of all the rotten luck, it was witnessed by a plainclothes copper, just passing in the street. To cap it all, DC Simms from Denton CID had just requested he come in to go through photos and maybe even a line-up, along with 'other unfortunates', as the detective called them. Well, none of them was as bloody unfortunate as him, he thought, sipping his fourth coffee of the day.

Originally he thought that placing the video recorders in the chimney sweep's van was a good idea, a great idea, in fact. A red herring, leading the police to assume the old boy was mixed up with dodgy dealings. That, of course, was before there'd been the slightest risk of Everett being caught for house-breaking.

Those bloody kids. His carefully woven plans were starting to unravel all over the place.

He looked nervously out through the plate-glass of his office into the open-plan area beyond. The girls were going about their business, placing new listings in the window, but they knew something was up; he knew they knew. He shouldn't have cancelled that viewing at Two Bridges. Keep things looking normal no matter what, that was the answer. He looked down at the list of clients: *Mullett, 3 Wessex Crescent*. The name was familiar, but he couldn't think why.

Those kids – those little bastards who grabbed his case – got more than they could ever have bargained for, more than an empty sandwich box and a copy of the *Denton Echo*, which is what he'd told the police the case contained. Suppose they handed themselves in, terrified they'd robbed a villain? No, they'd lie low, realizing they'd been lucky. Which was more than could be said for him. It was unheard of, daylight robbery in a nice part of Denton, where respectable, well-to-do people lived. People who murdered chimney sweeps.

The phone rang, and he could see Vicky through the glass mouthing something at him. As well as cancelling the viewing, he'd said he didn't want to be disturbed because of bad tooth-ache. He cringed at how lame it sounded. He gestured to Vicky to put the call through.

He sat in silence for what seemed like eternity, waiting for the caller to speak, expecting the police again.

'Christopher?' It was Fiona, his wife. 'Christopher, are you there, darling?'

'Yes, darling, I'm here. What is it?' he snapped. He was relieved it was only his wife but irritated with her for disturbing him at the same time.

'Darling, you know when that chappie was working on the chimney on Tuesday, did he say there was a problem?' Everett sat looking intently at the surface of the fake-wood desk.

'Darling? I can still hear cooing. Did you hear me? The pigeon, darling, I can still hear it cooing.'

Waters ejected Frost's jazz cassette and rooted around in the glove box for something more current. He could have brought something from the Vauxhall, but he had other things on his mind.

As well as a slight hangover he was still dazed from the attack last night. He knew he'd made a mistake going to *that* pub with Myles. A police pub with a very cute female police officer; how dumb was that? He'd let his guard down; he'd been lulled by Denton's simplicity and Myles's carefree confidence. Yes, just for a brief moment he'd started to enjoy life – more fool him. He felt OK in himself, but it was the slashed tyres on the Vauxhall that really hurt. He loved that car.

12 Gold Bars by Status Quo. It would have to do. He slipped the cassette in, and wound down the window too to get rid of the unpleasant smell. He'd not been in Frost's Cortina before, having driven the Vauxhall yesterday. Whatever it was, the smell was pretty pungent, and even the volume of cigarettes that was clearly smoked inside the car – the velour roof was stained yellow – was unable to mask it. Could be anything in this motor, he thought; the footwell was full of discarded fast-food cartons. Jesus, something could be living in there. Waters reached under the seat to adjust the leg room, nudging a size-able Jiffy bag out of the way as he did so.

'What the bleedin' hell is this?' Frost spluttered as he climbed back in after stopping to buy some cigarettes. 'Heavy Metal?'

'Chill your boots,' Waters said. 'It's just music.'

'Bit loud!'

'I found it in your glove box.'

'Must be Arthur's,' Frost said, his glance briefly taking in Waters' black eye. 'Got a bit of rhythm this, actually. The jazz didn't really do it for me, I must admit. The tape was my mother's. More curious to know what she listened to as much as anything . . .'

To Waters' surprise Frost had failed to remark on his bruised face when he'd picked him up from Eagle Lane twenty minutes ago. Mullett had ignored it too, but that was less of a surprise; with Frost he felt he'd built up some kind of rapport. Up to now he'd found him chatty and jolly; today he was subdued and uncommunicative. Waters doubted he was the sort to be troubled by a murder scene – the sweep's was the third dead body Frost had seen this week alone – but he didn't feel he knew him well enough to ask if there was anything troubling him.

So he'd changed the music in the hope of sparking off a conversation. But after the surprise mention of his mother, Frost had become sullen and lost in thought again.

They were now on the way to St Mary's, to check the background of Emily Hardy, Tom's sister, who was still missing. Uniform had been all over the school yesterday, but Frost was determined to see the headmistress for himself. Apparently they'd crossed swords before. No surprise there, thought Waters; everywhere in Denton he seemed to be a well-known character.

They drew to a halt at the end of the sweeping drive. The school was by far the strangest place Waters had come across since arriving in the area. A musty old Victorian edifice, the like of which he'd seen only in black and white films.

Girls stopped to stare wide-eyed as the incongruous figure of DS Waters – over six feet tall, chestnut skin, bruised and swollen face – stepped over the stone threshold.

'Boo!' he said, grinning at a gaggle of girls who were loitering in the polished hallway. They burst into giggles and ran off.

'Told you you'd go down a treat here. The headmistress may take a shine to you – but watch it, she's into taxidermy. Before you know it, you'll be stuffed and mounted as a curiosity.'

194

The ancient school porter showed them into Sidley's study. She was staring out of the window, smoking a cigarette, and as they entered she turned. Dressed from head to toe in black, she struck a tall, elegant, slightly Gothic figure. A teased mane of mulberry-coloured hair framed an angular face of the type that would sooner raise an eyebrow than a smile.

'Sergeant Frost,' she said, 'it's been a while.' She failed to acknowledge Waters. He shrugged off the slight and instead took in the peculiar array of stuffed objects – an owl, a raven – placed around the bookcase-lined office.

'Yes,' Frost was saying. 'I considered applying for the PE instructor vacancy but I wasn't sure I had the physique for it.'

'Well, don't hold your breath,' she answered curtly. 'I assume you're here about this?' She was indicating the copy of the *Denton Echo* on the enormous, empty oak desk.

Frost picked up the paper and read the headline: *Teenage Boy Found Mutilated by Golfing Chief of Police.* Ha – Mullett would love that. So much for the press conference. 'Yes, it's about the lad's sister, Emily, a pupil of yours. Must keep a better grip on your girls – they're forever going astray.' He tutted.

'Yes, your uniformed colleagues were here yesterday – quite a few of them. Very upsetting for the girls.'

'Of course,' Frost said gently. 'They can be a bit heavy-handed at times. In fact, that's part of the reason I'm here . . . and of course to see you again, Miss Sidley.'

Waters was taken aback. Was Frost flirting with the old dragon? An ageing Morticia Addams who surrounded herself with stuffed carcasses?

'Yes,' Frost continued. 'There seems to be some confusion among my colleagues regarding the time young Emily disappeared. As I'm sure you understand, it's crucial to our inquiry to know whether she went missing before or after learning of her brother's death.'

'She was here first thing for assembly and when the register was called in the morning, but she did not attend afternoon lessons.'

'Did nobody notice her absence?'

'She was going to the afternoon hockey match, so anyone who knew that would not have thought it odd that she wasn't in school.'

'So she was at the hockey match?' concluded Waters.

'Well . . . no,' said Sidley, wringing her pale hands. On one finger she wore an oversized ring in which the stone had been fashioned to look like an eye. 'Originally we reported she'd gone to hockey, but upon enquiring further we discovered she wasn't in fact with the hockey group.'

Waters raised an eyebrow. 'Is it normal to have quite such a relaxed approach to your pupils' whereabouts?'

'Well, Detective . . . ?'

'Waters.'

'Waters. We do keep as close a check on our pupils as the regular school day allows, giving due consideration to the age of the girls. After all, these are not infants. Some are mere months away from adulthood.'

'Legally perhaps,' Waters said, earning himself a withering look of disdain from Sidley.

'But in any case, a pupil's response to discovering that her brother has been found mutilated on a golf course isn't something we could feasibly foresee, now is it?'

Hard-hearted cow, thought Waters. He was about to express his surprise that someone who worked among young people wasn't more visibly distressed by recent events, but luckily Frost intervened.

'If Emily went missing in the early afternoon, she wouldn't have known Tom was dead. Her parents hadn't told her yet. All she knew was that he'd disappeared. His parents reported him missing on Tuesday morning, but our Forensics people think he was killed at the weekend – keep that to yourself, that's not been reported in the press.'

'So, in other words,' summarized Waters, 'when she came to school on Wednesday, all Emily knew was her brother had been missing for several days.'

'Miss Sidley,' Frost continued, 'I'm sure I don't have to tell you that teenage girls run off all the time, often for the oddest reasons, but in this case we're terribly concerned, and that's nothing to the anguish her parents are going through. We don't yet know how Emily's disappearance is connected to her brother's. It's possible she just got scared. Or perhaps there's something deeper at the heart of it. Anything you could tell us might be of help.'

Sidley reached for another cigarette and slowly fixed it into an ivory holder. 'You might want to talk to her friends. She's particularly close to two of the girls here, I understand. On Wednesdays, instead of going home to Denton, Emily always goes to Two Bridges. I believe she attends Girl Guides with her two friends who live there.'

'I see,' said Frost. 'That's interesting. We interviewed a couple of girls from Two Bridges in connection with another case – the girl found dead beside the train track on Monday morning.'

'My girls? Which ones?' Sidley asked, concerned. 'Wasn't the girl on the train from Denton Comprehensive?'

Frost was surprised to hear that she was unaware of their enquiries, given that Simms had called the school to verify whether the Two Bridges girls attended St Mary's. Of course, a secretary would have taken the call, but for the head to be left unaware that the police were asking questions seemed lax. This interview had revealed an unexpected number of holes in St Mary's procedures, and the head was looking more and more uncomfortable.

'Sarah Ferguson and Gail Burleigh,' replied Frost. 'We're

appealing for witnesses. We thought they may have seen the Ellis girl, or even known her.'

Sidley stubbed out her cigarette while processing this information. 'Well,' she finally said, 'I've heard nothing in school about this, and couldn't comment on what or who the girls have seen. But I can tell you that they both know Emily Hardy. They're the girls she went to Guides with.'

Thursday (3)

'Bloody French!' one uniformed officer snapped. Wells didn't catch who said it, as he put down the phone. It had been ringing constantly all morning – either Hartley-Jones again for the super, or the super's wife, or the flipping press. A bunch of uniform had gathered in the lobby and were noisily debating the latest news from the South Atlantic that had just broken.

'You can't say that – we've got the same bleedin' missiles!' bellowed PC Jordan. The British destroyer HMS *Sheffield* had been hit by an Exocet missile. The Defence Secretary, John Nott, had addressed the House of Commons late last night, and it was all over the wireless this morning.

'Yeah, but the Frogs gave the Argies the planes, too.'

'What? Like they just *gave* them away? Don't think so, mate . . .'

The phone went again, and Wells waved at the officers to keep it down. 'Denton Police.'

'Detective Frost, please,' said a voice Wells recognized.

'He's out, I'm afraid.'

'It's Harding from Forensics. We're at Kenneth Smith's house.' The sweep, of course. They'd located his address straightaway since Denton had only two chimney sweeps and both were listed in the *Yellow Pages*. 'Tell Frost we've found no clues to Smith's movements leading up to the crime, either here or in the van. He's a bachelor, which doesn't really help us, and we can't find an appointment book. Could you be so kind as to let him know?'

'Looks like we'll be visiting our young lady friends in Two Bridges again,' Frost said. 'First we'd better stop off at the lab to see what Drysdale's found out about the murdered sweep.'

Frost clumsily reversed the Cortina, narrowly missing an ancient-looking stone lion in the forecourt of St Mary's. The heatwave had returned with a vengeance, and the car's vinyl seats were like hot coals.

'So what are these Girl Guides?' Waters asked, winding down his window urgently.

'You know, big Brownies,' Frost said.

'You what?'

'Little girls who do good deeds in brown uniforms – the female version of Boy Scouts. You know, bob-a-job week, and all that.'

'Sure, I know what Boy Scouts are, the ones who made those tents out of leaves in the woods that Clarke mentioned yesterday.'

'The very same. Perhaps Brownies and Guides are more of a provincial thing,' Frost mused, pulling out on to the main road.

'These Girl Scouts camp too?'

'I would guess so – though not in the same tent. Why?'

'On Tuesday, when Simms and I went round to see Gail Burleigh, her snooty old dear was spouting on about how her Gail was one of these Guides. The girl was really embarrassed about it.'

'What? And neither of you said anything about it last night?'

'Didn't think much of it – the girl was so dismissive. We were more concerned with what she was up to on Saturday. Now I think of it, her mother did mention something about camping.'

'Simms is a clueless dork. He really should have told me this. Good lad in the field, but when it comes to engaging the old grey matter he's next to useless.' Frost sighed. 'Though it's probably nothing. Just because the golf course is next to the woods it doesn't definitely follow that the kid was in there. He was just as likely dropped off by a golf buggy. Still, Simms better have a list of all those kids who were in Denton Woods by the time we get back to Eagle Lane . . . if we ever do get back. Bloody farmers.'

In front of them a tractor was towing a trailer full of pigs. The farmyard smell wafted in through the open Cortina windows. Aah, the English countryside, thought Waters, but as he sank back in the passenger seat his ribs twitched, causing him to grimace.

'I guess the Scouts might have seen something,' Waters reasoned, 'but you don't honestly think it was them who sliced the kid open, do you?'

'Why am I driving?' Frost asked, annoyed, ignoring his question. Turning, he said, 'Was it the same people who vandalized your car who vandalized your face?'

'I dunno,' he said, staring out across the fields.

'What's the damage, anyway?'

'Couple of tyres slashed,' Waters replied. 'Don't worry, it should be sorted by this afternoon.'

'Coppers, was it?'

Waters didn't know what to make of Frost's direct, offhand approach. Perhaps it hid an underlying concern? He wasn't too sure. 'It's possible, I guess.'

'You *guess* or you *know*?'

'OK, well, I caught a whiff of aftershave as I hit the deck –

Brut, I think – and it was certainly familiar.' Waters turned and looked at Frost's sweaty profile. 'I wouldn't wish to levy accusations without being one hundred per cent certain, but on the other hand . . .' The fact that Frank Miller's green bottle was there taunting him under the shaving mirror at Fenwick Street, and that every morning Miller drenched himself in the stuff, he chose to keep to himself.

'On the other hand, it's hard to imagine who else you might have upset in such a short space of time,' Frost finished the sentence for him. 'Christ, that bloody truck stinks to high heaven!'

'Surprised you can tell, given the pong in this motor,' Waters couldn't help but say. 'Could do with a dose of Brut in here.'

'I beg your pardon, son? Are you saying my vehicle has odour issues?' Frost retorted.

'As it happens, I am,' Waters said.

'And there's me thinking you'd let rip.' Frost smiled. 'Only joking. There's not a Jiffy bag down there somewhere, by any chance?'

'Yep, there's a package.' Waters reached down and picked up the Jiffy bag, giving it a squeeze.

'Forgot about that. It's a cat for DC Simms.'

Waters froze before chucking the thing to the floor.

'Dead one,' Frost added, as if there could be any doubt. 'I guess the hot weather hasn't done it much good. I thought the car was a bit ripe this morning myself, in an unkebab-like way.'

'Ditch it, for Christ's sake!' Waters said, aghast.

'Nah, you keep hold of it, son, young Derek will be eternally grateful to you this afternoon. It belongs to one of Hornrim Harry's mates, the one who was turned over last weekend. Be hell to pay if we don't hand it back.'

'And there won't be if we hand it back like this?'

'Good point. Maybe shove it in the fridge – take the edge of it.' Frost grinned. 'After all, that's where it was found.'

*　　*　　*

'Right, here we are, right back where we started,' Simms said with a hollow laugh. He had the OS map spread out on the car's bonnet, which was parked at the bottom of a cul-de-sac beside the overgrown entrance to Denton Woods. He and Clarke had set off from here once already, wasting ten minutes traipsing along the path before discovering, when it broke off in three different directions, that they'd forgotten the OS map.

The temperature was rising steadily and the air was humid. Even beneath the shade of the trees it was hot. 'Are you all right?' Simms asked.

Clarke was tired already. Her fuzzy head was made worse by the events of yesterday jostling for position. Pangs of guilt and shame kept flooding through her, making her feel like she was going to throw up. Why did she do it? Why did she sleep with a stranger? Initially she'd felt liberated, but as the morning wore on the gloss faded and all that lingered was disgust.

'I'm fine. Leave me alone,' she said defensively. 'I'm not even sure why we're here. I was here with uniform late yesterday, after they'd trampled all over the bluebells.' She sighed.

He scrunched up the map and squared up to her. 'No, I won't leave you alone – we're here to do a job. Pull yourself together, bloody drama queen. They only made a cursory sweep to look for clothing. Now we've got this' – he waved the Ordnance Survey map at her – 'we're going over the area properly. Got it? God, you stink of booze.'

She was taken aback by his vehemence, and stumbled into a bramble, which caught her bare leg. She winced. Having got up late she'd rushed to get ready, forgetting to think about appropriate clothing. A short, pale-yellow summer dress and open-toed sandals weren't really the best things for tramping about in Denton Woods.

They set off along the path again, but within seconds the car radio crackled into life, a distinct burst of noise in the peaceful surroundings.

'That'll be Myles.' Simms turned on his heel and marched back. He was quite attractive when cross, albeit in a sort of boyish way. He leaned into the car to pick up the handset, his white T-shirt riding up as he did so.

Clarke picked up the map he'd dumped on the ground and walked back to the car with it, unfolding it on the bonnet as Simms had done. It was years since she'd looked at one of these – not since orienteering field trips for geography A level. Frost was right, she thought, flicking her hair behind her ears, you see the terrain differently on a detailed map; the contours of the land – dips and rises – give it proper definition. Yesterday afternoon uniform had been stumbling around blindly. She looked in fascination at the dotted paths, the markings for woodlands and orchards, the strangely named farms and the symbols for churches. Familiar names and sights linked up with less familiar ones to form a complete picture, like the pieces of a jigsaw. How much simpler everything seemed with a bit of perspective.

They were on a bridleway that started at Wood Vale. It was a popular entrance for Sunday strollers, particularly at this time of year when for a mere ten days, beginning around the end of April, Denton Woods became one of the most beautiful places in England. It was reputedly one of the largest bluebell woods in Europe. Clarke remembered the planning application for a new housing development being successfully opposed last year by conservationists.

She followed the path on the map with her thumb nail. The clearing where the scouts had camped was midway between where they stood now at Wood Vale and the golf course where Tom Hardy had been found. It appeared to be a good mile and a half from the camp to the fringe of Denton Golf Club, she reckoned. They'd parked at the same entrance the Scouts had used. Door-to-door enquiries in the cul-de-sac had confirmed the comings and goings of many young people at the weekend, but neither the Scouts nor the Guides had been in uniform, so it was harder to be sure how many had been part of the exercise.

'That was Myles,' Simms confirmed, hanging up the radio. 'Tom Hardy wasn't part of any camping trip to Denton Woods. But his sister Emily was. Myles is going now to Forest View; she'll start from there and meet us in the middle.'

'Right. That doesn't really help us much, does it? Emily didn't disappear until Wednesday, so who cares what she was up to at the weekend?'

Simms shrugged. 'Forensics said that on the green there was no blood around the body or any signs of frenzied activity such as you'd associate with a violent murder, so that implies he was murdered and stripped elsewhere. And the only place with unhindered access to the golf course is here,' he suggested, nodding towards the woods. 'Besides, you said yourself the search yesterday wasn't all that thorough – more of a ramble through the flowers looking for his clothes.'

Clarke was still studying the map's network of footpaths, which seemed to follow a distinct pattern, unless it was the glaze of her hangover playing tricks with her vision. Something caught her eye, within the maze of dotted lines. She consulted the map key.

'*Tumulus*,' she said to herself, a word she'd not heard since school.

'You what?' Simms asked, peering over her shoulder.

'It's Latin. It means mound or small hill.'

'Get you!' Simms whistled, fishing a crumpled pack of Bensons out of his back pocket. 'So?'

'A burial mound, an ancient burial site, thousands of years old,' Clarke continued, studying the map. 'I remember some-thing similar from a field trip at school. Not much to look at – in fact, unless you know it's there you'd walk straight past it, but thousands of years ago it would have been deeply significant.'

'A sort of prehistoric graveyard, you mean?'

'More than that. It's where the ancients would make offerings to their gods.'

'What are we waiting for?' Simms said, suddenly interested. Drysdale's theory of a ritual killing wasn't lost on him either. Flicking away the unfinished cigarette, he lifted up the police tape across the bridleway. 'Let's go take a look.'

Thursday (4)

'Can we say this is suicide?'

Mullett glared at Frost, who was banging away on the barely visible Smith Corona; the typewriter was shrouded by a disgraceful mound of paperwork and its operator wreathed in cigarette smoke.

'We can *say* whatever we like at this stage.' Frost squinted up at him, slapping the typewriter carriage across. 'I'm just typing up my report on the findings so far.'

'Well . . . is it?'

'There's a possibility, yes. Nobody saw the girl on the train – she was in a compartment on her own, we think. The train stopped at Denton due to engineering works instead of chundering on through to Wales, thereby allowing us to identify the other passengers, and we interviewed more or less everybody who got off the train.'

'More or less?' Mullett tapped his fingers rapidly on the door frame. 'That doesn't sound very conclusive to me.'

Frost shrugged and stubbed out his cigarette. 'That's where

we're at. There's a woman passenger who we've not been able to trace. We've interviewed the other three and failed to pin anything on them.' He raised his eyebrows. 'Three out of four are in the clear – so you can say there's an eighty per cent chance it's suicide.'

'Seventy-five, Frost, seventy-five.' Mullett puffed out his cheeks in exasperation. 'What about the post-mortem?'

'Inconclusive. I've just come from the lab. I've got the file here.' Frost shoved the ashtray off a beige lab-report folder, and flicked the file open, sending ash everywhere. 'We'd initially suspected a struggle because skin was found under the fingernails, but tests have shown it's likely to be her own.'

'Her *own*?' Mullett said incredulously.

'Drysdale noticed angry blotches on the girl's body. He called the Ellises' GP for her medical records and it transpires she suffered from a form of eczema.'

Mullett stepped aside as Waters entered the room with two mugs of coffee. What had that lad done to himself? he thought for the second time that day. Mullett didn't really want to know, but he would have to ask. On top of everything else. He sighed and felt increasingly irritable.

'Eczema? Do people claw their own skin? Seems a bit extreme to me,' he said finally.

'I'm allergic to cats – the slightest contact with fur, and my eyes run and my skin crawls. If it's anything like that, well . . .'

Mullett considered the Detective Sergeant with a mixture of exasperation and contempt. 'Get on to that ferrety fellow at the *Echo*,' he said, meaning Sandy Lane, whose name he'd all but wiped from his mind after the press-conference debacle yesterday. 'Tell him preliminary investigations indicate suicide, and then shelve it. And square it off with the parents first.'

'Shelve it?' Frost looked astonished. 'The girl was only discovered on Monday morning. The parents won't take too kindly to being told we've given up after less than a week. We've barely scratched the surface, if you forgive the pun.'

'*For now*, Frost, shelve it for now,' Mullett said. 'Buy ourselves some time and credibility with the public while we're dealing with the lad on the golf course. What other news from the lab? The body discovered this morning?'

The phone rang and Frost hastily answered it. Mullett could swear he was ignoring him on purpose.

'Fellow died of a wound to the throat,' Waters said.

'From a knife?'

'No. Judging from the wound, the pathologist thinks it was more like something like a butcher's hook.'

'A butcher's hook? How extraordinary.'

Mullett turned to go, and then remembered he had Frost's expenses, which looked dubious, though he hadn't the energy to take him to task over them. With the price of petrol rocketing past £1.50 a gallon there was a slim chance the figures were genuine, though he suspected not. He'd get him when things settled down – if they ever did.

Frost hung up the phone, mumbling to himself.

'Here,' said Mullett, 'these are yours. Given your dismal display of elementary mathematics just now, you may well be unable to calculate mileage allowances. You can have the benefit of the doubt this time. But next time . . .'

Frost flicked open Samantha Ellis's lab report, which he'd swiped from the lab, as soon as Mullett was out of the door. Something he'd noticed earlier in the girl's file had been playing on his mind. He hadn't time to deal with it now, but he ringed *distinguishing marks*. Drysdale may be good, but somehow he'd missed this.

'What was all that about?' Waters asked.

'Fractions,' Frost said, taking a proffered JPS.

Waters, confused, reached over with a lighter.

'And percentages,' Frost added, puffing enthusiastically.

'No, I meant the phone call.'

'Oh. That was Mrs Hardy. She and Mr Hardy are coming in later, which means we've a spot of time to kill. Which is great, because I'm starving. First, though, answer me this. How many people can want a sixty-five-year-old chimney sweep with nothing more than rent arrears to his name dead?'

Waters looked blankly at Frost. 'Not too many, I suspect.'

'Agreed,' said Frost, flipping the Rolodex round. 'So, while we wait for the boys and girls to get back from their ramble in the woods, let's do exactly what Hornrim Harry has asked.' Frost winked at him, a finger catching the card with the *Denton Echo* number, and began to dial.

'Ah, good morning. Sandy Lane, please.'

Denton Woods lived up to its reputation; the bluebells were truly spectacular, even more so now as the sun rose higher, and was refracted through the beech canopy, creating a hazy purple carpet as far as the eye could see. Yesterday, in the company of a dozen uniform, and rather the worse for wear, Clarke hadn't been able to appreciate it properly, but now, nearly alone, it seemed almost surreal. Derek Simms, by contrast, seemed not the least concerned where he trudged with his size nines.

'Isn't it beautiful?' She sighed, and for the first time that week felt cheerful. Maybe last night with Danny the farm boy had done her good, she thought. Though he wasn't so much of a boy . . .

'What is?' Simms barked, looking up from the map.

'The flowers. They're amazing. Mind where you tread, Derek.'

'Yeah, right . . . lovely.' His large, pale face frowned. 'But they don't really help.' He reached down to examine a specimen. 'I'm no expert, but these look like they've just bloomed or blossomed, or whatever the word is, which makes it difficult for us, when there's something covering the ground like this.'

Clarke was impressed with his thinking. He was smart, and would cut it as a detective, probably more so than she. Shame he was so childish in other ways. But she didn't want to dwell on the past.

She looked around her. Well, they're beautiful, regardless, she thought.

Suddenly she caught a flash of red out of the corner of her eye. There was something moving in the distance. But nobody should have been in here; the area had been sealed off until further notice.

'Derek,' she whispered, tapping him on the shoulder, though the figure was a good distance away. 'Look!'

Simms stood up. 'Oi!' he bellowed. 'Stop! Police!'

Very subtle, Clarke thought. The figure paused momentarily, as if weighing up the options of fight or flight. It was someone in a red-hooded coat, but they were too far away for her to be sure of sex or age. Not surprisingly, they opted for flight.

'Not thinking of a pursuit, then?' she asked the stationary Simms.

He looked at her as if she were mad. 'There's close on a couple of hundred feet of tightly packed undergrowth between us,' he cried, adding, 'Not to mention the pretty flowers.'

'Let's have the map a sec,' Clarke said. 'We'd never get back to the car quick enough to radio for back-up. But let's see which way they were heading. Whoever that was shouldn't have been in here, and knows it.' The figure had continued running in the same direction it had been moving in.

'Do you reckon they saw us?' Simms asked.

'Until your almighty bellow, no, I'd guess not. They were running across our path,' Clarke mused, folding the map over.

'Where were they heading?'

'North, according to this. It's residential up there. What's the area called with those really grand houses that back on to the woods?'

'Forest View?' Simms suggested.

'Possibly,' Clarke said. 'And where they were coming from – over there – it's where we're heading.'

'Your mound?'

Clarke squinted through the trees. 'That's it!' she said, pointing to a slight rise in the woodland floor, fifty feet away.

It didn't look much, Simms thought – you'd walk right over it if you didn't know it was there. 'Are you sure?' he asked, turning to look at her. The colour had risen in her face, and the sun through her thin cotton dress revealed her full young figure. She suddenly struck him as remarkably beautiful. Get a grip, he told himself. It was only an hour ago she'd been driving him crazy. Must be the tranquillizing effect of nature, or something. He wiped the sweat from his brow; he was getting thirsty.

'I'm positive,' she said in answer to his question, pointing at the map. She left the path, treading tentatively through the bluebells. 'I wish I'd worn different shoes. Come on.'

'Doesn't look much to me,' Simms said, following. 'I wish we had something to drink.'

'It's been here thousands of years. What do you expect?' Clarke tutted.

Derek Simms didn't really know what he expected. As they approached the burial mound, Simms noticed that the vegetation increasingly fell away and the flowers thinned, exposing a crust of earth, still damp after the recent downpours.

'I'm sure we didn't come here yesterday,' said Clarke.

'Hush,' Simms hissed, 'get down!' He could see a figure crouched beyond the mound. 'Slowly creep forward,' he said in a whisper. Clarke did as instructed.

They moved quietly, approaching to within a few yards of a crouching figure in a denim shirt, then Simms made a dash.

'Blimey, you scared the life out of me!' screeched a flushed DC Myles, getting to her feet and brushing woodland debris from her bare legs. She was wearing a matching denim skirt that was definitely too short, Simms thought, regardless of how hot it was.

'Sorry,' Clarke said. 'We thought you were . . . well, to be honest, we didn't know *who* you were. We just saw someone and . . .'

'Doesn't matter, though I did tell *him* I'd meet you here.' Myles pointed an accusatory finger at Simms. 'Never mind. Come and have a look at this.' Myles sank to her knees. Clarke and Simms followed suit.

She pointed out some small white lumps on the earth.

'Wax?' Simms wondered. 'Candle wax?'

'What on earth is candle wax doing out here?' Myles asked, perplexed.

'This is an ancient burial mound, so I'm guessing it could be from some sort of ritual.' Clarke got up, brushing soil from her knees and glancing meaningfully at Simms. 'So, Drysdale and Jack might be on to something.'

'Never mind why or what – the question is who,' Simms said uneasily. He realized they really had to get a handle on who had been camping out here. Until that moment he'd dismissed the theory of a ritual killing as laughable. Suddenly he wasn't so sure.

Thursday (5)

'Here we are. Time for a spot of nosh,' Frost said, holding open the door.

He removed his Polaroids but kept the panama hat firmly on his sweaty head. He wouldn't look so bad if he shaved every once in a while, thought Waters. In his cheesecloth shirt he wouldn't look out of place in Acapulco.

'Billy's Café: best fry-up in North Denton.'

'What, surely not in the *whole* of North Denton?' Waters smirked as they entered the smoggy café. Hell, he thought, this is the last place anyone sane would wish to be on a sunny day like this.

They slid into a booth. The place looked full of people who'd yet to come out of hibernation from last winter, dressed in overcoats and barely conscious.

A buxom waitress in a blouse that left little to the imagination took their order. Frost asked for a fried-egg sandwich and coffee, Waters settled for tea and toast.

'The rack on that!' Frost beamed as the waitress sashayed

away. He'd cheered up, or so it seemed, and the sight of an impressive cleavage on a girl half his age brought the sparkle back into his eyes.

'In with a chance there, pal,' Waters teased. 'See the smile she gave you?'

'Leave it out, son, I've got Y-fronts older than that bit of crumpet.'

Waters laughed.

'Behold, the prince of darkness himself,' Frost said, looking towards the door at a thin man wearing a fedora, pencil tie and raincoat, despite it being nearly eighty degrees. He'll fit right in with the clientele in here, Waters thought. He and Frost looked like alternate seasons from a budget fashion catalogue.

The man looked shifty and uncomfortable as he slid in next to Waters. 'All right, Jack?' he said.

'Sandy,' Frost acknowledged.

'Who's your boyfriend?' Sandy Lane said, nodding abruptly at Waters.

'Detective Sergeant Waters of the Metropolitan Police, may I introduce you to Sandy Lane, of the *Denton Echo*.'

Lane's eyebrows shot halfway upwards. 'Very exotic,' he said. 'Looks like you've been in the wars, old son.' Then his eyes flashed with excitement. 'Say, did that happen here? A race-related assault? Not been one of them since I don't know when.' He pulled out a tatty A5 notepad excitedly.

'No, it did not, Sandy,' Frost said, as the tea and coffee arrived. Lane waved off the waitress, wanting nothing for himself. 'John likes to do a bit of boxing in his spare time. He came a bit of a cropper in the ring, is all.'

'Oh.' Lane looked genuinely put out. 'What have you got for me, then?'

'We need you to make an appeal.'

'An appeal?'

'Yeah, you know' – Frost took a swig of coffee – 'a plea for help from the public.'

Waters thought Lane looked bemused. '*Help from the public?*' he said with a wry smile. 'Overstretched again, are we, Jack?'

'It's about a dead chimney sweep,' Waters chimed in.

'Outside Baskin's boudoir,' Lane affirmed, sounding slightly bored. 'I was there this morning, but you'd already gone. It's in the evening edition. Bet Harry Baskin's none too pleased, a dead bloke in his car park. 'Ere, I've heard rumours that it's more than a massage parlour – it's a knocking shop.' His journalistic interest was clearly rekindled at the thought.

The waitress hovered uncertainly with their late lunch, then gave up waiting to be acknowledged and placed the plates at the edge of the table, not daring to touch the ashtray which was seeing some heavy use.

'Disgraceful talk, Sandy,' Frost snapped, 'in front of a young lady, too. Of course not.'

'So, what about the deceased, then?' Lane enquired. 'Not much to go on, from what I hear.'

'People having chimneys swept in May are pretty thin on the ground, so finding witnesses and piecing together his movements could be tricky. You can help by putting in something every day. When did you last see this man? That sort of thing.'

'I told you, we're running the story this evening. I'm not sure how much more you want from me. I mean, who cares about some sad old geezer living on his own?'

'Maybe, but even so, run it again tomorrow,' Frost insisted.

Waters could see the dismissive look in the cynical hack's eyes. He attempted a further appeal. 'Why not print that he *wasn't* just some sad old man that nobody gave a toss about, he was a hardworking chimney sweep, a pillar of the community. Somebody's mate. Somebody's son. Strike a chord; run a photo of the van and equipment. Give him some humanity.'

Waters observed the tired old hack as he took this in. He

looked suddenly forlorn. Perhaps he was picturing himself in the role of the lonely, forgotten loser in just a few years from now. His sullen, creased eyes glazed over.

'All right.' Lane sighed. 'But what have you got for me?'

'What d'you mean?' Frost asked, surprised.

'Mullett's press conference yesterday was bloody useless. I mean, he actually found the kid himself, so you might be forgiven for thinking he'd have something to say, but no, just the usual clueless waffle. No idea when the boy was done in, even – nothing. Tell me something useful.'

'Sandy, you must understand Mr Mullett is not used to being at the coalface. He's a bit of a delicate flower.' The reporter shrugged, unimpressed. 'OK, here's a scoop. We suspect the Ellis girl – you know, the one found by the train track – was a suicide.'

Waters shot Frost a glance. It struck him as incredibly irresponsible to break this to a reporter when the parents hadn't even been informed. They should have been given at least a day's notice prior to it being made public. Although Mullett had keenly advocated the suicide angle, Waters could see repercussions for Frost for handling it like this.

'Really?' Lane said. 'Why?'

'Why what?' Frost said, reaching for Waters' cigarettes after discovering his pack was empty. 'Why do we suspect it was suicide?'

'No, why did she kill herself? Depressed? Mad?' Lane licked the tip of a stubby pencil, notepad at the ready.

'We can't comment as yet,' Waters cut in, fearing the worst for Mrs Ellis and her partner.

'That's not much of a story, is it?' Lane said indignantly. 'I need something a bit more juicy.'

'I'm sure you'll think of something,' Frost said. 'Clever chap like you.'

*   *   *

'Well played, son,' commented Frost as they left the café, putting on his Polaroids. 'About the sweep, I mean.'

'I see it all too often round my way,' Waters said. 'Lonely old bloke croaks in a tower block, for weeks nobody notices until a neighbour complains about a nasty smell from next door. You get to a certain age and people stop giving a damn.'

'Yep, we've had one or two of those down here,' Frost said, 'although you'd think a butcher's hook through the neck would cause more of a stir in the public's emotions.'

'I reckon it will,' Waters said. 'Not everyone's as jaded as your charming Mr Lane. Anyway, don't you think we'd better get over to the Ellises'?'

But Frost's attention was elsewhere. At the bus stop across the road was a striking brunette in a floppy sunhat and sunglasses. 'Look over there at that bird!' he hissed to Waters, removing his shades and shielding his eyes.

'Haven't we got better things to do than check out the crumpet?' Waters exclaimed.

A green double-decker had pulled in at the stop. When it pulled away the woman was gone. 'Did you see her?' demanded Frost. He seemed oddly agitated.

'The Brooke Shields lookalike, you mean?'

'Who?' Frost asked, perplexed.

'You know, that skinny teenage girl from *The Blue Lagoon*. Did you not see that? The one that came out last year or the year before.'

'She wasn't a girl, she was older.'

'More of a young Charlie's Angel, then? The one in the blue dress at the beginning?'

'How do I know?' Frost said wearily. 'My telly's black and white. Just thought I recognized her from somewhere, though for the life of me can't think where. Now, where were we?'

An old woman in a headscarf had appeared to Frost's left, as if

218

out of nowhere. She proffered what looked like a twig wrapped in silver foil.

'That for me, is it?' Frost said patiently, taking the gypsy's heather. 'Be a good chap, Waters, and give the lady a few coppers. Now then, my love, you've just reminded me of something . . .'

Frost pulled off the Bath Road towards the gypsy camp, and drove along what was little more than a mud track.

'Tell me again why we're here?' Waters asked. 'Surely we should head back to the station. What time did you tell the Hardys you'd see them?'

'All in good time, son. That old dear flogging heather outside the café reminded me to drop by.' Frost paused. 'Two reasons. One: Mullett wanted our visitors to be made to feel unwelcome. I bet he'd be only too pleased if we pinned those smash and grabs on a couple of gypsies; and I don't want a young hothead like Simms down here creating a stir. Uniform have already been tramping around.'

Frost concentrated on the uneven track. The cigarette clenched between his teeth dropped ash over his trousers as the Cortina clunked over potholes.

'And the other reason is?'

'Eh?' Frost's concentration was on the road, which was getting progressively worse. 'How they got the caravans down here I'll never know.'

'You said two reasons.'

'Flamin' hell!' said Frost, exasperated as he saw the camp pass by in the field to their left without their having found a way in. 'We've come up the wrong way or something. Let's get out and walk.'

They stopped the car and strode across to a dilapidated section of fence. Beyond it was a huddle of gypsy trailers arranged in an abstract pattern. A couple of small children were running around, and there were dogs of assorted shapes and sizes snuffling amongst the litter. A fair-haired man with a beer gut and a ragged goatee emerged from one of the trailers.

'Mr Frost!' he said. The gypsies were regular visitors, returning to Denton year on year, despite the condemnation of the likes of Mullett. The bearded man recognized Frost because of an incident a few years back when a young girl from the camp had been hit by a car.

'Hello there. Mind if we have a look about?'

'The police have already been here, Mr Frost.'

The presence of a pair of invaders had clearly been sensed throughout the camp. From every corner men and women of all ages began to appear, staring suspiciously at Frost and Waters. Although there was no outward hostility, Frost sensed that the gypsies were ready to stand their ground against further infringements of their privacy. Undeterred, he began to pick his way through the camp. There was little to see: a fire, children playing beneath a clothes line, scrap metal.

The bearded man had followed him. 'Anything in particular, Mr Frost?' he said, falling into step.

'Nope, just a general snoop around.' Frost took special note of a few adolescents on bicycles, but these were old, tatty objects, not the new BMX types scooting around Denton. He stood in the middle of the encampment, shielding his eyes and looking from left to right. 'Been into Denton much?' he asked the gypsy.

'We keep to ourselves mostly,' he replied, rolling a cigarette.

Waters caught them up. He had two children in tow, who regarded him curiously, no doubt mesmerized by his wraparound shades and Hawaiian shirt.

'I saw one of your number selling heather in the street.'

'Ain't no law against that!' The man looked affronted.

'Not saying there is, chief,' Frost replied with palms half raised in a placatory gesture. Someone was prodding lethargically the recently lit fire. 'Smoke'll get into the laundry,' he observed.

The man was unmoved. 'Look, I just wondered if anyone here had seen or heard anything untoward. It's like the Wild West, Denton, at the moment. More burglaries, robberies and muggings than you can shake a stick at . . . not to mention—'

'Now, just wait a minute, Mr Frost, we just got 'ere . . .'

Frost held up his hands again. 'Whoa there, let's keep calm. I'm not accusing anyone of anything, I just need a bit of help. Perhaps a couple of your kids might like to earn a few pennies?'

The man squinted; whether in distrust or because the sun had got the better of him Frost didn't know, but he took a step closer nonetheless. 'How do you mean?' he said, waving away a cloud of thunderflies that had gathered between them. He was probably of a similar age to Frost, but his rough, weathered skin made Frost's pale complexion appear almost youthful.

'The two kids on bikes over there, call them over.'

'Sam! Megan!' He beckoned to them.

The children, instantly alert, came cycling towards them. Frost regarded the pair and their rusty bikes with interest. They had the same big brown eyes and were clearly brother and sister. The bloated beardie looked on warily – whether he'd spawned them or not was difficult to tell.

'What sort of bike is that?' Frost asked the boy, who was the elder of the two and looked around twelve. The bike had tall handlebars sprouting out of a much smaller front wheel.

'A Chopper.' The lad grinned, embarrassed. The girl giggled beside him.

'Bet you can pull a few stunts on that, eh?'

He nodded confidently.

'And you,' Frost said to the girl, who had light-brown ringlets of hair that were falling over her eyes. 'Quick on that, are you? I bet you could overtake your brother.'

She smiled, head tilted to one side.

Frost bent down closer to their faces. 'Kids, how'd you like to earn some pocket money? I want you to do me a favour.'

'Visiting gypsies, I might have known.' The superintendent sighed. Wells noticed with unease how the heat disagreed with his commander. He was red in the face and his moustache looked decidedly damp. Perhaps if the uptight commander undid his tunic he might not get so wound up – it was bleedin' hot in here, after all. It was nearly three in the afternoon and Wells had the fan on his reception desk going full pelt.

'Hmm.' Mullett pondered, eyeing Wells suspiciously. 'Gypsies, travellers – can't trust anyone without roots. I did tell Frost to check them out, but I was clear I wanted an update this afternoon. When is he expected back?'

'Not spoken to him myself,' Wells admitted. 'Control has been trying to reach DS Frost for me all day, regarding the dead chimney sweep.'

'Yes, the chimney sweep,' Mullett repeated. 'Another body. Troubled and turbulent times, Wells. If we were suitably re-sourced would things be any different?'

Wells, unsure whether a response was required, said nothing. The super turned round and stood looking expectantly through the bright glass front doors opening out on to Eagle Lane. Hands on hips and pouting, as was his way. Wells had a sudden vision of him as some besieged Second World War commander in the midst of an enemy onslaught and deserted by his troops. The super didn't weather stress well on his own.

'Mr Mullett.' Wells looked at his notepad. 'Mr Hartley-Jones called again.'

'Did he?' Mullett replied without turning round, foot tapping on the polished floor. 'Is Simms making progress with that line-up, I wonder? Not that some teenage oik will be the one responsible for stealing my friend's wife's eternity ring. I don't suppose you know Simms's movements either, eh, Wells?'

'DC Simms is still in the field, sir, with DC Myles and DC

Clarke,' Wells said hopefully. 'Though he was calling with regard to his niece, sir, not the burglary.'

'Of course he is, of course he is,' Mullett replied with a hint of exasperation.

Just then the swing doors opened and two figures entered. Wells couldn't make out their features – they were in silhouette, because of the sun – but their shuffling gait and the way they leaned against each other told him who they were: the bereaved parents of Tom Hardy.

Waters finished talking to Control and replaced the radio handset. Frost should have asked what was happening at Eagle Lane but couldn't quite bring himself to do so. It was unlikely to be good news. Unwelcome thoughts still clouded his mind: Mary, her mother, the School of the Five Bells. Frost hadn't mentioned this last development to Waters. Was it embarrassment at his own wife being embroiled in some bizarre schoolgirl cult? No, it was twenty years ago. He needed to check with Records before going public with such information, that was the reason. But in any case, what was he driving at with this theory of a witchcraft link to both St Mary's and the murder? Would teenage girls really do something that horrific? It wasn't a thought he could countenance.

'Jack?' Waters was saying. 'Hey, Jack?'

'Sorry, pal,' Frost apologized. 'Lost in thought.'

'Mullett's on the warpath, Jack. The Hardys have turned up. They're with him now.'

'Shit,' Frost said. 'We're late. Better bite the bullet, then, and head back to the station. He's the last person you'd want to get any comfort from.'

Thursday (6)

Superintendent Stanley Mullett paused while his secretary placed glasses of water on the coasters on his desk. He looked over at the Hardys. It was a good few years since he'd been in such direct contact with grief. Where the bloody hell was Frost? It was him they were here to see.

'Thank you, Miss Smith,' he said deliberately, eking out the moment as long as possible.

Mrs Hardy finally moved the handkerchief which had obscured her features since she'd entered the station and began to speak. 'We thought, Mr Mullett, as Mr Frost was delayed . . . and as you found . . .' she shuddered, searching for the right word, '. . . T-Tom. We thought, as you found our son, it was best we come to see you directly. After the TV and everything.'

'Of course, and so you should,' Mullett said, trying to sound sincere. 'I want you to know we have our very best men and women working on this terrible, terrible tragedy.'

'But, sir, the bigger concern now is our daughter. She must

be found alive. Yes, we want our son's killer caught, but it won't bring him back.' The mother sobbed.

'We need everything focused on finding Emily,' reiterated Mr Hardy, who looked as though he'd not slept in days. He wore glasses not dissimilar to Mullett's, behind which his eyes were livid red.

Mullett swallowed hard. 'Yes, we're exploring every avenue,' he insisted, conscious of having little idea which avenues these were and how they were proceeding. Hadn't Frost been to the girl's private school this morning? That was all he really knew.

'But you're the one leading the investigation,' Mrs Hardy sobbed, 'so why are you just sitting here in your nice office? Why aren't you out there combing the streets?'

'Now, Mrs Hardy, please try and stay calm.' Mullett was terrified she would become hysterical. 'I have to remain here to direct operations.'

'But where is she?' Big, racking sobs had now engulfed Mrs Hardy and her face disappeared into her handkerchief again. The father seemed lost in a world of his own. Mullett's own pulse was soaring.

Suddenly the door flew open. In came Frost and Waters. Thank heavens.

'I'm sorry we're so late. Traffic . . .'

'Yes, please come in, both of you.' Mullett felt able to regain some composure, all eyes now being on the two dishevelled detectives. 'Mr and Mrs Hardy – have you met Detective Sergeant Frost?'

The Hardys looked less than impressed. 'We've spoken on the phone. We've met Miss Clarke.'

'Detective Constable Clarke reports to Detective Sergeant Frost who is heading the operation – in the field,' he added, as if to emphasize his own importance.

'Mr and Mrs Hardy, I'm so very sorry to meet you under such

circumstances,' Frost said solemnly. 'Apologies for not getting to you sooner. My colleague DS Waters and I have been out to St Mary's to see Miss Sidley.'

The parents looked expectantly at Frost. Mullett felt a pang of irritable envy. They now clearly thought this untidy individual held the key.

'Now,' Frost continued, 'how can we help?'

'We thought you should know,' Mrs Hardy said, 'that usually we wouldn't expect Emily home. She sleeps over at a friend's on a Wednesday.'

'At Two Bridges.' Frost nodded. 'Which reminds me, and I hate to bring it up at a time like this – Emily is only fourteen and really should not have been left alone for the duration of the holiday weekend.'

Mullett felt the colour drain from his face. He watched the distraught parents regard each other. Their expression betrayed the anxiety of guilt; they knew they were at fault and the blame was just beneath the surface.

But Frost was swift to move on. 'Am I correct that Emily was expected at Two Bridges?'

'Correct,' said the father.

'Yes. It was that evening when her friend at Two Bridges – the one she was supposed to be staying with – telephoned to ask where she was,' Mrs Hardy added. 'We thought you should know . . .'

'Which friend might that be, Mrs Hardy?' Frost asked.

'Gail. Gail Burleigh.'

'We appreciate you coming in like this,' Frost said diplomatically, 'but it's best all round if you let us get on with finding your daughter, which is our prime concern at the moment. I understand it's tough to sit at home just waiting, but I'm afraid it's the best course of action.'

Mullett watched the exhausted parents rise to their feet to take their leave. He had to hand it to Frost; vulgar though he was, he knew how to deal with civilians. At certain times, at least.

'Well done, Jack,' he said after a WPC had led the Hardys out. 'What do we reckon on the girl? Dead, do you think?'

'That's a bit premature, sir. I believe she may well still be alive.'

'Well, let's hope so. Keep up the good work.'

'Thank you, sir.'

'Oh, before you go, Records asked me to hand you this.' He passed across a faded foolscap file. 'Girl's suicide from twenty years ago.'

The dazzling afternoon sun caused DC Simms to brake suddenly as he pulled into Eagle Lane station.

'What the . . .'

A huge truck was obstructing half of the car park. In front of it was Superintendent Mullett lambasting PC Pooley, his face glowing with anger and sweat. He was holding something on hangers encased in plastic wrapping. Was that his dry cleaning? Simms wondered.

'What's going on here?' Clarke asked.

'Looks like the skip-hire people are in a jam.'

Clarke pulled up the handbrake. 'Well, this'll have to do.'

'Oh Christ, he's coming over.' Simms folded his sunglasses and hung them from the neck of his T-shirt.

'No way, I've had my fill of him this week. Wind your window up,' she said, getting out of the car.

'Afternoon, Super,' Simms said as Mullett approached, clutching a bunch of shirts on wire hangers.

'Well, what's happening with these burglaries?' Mullett demanded, blinking in the sun.

'See ya.' Clarke waved, hastily making her escape up the steps to the main entrance.

'Hold up there, Clarke, I want you too!' Mullett called after her. She stopped, deflated. Mullett turned back to Simms. 'Wells tells me we still don't have a line-up. I specifically asked you to organize a line-up of possible suspects with a view to making an arrest for this spate of burglaries.'

'I'm sorry, sir, I'm a little confused. I thought the line-up was for the crimes where those kids were the culprits, like the mugging of the guy with the briefcase and the robbery at the jeweller's on Merchant Street. What have they got to do with the burglaries?'

'*Jewellery*, Simms, use your head,' Mullett snapped.

Simms struggled to see the connection. 'But the street-robbers were opportunist kids on bikes. They're hardly likely to be carrying out carefully planned house burglaries.'

'You don't know that. If you had a suspect, which you don't, perhaps you might be able to find out, but you don't, do you?'

Simms felt he was in a no-win situation. The super was perspiring heavily and in no mood for disagreement. Nevertheless, it was true that he had yet to organize a line-up so an explanation was needed. 'A line-up with minors would be complicated,' he began. 'I thought it perhaps wiser to have the victims come in and go through photos of known offenders, so they're coming in this evening at six o'clock.'

Mullett turned away without comment. 'And you, Detective Clarke, I want you to try and remember something about your attackers.'

'But I already said—'

'I know what you said – but I want you to think harder. I need a result.' His look was intense and piercing. Even Simms felt uncomfortable on behalf of his colleague.

Suddenly, making all three of them jump, a terrific crunch came from behind Mullett. 'What in heavens . . .' he exclaimed.

In attempting to back out on to the road the lorry had taken the top off the wall between the station car park and the neighbouring garage. Pooley stood there shouting, 'Whoa!' and gesturing wildly, but the driver either hadn't seen him or was more intent on escaping than on paying him any heed. Mullett scuttled off to intervene.

'Is he trying to do what I think he's trying to do?' said Simms in amazement.

'What do you mean?' Clarke was sporting a pair of aviator sunglasses, making it impossible to gauge her reaction.

'I mean, is he trying to use you to nail someone for these break-ins?'

Clarke took off her shades, shook her hair and looked at the tarmac. 'I guess I didn't really take on board what he was saying to me yesterday. I was too busy being insulted and trying not to throw up to realize he was patronizing me.'

'What? You're not making any sense, Sue.' Simms looked up at her anxiously.

She reached up and playfully tugged his cheek. 'Nothing for you to worry about. C'mon.'

Thursday (7)

'The Crime Scene guys are there now,' said DC Kim Myles. Frost thought she looked very pleased with herself, and rightly so. She had located potentially important forensic evidence: candle wax in Denton Woods more than likely matching that found on Tom Hardy's face. The others looked less enthusiastic.

DCs Clarke and Simms both appeared tired and bedraggled, although to be fair, thought Frost, they were all starting to flag. The heat takes it out of you, he reasoned, shifting uncomfortably, perspiration having glued his shirt to the back of the cheap plastic chair. They had only the one fan going in the airless Incident Room.

'They've got another couple of hours of decent daylight,' Frost said, glancing at the wall clock. A quarter past four. 'What I don't get, though, is that the body was clean,' he continued as Waters elbowed his way through the door. 'If you hack a body to pieces in the woods and then drag it half a mile on to a golf course, you'd expect the odd cut or graze. A twig in the hair, that sort of thing.'

'Maybe the body had been out in the rain,' Simms suggested, sipping his coffee. 'Washed it down, like.'

'Nope,' Frost said decisively. 'Yesterday afternoon's downpour was the first heavy rain in over a week.'

'Which was an added problem,' chipped in Myles. 'The SOCOs weren't too hopeful that we'd find anything in the woods. Harding said the rain would have washed away the blood if there was any there to start with.'

'So where does that leave us?' snapped Clarke. Frost thought she looked rankled. Could it be because Myles, the attractive blonde, was stealing all the limelight?

'Where are the boy's clothes, that's what I want to know,' Frost said crossly. 'Uniform couldn't find the nose on the end of their faces. Was there a dog unit in the woods yesterday?'

'There were dogs, but they found zilch.'

Frost frowned. 'Somebody must have seen something. That boy didn't just materialize out of nowhere like an extra from *Star Trek*. One minute he's lying at home fantasizing about his French teacher, the next he's sprawled on Denton Golf Course in the buff with half his insides missing. Someone must have seen him leave the house. Myles and Waters, get over there when we're done and go door to door again. Map out any possible route. The family live off the Wells Road so try all the routes between there and the woods. Check in the local shops and newsagents; you never know, he may have got peckish and stopped for a Curly Wurly.'

'This puzzle about the body being clean,' Clarke said. 'Well, maybe he wasn't killed in the woods at all.'

'What, he was just out to look at the flowers,' Simms said, directing smoke rings towards the ceiling.

Frost ignored him. 'How do you mean?'

'Well, there's nothing to indicate that *anyone* was murdered in the woods. OK, we now have candle wax that matches. But so what? Doesn't prove there was a murder – only it's possible Tom

Hardy was there. There's no denying the burial mound itself has importance. Something happened there, undoubtedly. It's just a question of what.'

Frost thought this remark over, grabbing Simms's cigarettes off the table. He felt they were going nowhere. Was it time to relay what Mary had told him last night? Or should he just forget it? He didn't place much credence on schoolgirl pranks in the sixties being connected to a dead boy found on the golf course. Self-harm, tattoos and even suicide were one thing – what happened to that lad was a different matter altogether. 'Simms, where are you with who exactly was in the woods over the weekend? Didn't I ask you last night?'

'I'm on it, Sergeant. End of the day, promise. It's just that—'

'I don't want excuses. If I don't know by seven o'clock this evening the name of every individual who was in Denton Woods, I'll pull you off the case and do it myself. Is that clear?'

'Sir.'

'Right. Now on to the boy's sister, young Emily.'

'Uniform have pulled in her sleepover buddy, the Burleigh girl,' said Waters. 'Her old man the lawyer was none too pleased. He was making a fuss in the lobby when I grabbed the coffees – spouting off about human rights and Social Services.'

Frost felt Clarke's eyes on him. Be careful, her look warned. Social Services.

'She's helping us with our enquiries,' Frost said. 'Flamin' hell, you'd think the girl might want to help us find her friend . . . wouldn't you?' His question was met with raised eyebrows. The silence was broken by Superintendent Mullett barging into the Incident Room.

'Why do I do it?' he yelled, flinging a newspaper at Frost and causing him to spill his coffee down his light-cotton shirt. 'Why? *Why?*'

'Look what you've done to my shirt,' Frost retorted. 'It's my summer uniform.'

'Never mind that – look at this!' the superintendent bellowed.

Frost retrieved the paper from underneath an orange plastic chair, and looked at the headline: TRAIN GIRL WAS SUICIDE, SAY POLICE.

And underneath was a photo of Frost. An old one; those mutton-chop sideburns had been a mistake, he thought. 'Bloody annoying, that. I've told Sandy not to use that photo.'

Frost handed the paper to Waters, who grimaced. 'Not a good look.'

'Frost, this is serious!' Mullett fumed.

'Why?' Frost showed his palms plaintively. 'You told me to notify the press.'

'Yes! But not before you soothe the parents. Imbecile!' Mullett looked fit to burst. Clarke, Simms and Myles sat watching the superintendent's outburst in silence.

'Damn, I knew there was something else I meant to do.' Frost looked accusingly at Waters, who ignored him and continued to leaf through the paper. 'John, didn't I say, remind me to speak to Mrs Ellis?'

'I've had Michael Hartley-Jones, the girl's uncle, on the phone, accusing me of incompetence. Me! Incompetence! These people aren't just anyone, you know. They're not riff-raff. These are well-connected people. They're friends of mine!'

'So it's not actually the girl's parents you're worried about, sir?' Frost replied flatly, turning his attention to the centre-spread of the *Echo* that DS Waters had laid out on the table.

'Done us proud there,' he said, surveying the pages.

KEN SMITH: A TRAGEDY. WHO COULD HARM THIS MAN? And underneath, a poignant photograph of the murdered chimney sweep – bald, bearded and bespectacled with a cheery, sooty smile. Frost skimmed the editorial and accompanying photos. Lane had done a thorough job. If you'd seen this man or his van in the last week your attention would certainly be grabbed, Frost thought. The fact the man's appointment book couldn't be found had the DS convinced that the man had been killed by a customer – a customer who did not want to be traced.

'. . . after last year's fiasco.' Mullett was filling Waters in on Frost's previous dealings with newspapers. 'This cretin almost brought the country to a halt with a rabies scare! You are forbidden to talk to the press – do you hear me, Frost?'

'Loud and clear, sir. Does that mean TV appearances are off?'

Chris Everett poured generously from a bottle of Gordon's. Shaken, he had returned straight home after valuing the place on Wessex Crescent, to which he'd already been given the keys, as the lady of the house was not available to show him around that week. The shock of seeing, carefully arranged throughout the modern detached property, various framed photographs of the haughty policeman from the TV news had nearly given him a heart attack. He would undervalue the place just to get shot of it – and its owner – quickly. He already had people viewing it tomorrow morning.

Even with nerves bubbling, however, he couldn't resist a snoop. What he'd found under the bed in a shoebox was enough to give him a nose bleed.

'Wasn't this the little man who came to remove the pigeons?' Fiona Everett said, spinning the newspaper round on the kitchen table.

'I've no idea, darling,' Everett said carefully, gulping from the cut-glass tumbler as if it contained some sort of elixir. It was a bit early in the day, but he needed it. 'I told you, he'd gone by the time I got home – if he'd ever been.'

'Don't be silly, Christopher – of course he was here when you arrived home. I saw your car turn into the street just as I was leaving to drop the girls off.'

'I don't recall, I really don't, sweetheart.' Everett fumbled nervously with a pack of Dunhill. 'Best not mention it, anyway. We don't want the police to come snooping around here. It'll upset the girls.'

'But there's an appeal for help.' Fiona frowned tenderly. 'Poor little chap, I'm sure he wouldn't have harmed a fly. We really ought—'

'Fiona, think about it. What would the neighbours say?'

Mrs Everett paused for a moment, struck by a new thought. 'Oh, quite, the neighbours – we can't have that.'

Everett relaxed; that was his wife off his back, at least. But the missing briefcase was still a problem. Fiona knew nothing about the mugging and his summons to the police station. Nor would she – he would fob her off with a tale about an evening viewing when he left in half an hour or so.

He had to be at the station at six. Just thinking about it, he started to tense up again. He would say he didn't recognize anyone – the last thing he wanted was the little bastards being caught.

'Nice of him to pop by,' Frost muttered as Mullett left the Incident Room. Clarke noticed a tangible sense of relief as the superintendent stormed out. Desk Sergeant Bill Wells had interrupted him in full flow with the news that Mrs Mullett's car had broken down on the M3.

'Now, from one pain in the arse to another – Social Services. What's all this about the Burleigh girl?'

'Not a pain in the arse yet, Jack,' Waters said. 'I just overheard her old man banging on about procedures regarding questioning a minor. It's illegal without Social Services' involvement, he reckons.'

'Probably a mistake bringing her in. Maybe we should have called round. But she's here now, anyway. Clarke and myself will have a chat,' he said, undaunted.

Clarke regarded Frost with affection. There was something

endearing in that hapless but determined approach of his. Here he was juggling three, possibly four fatalities – Ken Smith, Samantha Ellis, Tom and Emily Hardy – fielding everything that came his way, and despite spending half the time looking lost and desperate, he always kept going. She didn't know how he did it. She felt lost herself, but had the likes of him to look to for support. Jack would always win through, somehow. His drive and dedication was unfaltering.

The phone went. It was Desk Sergeant Bill Wells.

'DC Simms,' said Frost, 'it appears you have visitors.'

'Shit – that'll be the robbery victims, here to go through mugshots.' Simms lifted his feet off the desk.

'You'd better get on with it, then. Waters and Myles, get over to Denton Close and the surrounds. Check the corner shops first, they might still be open.'

The phone rang again. 'Flamin' hell, anyone would think we've got nothing better to do than answer the phone. Yes?' he snapped.

'Jack, it's Mrs Ellis . . .'

'Tell her I'll call her back.' No doubt she was terribly upset at the *Denton Echo* headlines – claiming her daughter's death was suicide – and rightly so. He should have called round first.

'She says she called you yesterday too—'

'I'll ring back tonight, I promise,' he said, nudging his coffee mug across the blotter and underlining the word 'Ellis' that he'd written the previous evening.

Thursday (8)

Everett sat in the lobby of Denton police station. It occurred to him that he'd never actually been in a police station before. He had no preconceived ideas of how one should be, but somehow the magnolia emulsion struck him as peculiar.

Next to him on the bench was an Asian gentleman, softly mumbling to himself. Overhead the wall clock ticked steadily. He flinched as something touched his neck; one corner of a warning poster – something to do with beetles – had lost its fixing on the noticeboard behind them.

The revolving door spun and a middle-aged man walked up to the front desk. He was asked to join Everett and the Asian man on the bench.

The door went again and in came a gaunt officer in uniform, immediately followed by the man whose portrait Everett had seen all over the Wessex Crescent property this afternoon, the moustachioed policeman off the TV. He was in the middle of berating the younger fellow, something to do with a skip and a damaged wall, but after laying eyes on three men seated beneath the noticeboard, he stopped in his tracks. Everett was alarmed to see him standing there, one hand on hip, the other stroking his moustache. His glare was menacing. But it was over in an instant and he marched off yelling, 'Wells!', giving the man behind the front desk a start. Everett guessed he was the next unlucky victim of the angry fellow's wrath.

The young detective in denims who'd found Everett in the street had appeared before them. 'Sorry to keep you, if you'd all like to come this way.'

They looked at one another, realizing for the first time that they were all victims. Everett felt decidedly uneasy. He followed the CID man down the corridor, just wanting to get this risky situation over with. Suddenly, through a swing door came the scruffy guy he'd seen at the train station. By the looks of him he hadn't shaved since Everett had almost bashed him with his briefcase on Monday. Everett looked away far too obviously, which triggered from the man a cursory glance of suspicion.

'Right, Bill.' Frost banged his fist on the desk, causing Desk Sergeant Bill Wells to jump again. Before him were DS Frost and DS Waters. 'Where's this teenage girl, then? Not under there, is she, giving your shoes a polish?' Frost rapped his knuckles on the desk surface.

'Don't do that, Jack. The super's been doing my pieces all afternoon,' Wells said, rubbing his forehead. 'The skip-hire people have taken the wall off the garage next door. The girl and her father are in Interview Room 2. DC Simms has number 1.'

'Yes, with his robbery victims. A motley-looking trio, they are,' Frost mused. 'The shifty-looking blond chap – he definitely looked familiar.'

'Everyone looks familiar to you, Jack,' Wells said. 'It doesn't mean they've done anything. You're too suspicious for your own good.'

'That's where you're wrong, Bill. Everyone's done something wrong at some point – even you. Isn't that so, Johnny boy?'

'Reckon so. Life'd be dull otherwise.'

'Looks like it's not been dull for John just lately. Nice shiner you got there,' Wells said, noticing Waters' black eye. 'Would have to have been a big lad brave enough to have a crack at you.'

'Big or not, we'll have them. What are you still doing here anyway, Waters? Where's that little blonde strumpet?' Frost joked.

'Powdering her nose,' Waters replied.

'I bet she is, and the rest. Try not to get beaten up this time – at least not until you've finished your house calls.'

Wells shook his head despairingly and answered the phone which had been ringing throughout the exchange. Its shrill jangle had been almost constant throughout the day – in fact, it had reached the stage where he was more aware of it when it wasn't ringing.

'Denton Police.' A voice announced itself to be from Denton Council. Heavens, thought Wells, it'll be about that infernal skip.

Waters was surprised by Frost's remark to Bill Wells about catching the people who had given him a beating after walking Kim Myles home from the pub the previous evening. Frost had not commented on the incident apart from an aside in the car that morning. Also, it was strange the way he'd casually revealed his knowledge that Waters had been out with Myles. How did he know? Frost was a difficult guy to fathom; his mind might seem to be elsewhere, but he was taking things in all the time, and would let them slip out when you'd least expect it.

Myles emerged from the Ladies. 'Sorry I took so long,' she bubbled. 'Jesus, what the hell happened to you?' She reached out to touch his face but he instinctively pulled back. He'd not had a chance to talk to her and explain, and now she was here, he really didn't feel like doing so.

'Hey, I'm fine, let's get out of here.' He ushered her towards the door and out into the last of the sun. 'Someone's made a mess of that wall,' he remarked, pointing at a pile of bricks at the edge of the car park.

'And someone's made quite a mess of your face,' Myles said. 'So when did it happen?'

'After I dropped you off. Two guys.'

'Bastards. Bet it was those pigs from the pub.'

'I don't know about that. There are lots of muggings around here, it seems. Couldn't say for sure who it was.' As he said it, Waters tried not to think about the pungent smell of Brut which he'd detected just now in the corridor of Eagle Lane, as a group of other officers walked by.

'Don't be ridiculous. It wasn't a bunch of kids on BMXs that jumped you, was it? The Eagle is a coppers' pub. You know who it was; why cover up for them? We must've been followed.'

'I don't think we were followed,' he said seriously. 'Denton's hardly a crowded metropolis – the streets were empty. We would have noticed if someone had left the pub and followed us. Maybe they were lying in wait? But then they'd have to know where you live.'

'What are you suggesting?' she snapped.

'I'm not suggesting anything! Just leave it. Are you OK to drive?'

'I'd prefer to go in yours. Far better than a beat-up Escort.'

'It's in the garage.'

'What d'you mean?'

He shrugged.

'Shit, no, don't tell me they've done your car as well. Why didn't you say? It's obviously not just some opportunist loser from the pub. Have you told Frost?'

'The chance hasn't presented itself.'

'Well, present it, then. Get in.'

*   *   *

Simms left the three men to page through the mugshots of youth offenders. He'd not removed the snaps of those already convicted and holed up in borstals, just to see how reliable they turned out to be as witnesses.

The jeweller, the estate agent and the newsagent sat carefully studying the assortment of absconding schoolboys and minor teenage felons in silence; he'd told them not to confer.

Simms sat on the corner of the desk, lit a cigarette and pulled the marker from the *Yellow Pages*. He studied the four phone numbers he'd scribbled down that morning. It was gone six thirty – they'd probably be home by now. With a sigh he picked up the phone and dialled the first number. 'Hello, Mrs Tindell? Denton Girl Guides? Hi, this is Detective Constable Simms of Denton CID.'

'Good evening, Gail, Mr Burleigh.' Frost nodded, as the duty constable opened the door to Interview Room 2. 'Thank you for coming in, though there really was no need. A misunderstanding on my colleague's part. We have a missing girl who—'

Burleigh got to his feet, seething with fury. 'This is an outrage!'

'Sit down!' Frost shouted. 'Now! Or the constable here will take you down to the cells.'

The man was instantly silenced. The constable shut the door and stood against the back wall, and Frost winked at him in assurance that everything was under control.

'I have two dead teenagers on my hands and another missing. What I don't need is a load of verbal aggro from you, thank you very much. Now, if you can just see your way clear to answering a few questions?' Frost paused, turning to address Gail. 'Presumably you are mildly concerned about your friend Emily Hardy?'

'Yes, of course,' answered Burleigh senior.

'Please, sir, let your daughter answer.'

The father glanced uncertainly at Gail, who until now had said nothing. She lifted her precocious dark brown eyes and fixed her gaze squarely on Frost. 'Of course, I'm very worried. But I don't see why it's me who's singled out.'

'Well, funnily enough, it has something to do with Emily spending most Wednesday evenings at yours, so on the day she disappeared some people thought she was with you,' he said testily, knowing this not to be the case.

'But she wasn't.' The girl smiled. 'I rang her parents.'

'Tell me,' Frost said, lighting a cigarette. 'What did you two girls usually get up to of an evening – you know, now you're growing up. It used to be the Girl Guides, according to your headmistress.'

'Is that relevant?' Burleigh snapped.

'Ever the lawyer,' Frost said. 'You know, if I'm to have any chance of finding this missing girl, I need to know as much about her as possible, presumably by talking to someone who knows her well.'

'Why not try the parents?' Burleigh huffed.

'Oh, believe me, we do. But as children reach a certain age' – Frost regarded the girl in heavy make-up before him – 'it often transpires that the parents are the last to know what the kids are up to.'

The father looked expectantly at his daughter, rubbing his beard thoughtfully. Frost repeated his question to Gail.

'We play records and stuff. We're quite into our music.'

'Of course you are. I understand that on Saturday night you went up to the Smoke with your mates.'

'Yes, yes,' Burleigh interjected. 'We've been over all that with your colleague, the dark chap.'

'Sergeant Waters?' Frost replied, almost tempted to say something further to antagonize the buttoned-up lawyer, but thinking better of it. 'OK, Gail, when was the last time you saw Emily?'

'Lunchtime at school.'

'And? Did she intend to come home with you that evening?'

It was like getting blood out of a stone. She sat there chewing gum; he had to forcibly stop himself reaching across and . . .

'Yeah, she was coming over. But she had to meet someone first. She said she'd meet me after hockey.'

'Any idea who?'

The girl shook her head.

'What state of mind was she in?' Frost pressed. 'You know, happy? Sad?'

'She was, you know, all right. Happy, I guess.'

'And at this stage neither of you had heard about her brother's fate?'

The girl shook her head. Frost got up and stretched. He was none the wiser; he still had no clue as to how the missing girl had reacted to her brother's death. Was she frightened? Scared? Had she even known that he was dead?

'Did you know Emily's brother, Tom?' Frost asked.

The girl considered the question before answering, 'No, not really. Only by sight.'

'Did you ever go to the Hardys' house?'

There was a rap on the door. A face appeared at the small, rectangular window – it was Simms. Now what?

Frost stepped outside, pulling the door to. 'Yes?'

'We might have found the Hardy boy's clothes,' Simms said excitedly. 'And . . .'

Frost stepped back into the interview room. 'OK, you can go. Thank you for your time. We'll be in touch very soon. Gail, please try and think a little more about the last time you saw Emily Hardy . . .' The pair looked surprised to be released so abruptly but weren't about to argue. 'Constable, show the gentleman and his daughter out.'

Frost waited until they were out of earshot down the corridor.

'Well, where?' he asked Simms.

'Municipal dump. Clarke took the call.'

Thursday (9)

The clear skies brought a chill to the evening air when the sun disappeared behind the old mill across the canal. Clarke pulled a crumpled raincoat from the boot of the Escort, slipped it on with a shiver and picked up the torch.

The slowly rotating blue light of the area car advertised the presence of two uniformed officers, who were accompanied by a council worker. The municipal dump was brilliantly lit with huge arc lamps reminiscent of a sports arena, except all there was to see was garbage.

The officers nodded as Clarke approached. The council worker, dressed in a woollen hat and a tatty denim jerkin, regarded her disdainfully. He was in full flow, explaining the complexities of rubbish collection. A *woman*, was what his expression said.

'. . . because of the bank holiday there's always some confusion, you see. There's those that read the flyers with all the revised collection dates on them, and those that don't.'

One of the PCs turned to Clarke in order to elucidate the

topic at hand. 'What the gentleman is saying is that it's difficult to ascertain when the—'

'Whoa . . .' Clarke protested, looking over her shoulder as an unmarked black van pulled up. She had asked for an initial on-site forensic analysis, thinking it best before moving the clothes to the lab. 'Let's take this in reverse order. So, start with when the discovery was made.'

'It was the rats.'

'Rats?' Clarke looked to the PC, who shrugged.

'Yep, rats. You'd think this being a refuse site we'd be used to seeing 'em all the time. Well, to a degree that's true. But when there's so much to choose from' – the man made a sweeping gesture – 'they get fussy. You only see a real frenzy when there's fresh meat to be had. By fresh I don't mean literally fresh, just uncooked.'

Clarke felt suddenly colder. 'I'm sorry,' she said, 'but what does this have to do with the clothes?'

'It's what the clothes contained,' the man said with a grave look.

He didn't need to say any more. The organs and entrails of that poor, eviscerated boy, she thought, that's what the rats had been feasting on. She fought back a wave of nausea and was barely aware of the conversation between the dustman and Forensics men as to where the objects had been found.

Clarke recovered her poise and followed the others into the landfill area.

The dustman continued his story: 'So, come this evening, we tramp across the mound, just to see if there's anything worth having – you'd be surprised.'

Clarke was more intent on watching her footing as they clambered across the landscape of rubbish.

'Here you are,' he said, bending down to cast aside a large hessian sack. 'I put this over it to stop the rats from 'aving it away.'

Clarke flashed the torch over a supermarket carrier bag. What looked like a heavily blood-stained sleeve of a white tracksuit lay poking out of the top.

'As soon as I saw the blood I called the police.'

'That's about it, thank God,' said DC Kim Myles. 'My feet are so sore. We've covered every street and cul-de-sac on this blinkin' estate. And a fat lot of good it's done us. We've basically retrodden uniform's path.'

'Apart from that row of shops.' Waters pointed towards a parade of half a dozen shops all in darkness except for one, on the corner of a modern housing estate and the Wells Road.

'Let's grab a few cans at the offy,' Myles suggested.

Waters nodded. He felt deflated and fancied a drink; it had been a long day and it seemed to him that the investigation was going badly. They should have questioned Emily immediately upon discovering her brother's body. It stood to reason that she was in all probability the last one to see the boy alive, the pair being alone in the house. OK, Denton division were chronically understaffed, but Mullett's preoccupation with the press and keeping up appearances did nothing to help.

He pulled open the door of Unwins and allowed Myles in first; he liked her all the more for respecting his preference not to discuss the caning he'd received last night. She'd not mentioned it again since they'd left the station.

As he paid for the beers, Waters raised the subject of the boy and his missing sister. The off-licence owner had yet to be questioned; he'd been closed when the initial sweep by was made on Wednesday morning.

'Yes, I know both of them,' the shopkeeper said. 'They've been coming in with their parents since they were knee-high. The boy would come in from time to time on his own, for crisps and so on. And he tried to buy a bottle of cider only the other week. I refused him, of course. Terrible tragedy.'

'When exactly? Can you remember? It might be important.'

'Possibly at the weekend. Let me see.' The man tugged thoughtfully at an earlobe. Waters realized immediately that the shopkeeper might have been the last one to see the boy alive, a fact he'd be unaware of since it had still not been reported in the press that Tom had been dead for several days before the discovery of his body. 'Yes, it was a Friday; he asked me about bus times.'

'Bus times?' Myles repeated anxiously.

'Yes, whether they ran to the same schedule in the evening as during the day. The timetable at the bus stop on the Wells Road had been defaced.'

'Where was he heading?'

'Other side of town. He wanted a number 4, which runs up the Bath Road out west, past Denton Woods.'

Waters' heart started beating fast. 'Can you recall what he was wearing?'

The shopkeeper squinted with the effort of remembering. 'A tracksuit, I think.'

'Time?'

'I'd guess around 7.30.'

'Thank you, you've been a big help.'

Waters made to leave but the man was still pondering. 'Yes, I remember it now – a white top – a complete contrast to the girl all in black.'

'The girl?'

'Yes. The girl – I think it must have been his sister.'

Shortly after 10 p.m. Simms knocked on Frost's office door. As he entered, he thought the DS looked pained in the glow from the desk lamp. His fingers were working his temples in a motion suggesting either deep thought or worry, Simms couldn't tell which. In front of him was a large-scale map of Denton with highlighter marks across the middle.

'Hello, son, come in. What's up?'

'The smash and grabs and the mugging. I've drawn a blank, I'm afraid. The victims didn't recognize their attackers.'

'What, between the three of them they couldn't come up with even one possible?' Frost said in amazement, picking his cigarette up from the ashtray.

'The estate agent and the jeweller, nothing. The newsagent, well, every single photo was a candidate from his position; literally every white kid that came up.'

'Hold on – surely he's the one least likely to make a match? They were *all* wearing balaclavas in his shop, am I right?'

'Yep.' Simms pulled up a chair.

Frost reached into the lower drawer. 'Time for a nightcap?' he said, waving the bottle of Black Label.

Simms nodded, remarking, 'I reckon the newsagent has convinced himself it's race-related. Some weird persecution complex . . .'

'Nothing weird about it. He's probably right to be concerned; that estate is going downhill fast.'

Frost endeavoured to find some cleanish mugs, opening the office window and slinging out coffee dregs, while Simms wondered, not for the first time, what Frost's thoughts were on Waters' beating. The DS clearly wasn't going to discuss it, not with him at least.

Simms's thoughts turned back to the robberies. 'Well, maybe we're wrong to think it's the same gang that's done all three,' he said. 'After all, in the newsagent's job they were armed, and they all had balaclavas.'

'We don't know they were armed. Nobody actually saw a gun. And the kid who did the bike trick outside the jeweller's was in a balaclava. The other attack was more opportunist, so they hadn't had time to get their masks on, and it was in broad daylight too – and yet the estate agent can't offer us anything to help us ID them?' Frost rolled his eyes.

'Nothing. I picked him up off the street, remember. He was pretty dazed, and visibility was quite poor; the sky was very overcast.'

The Scotch burned Simms's throat. He looked over at Frost; he had to hand it to him, he may look a tired wreck of a man, but you couldn't fault his sharpness. According to station gossip his marriage was in trouble, perhaps seriously, and yet here he was, still giving his all to the job.

'I take it DC Clarke has been through these too?'

Simms nodded. 'She can't point to anyone either, despite her tussle with one of the assailants, same as the estate agent.'

Frost grunted. 'Never mind. We'll catch them. I've enlisted some outside help . . .'

Simms was about to ask what but decided he was too weary.

'And talking of Ms Clarke' – Frost looked at his watch – 'she should be back from the tip soon . . . which leads us to Tom Hardy and the jolly campers in Denton Woods. They're our biggest chance of a breakthrough. We have the candle wax to suggest he was in the woods, so chances are the Scouts saw something. Any progress?'

'Yes and no.' Simms sighed. 'The Scouts did camp this weekend. But not at Denton. They were on Rimmington Meadows.'

'Arse.' Frost sighed and looked nonplussed. 'But hang on . . . Witnesses at Wood Vale saw groups of teenagers traipsing into the woods on Friday. What were they doing, going flower-picking?' He snorted in derision.

'Well, yeah, actually – more looking at them than picking. I don't know exactly, but the Scout and Guide leaders mentioned something to do with a nature badge.'

'What about the huts made of twigs and what-have-you?' Frost puffed.

'Bivouacs? They'd been there weeks, left over from their Easter camp.'

'So let me get this straight – there was *nobody* camping out in Denton Woods last weekend?'

'Not that we can verify. But I asked the leaders for names and addresses of everyone in their troops.'

'Get that list,' Frost said urgently, then looked back at the map before him, prompting Simms to ask, 'What have you got there?'

'Well, it's not all bad news. Myles and Waters have had a breakthrough on Tom Hardy's movements.' Frost reached for another cigarette. 'Well, I say it's a breakthrough – we've at least found out when he left the house on Friday evening and where he was going. He stopped in at a shop around seven to make enquiries about bus times . . .'

'Which bus?'

'The number 4, which runs up the Bath Road.'

'And past Denton Woods.'

'Exactly. Waters has gone to question the bus driver, to try and find out where the poor kid got off the bus. And Clarke has been to the dump where the kid's clothes were found, and they match the description from the shopkeeper, so we know he wore a white tracksuit top on Friday evening, the same as when he was murdered.'

'So, Friday looks to have been D-Day then,' mused Simms.

'Yes, so some progress. Clarke also found . . . Well, no need to get into that now . . .'

When Simms finally closed the door behind him at ten thirty, Frost pulled out the Samantha Ellis file and leafed through the pages until he found what he was looking for, the detailed pathologist report made by Drysdale's sidekick. There it was under 'distinguishing marks': *inside left thigh, a small brown mole/ birth mark (?); sickle-shape / inverted '5'*.

He thought back to the girl's bedroom which he'd briefly seen on Monday, filled with astrological mumbo jumbo. He had no daughters or sisters of his own, so couldn't presume to offer any expert understanding of how adolescent girls' minds worked, but if he had to hazard a guess, then turmoil, melo-drama and a burning quest for self-expression would all figure highly. It was the question mark the pathologist had added that had caught his eye. Suppose the mark were not a birthmark but instead a makeshift tattoo in brown ink? A sickle could mean a couple of things – a rural peasant's farm tool; the emblem of the Soviet Union – but it was the final description that interested Frost: *an inverted '5'*. Inverted 5? Where had he read that before? He reached over for *A Brief History of the Pagan Calendar* and flicked to the glossary at the back. There it was, pentagram. '*The five-pointed star drawn with straight strokes. The word originates from the Greek . . .*' Yeah, yeah. He read on, '*Symbol of the Wicca faith. An inverted pentagram, with two points upwards, is often regarded as the sign of the witch.*'

Frost's mind was racing. He snatched up the autopsy report from twenty years ago on Nancy Edwards, the girl who had hanged herself. A few pages in, there it was in faded ink, a description of the tattoo the girl had been caught, compasses in hand, disfiguring herself with: *The number five; the bottom resembling a blade or scythe.* Five. The School of the Five Bells. The members of which, according to Mary, had numbered five, all similarly marked with a tattoo. But could the connection between past and present take him any further? The original members certainly committed no serious crimes – the only injury was to one of their own, and by her own hand. Something wasn't right.

He stubbed out his cigarette, got up from his desk and made his way down the corridor. The Incident Room was in darkness. He switched on the lights and waited briefly for the fluorescent tubes to flicker into life. Scanning the dozens of photos on the two boards, he found what he was looking for – the landscape shot of Tom Hardy's body. It had been positioned on a slight rise a few yards from the ninth hole, with the head on the downward slope, at an angle of 45 degrees to the neck. As previously established, the victim had been laid out that way on purpose, but now it struck Frost. It was another inverted 5. He unpinned the photo and made his way back to his office, just as the phone began ringing, reverberating eerily through the empty corridor. Mary? He increased his pace to almost a jog or the best approximation he could manage.

'Hello?'

It was Desk Sergeant Johnny Johnson – he had Sue Clarke on the line.

'Sue, love, everything all right?' Where were his cigarettes, or was he out of them again?

'I just wanted to apologize.'

'It's fine,' he said, without the slightest idea of what she meant.

'And tear up that letter. I know you've not read it . . . It was stupid. You've enough on your plate, what with . . . Shit. Wait a sec. The bath's about to overflow.'

He poured another measure of Black Label into his coffee mug. His mind, stirred by the thought of Sue and her bath, began to wander.

'Sorry, where were we?' she said.

'Sue, I've been trying all week to catch up with you . . .' It was a lie. Since Tuesday's awkward showdown he'd barely given his personal feelings for Clarke a second thought, until the image of her curvaceous naked body about to slip beneath the suds floated by.

'I'm glad. I know you're in a difficult position. Come round for a chat maybe?'

'Yes, of course, good idea,' he said. A 'chat' was the last thing on his mind, but one thing could lead to another. Mary was most likely still at her mother's; she'd expressed no intention of returning home any time soon. Could he? How big a stinker would that make him? 'It's getting late, though, and I've one more call to make. It's important,' he said reluctantly, having just noticed the underlined 'Ellis' on his blotter from the previous day.

'OK. Yes, maybe it is a bit late. I need an early night too.'

He hung up and rifled through the Ellis file to find her mother's telephone number. He unearthed his cigarettes and lit a Rothmans.

'Mrs Ellis? Good evening. It's Detective Sergeant Frost here. I do apologize for the lateness of the hour.'

'Mr Frost, I've been trying to reach you . . .'

'I'm terribly sorry about that article in the *Echo*. It's the press, they'll do anything for a story – totally unscrupulous . . .'

'I quite understand. It wasn't me who complained. My late husband's brother, Michael Hartley-Jones, was furious, and he thinks because he knows your station chief . . . Anyway . . .' the woman stuttered, 'I completely understand that it's not your fault. No, I called about something else . . .'

'Oh, really?' Frost was relieved and intrigued. 'What might that be?'

'I saw a police statement on the television – a lad was found dead on the golf course yesterday.'

'Yes. Tom Hardy.'

'Yes, poor Tom. I'm not sure whether it's relevant, but I thought you should know that Sam was going out with Tom.'

'I'm sorry . . . "going out with"?'

'You know, dating.'

'They were boyfriend and girlfriend?'

'Yes.'

Well, well, thought Frost, that's an unexpected piece of information.

Friday (1)

'The heart is missing,' the pathologist said, tapping the metal tray conclusively with a scalpel.

'Are you sure?' Frost said, as Clarke shuffled uncomfortably next to him. 'Couldn't the rats have eaten it?'

'Sergeant, the heart is one of the larger of the organs – I wouldn't miss it if it was here. The liver and kidneys are here in part, here and here' – Drysdale poked the half-eaten organs again – 'and are widely considered more edible, whether by rodents or others.'

Drysdale was right of course, Frost realized. The heart had probably never been among the organs in the plastic bag in the first place.

The clothes and body parts discovered at Denton Municipal Tip had been confirmed as belonging to Tom Hardy.

'Everything is pointing towards a ritual killing, as you yourself wisely suspected, Doc.' Frost was flattering Drysdale, biding his time before bringing up what really interested him. 'Anything useful on the clothes?'

'As a matter of fact, yes.' Drysdale pulled two further trays from beneath the counter. Inside each were bagged items of clothing.

'Though they were blood-soaked, I am certain the victim was not wearing the clothes when he was killed. The markings would indicate the clothing was used to "mop up".'

Frost sensed Clarke wincing; she had his sympathy there. There was a chilling absence of emotion in the jaded pathologist's delivery which Frost had long ago got used to.

'I'll trust your opinion on that, Doc. Now, if I may—'

'Not so fast, Sergeant. I've not finished.' Drysdale reached over for a microscope. 'These are the socks.'

'Socks?' Clarke asked. 'Were there socks? Forensics didn't mention that.'

'The socks were there, along with the underpants. If Harding and his Forensics chums took the trouble to look—'

'We were intent on getting the garments back here to confirm the blood type,' Clarke said defensively.

Drysdale barely acknowledged her. 'I took the liberty of examining the socks. I thought they might be significant, given there was no footwear found initially on the corpse, although the shoes have since been found. I thought perhaps a closer look at the socks might give some indication of where the victim last walked.'

Frost was getting impatient – who gave a monkey's about socks? – he wanted to examine Samantha Ellis's body for evidence of a tattoo. 'Very good, Doc – you should consider branching out into Forensics. God knows, they need the help. Been bugger-all use so far with this poor sod.'

Drysdale was hunched over the work surface, fiddling with the microscope. 'Come here, take a look at this.' He waved them over.

Frost bent before the instrument. Drysdale began to explain the mechanism but didn't get far.

'I know, I know how these things work,' Frost insisted. He screwed up his face and twiddled the knob back and forth wildly until he had the slide in focus. He squinted for several seconds at the object on the glass. 'A pubic hair?' he said.

'A wool tuft,' Drysdale replied airily.

'Call it what you like, Doc, a pube's a pube where I come from – although not usually in this colour . . .' Frost adjusted the focus further. 'Blue?'

'Indeed. Ice-blue. I would say an Axminster.'

Frost looked up.

'A carpet, recently laid,' Drysdale added, lest there be any doubt.

'Very good!' Frost clapped the grey-skinned pathologist on the back. 'Maybe the boy was killed indoors after all. This could turn out to be a key piece of evidence. Well done! Now then, Samantha Ellis – is she still here?'

'Er, yes,' Drysdale said, clearly surprised by the sudden jump. 'Why?'

'There's something I'd like to check up on.'

Drysdale led them down the corridor and into the lab morgue itself.

'You're in luck – this one goes today,' he said, releasing the cold-storage lock and sliding out the drawer containing the corpse. He turned back the sheet to reveal the unearthly bluish face.

'That's her,' Frost said, 'but I want the other end.' Unceremoniously he flung the sheet off the lower half of the body and peered at the inner thighs. 'The trouble with stiffs,' he said, parting the legs, 'is that they tend to be stiff.'

'Jack, what are you doing?' Clarke cried in alarm.

'It's the cold storage that makes the body stiffen,' Drysdale said. 'May I ask what you hope to achieve by manhandling the body like this?'

'According to your assistant's report, there was a distinguishing mark on the inner thigh, possibly a birthmark, or possibly something else.' Frost looked across to Drysdale for help.

Drysdale raised an eyebrow. 'I never thought you read them, to be totally honest.'

'Of course I . . . Wait a minute – there we go. Doc, magnifying glass?'

Drysdale passed him a glass from his overall pocket.

Halfway down the left thigh was a brown mark the size and colour of a well-used two-penny piece. To the naked eye it looked like a large, crescent-shaped birthmark, but under close scrutiny it did appear to be a crude tattoo – a sickle with a line perpendicular to the handle: the number 5.

'Here, have a look.' Frost passed the glass over to Clarke. 'I'd hate you to think I was some sort of pervert.'

She rolled her eyes towards the ceiling before scrutinizing the mark. 'I agree, it's some form of tattoo. But what does it mean?'

Frost stepped back from the corpse. The half-light of the morgue gave his tired features a somewhat sinister appearance. 'I think it means she belonged to a secret society, one which first existed here in Denton twenty years ago, and was formed by disaffected schoolgirls.' He fiddled nervously with his cigarette packet; the nicotine jitters always got to him in here. 'Back then, St Mary's School for Girls had a reputation for strict discipline verging on brutality. This was in the sixties when most girls boarded. One end of term, five of them, all aged about fifteen or sixteen, arranged a tryst with some boys from Denton Comprehensive, in the sports pavilion in St Mary's grounds. The boys arrived late one night, after "lights out", loaded with booze and cigarettes.'

Clarke was watching him carefully, hanging on every word.

'This was all well and good to begin with but, while rebellious, these were well-brought-up girls at heart, so when they didn't put out, the lads became fractious and disgruntled, as well they might . . .' Frost paused in thought, as though imagining himself on the scene.

'Well?' Clarke prompted.

'A tussle ensued. They'd used candles to light the pavilion and in the upset a curtain caught fire. They were spotted from the main school building by a matron doing the rounds. The girls were all caught but the boys, of course, got away . . .'

Drysdale pulled the sheet over the body and slid it back into the deep freeze.

'The punishment delivered by the then headmistress was ingeniously cruel,' Frost continued. 'They were, of course, initially caned. Expulsion should naturally have been their punishment, but they were allowed to remain at the school. However, they were starved of education, the ultimate humiliation for intelligent girls like that.'

'How do you mean?' Drysdale asked. He and Clarke were both intrigued by Frost's story.

'The girls were given a choice: either be expelled and their disgrace laid bare for all to see, or accept demotion within the school. They would be removed from the top class where they all sat, to the lowest set where they'd learn nothing. The parents would be baffled by their lack of exam success but would never know the reason, unless the girls revealed their scandalous behaviour.'

'But surely they could swot up in their own time?' said Clarke.

'Yes,' added Drysdale. 'If they were clever enough they could catch up at home.'

'Ah, if they *went* home – but these girls were boarders, remember. All of their free time was strictly supervised. Most of it from then on was spent pointlessly copying out pages from the *Encyclopaedia Britannica*. A further edge to their punishment.' He paused. 'The girls opted unanimously for demotion. They came from respectable backgrounds and couldn't face the humiliation and the shame it would bring to their parents.'

Clarke shook her head in dismay. 'So what happened to them?'

Frost rubbed his eyes before continuing. Clarke and Drysdale could have no idea of the personal resonance this tale had for him. 'They formed a pact to exact a double revenge: on the institution that had inflicted this punishment on them – the Catholic Church – and on those who had got them caught – the boys. They called themselves the School of the Five Bells.'

'Sounds like a pop group.'

'You've got the racket part right – though only metaphorically. The Five Bells allude to the five church bells in St Jude's. They used to ring them during air raids in the war – not that Denton was ever bombed. My mother told me they all thought the Luftwaffe had its eye on the old cotton mill . . . Anyway I digress. The ringing of the bells was a muster call of sorts, and being five girls—'

'And let me guess,' Clarke leaped in eagerly. 'The tattoo – the "5" shape – is a sign of membership.'

'Exactly.'

'How do you know all this?' she asked, flummoxed.

'Let's just say, I've been making enquiries.'

'And what exactly did this School of the Five Bells get up to? Are we seriously talking witchcraft?'

'No . . . not in the same league by any stretch, if indeed witchcraft is behind the death of Tom Hardy.' Frost sighed. 'No, the Five Bells was no more than some silly schoolgirl prank that went wrong, ending in the pointless suicide of one of the girls, and if Samantha really did top herself, then that's where any similarity ends.'

'So, first things first – what happened to you last night? Thought you were coming over?' Clarke asked Frost on the way out of the lab to the car. Though she already knew from the smell of him and the fact that he'd slept all the way from the station to the lab that he'd spent the night at Eagle Lane.

'Must have dozed off,' Frost said quietly. 'Besides, you said yourself, it was late . . .'

Clarke positioned herself between him and the passenger door of the Escort.

'Look, Jack, I don't quite know how to say this . . . so I might as well just come out and say it. The other night I met someone. A man.'

Clarke registered the resigned look in Frost's tired eyes as he took in what she'd said. She instantly regretted it.

'Oh,' he said simply. He moved forward to get into the car and she stepped aside with a sigh, both disappointed and sad.

'I thought you should know,' she added.

'About time you met someone your own age.' He smiled wanly.

Clarke had been playing this scene in her mind ever since the night with Danny but it was not going how she'd imagined. His polite acceptance, encouragement even, was infuriating.

She started the car and pulled away with a jolt. Frost was thrown forward, losing his cigarette in the process. He let out a stream of expletives.

'Look, if you don't like my driving, wear a bloody seat belt! Better still, drive your bloody self.'

He ignored her outburst. 'The boy, Tom Hardy. He was killed by someone he knew, don't you think?'

Mind always on the job, she thought sadly. It's almost as if he's incapable of dealing with anything else. She glanced across at him, unshaven and ragged, chucking the bent cigarette out of the car window and fishing for a new one. She swallowed hard. Had her admission of a new lover driven a wedge between the private and the professional? Even if he cared, he was unlikely to let on, for now at least.

'I suppose,' she replied sullenly.

'To pad about in your socks in someone else's home suggests familiarity.'

'Makes sense.' Though Frost's train of thought didn't. Or she felt unable at times to follow it – when the pathologist had tried to engage Frost in the lab he'd been quick to move on to the business of examining tattoos on dead thighs. She indicated to pull out on to the Rimmington Road and head back to Denton.

'It reminds me of something,' Frost said. 'From the time we first started dating, Mary's parents would always make me take my shoes off before I was allowed in the house. It's a house-proud middle-class thing; everyone has to take their shoes off to avoid messing up the Wilton . . .'

'Axminster.'

'Whatever. The carpet.'

'Clutching at straws a bit, aren't we?'

'You're probably right. I only thought of it because I was round there the other evening . . . Anyway, that's irrelevant now. Let's hope the bus driver remembers Tom Hardy getting off the bus. What's the time – tennish? Waters should have cracked that by now.'

'Look, Jack, one thing at a time, OK? The girl's tattoo – are you saying Samantha Ellis is, was, practising witchcraft?'

'It's a stretch of the imagination to think a pretty little thing like that was a bona fide witch, I'll grant you . . . But if Tom Hardy was killed in, let's say, a sacrificial fashion, it makes you wonder. I spoke to the Ellis girl's mother last night. Tom and Samantha were dating.'

'Jesus!' Clarke looked at Frost in amazement. 'You think their deaths are linked? Or is it just coincidence?'

'The boy was killed, we now think, on the Friday. The girl died on the Saturday. It's possible she could have killed her boyfriend in some sadistic frenzy and then thrown herself off the train in remorse, but I think it unlikely. There's more to it. There are others involved, wouldn't you agree?' He looked across at her, a keenness to discover the truth enlivening his weary eyes.

'And hence the idea of the School of the Five Bells?'

'Yes, but the original Five Bells didn't do much except tattoo themselves; and rather poorly at that. The only harm was to themselves. One hanged herself after her mother caught her making a second tattoo with a pair of compasses and school ink. No, this is in a different league altogether.' Frost lit another cigarette. He appeared to be having difficulty believing the conclusions his thoughts were taking him towards. 'The boy's heart,' he continued, looking distractedly out of the car window, 'the removal of it has to be part of some sort of ritual; pagan or Wiccan or Satanist – I'm not sure of the differences. But the motivation of the original Five Bells was revenge . . .' He paused.

Clarke glanced at him expectantly.

'Revenge,' he said to himself again. 'Hardy was Ellis's boyfriend. Maybe he'd betrayed her in some way and "the gang" killed him as a result; it's all I can think of. The girl was pregnant, too . . .'

Clarke now realized why Frost was so preoccupied; there had to be a connection.

'So,' she pondered, 'if we're dealing with witches or occultists, and we're assuming Samantha Ellis was part of a group that murdered Tom Hardy, why would she end up dead herself?'

'Who knows. Guilt?'

'We need to know who else was in the gang. Not easy when all those we think so far are connected with it are dead. Unless there's a connection with the original Five Bells?'

'I have a file here that lists the members.' Frost opened a foolscap wallet and began fiddling with loose sheets of paper. 'None of the names are familiar, apart from one. Simpson, Parke, Lewis . . . not much use really.'

'Which one is familiar? Why?'

'Simpson . . . I . . . relative. Er . . . friend of a relative.'

Clarke swung into Eagle Lane car park at speed. The entrance was partly obstructed by a white Ford Transit bearing the legend *Baskin Construction & Co.* Two bare-chested men were already repairing the car-park wall hit yesterday by the skip lorry. Had Frost been paying attention to Clarke he would have noticed a flicker of shock cross her face as she recognized the fair-haired one, with the sunburnt shoulders.

Oblivious, he lit another cigarette. 'I wonder,' he said, 'where the rest of the Five Bells are now.'

Clarke frowned. Her mind was elsewhere. Here was the last place she'd expected Danny to turn up. He'd told her he was a farm labourer.

'OK?' Frost said, patting her thigh.

The intimacy took her by surprise. It was the most physical contact there'd been between them in over a week. She tried to drag herself back to the business in hand. 'So, what now then?'

'We need to find out two things. One, where exactly Tom Hardy was heading on Friday evening, and secondly, who Samantha's close friends were, which should lead us to the other four member of the Five Bells. And friend or not, the one we need most is Tom Hardy's sister, Emily. She's the key.'

'Let's hope she's alive, then,' Clarke said, rooting around in her handbag for her sunglasses.

Friday (2)

The trouble with Frost, thought Simms as Waters accelerated down King Street, was that although he was undoubtedly a great copper, his lack of organizational skills left everyone else floundering. Take this morning, for example, when they got the call from the pawnbroker's. Simms was happy to go – after all, he'd been working on the robberies anyway – but why lumber him with Waters? Simms liked the bloke, no question, although he didn't like the feelings of inadequacy he provoked, being that much more senior and sharp with it. But Frost had shot off with Clarke and he didn't want Waters left milling around under Mullett's gaze, especially as Kim Myles had taken a shine to the big man. That rattled Simms too. It seemed everyone was getting some action apart from him . . .

'Here?' Waters nudged him. 'Wilson's Pawnbrokers?'

'Yep,' he confirmed, glancing across at the shop front. 'Right shifty little sod, this bloke is. I'm amazed he came forward.'

A bell chimed as they entered the dusty shop rammed full

of bric-a-brac. At the back of the store, behind an enormous counter, sat a creased old man in waistcoat and green visor.

'Wotcha, Sid,' Simms called.

'Very prompt of you, young man,' Wilson replied. 'My, look at you! Straight out of *The Sweeney*.' Simms was growing increasingly tired of this joke. Why was it only him, out of the whole plainclothes division, who was constantly ribbed for his attire? He and Wilson knew each other well from his time on the beat.

'Unlike you to be forthcoming with stolen goods?'

'That ain't fair. I have to take items on good faith. Can't go suspecting every Tom, Dick and Harry, can I? I would never do any business. But come on, I ain't stupid. When a bunch of kids come in 'ere with ten grand's worth of jewellery, I knows something's amiss.'

'All right, all right,' Simms said in a placatory tone.

''Ere, who's yer chum?' Wilson said, having suddenly noticed Waters, who was nosing around some ancient taxidermy at the front of the store.

'Him? Drafted in from East London. A specialist in thieving swindlers like you. You'd better watch out.'

'Bit of respect. I'm due it. I'll tell Mr Frost.'

'Calm down. What exactly did they try to pawn?' Simms took out his notebook.

'Necklaces – two of 'em – one diamond and one pearl.' Wilson opened his tobacco tin and with shaky hands began to fashion a roll-up. 'Now, if it were just the pearls I might have let it go; he said they were 'is nan's, but the styles were poles apart. I've got a nose for this sort of thing. Knew he was a wrong 'un . . .'

'OK, these kids – description?'

'Two of them, there were; hooded tracksuits and sunglasses. Only got a proper butcher's at one. 'E was wearing – whatchercall'em – mirror glasses. I knew there was something fishy about it. I mean, it's sunny as you like outside, but in 'ere it ain't quite the same.'

'Certainly isn't,' Simms replied, eyeing a sickly-looking spider plant on the counter. 'This lad, anything else you can tell me?'

'Average height – about five nine, five ten, cropped hair. Crooked hooter.'

'Crooked or broken?'

'Like this.' Wilson pushed his nose to the left.

'Wait a minute – how old do you reckon he is?'

'Dunno. Seventeen, eighteen?'

'Hardly a kid, then.'

'When you're as old as me they're all babies.'

'What gives?' said Waters, sidling up.

'Martin bloody Wakely is what,' replied Simms.

Chris Everett peered through the plate-glass window of the estate agent's. Fooling about outside the supermarket on the other side of the High Street were three kids on BMX bikes. Yesterday evening down the station he had drawn a blank; he'd not identified any of the juvenile delinquents who'd attacked him from the photos he was forced to wade through. Though of course *had* he recognized anyone he wouldn't have said. Fortunately, neither the jeweller nor the newsagent had come up with anyone either, but Everett couldn't help but feel the detective had expected more from him – perhaps because he had also seen the attack?

Was he being paranoid or were those kids watching him? Wait a minute, were they the same three that had attacked him? They suddenly looked familiar. Or had he just seen them around a few times? Come to think of it, he'd definitely seen some very similar-looking kids yesterday, hanging around near his house.

The thought hovered sickeningly at the back of his mind. Blackmail. They'd been hanging around outside for most of the morning. When the mugging was mentioned in the paper his name and occupation were printed, so it was easy enough for them to find out where he worked, where he lived. They weren't stupid – a man carrying thousands of pounds' worth of jewellery around in a briefcase was clearly up to no good.

Suddenly the kids made off in haste; Everett nudged the Lettings board aside and saw the reason – a bobby on the beat. Two smaller children on bikes loitering by the rack of super-market trolleys took off after the others.

'Chris, there's a Mr Mullett on the phone for you.'

It was the policeman whose house he'd valued. Not for the first time, he thought about cutting his losses and getting on a plane to Australia; holing up with his brother until things blew over. Although such action would throw Fiona into turmoil and probably make her suspicious, not to mention the effect it would have on the children, he might soon have no other option. The scales were tipping: he'd taken a risk too many.

Friday (3)

Frost was famished; he couldn't remember the last time he'd eaten. Was it yesterday lunchtime at Billy's Café? He'd not had a thing this morning before he'd left the station for the lab. Perhaps a sense of progress with his caseload had made his appetite resurface with a vengeance. They had certainly made some headway; there were leads to follow up . . . and yes, if he was honest with himself, he couldn't deny a sense of relief on learning that Sue Clarke had got herself a boyfriend. At first he'd felt put out by her confession, but the feeling was fleeting. It was telling that he suddenly felt better disposed towards her than he had done for weeks, and as a result they were on their way out to get some early lunch. Maybe a liquid lunch.

'Jack, wait a sec,' Desk Sergeant Bill Wells called after him as he reached the front door. 'You've got some visitors.' He nodded towards the bench in reception. Frost instantly recognized the two scruffy children from the gypsy camp. He wondered how he hadn't noticed them.

Just then, Simms burst through the revolving door, almost

colliding with Clarke. 'Guv, we've had a breakthrough on the burglaries.'

'Nothing all week and then bang – like buses.' Frost swung round. 'Kids, I'll be with you in a sec. Derek, slowly now, what have you got?'

'Sid Wilson, the pawnbroker, just gave a description of the kid offloading the gems; it was Martin Wakely.'

'Martin Wakely? Bit big to be charging around on a BMX, isn't he? I remember when his mum was up the spout with him. I was in uniform. I nabbed her shoplifting in Bejam's when she was eight months gone. From the size of the bulge she had, you'd have thought she was pregnant with an elephant.'

'He does have a younger brother, Gary. I just checked with Records. He's fourteen.'

'Has he? Interesting.' This was starting to make sense; kids scooting around on bikes like little Dick Turpins, nabbing stuff and passing it to big brother to offload. 'Did Sid take any gear off Wakely senior?'

'Nope, he was too suspicious. Called us instead.'

'Shame, Sid developing a conscience all of a sudden at his time of life. If we actually had an item we could nail the little bleeder and pinpoint where it had been nabbed. What exactly did Sid say? Nothing to get him spooked, I hope; that's all we need, him heading for the hills and the kids all going to ground.'

'He asked Wakely how he'd come by such quality necklaces. He said he'd inherited them from his nan or something. Sid told him they were too valuable for him personally, and suggested he try Sparklers in Merchant Street . . .'

'Where they probably came from in the first place. What did Wakely say to that?'

'Just shrugged and left.'

'You'd best go wheel him in, then. Don't go alone; our Martin's a little bit tasty with his fists and has a short fuse. Take John. You two make such a lovely couple.' Whilst they'd been talking,

Waters had entered the building. He stood placidly behind Simms, although his black eye still looked nasty.

'Oh and Simms, you haven't got a couple of quid, have you?' Frost asked.

'Brassic, sorry.' Simms patted himself up and down.

'Here.' Clarke pulled her purse out of her shoulder bag. 'How much do you want?'

'A pair of ones.'

Clarke handed him two pound notes.

'Now,' Frost said, bending down to the two kids, who had sat quietly on the bench in the lobby throughout the exchange with Simms. 'What have you two found out?'

'We did what you asked, Mr Frost.' It was the boy who spoke first. 'We went to the town centre and looked around for bigger kids on them smart new bikes – BMXs – and followed them.'

'Yes, it was easy,' the girl added, ''cos most kids were in school apart from them and us!' She giggled.

'They stuck mainly to Market Square, bumping up and down the kerb, then headed off down Foundling Street when it got dark. We didn't cross the canal.' He looked anxiously at Frost.

'No, the houses are scary over there.' The girl pulled a face. 'Bad people.'

'The Southern Housing Estate?' Frost offered.

'Yeah,' the boy said sullenly, but quickly brightened up again. 'Then this morning, we found them again at Market Square.'

'They spoke to us,' the girl chipped in.

'Really? What did they say?'

'They wanted to know why we weren't in school,' the girl said.

'Yeah, they thought we were pretty cool.'

'I'm also wondering why you're not in school,' Clarke added drily. Frost had forgotten she was there.

'How old do you reckon they were?' he asked.

'Hard to say.' The boy frowned. 'Bit older than me . . . Fifteen?'

'They sped off really fast when the policeman came up to them this morning while they were waiting for the man in the house shop,' the girl said excitedly.

'House shop? Estate agent, you mean?' Frost asked.

'Yes. We were hanging about on the other side of the High Street while they waited for the man to come out.'

Frost stood up straight, his back creaking from an uncomfortable night slumped on his desk, and addressed Clarke, 'Hmm . . . Bit young to be thinking about getting on the property ladder.'

'Don't know,' Clarke said. 'Maybe they've enough for a deposit already with their ill-gotten gains?' He could tell from her face that she disapproved of his unconventional use of informants.

'Estate agent. Estate agent,' Frost repeated. 'Wasn't there one in here the other day? Where's Simms? Blast, he's just left. Right . . .'

'Hey, what about us?' The girl tugged on his trousers. 'We were here at twelve o'clock, like you asked.'

'Yes, of course. Well done.' He handed them each a pound note.

'Now, I don't think Mr Frost needs your help any more,' Clarke cut in. 'Stay out of town for a while. These boys might seem fun but they're very, very dangerous.'

Frost noticed both children's faces light up at the thought they'd been courting danger. He realized with hindsight that Clarke was right: it had been irresponsible of him, especially if those BMX kids had anything to do with the Wakelys.

'Now off you both scoot,' Clarke said, 'and whatever you do, don't tell anyone you've been here. Got it?'

They both nodded and ran excitedly towards the door clutching the pound notes. Frost made off down the corridor to look for Simms, already forgetting that he'd only just recalled sending him to look for the Wakelys.

'Jack, that was dumb.' Clarke was at his side. 'What if those animals knew you were using the kids and found out they'd been grassing?'

'Yes, yes, but it's fine, no harm done. And even if they found out, the gypsies will be off in a week or so.' Frost paused to hold the door open. 'Besides, what have they told us other than the kids on bikes were doing a little house-hunting?'

Clarke entered the CID office. 'That's not the point; it's irresponsible,' she said brusquely.

'No.' He looked at her sternly. 'The point is, why would a bunch of BMX bandits be interested in an estate agent – possibly one they've already mugged, one who could ID them?'

Superintendent Mullett placed the phone back in its cradle. It was the second time today he had spoken to the estate agent. The regional manager no less, a chap named Everett. A decent sort, well educated. Everett had valued the Mulletts' detached four-bedroom house in Wessex Crescent at £27,000, a respectable amount; though, with the recession dragging on, how long it would take to shift the place was anyone's guess. Mrs M would have to bide her time if she wanted a Victorian townhouse in Rimmington.

He sighed and spread the *Telegraph* out on his desk. Economic woes were prominent across the spread of the broadsheet. If only those damn Argentines would behave, the Iron Lady would have more time to focus on Blighty. Peruvian peace-plan? Whatever next, he tutted. What had Peru ever done for Britain apart from sending a talking bear in wellington boots?

Thankfully, Mullett still had his sanctuary that was un-affected by the nation's dreadful state, and it was tee-off at three. The new club would open as planned this afternoon in spite of Wednesday's awful business.

'Stanley.'

'Assistant Chief Constable.' Mullett stood up abruptly. How

the devil had he crept in here? He'd be having words with Miss Smith. 'Just having a five-minute catch-up on the action in the South Atlantic. The Argies have only gone and sunk one of ours.'

'Really?' Winslow sniffed. 'Your secretary said you were on the phone to your estate agent.' The ACC flopped into the guest chair, rubbing his jaw.

'Teeth still playing up, sir?' Mullett asked, hoping they were, and would thus put him off his game. They were both on the green this afternoon.

He nodded. 'Dashed fellow didn't tell me it would be this sore. Not much point having them out if one still gets this much gip.'

'I suspect the gums are bruised.'

'Perhaps so. On the subject of bruising, I saw the coloured chap in the corridor. Looks as though he's been in the wars.'

Mullett got up and fidgeted nervously about the office, twiddling with the blinds and adjusting the desk fan. 'I can't say that I've noticed,' he lied.

'Not noticed? Are you blind, man? He's sporting a shiner that Muhammad Ali would be proud of.'

'I think you exaggerate, Nigel.'

'So you have seen it?'

'Yes, now I think of it, yes.' He squirmed. 'As I said, I have placed Waters in Frost's care. I think there's a lot going on. They've barely been in the office.'

'Frost? Waters was on his way out with the young, moon-faced chappie?'

'Derek Simms.' Mullett sighed.

'Yes. Promoted recently to CID, wasn't he? Bit green, I would say. Frost is far more suitable. Big chap, that Waters. I don't remember him being that big when we met at the Ethnic Liaison Meeting in March. One would think he'd be able to look after himself. Find out what's going on; I don't want an incident to develop. This isn't Brixton. If this happened at our own hands, I want it nipped in the bud. Do I make myself clear?'

'Crystal.' Mullett knew he should have acted sooner, but finding the body on the course had distracted him.

'Right.' The bald, bespectacled ACC propelled himself out of the chair. 'I'm off to meet a chum for a spot of lunch in that pub down the road, the Eagle. Any good?'

A poisonous rathole, Mullett thought, but said, 'Nice food. Try the pickled eggs. I hear they're rather good.'

'Splendid. See you later?' Mullett showed him to the door. 'Someone made rather a mess of the car-park wall, what?'

'Yes, when the skip was collected.'

'Builders not finished the repairs yet?'

'I fear the new clubhouse may have taken priority.' Mullett smiled, his feelings on the matter mixed.

'Ah yes, same chaps. Reputable, by all accounts.' And with that he was gone.

Mullett closed the door behind him, but remained clutching the door handle, head bowed. He sighed and rubbed his temples wearily before opening the door again. 'Get me Frost. Now!' he hissed at Miss Smith.

All he'd wanted was for Frost to look after Waters for a week or so, show him the ropes, exchange ideas – was that really too much to ask? Heavens, he thought, Frost makes do with that useless great oaf Arthur Hanlon ninety per cent of the time, whereas this chap might actually have something to bring to the party. But no, good ol' maverick Jack Frost fobs our guest off back on to Simms and the fellow is left meandering around Eagle Lane half beaten to death.

Waters waited for Simms in his car, once again fully operational, in Denton Comprehensive School's staff car park. The new tyres had certainly set him back a few quid. He was more annoyed about that than anything else.

Simms burst through the swing doors, almost sending a first-year flying. He'd been visiting a dinner lady with access to the register for Denton's Girl Guide population; though why they needed it now was a mystery – there had been no Guide camps last weekend in Denton Woods – but Frost had insisted Simms get it.

'Right, let's go,' he said, stuffing folded sheets of A5 paper into the top of his leather jacket.

Waters would have liked to see the list, but felt obliged to roll with his young hot-headed colleague who clearly had his mind set on the Southern Housing Estate.

'Take a left here,' Simms said, 'then hoof it down to the next set of lights.'

Waters floored the accelerator. The sooner they nailed this second-rate thug that everyone appeared to be frightened of, the sooner they could tackle the Hardy case which seemed to be falling into place.

His focus on the task in hand soon wavered, however. He couldn't help but notice the number of pretty girls brought out of hibernation by the fine weather. He caught sight of two in short skirts and his thoughts drifted to Kim Myles.

'So you and the pocket Venus? What's the story?' Simms said, as if reading his mind.

'No story, man, just a cute girl. Just friends.' He smiled innocently, last night's bedroom acrobatics flashing through his memory.

'She is cute. That much is true . . . that much is true,' Simms mused. 'Anyway, open up your ears, son, and get a load of this.' He rammed in a TDK excitedly.

'What's this?' Waters asked warily, though anything was better than that McCartney/Wonder duet which was monopolizing the airwaves – Jesus that was nauseating.

'*Hot Space*. I told you, the new Queen record. Not out till later this month, but a mate got me a bootleg. Terrific.'

'You really love these guys, don't you?'

'This is the real deal. Feel that pumping through.' Simms drummed his thighs enthusiastically.

'You can keep your pumping to yourself.'

'What do you mean? This is music for real men!'

'Call me old-fashioned, but a bloke in a leotard fronting a band called Queen doesn't exactly shout "real men" to me.' Waters couldn't help but smile at the boy's naivety.

'Hey, look, over there!' Simms pointed out of the window. 'Pull over. See that bovver boy in the knee-high red Doc Martens? See him? On the left by the bus stop.'

Waters clocked a fair-haired skinhead in his early twenties, red braces overlaying his check shirt, lolling against a bus shelter. Two old dears with pull-along trolleys stood at a respectful distance. Waters drew up around thirty yards from the bus stop and Simms leaped out of the car before he'd yanked up the handbrake.

'Oi, Wakely, you flat-nosed toe-rag! A word in your shell-like!'

The skinhead – who did indeed sport a bashed-in nose – jerked up as if woken from deep contemplation. In a flash he was pegging it across the road and into oncoming traffic. Cars from both directions screeched to a halt, horns blaring angrily. The gangly Simms tore off after him. Chasing people in the street was beginning to seem to Waters very much the Denton way, but, not to be outdone, he got out of the Vauxhall and hot-footed it after them.

Simms quickly caught up with the stocky thug, who proved not to be much of a sprinter. Wakely, realizing he was about to be collared, stopped abruptly and spun round. The burly youth ducked Simms's lunge and cracked the young DC a sharp one to the ribs, the force of which sent him sprawling to the concrete.

Wakely looked up and was surprised to see Waters bearing

down on him. He hesitated, clearly reckoning the six-foot-plus DS to be more of a match than his prone colleague.

'What tree did you just swing from, Sambo?' he sneered. Waters edged nearer. Squaring up, Wakely threw caution to the wind and took a swing. He missed, and in annoyance lashed out with an angry left, causing him to lose balance. Waters moved behind him and got him in an armlock. The skinhead thrashed around manically. Suddenly he tensed up; Simms had staggered to his feet and was wading in.

'Assault a police officer, would you?'

'You collided into—' Wakely began unwisely and was instantly winded by Simms. 'Didn't recognize . . . you . . . not in uniform . . .' he managed to squeeze out.

'Sorry? Didn't hear that, mate.' Simms continued to pummel away.

Waters spoke up. 'Ease off. He's done. Aren't you?' The cropped head nodded dejectedly. Waters loosened his grip.

Simms stepped back, looking ruffled. 'Right – down to the station, sunshine,' he gasped.

The three of them stood there, panting. Waters assumed Wakely was reaching for cigarettes inside his jacket and froze in disbelief when instead he pulled out a snub-nosed Smith & Wesson pistol.

'What the—' Simms exclaimed.

'No station for me, boys,' Wakely said with measured poise. The civilian audience that had gathered round now shuffled nervously back. 'Just ain't going back inside, sorry,' he said, raising his free hand in a warning.

'Unless you put that down sharpish, that's the one thing guaranteed from this situation,' Waters said calmly.

'What do you want?' snapped Wakely nervously. Waters perceived in the angry eyes a man weighing up the odds. His fate hung in the balance; the next few seconds were crucial.

*　　*　　*

Frost sighed. Martin Wakely. He needed this like a hole in the head. His mind was whirring: Ellis–Hardy–Hardy–Ellis. He didn't need distractions, not now. He slammed the desk in despair. Hopefully they would unearth the other members of the Five Bells sooner rather than later. He knew that not all five girls were from St Mary's – there must be another connection, he thought. But it would have to wait; in the meantime, he had this flamin' robbery case to sort out, and Martin Wakely making a tit of himself waving a hand gun around in the middle of Denton.

Frost knew he'd taken his eye off the ball with the robberies. As the week went on, they'd slipped down his list of priorities and he'd left them for others to deal with. He should have known better. With Hornrim Harry putting pressure on for an arrest it was inevitable that things would go pear-shaped, and now the whole of Eagle Lane was confusing the spate of daylight raids by kids on bikes with a raft of cat-burglaries, the only similarity being that jewels were involved. He shook his head in despair.

Simms stood waiting expectantly in the doorway of the office. Frost took a slurp of cold coffee and stubbed out his cigarette. It occurred to him that he'd still not eaten all day. Every so often hunger would overcome him in an urgent craving, but generally he was oblivious. He did miss Hanlon; the tubby detective always kept himself in close proximity to food, and Frost would certainly have had more than two cups of coffee and half a pack of Rothmans to survive on.

'I'll take over from here, Simms.' Frost could tell the lad was crestfallen, but it was too risky having Simms flare up in the interview room. Whatever he could get out of Wakely he'd achieve it far better without the feisty DC. 'You've done well, son, but we don't want Wakely antagonized unnecessarily. It was quite a pasting you gave him back there.' Simms started to protest, but quickly realized Frost wasn't budging and slunk off down the corridor, shaking his head in disbelief.

'Wait a minute!' Frost hollered after him. Simms spun round in hope. 'You get that list I asked for? The Girl Guides?'

Simms waved a scrap of paper at Frost as if the taxman had just asked for his last fiver.

'Good lad! Don't disappear!'

DS Waters appeared at Frost's side with two coffees. 'Perfect,' he said as he took one, 'and well done for talking down this guy with the gun. Had it been left in the hands of young Derek there . . . well, let's just say things might not have turned out so well.' He paused. 'Right, let's go and talk to Mr Wakely about his recent trip to the pawn shop. We can safely assume he was trying to offload the stuff the BMX bandits nabbed from Sparklers . . .'

'Not necessarily. These items weren't new.'

'Oh?' Frost was puzzled. 'Why'd he leg it, then? It's not a crime to try and pawn jewels. If they really were his nan's then this all seems a bit of an overreaction. No, he's clearly got a guilty conscience, of which we should take full advantage.' Frost took a sip of coffee. He narrowed his eyes and stared off into the middle distance; an idea was forming in his mind. 'Have we got any photos of stuff stolen by the cat burglar?'

'Yep. The Hartley-Joneses had some Polaroids.'

'Go grab them and bring them in here.' Frost opened the door to Interview Room 1 and gestured for the WPC to leave. As he stood back to hold the door open for her – she was cute, not one he'd seen before – his attention was caught by two uniform in the corridor. One was Miller. 'PC Miller?'

'Sergeant Frost?'

'I'd like to see you this afternoon. Something's come up.' The PC looked bemused. 'My office at four,' was all Frost said before stepping into the interview room, closely followed by Waters.

*   *   *

Simms sat disgruntled at his desk. Wakely was *his* collar; Frost couldn't just boot him off the case and sort it out instead. And he'd taken Waters in, too. OK, so the guy was on secondment and needed to see how things worked, but it wasn't fair that it had to be at his expense. He sighed and unfolded the list of Girl Guides.

'Afternoon, Derek.' DC Sue Clarke sat down opposite with a sandwich. He grunted and gave her a cursory glance. The list he had covered the two Girl Guide troops in the Denton area. Both columns were in alphabetical order, and included all members as of last September; 'guiding' activity apparently followed the school year. And there they all were before his eyes: *Samantha Ellis, Gail Burleigh, Sarah Ferguson, Emily Hardy.*

'Lying little mares,' he muttered. So the pair from Two Bridges knew Ellis after all. But so what? Had the Guides been camping last weekend it would have put all four girls in the possible area of Tom Hardy's murder – but they weren't, so that was that. Simms yawned.

Just then he spotted a message saying Denton Hi-Fi had called, regarding the girl's cassette – it was unintelligible. What had he been expecting – the Lord's Prayer read backwards? He realized he should tell Frost about Ferguson and Burleigh lying about knowing Ellis; he'd do it once he'd typed up this damned witness report Mullett wanted on Chris Everett.

Friday (4)

Considering the fracas he'd just been at the centre of, the youth in the airless interview room appeared uncannily fresh. Violence was no novelty to Martin Wakely and he was also no boy, as the aged pawnbroker had claimed to Waters and Simms, but a grown man, and a very nasty one at that. Wakely had been in and out of borstals across the country since the age of twelve. The rest was predictable – two years in the Scrubs for robbery, out for a breath of air, and then before he'd turned twenty-one back inside for six months for GBH.

'Martin, Martin, Martin,' Frost clucked as he pulled up a chair. 'You have been a very naughty boy.'

Wakely puffed angrily on a cigarette, not looking up. Waters stood to the side, observing quietly and holding a large white envelope.

'What have you got to say for yourself, eh?' Frost reached across and punched the fan in vain – it was already switched to maximum power.

'Think me ribs are bust,' he grunted. 'Wanker.'

'Manners, Martin. That'll be DC Simms. What he does in his spare time is no concern of yours.'

'Shagging me cousin, that's what,' came the surprise response. Frost glanced at Waters, who shrugged.

'Be that as it may, we can't have people waving shooters around on Friday morning in Denton, now can we? Not good for the tourist trade or the grannies waiting for the number 19 to Market Square.'

'Was defending meself.'

'From what?'

'From them that were chasing me.' Wakely looked up, fixing his pale-blue, steely eyes on Frost. 'They wasn't in uniform. Could have been anyone. Can't take a chance when there's a few that ain't too keen on you.'

'Do be brief, son! "A few that ain't too keen on you"? I'd be surprised if anyone was "keen" on you. Not even your poor old mum.'

'You leave my mum out of this.' Wakely stubbed out his cigarette.

'Are you seriously trying to tell me you didn't recognize DC Simms? His beat was your estate for years.'

'He looks different. Weren't one of your plainclothes mob when I went inside. And' – Wakely thumbed behind him – 'Sooty here spooked me a bit. Thought he was . . . well, to be honest, had no idea who he was . . .'

'Oi, oi!' Frost snapped. 'A bit of respect, if you please. He is Detective Sergeant Waters to you, and you're not fit to clean his boots. Remember that.' Frost leaned across the desk, meeting the young man's eyes. 'Now, let's get this straight before we go any further: as far as I'm concerned, you could claim you were pursued by Basil Brush armed with a tommy gun – but you are not, to my knowledge, part of either the ATB or Her Majesty's Forces, and therefore are not authorized to carry firearms, got it?'

Wakely looked at him sulkily.

'Right, enough of this nonsense, we haven't got all day. Sergeant, the photos, if you please.'

Waters handed Frost the white envelope, and Frost slipped out three small Polaroid photographs.

'Sid Wilson informs us you tried to pawn these items yesterday.' Wakely frowned. 'These snaps were taken for insurance purposes, and the pieces in the photos were stolen from a home in Denton last Saturday. Yes, Martin, you have been handling *stolen goods*.' Frost looked at his watch; it was close to two o'clock and he really needed some lunch. 'I'm going to give you an hour to think things through, all right? I've more important things to do than deal with a second-rate tea-leaf like you . . .'

'I didn't steal anything . . .'

Frost put his finger to his lips, saying, 'Think about it, Martin – think about what's happened. Assault on a police officer, and unlawful possession of a firearm? And then add to the mix that I'm very busy and not my usual tolerant self. Got it?'

Frost allowed the silence to hang in the stifling room. Only the hum of the fan accompanied Wakely's slow nod.

'Good lad. Right, John, let's leave him to stew for a bit.' Frost retrieved the photos and slipped them back in the envelope, not wanting to let Wakely scrutinize them for too long. He closed the door behind him, indicating to the WPC to wait outside the room. 'Bleedin' stuffy in there,' he said to Waters, who he suddenly realized was looking at him in amazement. 'What?'

'Those photos were the stuff that was nicked from Mullett's mates, the Hartley-Joneses. It's hardly likely to be the same gear.'

'So?'

Waters stared blankly and said nothing. Frost cuffed him round the shoulder playfully and headed off down the corridor to the main CID office. It wasn't that Waters disapproved of

Frost's tactics – photographic evidence of any crime waved under a villain's nose always brought reality crashing home – no, he was merely surprised at how swiftly Frost had reduced such an obviously tough man to a worried heap.

Waters followed Frost into the CID office, which fortunately was better ventilated than the interview room they'd just left. Situated at the back of the building, the office had large windows which were open, allowing a gentle breeze to nudge the blinds.

Simms and Clarke were both there, the former bearing down on an old typewriter and the latter hunched over the telephone, talking softly. Kim Myles had the day off – her first in ten days.

'We've bigger fish to fry,' Frost was saying. 'We'll let him sweat. Want to talk to me about buses? Did you find out where Tom Hardy got off?'

'Yep. I'm parched, though. What's the point of having a fridge if all you keep in it is sour milk?' Waters closed the door on the tiniest, dirtiest fridge he'd ever seen. He was thirsty as hell; after calling at the bus station first thing, he'd subsequently had to chase all over Denton in pursuit of the driver who had dropped Hardy off. It was worth it, though; the driver had remembered.

'There's no law stopping you filling it up,' Simms chimed in, clattering away on the Corona.

'Now girls,' Frost tutted, 'that'll do.' He pinned a Western National bus-route map lopsidedly on the cork board and stepped back to admire it.

'OK, John, so what did our bus driver have to say about Tom Hardy? Did he see him get on or off the bus?'

'He did. His story tallies with the offy man's description – a boy in a white tracksuit and a girl dressed in black. They got off on Bath Road, at Union Street.'

'Aha . . . Union Street . . .' Frost carefully circled the area, a cigarette tenaciously gripped between his teeth, the smoke doing its level best to blind him, curling round his sandy-brown hair. 'You'll see the stops become less frequent past here.' Frost jabbed at the map. 'Though there are other buses . . . and on that basis we could rule out anywhere running down Union Street – if he wanted anywhere near the canal he'd have got a 7 or a 13 . . .'

'Thirteen doesn't run down the Wells Road,' Simms pointed out.

'He could change at Market Square, smartarse. So . . .' Frost said, taking a step back. 'There's not much in the way of residential property on that stretch of the Bath Road – that leaves us with either Bath Hill or Forest View.'

'Forest View,' Waters pondered, remembering his first day at Denton – unbelievably, only last Monday. It felt like he'd been here an age. 'That's where the Hartley-Joneses' place is. Sam Ellis's aunt and uncle. She was feeding the cat.'

'Cat? Really?' Frost exclaimed. 'Of course, she missed feeding the cat on Sunday, that's how we know about the connection, although by that time there was no cat to feed . . . So, the house is empty, it's Friday night, no grown-ups around because they've already gone off for the weekend. Seems likely to me he was heading there for a bit of rumpo with his girlfriend, the late Miss Ellis . . .'

Waters could almost see Frost's mind whirring.

'Simms, find out if the Hardys have a pale-blue carpet – I doubt it, but we'd better rule them out. Then get over to Forest View, the Wotsit-Joneses, and find out whether it's them who've got the new blue carpet. My money's on the latter.'

'What, guv?' Simms grunted, looking up from the typewriter.

'A pale icy-blue one, to be exact. Probably quite new.' The boy was at a loss. 'A fibre from such a carpet was found on Tom Hardy's sock. Clarke found the clothes at the dump, remember?' Frost tapped the side of his head.

'What? I can't just go over there and ask that. Besides, they'll nag me about the cat . . .'

'Cat? Well, you can relieve them of their worry, then. Whiskers is in my car.' Frost tossed him his car keys. 'Been keeping me company. But let me have the Girl Guides list before you go.' Frost stood in front of Clarke and Simms's adjoining desks, holding his hand out expectantly.

'Here,' Simms said, passing him the paper. 'Meant to tell you . . .'

'Well, well!' Frost exclaimed loudly. 'Lying strumpets! Burleigh and Ferguson claimed not to know the Ellis girl. Why on earth would they think we'd not find out? Such a stupid lie.'

Clarke spun round on her chair, tying back her hair. 'Do you think these might be the girls we're after? Perhaps they were frightened.'

Waters turned to Clarke. 'You've not met them. These are cunning little minxes. They'd pull the wool over your eyes as soon as look at you.'

'Oh, and you're an expert on teenage girls brought up in the south of England, are you?' she snapped.

'Sue, for Christ's sake,' Simms interjected, 'the guy did interview both girls . . .'

Waters slumped down at the spare desk, wishing he'd kept his mouth shut. Clarke could be spiky as hell at times.

'Flamin' hell, the temperature goes up a couple of notches and everybody gets bad-tempered,' Frost said, looking as though he could do with a hose-down himself. 'Will everybody just sit and think for a second.' Frost raised both hands, exposing two damp underarms in his cheesecloth shirt. 'A group within a group, that's what we were looking for – and here we have a bunch on a plate. Now,' he said calmly, walking back to the map of Denton, 'we need to find out exactly where these young ladies were on Friday night.'

'Which ladies?' Simms asked. 'There are dozens here.'

'Use your loaf, son,' Frost said. 'Burleigh and Ferguson. My money's on Hardy and Ellis having been there too.'

'But Jack, we're still a girl short,' Clarke said. 'Aren't we looking for five, as in the School of Five Bells?'

'True – for now – but it's only a matter of time before we have the fifth one.'

Waters noticed a gleam in Frost's eye he'd not seen until now; they were finally making some headway with the case.

'Frost!' Mullett barked, as he and the Assistant Chief Constable strolled into the lobby. The superintendent immediately regretted bellowing; he wanted to express authority, but didn't want Winslow to think that he could only keep control by shouting.

Frost, who was heading outside with DC Clarke, turned to face the two men. Heavens, what a state! Was it really beyond him to shave and change his clothes once in a while? Mullett immediately wished he hadn't stopped him, but to his relief the Assistant Chief Constable showed no adverse reaction. Mind you, Winslow himself reeked. Mullett wondered how many he'd had at the Eagle over lunch.

'Afternoon, sir,' Frost said, addressing Winslow and ignoring Mullett. 'Off for a spot of golf? Glorious day for it. I'm thinking of taking it up myself if I ever—'

'The Assistant Chief Constable is not interested in your blatherings,' Mullett interjected. Insolent oaf, he thought to himself.

'Nonsense, Stanley,' Winslow slurred. 'You certainly should take it up. Stanley here will vouch for you at the new club, won't you, Stanley?'

Mullett could feel himself colour uncontrollably with anger. What on earth was the hairless loon playing at? He'd rather impale himself on a 9 iron than have Frost anywhere near the club.

'Would you, sir? That's very kind. I might need some help with the . . . er . . . attire. Perhaps a nice pink jersey like you're wearing . . . ?'

'Now, look here.' Mullett was losing patience and didn't care what Winslow thought. 'Where's DS Waters? I placed him in your charge.'

'He's off with Simms, sir,' Frost said. 'We've had a break-through on the Tom Hardy case. We believe we've traced his last-known movements.'

'I see.' Mullett would always remain cynical until he actually saw someone arrested. He found it difficult to allow his confidence to rise. He glanced at Clarke, standing just behind Frost. 'And where exactly are you two off to?'

'To find the boy's sister, Emily.'

Friday (5)

'Forest View, eh?'

Simms tutted, removing his sunglasses. It seemed ludicrous to imagine that anything so brutal as Tom Hardy's murder could occur in such a serene setting. Had a bizarre satanic ritual really taken place within this modern detached house in a leafy cul-de-sac?

Simms was unconvinced. 'I ask you though – how? How on earth could they get the body to the golf course? And why?' he implored.

'Man, I don't know,' Waters conceded as they got out of the car.

'These schoolgirls can't drive. What did they do, fly him there on a broomstick? No, he was killed in Denton Woods, he had to be, and then the body was moved to the golf course.' He popped the boot and regarded the cat-size package distastefully. 'Not sure how this is going to go down, either, especially the bin bag.' The original Jiffy bag was now wrapped in additional layers of black plastic to contain the smell.

He spun the package irreverently in his hands and then stopped abruptly, looking at the bin-liner wrapping. 'Hey, maybe they used some sort of liner? A giant polythene bag. It would keep the body clean and also the killer could drag it' – he sighed – 'for whatever perverted reason.' He rang the doorbell.

The supermarket manager led Frost towards the checkout till, behind which sat Mrs Ellis. At the morgue on Tuesday her beauty had been largely disguised by a mask of grief, but today she was strikingly attractive, with glossy red hair. Seeing her working at a checkout, Frost felt a pang of indignation; the spotty schoolgirls either side of her belonged here, but Mrs Ellis seemed to deserve better. As they drew nearer and she looked up, recognizing him, her face betrayed a rapid flurry of feelings. Frost was saddened that her initial look had been one of hope; maybe her little girl wasn't really dead, maybe it was all a bad dream? The look vanished as quickly as it had arrived.

Frost and Clarke stood politely to one side while she finished serving a customer. In an effort to find out more about the so-called Five Bells, Frost had decided to talk first to Mrs Ellis, who he was sure would be more candid and helpful than the slippery pair from Two Bridges, although he realized he needed to tread carefully so as not to upset her unduly. Mrs Ellis had said on the telephone that it was likely Samantha and Tom had spent Friday night together, although where they went she couldn't say. Frost now believed it was Forest View.

The store manager left the three of them in his office, shutting the door behind him as he left.

'I thought it best that I went back to work as soon as I could,' said Mrs Ellis, her unsteady hands struggling with a pack of cigarettes. 'Nothing can bring my little girl back now, so sitting around at home isn't going to help me.' She looked across the desk at Frost. Viewed closely, her eyes were lined beyond her years. 'Most people think I was mad to come back to work, what with Sam not even buried . . .' She ground to a halt.

'Besides,' the woman continued, 'the bleeders won't pay me if I don't turn up.'

Frost was perplexed; here was Mrs Ellis, a bereaved mother, worrying about the paltry earnings from a supermarket job, whereas her relatives, the Hartley-Joneses, were sitting comfortably in Denton's most exclusive neighbourhood. The Ellis family were clearly the poor relations. It seemed a shame, not to say peculiar, that Samantha's uncle couldn't have helped out in a practical way instead of just making a fuss about the *Echo* running the story about the suicide theory. Frost was yet to come across Mr Hartley-Jones, a man he'd dismissed as a mate of Mullett's who'd been burgled and who was, in short, a pain in the arse, but he felt a sudden keenness to pay him a visit.

'Mrs Ellis,' he said, 'I wonder if you could help us. It hadn't really occurred to us that your daughter could be linked to Tom Hardy's death, but we've uncovered certain information that suggests a connection.'

'Really? And what's that?'

'It's difficult to explain. As yet the lines aren't entirely clear. But we're very keen to know who Samantha's closest friends were, and the sort of things she and her friends got up to. For instance, we understand that she used to be a Girl Guide.'

'Yes, that's right. She was particularly close to a few of those girls – there's Sarah and Gail out at Two Bridges, and Emily, Tom's sister. She's known them all for years.'

'Mrs Ellis, when we interviewed those girls they denied knowing your daughter. Would you have any clue as to why that might be?'

The mother's pleasant face morphed into a haggard mask of anger. 'Because,' she said, trying to regain composure and hold back the tears, 'since my husband's death, those snooty bitches and their parents considered themselves too good for my girl.'

Frost looked at the woman intently. Class snobbery was something he met all the time and yet still found hard to comprehend. Considering himself 'classless' he struggled to understand those who acted from such motives. Burleigh was a lawyer; surely he must know the implications of lying to the police? Did he seriously consider his class prejudice to be more important than that?

'Fucking snobs,' sniffed Mrs Ellis.

'Anyone else?' Clarke asked. Frost had all but forgotten she was there. 'Anyone else she was close to?'

'Her cousin Nicola. She lives at Forest View.'

'Her *cousin*?' Frost exclaimed. 'What, the Hartley-Joneses have a daughter?'

Mrs Ellis nodded. Frost pulled out the list Simms had given him and ran his finger down it, although he knew he would have spotted a name like Hartley-Jones. 'Nicola not a Guide, then?'

'Well, she was.' Mrs Ellis peered over to see what Frost was looking at.

'It's a list of all the Girl Guides in Denton,' he said, passing it over.

'There she is – Parke. Nicola Parke. She's more often than not the ringleader. Very pretty and very full of herself. Captain of the hockey team at St Mary's, no less.'

'Parke?' Frost's mind raced. The name Parke had appeared in the Records file Mullett handed him yesterday. It was one of the names of the original Five Bells.

'Her mother's maiden name. She doesn't get on with her stepfather – my late husband's brother.'

'But you're *Ellis*?'

'I told you, he's dead. I reverted to my maiden name. Sam started using it as well. I'm not sorry to be no longer part of that family. Those men were spoilt brats, the pair of them,' she said bitterly, lighting a second cigarette.

Frost scratched his head. So, Mrs Hartley-Jones had a *daughter*. Where on earth was *she* last weekend? Evidently not at home, otherwise the niece wouldn't have been drafted in to feed the cat. 'And this Nicola, where was she last weekend?'

'With her natural father, I'd guess. He doesn't live round here. The girls had a bit of a falling-out, so that's probably why she decided to go there.'

'Any clue as to why they'd fallen out?' Clarke asked.

Mrs Ellis shot her a glance. 'Girls can be very cruel to one another,' she said. 'Especially when it comes to boys, don't you find?'

'At a certain age, yes, I suppose so,' Clarke answered diffidently. 'Was it because Sam had a boyfriend, then?'

'Not especially.' Mrs Ellis sighed. 'They're evil to each other for no apparent reason.'

Frost glanced at Clarke. He couldn't fathom where this was leading. 'Tell me,' he asked, 'and I appreciate this must be painful for you; when Gail Burleigh and Sarah Ferguson were interviewed about your daughter's death they denied they ever knew her. They must have known there was a huge risk of us finding out the truth, and yet they felt the risk was worth it. Can you think of any reason why?'

Mrs Ellis looked unmoved. 'No idea, but they could lie for England, that lot. And make no mistake, they're not stupid, not by any stretch.'

'Thanks for that, Mrs Ellis. Very helpful,' Frost said.

Clarke met his eye.

They had found their fifth Bell.

'What's your take on this Two Bridges lot?' Frost asked, perplexed, as he and Clarke stood on the street outside the supermarket. 'If they're that clever, why would they blatantly lie to the police?'

'Like she says, they would have lied for a purpose.'

'But what purpose?'

Clarke shrugged. Frost sparked up a Rothmans, noticing as he did so the estate agent's over the road, and in particular the fair-haired young gent he'd seen yesterday with Simms at Eagle Lane, visible through the plate-glass window.

'Maybe Mrs Ellis was right first time, it's simply the snob in them not wanting to be associated with the riff-raff. Anyway, let's pop over there for a second.' He moved to cross the road but suddenly spotted a traffic warden eyeing the Cortina, which was parked half-on half-off the kerb. He knew full well that the High Street was a double-yellow zone and that the supermarket had a car park, but if you couldn't break the rules when on a murder investigation . . .

'Oh, for the love of . . . Oi, you! That's a police vehicle!'

'I am well aware of that, sir,' said the warden who, buttoned up tightly in his pristine uniform, resembled a youthful Mullett. 'You left your windows down and the radio has been—'

Frost reached inside and snatched up the handset. It was Bill Wells. Frost had left Martin Wakely stewing in Interview Room 1. He'd clean forgotten.

'Blast!' Frost said. 'Just lock him up.'

'What for?' came the crackled response. 'Well, if you're sure. Oh yeah, Jack, we've got some leads on the chimney sweep; a couple of calls have come in following the *Echo* splash . . .'

'Get Simms on it. I'm tied up in town and about to nut a traffic warden. As for Wakely, wave a Receiving Stolen Goods or a Possession of a Fire Arm charge under his nose; the smell of that should bring him round.' He chucked the handset on the passenger seat. The traffic warden had gone, but had left his hateful yellow calling card under the windscreen wiper. Frost swore and made to cross the road.

My God, he's coming here! thought Chris Everett in panic. The policeman in sunglasses, whom he recognized from the station, was heading his way across the road, along with his attractive sidekick. What on earth did they want? He'd done what had been asked of him. Why couldn't they leave him alone?

Trying to remain calm, Everett adopted a welcoming pose as the two CID officers entered the office.

'Good afternoon, may I help you? I'm Chris Everett, the regional manager.' He proffered his hand.

'Getting muggy out there,' said the scruffy detective, ignoring the handshake gesture.

Everett speculated that he was only in his late thirties but he looked worn, and what was that smell on him?

'Wouldn't surprise me if the weather broke again later,' Frost persisted. He was smiling disarmingly, presumably expecting Everett to respond.

'Er . . . yes,' he said, wishing they'd get to the point of why they were there.

The female detective moved around the office and began to chat to the girls.

The policeman glanced cursorily at the For Sale board. 'Business good this time of year? Or is it too hot for punters to go traipsing around houses?'

Did he presume Everett knew who he was? He'd not introduced himself. Was this some sort of trick? 'I'm sorry,' he pre-empted, 'I don't believe we've had the pleasure . . . ?'

'DS Frost, Denton CID, and my colleague' – he waved at the young woman, who now seemed to be genuinely studying the To Let board – 'DC Clarke.'

'Ah yes, I thought you looked familiar. I think I saw you yesterday,' the estate agent said hesitantly.

'Yes, you may well have done,' the detective said casually. 'Tell me, Mr Everett, did you notice earlier today three youths on bikes matching a similar description to the ones who mugged you loitering across the road, outside Bejam's supermarket?'

How on earth did he know that? Everett glanced nervously

at the office girls, who were looking intently at him; he couldn't lie and say he wasn't here. Could he even lie and say he'd not seen them? He felt perspiration break out on his top lip. 'Er . . . no,' he forced out. 'When was this, exactly?'

'This morning, at about ten. Think hard, Mr Everett.'

The woman detective moved away from the window. Everett was having trouble keeping his eye on both of them at the same time.

She spoke up: 'They were there for at least half an hour. It would be surprising if you *hadn't* seen something, given the proximity of the supermarket across the way.' Her look was in-scrutable.

He knew he daren't admit to seeing them, or they'd be questioning why he didn't report it. 'I just don't recall,' he said. 'My office is at the back . . .' He gestured vaguely behind him. Would the girls give him away? Would they remember him peering nervously through the window at the boys in question?

'Ladies,' the detective said, addressing Vicky and Claire. 'Did either of you notice anything? A bunch of kids loitering, pulling wheelies over the road?' They both looked nervously at Everett before shaking their heads in unison.

The door chimed and a woman entered with a brown and white spaniel at her heels. Clarke made to fuss over the animal but Claire was quickly on her feet.

'No animals allowed, madam,' she said, pointing to a notice on the door. 'Mr Everett is allergic to them.'

'Is he?' Frost said, giving Everett a look that sent his blood cold. 'Well, he's not alone there.' The moment passed and the detective smiled thinly. 'We'll leave you in peace now, but keep a look-out. It's possible that whoever attacked you may come back for more. Anything *untoward* happens, you let me know.' Frost handed him a card. 'Well, good day, sir.'

Untoward? What on earth did he mean? Everett watched from the window as the pair returned to their unmarked vehicle.

The detective pulled a parking ticket from beneath the wiper and made a show of ripping it up. Everett didn't know what to think. Perhaps the police were merely concerned for his safety, but did he misread the penetrating look the detective gave him regarding the dog? Was he beyond suspicion? He felt a tingle of adrenalin. If only he could think of a way to deal with those little thugs . . .

'So, Mrs Hartley-Jones, can we run through this one more time? All the . . .' Simms began but then paused as a tall, slim, dark-haired man in his late fifties appeared in the doorway of the front room. The man was clearly dressed for golf, in an argyle sweater and plus-fours. The husband, Simms thought, and the pain-in-the-arse mate of Mullett's who kept pestering them to nail the jewel thief, and who complained about Frost's screw-up over the Ellis girl's supposed suicide.

Waters got to his feet and approached him with his hand out-stretched, whereas Simms elected to ignore him and continue to push his scatty cow of a wife to get her facts straight.

'To recap.' He cleared his throat. 'All the beds were made and there was no evidence of people sleeping here. Of, shall we say, teenage activity. And the rubbish bin was clear, exactly as you'd left it on the Friday afternoon.'

'Correct. When Nicola has been left alone before – only for a night, mind' – the woman looked shifty, clearly unsure of whether at sixteen her daughter could legally be left alone, and Simms saw no reason to put her mind at ease – 'there is usually a trace of something or other. Cigarette ends, cider bottles, takeaway wrappers – you know the sort of stuff.'

He did; he was more than familiar with that sort of debris at his Fenwick Street police digs.

'I still find it odd that you didn't mention you had a daughter when we called on Monday,' Simms probed.

'You didn't ask. And why would I need to mention it when

she wasn't here?' The woman looked indignant. 'She went to stay with her father for the weekend, which is why her cousin was feeding the cat. I'm still not entirely sure what this is about. Are you suggesting that there was some sort of a wild party held here while we were away, and that unfortunate boy was here before being murdered on the golf course?'

'It's a possibility we have to acknowledge, yes,' he said, and added, addressing them both, 'There was carpet fibre found on the boy's sock.'

'Ridiculous!' the tall man exploded, causing Waters to step back into the room. 'Do you think we're the only people in Denton with a new carpet! Vera, you're not to talk to these people any more. I shall call Superintendent Mullett this instant!'

Simms reached down and pulled a few strands from the recently laid carpet before making to leave. The woman looked flustered by her husband's outburst, and stood up from the sofa, unsure what to do next. Hartley-Jones stepped aside to allow them out.

As he passed him, Simms couldn't resist a parting shot. 'Sir, it is highly likely that Tom Hardy was in your house on Friday evening to see your niece. Both children are now dead. It would be useful if you assisted us with our enquiries rather than turfing us out on to the street.'

'Wait. Excuse me,' Waters said suddenly as they reached the porch. 'Last time we were here I remember stepping over a pile of large candles. They were here where the wellingtons are.'

'We do have electricity out here, just like you do in London,' snapped Hartley-Jones.

'Mrs Hartley-Jones, do you remember, you asked me to mind my step?' Waters persisted.

Simms noted the expression on her face: anxiety and confusion. He tapped Waters on the elbow to go. The woman was frightened – there was no point pushing her now.

At five past four Frost was on the verge of opening the Basildon Bond envelope that had been glaring at him accusingly all week from the untidy desk. The detective in him read the sharp capitals and understroke as signs of a missive written in anger. He toyed with the edge of the envelope, recalling that she'd said not to read it.

'Sergeant Frost.'

'Ah, PC Miller, come in.' Frost jolted upright in his chair, sliding the unopened letter to one side and reaching for his cigarettes.

'You wanted to see me, sir?' The police constable looked hot and bothered, like everyone else in Eagle Lane, but his sweaty sneer and the way the standard-issue black tie had been tugged casually to the side gave him the air of a malevolent school bully.

'How are you finding your new housemate?'

'Beg pardon, guv?'

'You live, do you not, in police accommodation at Fenwick Street?'

'Y-yes,' Miller stammered.

'Well. How are you coping with your guest? DS Waters, the black officer?' Frost waited for the PC to open his mouth, then snapped, 'Or had you not noticed? I won't beat around the bush, Miller. I have your personnel file in front of me . . .'

'You've no—'

'No what? Right? I think I'll be the judge of who has the right to do what, Constable.' Frost paused for a drag on his cigarette. 'I also have your duty roster here. You've done ten days straight – without a day off, including the bank holiday. For the overtime, no doubt.'

Miller nodded reluctantly.

'And you've the next three days off according to this, finishing today at the end of an early shift.' Frost flicked a buff folder on to the desk.

'Yes, guv.'

'Wrong, guv,' Frost stated. 'You're on a stake-out tonight. And tomorrow night, and probably into the small hours of Sunday.'

Miller's face fell and he opened his mouth guppy-like in protest.

'You'll be on duty outside the Pink Toothbrush with your accomplice from eight o'clock this evening. Understood?'

The chubby PC wasn't as stupid as he looked, Frost thought. He knew that by 'accomplice' he was referring to whoever else had jumped DS Waters on Wednesday. Frost had no authority over uniform, but Miller was not about to question Frost's request – he'd got off lightly, and they both knew it. Through formal channels Frost would probably get nowhere – racism polluted the ranks of the force from top to bottom – but this way the message might just get through. He could have gone to Mullett; Mullett would in principle have supported him, but then be too afraid to upset the apple cart to act. Life was too short. Frost had put his marker down.

'Good,' Frost concluded. 'There's a big do at the golf club tonight – lot of bigwigs who may well fancy a rub-down after a hard day's strolling around the greens. You're not to make an arrest. Observe only; watch the comings and goings, is that clear?'

'Yes, guv.'

'I'm glad we understand each other. And if DS Waters so much as breaks out in a sweat, I'll have your balls in a kebab.' The constable made to go. 'Oh, and by the way,' Frost added, 'you'll pay for the damage to Sergeant Waters' Vauxhall, too. Dismissed.'

Friday (6)

Frost had acted, and Clarke felt for him.

It had just gone six, and the four of them were sitting in the main CID office, all eyes on Frost sipping lukewarm Harp lager.

She could tell he was unsure of his decision; that it was only his instinct that told him it was the right move. But instinct had let him down previously.

First, he brought in both the girls from Two Bridges. He wanted to nail them for the murder of Tom Hardy, but couldn't press charges yet as he had no actual evidence. All he had on them so far was a charge of giving false information, and indeed, they'd lied so boldly that he was sure they were guilty of something. He hoped that with cross-examination they might unwittingly give one another away.

Second, an even bolder move, he'd sealed off the Hartley-Joneses' place at Forest View.

'Forensics are all over the place,' Waters said. 'Mrs H-J really wasn't happy. She was straight on the blower to the golf club, where her husband was playing with Mr Mullett—'

'I don't give a monkey's whether she's happy or not. Besides' – Frost checked his watch – 'they don't play golf in the dark, and Mr Mullett and co. will already have been on the lash for a good few hours. Did you tell them to check the garden for access to the woods?'

'Yes, they're checking everywhere with a fine-tooth comb.'

'That doesn't stack up,' Simms interjected. 'All right, there is access to Denton Woods that way but it's not as the crow flies, it's . . .'

Frost shot him an angry glance. 'I'm not interested in your avian observations. Schoolgirls could not have driven the body to the golf course, and they'd never risk it on foot, whatever the hour. No, they had to go via the woods.'

Clarke could tell Frost was tired and frustrated. She knew as well as Simms from the OS maps that this was an unlikely route and she reckoned that Frost probably knew as much, too.

'What about a motive, Jack? Or do you think they just did it for the hell of it?'

Frost's brow creased. She knew he was having difficulty believing pure witchcraft to be the rationale, even though everything was pointing that way.

'Revenge? For getting the girl pregnant?' he offered. 'We'll find out soon enough, I promise. Right, what are we waiting for?'

'Solicitors,' Waters said.

'Sod them,' Frost spat. 'Burleigh is one himself, for starters, and we're not even charging – yet.' He got up to take another lager off Simms. 'OK, Waters and I will take Sarah Ferguson, as we had her on Wednesday. Simms and Clarke: Gail Burleigh.'

Frost had not met Sarah Ferguson's father before. It was the mother who had greeted them at the family home on Wednesday. He appeared to be an ordinary middle-aged man, already worn down by life. Here, in the airless interview room he seemed more inconvenienced than cross, as if he'd rather be at home with his feet up in front of the telly.

Sarah herself looked a far cry from the pouting minx he'd interviewed on Wednesday. The heavy eyeliner and mascara were gone. Sitting before him was a schoolgirl version of her balding father, with acne. She flicked a strand of mousy hair out of her face.

For a moment he felt guilty about the accusations weighing on his mind. This was a schoolgirl! He tried to push away the doubts and focus on what was at stake – as a friend of Emily Hardy this girl was crucial to the investigation. He assessed her behaviour and appearance. He had to remember she was smart; it was always possible she'd 'dressed down' to give the impression of guilelessness and innocence.

'Thank you for coming in,' Frost opened, sitting down opposite the father and daughter. Waters remained standing. Frost had requested he observe only.

'That's quite all right. We'd be grateful if you could kindly let us know what the problem is, exactly.' The man spoke softly, not looking at his daughter.

'We have reason to believe that your daughter, Sarah, attended a party at number 7 Forest View last Friday night.' The girl raised her bowed head and Frost was struck again by her sparkling green eyes.

'Who lives there?' said the father, looking at his daughter with a bemusement verging on disinterest. What did he care for children's parties?

'Relations of Samantha Ellis.' Frost looked intently at Sarah.

'That was the girl you mentioned the other day,' she said unexpectedly. Frost was aware of Waters shifting his feet behind him.

'Yes, you claimed not to know her,' Frost said.

'Come to think of it, the name is familiar.'

'Is that so?'

'Yes.' The girl made a show of looking towards the ceiling, as if searching her mind, forefinger on bottom lip. Frost offered nothing. 'Yes, I do recall her . . . a blonde girl. She went to Guides.'

'Sarah was, I think, a bit intimidated by you the other day,' Mr Ferguson said. 'You know, it's not every day the police come knocking on your door.' He gave a stilted laugh, then gathered himself. 'Yes, quite intimidating.'

Frost kept his eyes on the girl, who fiddled with a hair clip. 'So,' he finally said. 'You'd have recognized her on the train, say, or at a party?'

The girl snorted defiantly, colouring. 'She was quite ordinary. I'm not sure I would.'

'Sarah,' Frost said firmly, pausing long enough for her to look at him. There was no point directly accusing her of lying. They both knew what she had said. 'You said previously you may have seen Samantha at a hockey match. Why did you not mention the Girl Guides?'

'My daughter is very active socially and meets many, many people,' Ferguson said lamely.

'Mr Ferguson, your daughter is a schoolgirl, not a foreign diplomat. Whether it's from hockey or Brownies, I'll wager she knows exactly who she's met.' He pulled out the Rothmans, noticing as he did so that Sarah Ferguson's fingers were as nicotine-stained as his.

'From memory,' the girl said, fixing Frost with a look, 'it was *you* who suggested I might know the girl from hockey. You didn't mention Girl Guides.'

Frost was unsure what he himself had said. Now he thought of it, perhaps it was the mother who'd suggested the connection? 'Of course. Yes. I beg your pardon,' he said, climbing down, 'though there was a Girl Guide camp planned for the bank holiday weekend at Rimmington Meadow which both you and the Ellis girl were down to go to. Which you, Samantha and one or two others pulled out of at the last minute. Why did you do that?'

The girl was caught off guard. 'I didn't say I didn't go to a party, did I?' she replied curtly.

'Sarah, will you please tell the detective what you did on Friday night and with whom, so we can go home.'

'It wasn't a party . . . I was just with some friends.'

'Where?' Frost asked.

'Yes, where were you?' repeated the father.

'Was it 7 Forest View?'

After a slight hesitation, the girl acquiesced.

'Was Samantha Ellis there?'

She shook her head. This surprised Frost. Was she still lying?

'Well, what were you doing there, then?' he prompted.

'Nicola invited us. Nicola Parke. It's her house.'

'Any boys?'

Again, she shook her head. Frost asked her to confirm who else was there.

'Gail, Emily and Nicola.' Sarah Ferguson crossed her arms, as if to indicate that was all there was to say on the matter.

Regardless, Frost pressed on. 'You're sure that at no point Samantha Ellis or Tom Hardy were there?'

She shook her head.

So four of the five. And no Tom Hardy. Frost didn't push her on this and just asked what they had got up to, to which she answered that it had been the usual teenage-girl thing, playing records and raiding the booze cabinet. It all sounded pretty convincing, but he was sure the girl was lying about Hardy and Ellis – she had to be.

He began to grow weary. His questioning became repetitive, and she had nothing useful to offer on the current whereabouts of Emily Hardy, although she did come across as genuinely worried. Finally, Frost brought up the School of the Five Bells. When she looked at him as if he was mad, Frost opted for a ten-minute break and promised they would not be kept beyond nine o'clock.

Waters and he went out and rapped on the door to Interview Room 2 to confer with Simms and Clarke.

'They'll have rehearsed this,' Frost said on hearing Clarke's run-down of her interview. Gail Burleigh had given much the same story as her erstwhile accomplice. His cross-examination ploy didn't appear to be working. He felt truly knackered, which probably wasn't helping. And he'd finally eaten – going out to grab a Wimpy in the High Street before going back to the CID office, and he always felt tired after eating.

'Is it worth getting hold of this Nicola Parke girl?' Simms suggested. 'She was supposed to be at her natural father's in Reading all weekend, and yet she's hosting house-parties-cum-satanic-rituals in Denton? Someone's telling porkies there.'

'You'll get the same story – thick as thieves, this lot – but we certainly need confirmation that Nicola Parke was there.'

'Jack, Jack!' It was Desk Sergeant Bill Wells bowling down the corridor.

'Shift finished, old son? You don't usually get so excited.' Frost looked at his watch. It was bang on eight thirty.

'Yes, but that's not . . . They've found it. Forensics have found it,' he said, struggling to get his breath.

'Found *what*?'

'The girl's diary. Samantha Ellis's diary.'

'Bingo! Where was it?'

'At the Hartley-Joneses' place. It's going to be picked up by an area car . . .'

'Great.' Frost made to move towards the front desk.

'Not so fast, mate. It's not the only thing that's on its way. The super will be coming along with it. He ordered the area car to pick them up from the golf club, he and Hartley-Jones, who's furious about Forensics crawling all over his house.'

'Right. I need the phone. I've got to speak to Forensics, before Hornrim Harry fouls everything up just because he wants to give his chum a lift home.'

The area car, a musty Austin Allegro, was slow going in the rain and not the smoothest ride. Mullett sat stewing in the back; next to him was the rattled Hartley-Jones. The weather had finally broken and there was another flash of lightning from the west. The constable flicked the wipers up a gear.

The afternoon had started well enough; Mullett had got round the course below par, more importantly beating those who annoyed him most: Hudson, the corpulent manager of Bennington's Bank; the lowlife club owner Baskin, and Hartley-Jones himself. The latter triumph surprised him; normally a far superior player, Hartley-Jones had seemed out of sorts and distracted even at that stage, and had played dreadfully.

The only one Mullett would have loved to have beaten but didn't was Winslow, the Assistant Chief Constable, who seemed rather pleased with himself, his boozy lunch apparently beneficial to his game. Yes, now that he thought about it, Winslow was in a remarkably good mood, and Mullett had noticed the ACC was on very good terms with Baskin. Try as he might to ignore it, there was no denying they did seem awfully chummy.

It wasn't until evening when the champagne and prawn vol-au-vents did the rounds that Hartley-Jones had got the call from his wife; CID had invaded his home and Forensics were hacking about in the back garden.

Mullett glanced at Hartley-Jones. Thankfully he appeared calm and remarkably sober as he peered out on to the dark Denton evening. He was beginning to regret what he thought was the generous offer of a chauffeur by way of an area car to the club and back. Frost had better have his facts straight this time, Mullett thought. He'd assured Hartley-Jones that there was no cause for alarm, and that all would be swiftly sorted out. He hoped he was right.

'Ah, looks like we're here,' Mullett said. As the car drew to a stop a constable approached the passenger window. Mullett had no intention of getting out in the rain. He wound down the window.

'Yes?' Mullett squinted. The PC leaned forward, rain cascading off his helmet and into the Allegro's interior.

'There's been a disagreement, sir, between the lady of the house and one of our Forensics officers.'

'About what?'

'Mr Harding has found evidence that he wants removed for—' Mullett was suddenly aware of the door being flung open and Michael Hartley-Jones hurriedly exiting the car.

Mullett instinctively realized something was amiss, and though woozy he now felt compelled to follow his friend into the house, which to all intents and purposes had been transformed into a crime scene.

Inside there was an argument in full swing involving Harding, the senior Forensics officer, and Mr and Mrs Hartley-Jones, who were flanked by a PC and a lad in overalls.

'Can someone please explain what exactly is going on?' Mullett boomed, brushing rain off his blazer.

'The lady here is withholding evidence,' Harding said matter-of-factly. 'Munson here found a diary in the girl's bedroom. The lady overheard that it had been found and snatched it away.'

'Is this correct?' Superintendent Mullett asked.

The woman nodded, moving closer to her husband for support. 'That belongs to my daughter. It's her personal property.'

'And where is your daughter?' Mullett asked.

'With her father,' the woman answered. Mullett looked in bemusement at the grim-faced Hartley-Jones, who said nothing. 'In Reading,' she added. 'Michael is Nicola's stepfather.'

'I see,' said Mullett. He knew that, though thought it prudent to keep a professional distance.

'The diary does not belong to Nicola,' Harding clarified.

'That's irrelevant,' Michael Hartley-Jones asserted. 'The diary is with my stepdaughter for safe-keeping.'

Mullett was struggling to comprehend why there was such an altercation over a child's diary. 'Mr Harding,' he asked. 'To whom do you believe the diary to belong?'

'Samantha Ellis.'

The girl found dead by the train track. What on earth was it doing here? Mullett's mind might still be cloudy from his over-indulgence at the club, but it was clear what the appropriate course of action should be. 'I see. Well, it's obviously a crucial piece of evidence and we must be allowed to—'

'Stanley, I beg you, please respect the poor dead girl's wishes. She wanted Nicola to keep it . . .'

'Nonsense, Michael. Vera, please hand the item over.' Mullett held out his hand.

'No.' Hartley-Jones stepped in front of his wife. 'I will speak to Winslow before anyone takes possession of any of my step-daughter's belongings.'

Mullett was now suddenly sober and fixed his stern gaze on the sweating husband. 'Michael, please think what you're doing before this goes any further. Vera, if I may?'

Hartley-Jones stepped back, and his wife passed the diary over.

'There, that wasn't difficult, was it?' The superintendent flicked through the diary. 'Most of the pages have been ripped out. Munson, is this how you found it?'

'Yes, sir.'

'Well, I can't see what all the fuss was about.' He slipped the diary into his blazer pocket and patted it reassuringly. 'Now, I suggest we call it a day. It's been a trying week all round. It's getting late. Mr Harding, has your team finished for the day?'

Harding nodded.

'Good evening.' Mullett nodded to his friends. 'Mr Harding, if you'd like to follow me outside.'

Mullett stood next to the panda car in the rain, which now felt rather refreshing, smoking a cigarette that started to fizzle as soon as he'd lit it. Harding joined him directly.

'For my benefit, can you explain to me what all the fuss was about – or am I missing something vital?'

Mullett stood listening intently to the debrief regarding the blue-carpet fibre found on Tom Hardy's sock, which matched the Hartley-Joneses' carpet. But that, essentially, was it; no incriminating candles had been found, and the thorough search of the garden and its fence had yielded nothing. Even so, Mullett felt something was fishy. His friend's behaviour was, at best, peculiar, and at worst, incriminating.

'. . . and when we arrived the lady immediately called the husband who was with you at the golf club.'

'Yes, yes, that much I know.' Mullett felt mild irritation at the Forensics officer. 'But what made her so protective over the diary?'

'Her husband had instructed her not to let anything be removed from the house.'

'And what else have you found? Apart from the diary – anything?'

The swirling blue light of the car and the rhythmic rain gave the scene a melancholy air. Harding shook his head.

Mullett absorbed this information and grunted a goodnight. He climbed into the Allegro and instructed the driver to head for Eagle Lane. On the journey to the station, he racked his brains trying to recall where the Hartley-Joneses had been holidaying last weekend. Was it Wales? He hoped so, or at least somewhere equally as far away from Denton, and completely removed from what looked like a very messy situation.

*   *   *

Clarke returned from the kitchen carrying four coffees, to be greeted by the sight of an ill-tempered Superintendent Mullett, his blazer and plus-fours dripping wet. He looked like a survivor pulled from a *Titanic* lifeboat.

'The girls are over fourteen,' Frost insisted, 'so we have no cause to call Social Services. Both fathers were present.'

'I'm not interested in the age of the girls,' Mullett fumed. 'What rankles with me is your sledgehammer approach to the case. You know Hartley-Jones was . . . is a friend of mine. If you'd suspected the house had been used to host a party of some description, you could have asked me . . . I'm sure Michael is in no way implicated. He was on holiday at the time. He would have been more than happy to help us with our enquiries, instead of having you lot barge in on his poor wife like a herd of elephants.'

Clarke didn't think Mullett looked convinced by his own argument. Frost said nothing; perhaps he too could sense a hint of doubt creeping into the station commander's tone. In any case, Mullett would know that if CID had good cause to go in, they didn't have time to fuss about chasing around golf courses for the super's friends.

'Well,' Mullett huffed, 'here's your diary.' He slung it across at Frost. 'Though what little help it is you can judge for yourself . . . Most of the pages are missing.'

Frost turned the item over in his hands then tossed it to Clarke. 'Forensics come up with anything else?' he asked. 'Candles?'

'Candles. Ah yes, the altar candles allegedly used in some satanic ritual. No.'

'Well, they were bloody well there!' Frost slapped the desk, and looked in the direction of Waters for support.

'It's true,' Waters confirmed. 'There was a whole pile of them on Monday, in the porch. And today the old lady almost re-membered, but her husband . . .'

Mullett raised his hand in a lordly fashion. 'Well, there are no candles there now, and that's all that counts. Harding confirmed as much.'

'What about the back garden? Any sign to indicate that someone may have forced their way through to the woods?' Frost persisted.

'The theory being that the body, after being brutally murdered in the front room, was somehow dragged out the through the woods over two miles to the golf course?' Mullett patted himself for cigarettes. 'No. Nothing there, either. And that reminds me, you' – Mullett pointed a cigarette at Simms, slumped in the corner, half-heartedly drinking a can of lager – 'if you were half the detective you could be, let alone think you are, and had been on the ball on Monday, you would have had Forensics either side of the garden fence looking for evidence of the housebreaker from Saturday night. Eh?' Mullett paused to light his cigarette.

Clarke felt embarrassed for the lad as all eyes turned on Simms.

'The forced entry was from the rear of the house, was it not?' Mullett shook his head despairingly. 'As it is, following the deluge on Wednesday, Harding informs me, you'd be hard pushed to find tracks made by something even the size of an elephant, such is the vegetation. What a shambles,' he said. '*Procedure!* If I have told you all once, I have told you a dozen times, the only way to get results is to follow procedure.'

'Knew you couldn't get a body through them woods – impossible,' Simms mumbled.

'Not impossible, DC Simms, impractical,' Mullett corrected.

'Sorry, sir,' Frost piped up. 'Are you suggesting you believe that Tom Hardy *was* murdered at Forest View?'

'I am interested in the facts, Frost. The facts and the evidence alone. It looks as if the boy was there; the carpet fibre matches the strand found on his socks. If something did happen in that house, above and beyond a burglary and a garrotted cat, I would hope that even you would manage to get to the bottom of it.'

The diary proved useless. Frost chucked it aside. It did, however, suggest a close link between Nicola Parke and Samantha Ellis. Parke was due to arrive by train from Reading first thing tomorrow morning.

'OK,' Frost said, wearily picking up his coffee. He had hoped the two girls would give contradictory statements, but he realized now how unlikely that had been. The girls were so close and had had ample opportunity to spend time getting their stories to match. To pin something on them he needed solid evidence; something that could be trusted. Suddenly it hit him. He slapped his forehead in annoyance: what on earth was he thinking of!

They had let the Burleighs go. The father had been moaning like hell, dishing out threats of all sorts. It was close to ten.

Frost opened the door to Interview Room 1. Both Mr Ferguson and his daughter sipped coffee that must surely be cold by now.

'Sorry to have kept you,' Frost muttered, pulling up a chair. 'This won't take much longer. Sarah, I'd like you to consider very carefully how you answer the next question.' He noticed the girl was blinking heavily. Had she been doing that all along, or was it a new sign of nerves, he wondered? 'Have you ever had a tattoo, either professionally or' – he watched intently – 'or home-made?'

'What sort of question is that?' Mr Ferguson blustered.

'I think Sarah knows exactly what I'm referring to. It's very important that you answer truthfully. Of course, if you don't answer, we could always call the General and request an examination.'

'Stupid cow,' Sarah Ferguson suddenly snapped angrily, 'spoiling everyone's fun.'

Frost took this as an admission of guilt. A tattoo could not be hidden, and as he rightly suspected they would all have one, as part of the membership requirements. 'Sergeant Waters, would you please pull up a pew and prepare to take Miss Ferguson's statement.' He addressed the girl again. 'The demise of Miss Ellis has proved a nuisance for you. The dead can't talk, but they can't lie either, especially if they've marked themselves indelibly. Now there's no way out, despite causing hapless detectives to jump to conclusions.'

'Would someone mind telling me what on earth is going on?' Ferguson said, exasperated.

'Oh be quiet, Daddy.' The girl sighed. 'Yes, the School of the Five Bells does exist.'

'And the members are?'

'Me, Samantha Ellis, Gail Burleigh, Emily Hardy and Nicola Parke.'

'Right, I will ask you again – did Tom Hardy arrive at the house in Forest View along with his sister Emily on Friday night?'

'Tom turned up with Sam.'

Frost looked askance at Waters. All they knew was that Tom had caught the bus with a girl dressed in black. They had assumed it was his sister, Emily.

'Tell me.' Waters looked up from his pad. 'What exactly is the School of the Five Bells?'

Sarah Ferguson looked at Waters as if for the first time. It wasn't quite contempt in her nervous eyes, but something very close to it. 'Just a group of girls who worship nature and the seasons in a sort of pagan way. And abhor men,' she said piercingly.

'What, like witches?' Waters asked.

'If you like.' She shrugged.

Frost was baffled by the girl's nonchalance. 'Tell me,' he said, 'what were you and your friends up to before Tom and Samantha turned up?'

314

'Messing around in Denton Woods.'

'Define "messing around",' said Waters.

'Bit of dancing and drinking. All part of our May Day celebrations.'

'Any candles?' Frost asked.

'Yes.' The girl frowned. 'As it happens, there were. Why?'

'Please don't toy with us – this is serious. We understand exactly what went on.'

The girl blinked again. 'We were celebrating May Day, as I've told you. OK, it is a pagan thing, but so what? At least we're not blowing up battleships on the other side of the world for a two-bit island full of sheep.'

'As I've said,' Frost pushed, 'we're trying to trace Tom Hardy's last movements. So where was he?'

'Tom Hardy?' said the father. 'I thought this was about Emily?'

The girl looked equally shocked. 'He wasn't in the woods with us. I told you, he came by with Sam about eight. He wasn't keen on what we got up to and always tried to talk her out of it, right up until the moment he dropped her off – on the doorstep. He wasn't welcome.'

'So he didn't step inside the house?'

'He came in, but not for long. Like I said, he wasn't welcome.'

'What did you think of Tom Hardy?' Waters asked.

'*Think* of him?' The girl almost sneered. 'I didn't think anything of him.'

'Which of you has a boyfriend apart from Samantha Ellis?'

'None of us.'

'I'm sorry?'

'None of us has boyfriends. Are you deaf?'

That would explain the hostility towards the boy, Frost thought. Man-haters at this age. Hell's teeth, what was the world coming to? 'Just a little hard of hearing; it comes with old age. Why did you call Samantha Ellis "a stupid cow" who "spoiled everyone's fun"?' he continued.

'Throwing herself off a train . . .'

'Detective, please, what has any of this got to do with Tom Hardy? He was killed on Tuesday . . .'

'Wrong. He was murdered on Friday night,' Frost snapped.

'No, you wait!' Ferguson's pitch was rising. 'We're here to help with the missing girl. Her brother was ripped apart by a madman . . .'

'Mr Ferguson,' Frost said, now standing, 'Tom Hardy was last seen by your daughter and her friends on Friday night.'

'What are you implying? That my . . .' Ferguson's face contorted in alarm. '. . . that my daughter is in some way involved in *murder*?'

Suddenly Sarah let out an ear-piercing scream.

'Jesus wept,' Frost said to himself, taking a step back. The girl looked terrified. 'Please calm down, calm down.'

'Mr Frost, we must call a halt to this,' said Ferguson, comforting his daughter, who now had tears streaming down her face. 'We'll not say another word without a lawyer present.'

Frost acquiesced. He realized he'd only get so far without the father shouting for a lawyer. He'd got what he wanted – a reaction – just not the one he'd expected. He thought she'd shrug off the accusation, but the outburst he witnessed was done out of sheer fright, that or a damn good impression of it.

Clarke made room as Frost precariously nudged the drinks tray on to the small circular pub table, which after two rounds was already crammed with glassware. She wasn't keen on the Eagle, a grubby coppers' pub, but at least it was unlikely she'd bump into her farmhand-stroke-builder lover in here. It was an incident she now regretted, and tried to blank from her mind. She had hoped to grab five minutes alone with Frost, but he'd invited the others along for a drink too, in an unusually gregarious gesture. She could only assume he was over-tired and this was a last surge of energy.

Clarke and Simms had failed to make much progress questioning Gail Burleigh. The girl's lawyer father had made things difficult, and all they'd managed to establish was that Emily Hardy was indeed at 7 Forest View on Friday night. Now, as the four of them sat drinking in an Eagle lock-in, the same fact ran through their minds: in theory, a child could murder another child, but it was hard to believe without evidence, and all they had thus far was circumstantial. One sock fibre. No blood was found anywhere at the Forest View address. This, coupled with the Ferguson girl's horror at being implicated had made them doubt themselves.

'Just because the girl screamed out,' continued Derek Simms, 'doesn't mean she's not guilty. She's a girl; she would have screamed if a spider ran across the table.'

'Derek, don't be so ridiculous,' Clarke said. 'For starters, a girl capable of murder is hardly likely to be squeamish of spiders.'

'Give me strength.' Simms tapped the side of his head. 'I *know* that. She's playing us, geddit?'

Clarke gave him a disparaging look.

'Women manipulate men,' he continued, 'one minute screaming at spiders, the next marching on American air bases, like all those Welsh lesbians at Greenham Common. Man-haters when it suits them.'

'What a load of twaddle!' Clarke spat. 'How much have you had?'

'Evening, all. Talking politics? That time of night already, is it?' Kim Myles had pulled up a stool next to Waters.

'Wait a minute.' Frost emerged from his reverie. 'John, what was it Sarah Ferguson said to you? About disliking men?'

'Just that,' Waters said, sipping his pint. 'Though her exact

317

words were something like "we abhor men". None of them had boyfriends except Samantha Ellis.'

'Exactly,' Simms said too loudly. 'And look what happened to her.'

'Oh, for goodness' sake.' Clarke sighed.

'No, no. Let's look at it differently for a second. The original School of the Five Bells was created for the purpose of revenge. The girls from St Mary's were caught one night messing around with local boys, and the group was formed to seek vengeance on those who'd punished them and those who'd got off scot-free, although no revenge was ever exacted. What I'm saying is, we should be looking at why this current incarnation of the Five Bells exists . . .'

'So, Jack, you're suggesting that the girls did kill the boy for some revenge motive?' Clarke asked.

'All I'm saying is, look to the motive for re-forming the Five Bells and see what that throws up . . . But I still think we're missing something.'

'The Fifth Bell. Miss Parke?'

'There's her, yes . . . but something else too.'

'She's coming back by train,' Simms explained. 'First thing tomorrow. I told her we wanted a chat and she suggested meeting her at the station.'

'Blimey,' Frost said, stifling a yawn. 'Someone actually being forthcoming, a first in this case.'

Clarke watched Myles and Waters link arms and make their way down the street, laughing together. Simms ambled off after them, swaying slightly and calling for them to wait up.

'Well,' she said to Frost. 'What's it to be?'

It was 12.45. Frost, though dishevelled and tired, looked sharp and sober in the moonlight, his eyes shining brightly.

'I'm needed at home,' he said.

'At this time of night? For what?' She huffed. She could feel herself getting emotional, no doubt intensified by the drink. She bit her bottom lip. 'Look, the lad I was seeing . . . it was nothing. I just did it to—'

Frost placed his hand gently on her shoulder. 'It's not that, love,' he said, bowing his head. 'Mary is . . .' He couldn't finish the sentence.

'I see.' Clarke could think of nothing else to say. 'You'd best go, then.'

He leaned over and kissed her gently on her cheek, then turned in the direction of the station. She'd definitely drunk too much to drive.

Myles had recently moved into the block next door to hers, a ten-minute walk away.

'Hey! Wait up!' she hollered and made after her three colleagues, who were stumbling off into the night.

'Evening, Johnny.' Frost nodded at Night Sergeant Johnny Johnson, sitting in a soft pool of light behind the Eagle Lane reception desk, doing a crossword. The rest of the station was in darkness. The comforting murmur of a small portable transistor radio took the edge off the silence.

'Just popping down to the cells. Left a friend down there . . .'

'Right you are, Mr Frost.'

Frost flicked the corridor light on and made his way downstairs. Propped in the far corner a PC sat dozing. He peered in the first cell: a drunk. He looked like 'Mugger' Moore. What was he doing still here? Never mind, he thought, and moved on to the next one. 'Ah, there you are,' he muttered before banging fiercely on the door. 'Wakey, wakey!'

The snoring skinhead leapt up, dazed, taking a moment to register where he was. 'Frost?'

'Martin. Bet you thought I'd forgotten about you.' In truth he had, until he'd sat behind the wheel of the Cortina five minutes ago.

The sleepy thug grunted.

'But no, I just thought you might like a taster of what you've got to look forward to.'

The PC had woken from his slumber and now unlocked the cell door so that Frost could step inside.

'Well, had any thoughts?'

'About what?'

Frost yawned. 'With your record, I won't have any trouble at all getting you banged up again; and that's just for your antics in Milk Street. But it's your visit to the pawnshop I'm interested in, and if you want to help yourself, then you'd better help me. The jewels – where did you get them?'

'Me nan's, just like I told that old bastard at the pawnshop.'

'I don't believe that for a minute. But what we're going to do is this: you're going to tell your little brother that I want to know where he got those jewels from. Do you know why?'

'Why?' Martin Wakely rubbed his tired eyes.

'Because if you don't, I'm going to pin every burglary that's happened round here in the last six months on you and your little brother. It's one thing running around jabbing people with a penknife, but armed robbery is something else altogether.'

'Armed robbery? What you talking about?' Wakely's cell bunk groaned in protest as he shifted position.

'A newsagent was robbed at the start of this week by a gang of kids. The owner swore blind they were armed. Don't believe it myself; reckon the old fingers-in-the-pocket routine worked a treat.' Frost shoved his hand in his mac to demonstrate. 'See? Now you or I would call their bluff, but not an elderly Asian shopkeeper who thinks every white face a vicious racist.'

'He was never armed!'

'Wakely junior? But what about the gun his big brother was waving around in Milk Street this afternoon?'

'What?' The burly skinhead got to his feet. 'My kid brother ain't never had my shooter . . .'

Frost pushed him back down. 'Calm down, or do you want me to call in the PC to witness our negotiation?' Wakely slumped back. Frost offered him a cigarette, sighing. 'Maybe it's a daft idea.'

'What do you mean?'

'I could never get the charges dropped for the assault on DC Clarke. Assaulting a police officer is a very serious offence.' Frost waved out the match. 'What is it with you Wakelys; such an aversion to the law . . .'

'It wasn't Gary.'

'What?'

'It weren't my brother. It were Justin Pile.' Wakely put his head in his hands. 'Bunch of dumb kids charging around on BMXs. Don't know what they thought they were playing at. All right if people are dumb enough to leave their motors un-locked, in this day and age they deserve to get stuff pinched – but after such a close shave with a pair of coppers you'd think they'd keep low. But did they? Nah, of course not – they go rob the Paki shop. Stupid. Like they're untouchable. I told him, he'd be in for a hiding off me if he didn't stay well clear of Pile.' Wakely looked up at Frost almost penitently. 'You know, they didn't realize at first it was a copper's car, not until they tried to leg it. Pile just lashed out at her to get away . . .'

'But the attack on the jeweller on Merchant Street? A knife to the neck is armed robbery.'

'It weren't my brother. I told him after the copper got stabbed to stay away from Pile. But the rest all got carried away. Any-way, the gems from Sparklers in Merchant Street, them weren't what I was trying to pawn.'

'We know that. Those were stolen twice,' Frost said to him-self. 'But what a mess. What are we going to do, eh?'

Wakely shook his head. 'He's not the ringleader . . . but I ain't no grass, and he ain't neither. I can take care of meself, but Gary's only fourteen – he'd get lynched on that estate.'

'You tell me now where the jewellery came from, and I promise you we'll nobble Justin Pile and brush Gary under the carpet.'

'What'll happen to me?'

'You can go. We'll forget about your little tantrum. But keep your nose clean.'

'None of this'll get out, right?'

Frost nodded.

Wakely sighed. 'All I know is they jumped some guy with a briefcase.'

'Where?'

'Rose Avenue.'

Well-heeled North Denton, thought Frost. 'A briefcase. Suited?'

'Yes, big tall bloke, put up a bit of a fight . . .'

'That'll do nicely,' Frost said. Wakely's description pointed directly to the estate agent he had visited today. Frost banged on the door. 'Officer!' he called.

'What you doing?' Wakely said, worried.

'Getting you released.' He looked at his watch. It was nearly 2 a.m. 'Now, off that bed, I'm getting in. Tomorrow's going to be another long day.'

Saturday (1)

Waters rubbed his eyes and blinked rapidly. He was still not quite awake. Frost had called him at Kim Myles's flat at 7 a.m.; no explanation, just a polite request that DS Waters join him at his earliest convenience at Eagle Lane.

It was now just after seven thirty and he was in Frost's office next to a hungover DC Simms. He looked over at Frost, who was, like himself, in the same clothes as yesterday, energetically shuffling paperwork and puffing on a Rothmans. Waters found Frost's smoking this early in the morning nauseating in the extreme. Clearly it didn't agree with Simms either; the lad looked decidedly green. If he hadn't gone home, Waters wondered, where had the DS ended up last night? He hadn't been with Clarke; she'd tagged along back to Myles's flat and sat up complaining about Frost into the small hours, much to his annoyance.

'Boys,' Frost coughed, 'I'm sure there are things you'd far rather be doing than spending your Saturday morning with me, in the nick.'

Simms raised a sly eyebrow in Waters' direction, prompting him to say, 'Not at all, Jack, there's nowhere I'd prefer to be than cosied up here with you and Derek.'

'You're a very sick individual if that's the case.' Frost snorted. 'I'm afraid it's likely to be a rather long day. I have here the Forensics report on Ken Smith, the murdered sweep from Baskin's sauna car park.' He opened the buff folder. 'The VCRs in the back of the van had a bunch of prints, probably the original owner's. The steering wheel had only three discernible prints – all the sweep's – otherwise it was clean, suggesting to me a gloved driver drove the van and placed the VCRs in the back of it. The provenance of these VCRs can be traced to burglaries in the Denton and Rimmington area over the last eighteen months. The deceased had spent the best part of forty years in and around chimneys, and soot was embedded in his very skin. Harding reckoned it would have been virtually impossible for the poor sod to move a muscle without leaving a trace of it somewhere. The VCRs are totally clean.' Frost paused. 'No, the man who stole these video recorders is more than likely the same man who stole the necklaces Martin Wakely was trying to pawn, and for whatever reason this thief killed Ken Smith . . .'

'Who, Wakely?' Simms asked.

'No. Chris Everett, the manager of Regal Estate Agents in Denton High Street, who was carrying a not-so-empty brief-case when mugged by a gang of kids on BMX bikes.'

Frost's theory was that Everett had been on his way to sell the gems and, unluckily for him, had encountered the BMX bandits en route. Frost knew Everett had lied about the contents of his briefcase, given what Wakely had told him last night.

There was one thing nobody could understand; OK, so Everett was a housebreaker, but a murderer too? Why?

'Maybe the sweep was a fence?' suggested Waters. 'You know, Everett offloads the VCRs and the sweep sells them on; they fall out, and Everett murders him.'

'Estate agent murders chimney-sweep accomplice? Given what's gone on this week, nothing would surprise me,' Frost huffed. 'But what was the trigger? Ken Smith was found in over-alls and' – Frost flicked through the file notes – 'was "sooty in appearance", which would lead one to believe he was disturbed mid sweep, as it were. Hence it's crucial we find out where his last appointment was.'

'Oh, that reminds me.' Simms stirred beside him. 'Johnson passed me a note on my way in. A member of the public rang early this morning, responding to the appeal in the *Echo*.' Simms rooted around in his jeans pocket. 'She's a hairdresser, and one of her Tuesday-morning clients said she was having a sweep round in the afternoon to root out pigeons or something. Wait a sec. Oh Christ!' he exclaimed. 'The client's name is Fiona Everett. Lives on Somerton Street, apparently. Jesus.'

Frost's eyes sparkled. 'OK,' he said eventually, after lighting yet another cigarette. 'Let's be clever about this. Bring him in, but easy does it. Tell him we've got the lads who mugged him and we've recovered some jewellery belonging to him.'

'And if he resists?' Simms asked.

'Any trouble, nick him,' Frost said. 'No dramatics, Derek. We don't want his missus getting ruffled when she's just had her hair done. In fact, John, you stay behind and have a natter with the wife – sound her out, she may not be in on it. Keep them apart so she doesn't twig there's something up. Softly-softly does it.'

'Sure thing,' Waters said. 'And what'll you do?'

'I'll pick up Miss Parke off her train. I'm sure you two can cope alone. But tidy yourselves up a bit,' he said disapprovingly. 'You look like something the cat's dragged in.'

Waters couldn't help but wonder what the young Miss Parke would think when DS Frost rolled up at Denton train station; true, he and Simms could have done with a shave, but Frost looked like he'd slept on a park bench. For a week.

Frost pummelled the car horn one more time, although it turned out there was no need; Sue Clarke had emerged and was bouncing down the pavement towards the car. And she looked gorgeous. He cursed himself for not going back to her flat last night. His tired brain attempted to grasp his reasoning – had it been discretion in the presence of junior officers, or had concern for Mary truly brought a change in his feelings? All he knew was that, right now, to be snuggled up with her was the most appealing thing he could think of.

'Did you really have to do that?' she scolded, slamming the Cortina's door. 'It's not even nine in the morning. You'll have people complaining.'

'Well, it'll give Bill Wells something to do apart from check out the racing fixtures.' He smiled.

'God almighty!' she exclaimed. 'Look at the state of you! I thought you were going home last night?'

'I got waylaid with Martin Wakely. Those cell beds aren't as comfy as you'd think. We might have prison reformers on our case if we're not careful.' He scratched his neck irritably. 'There are things living in those mattresses, I'm sure.'

'Oh, Jack,' she complained, 'and you smell to high heaven. No, I'm not going anywhere with you like this. You're a disgrace. What time does the girl's train come in?'

'Ten.'

'Come on,' she said, opening the car door. 'We've got half an hour to hose you down and make you less of a fright.'

Everett heard the doorbell. He knew it was the police. He just *knew* it was them. It was too late to run. He should have done it last night. He had an overnight bag packed with a change of clothes, a passport and £1,000 in cash. He could hear Fiona at the door.

'Darling!' The call came up the stairs. He braced himself and made his way on to the landing. 'The sergeant here says they have the boys who attacked you . . .'

Everett acknowledged the two plainclothes policemen. Shit, he thought, what does that mean? But in place of panic the thought that occurred to him was: nothing; it meant nothing. Now, when he really had his back against the wall, he suddenly felt very calm. He'd say the kids were lying, he hadn't been carrying jewellery, and who would the police believe, him or a bunch of little thugs? So long as they had no other way to pin the burglaries on him he'd be in the clear. And it may have been a blunder to put the VCRs in the dead sweep's van, inextricably linking the two series of crimes, but the police would never believe he could be guilty of murder.

'Yes, a result,' said the white officer who'd picked him up in the street after the mugging. 'We'd be very grateful if you'd accompany us to the station to identify them.'

'Now? But I have to open the office.'

'Sorry if it's inconvenient, sir. I'm sure you understand how important it is.'

Fiona smiled encouragingly. He did love her an awful lot. He assured her he'd be back soon enough and grudgingly slipped on a pair of loafers.

Outside he paused. 'Hey, wait a sec,' he said, realizing the black officer had stayed behind. 'Where's the other chap?'

'Detective Sergeant Waters has a couple of routine questions for your wife.' Simms smiled reassuringly, walking down the path to his unmarked car. Alongside it was a panda car, two uniformed officers standing on the pavement.

'Questions about what?' Everett demanded as an officer opened the Allegro's rear door.

'We understand that your wife recently procured the services of a chimney sweep,' Simms said, ushering him into the panda car. 'Nothing to worry about, only routine.'

*   *   *

327

'That's our girl,' Frost said, as the ten o'clock arrival's passengers swarmed out into the station forecourt. He was feeling refreshed and reinvigorated following the forty-five minutes he'd spent at Sue Clarke's flat.

'Which one?' Clarke said. There was quite a throng, it being the first fast train out of London on a Saturday.

'The small blonde one. You can tell by her bearing. She's got "head girl" written all over her.'

Clarke spotted a striking platinum blonde, petite but striding purposefully towards the taxi rank.

'In which lifetime would you have come across a head girl from a girls' boarding school?'

'It's the detective in me, darlin',' he grinned.

'Well, if you're sure . . . but you can't just pick her up; what about her mother, or stepfather?'

'This one is sixteen,' Frost said, opening the car door, 'and is expecting us. Simms spoke to her on the phone, remember? She's happy to talk to us alone. She didn't want her family involved.'

Clarke followed Frost out of the car. He was back in his grubby mac, the weather having turned again – though at least he'd had a bath and shaved, she'd made sure of that, knowing how fastidious teenage girls could be. She didn't want him scaring her off.

They approached the diminutive girl. 'Miss Parke?' said Frost.

'Yes,' she replied in a clipped, confident tone. Beneath the blonde hair was a delicate-featured, slightly pouting face of the sort that got middle-aged men into trouble.

'I'm Detective Sergeant Frost, and this is Detective Constable Clarke. Detective Simms spoke to you last night about helping us with our enquiries. Would you mind accompanying us to the station?'

'The station? Do you mean a *police* station? Yes, I would mind. How ghastly.' She looked horrified.

'But Detective Simms . . .'

'I know what I jolly well said to Detective Simms, Sergeant.'

Nicola Parke, the youngest and shortest of the three, had a convincing air of superiority. Clarke knew this to be Frost's weakness; in the face of a dominant woman he was prone to crumble. Maybe that's where she was going wrong. It was pointless writing heartfelt letters.

'I said I would gladly talk to you, but not at Forest View and certainly not at "the station",' Parke said, annoyed.

'Oh,' Frost said, almost meekly. Hell, Jack, pull it together, thought Clarke. 'Well, perhaps if you'd like to sit in the back of the car here, we can make a start.' Frost chivalrously opened the door.

'There is no way on earth I'm getting in there! It's revolting!' Nicola wrinkled her small, sharp nose in disgust. 'There are things growing on the seats. Yuk!'

'I agree with you there,' Clarke said. 'Look, there's a café over the road.' She pointed to the transport café opposite the station. 'Let's grab a coffee.'

Nicola's story was that, having been closeted away all week at her father's house in Reading revising for O levels, she'd not been in contact with any of her friends and hadn't known a thing about Tom Hardy's death until Simms's phone call yesterday. The story had been on national news but Nicola maintained that if she wasn't revising she was horse-riding or in the stables.

Frost found it hard to believe. Her mother had called her only the once, on Tuesday, to notify her of her cousin Samantha's death. The girl had pushed to return home, but her mother had refused; she'd insisted there was no benefit to be had from her presence in Denton, and she should remain with her father revising. Parke corroborated the other girls' stories about the party on Friday night.

'Both girls lied about travelling with, or indeed knowing,

Samantha Ellis,' Frost stated. 'Why do you think they'd do that?'

The girl thought for a second, stirring her milkshake with a straw. 'Because they think Sam committed suicide that night? Because they were frightened? That's what I would say. Wouldn't you?' As if it were the most obvious thing in the world.

'They knew we knew they were on the same train coming back,' Clarke said.

'Well, what did they have to say?'

'They claimed they were drunk,' Frost replied, remembering that both girls made a point of making the police aware of this fact.

Parke snorted with derision. 'So that they conveniently couldn't remember anything about the journey home?'

Frost lit another cigarette. The girl's confidence was starting to grate. He suspected the bravado was cover; she would have an Achilles heel and he'd find it.

'Tell me,' he asked, 'do you *really* think Samantha committed suicide? I mean, you knew her . . .' The café door went, and two lorry drivers came in laughing loudly. Frost missed Parke's response.

'I'm sorry?' he asked. 'Didn't catch that.'

'I don't know, Detective. I really don't. We weren't that close.'

'Don't you think it's odd, though, that both Samantha and her boyfriend are dead within the space of a week?'

'Odd? Is it *odd*. It's unfortunate, but the circumstances of the deaths, as far as I'm aware, appear unrelated.' She feigned a smile, displaying bright, pristine teeth.

Frost didn't smile back. Instead he said, 'So none of your friends tried to call you with the news of these two tragic deaths?'

'They couldn't – they don't have that number.'

'We can check with British Telecom, you know,' Clarke said.

'Check away,' Parke said dismissively, slurping on her milk-shake in a manner at odds with her precocious demeanour.

'You don't seem that shocked or surprised, or even upset,' Clarke added. 'One of your closest friends, your cousin no less, and her boyfriend are dead.'

Parke let the straw fall from her mouth. 'Do not presume to tell me how I feel, Miss Clarke.'

'It's Detective Clarke, if you please, Miss Parke.'

'I haven't slept a wink since that fellow Simms rang,' said Nicola, although Frost detected not a smudge of tiredness under the clear blue eyes. 'You can ask my father if you don't believe me,' she added, as if reading his mind.

'Tell me, Miss Parke, how did the School of the Five Bells come about?' Frost asked, abruptly.

'I founded it,' she said proudly.

'That's not strictly true, though, seeing as it already existed twenty years ago. If anything, you rekindled it.'

'My, you are the detective!' Parke said, impressed. 'Yes, it did exist. So you'll probably know that my mother was involved.'

'How so?' Clarke asked.

'If you know that much, then you'll know my mother was a founder member of the original Five Bells.'

'Then *you'll* know why the, for want of a better word, "secret society" was formed?' Frost said sharply.

The girl put her forefinger to her lips, and her eyes flitted from left to right anxiously.

'Let me answer that for you,' Frost said, finishing his coffee and lighting another cigarette. 'Revenge. Revenge on boys.'

'You have me, Sergeant,' the girl said suddenly, waving off the cigarette smoke. 'It's our mission to castrate every boy who's goosed a girl at the bus stop . . .'

'Please don't play games with us,' Clarke snapped. 'Two people are dead, and you – as the head of a secret society hellbent on revenge – are seriously implicated.'

'I am perfectly serious.' Nicola Parke flashed Clarke a look, but then switched to Frost. 'We live in a sexist, misogynistic age. Or perhaps not in the police force, Detective Clarke?'

Frost could see that Clarke was unsure how to answer.

'Or perhaps I'm wrong, eh? Present company excepted?' Nicola Parke glanced at Frost caustically. 'We don't all have to be unwashed lesbians chaining ourselves to the fences of US military bases to register our disapproval of the deep-seated inequalities in society. I hope you, Miss Clarke, would agree that there's a place for solidarity between women.'

Frost was at a loss as to how a girl of sixteen with no experience of the real world could form such forthright views; besides, where was the harm in having your bottom pinched at a bus stop? He couldn't see it himself, but what got the youth of today worked up was anyone's guess.

'I don't know, Miss Parke, my mind is on my job,' Clarke said sharply.

'Very noble sentiments, I'm sure, but let's not start burning our bras just yet,' Frost interrupted. 'What does your stepfather think of all this? He doesn't strike me as the sort of bloke who has much time for this . . . this sort of thing.'

'My stepfather? What has my stepfather got to do with it?' Frost noticed a dramatic change in Parke's expression. Was it fear?

He continued softly, 'Put it this way, Mr Hartley-Jones was not best pleased when the police marched in yesterday suspecting that a fifteen-year-old boy had been murdered in a ritualistic fashion in his front room.' A wave of shock washed across the face of the girl. Frost added, 'After being burgled on Saturday night, and having his cat garrotted, it's not been his week at all.'

'May I have one of those?' Nicola Parke indicated the Rothmans lying on the table. Frost nodded his assent.

'Miss Parke,' Clarke said, 'how much do you know about Tom Hardy's death?'

'Only that he died . . . was killed, I mean' – the girl took a puff – 'in what you just described as a "ritualistic" fashion, although I have no idea what that means.'

'It means,' Clarke began, 'that the boy was laid out in the manner of a sacrifice, his body eviscerated. His heart has yet to be recovered.'

Nicola Parke covered her mouth in anguish. If Frost didn't know better, he'd have thought Sue Clarke relished telling the girl the gory details. Nicola Parke was very obviously distressed at this revelation.

'So you see, Miss Parke,' Frost said, 'why we're treating the School of the Five Bells as something more serious than a suffragette youth movement. And that you and your friends' festive antics in Denton Woods could be viewed in a very different light. It's how it appears to the rest of the world. Understand?'

'Indeed.' The girl nodded solemnly. 'All is not as it seems. My goodness, I'd best be going.' Parke looked at her watch. 'They'll be expecting me . . .'

'Have you not told your parents you're talking to the police?' Clarke asked.

'No,' the girl said, and to Frost's eyes she at last resembled the schoolgirl she really was, all the bravado displayed when they first met completely disappearing. 'And I'd rather you didn't mention it should you speak to my stepfather.'

The girl was clearly frightened of Hartley-Jones. Samantha Ellis's mother had mentioned that they didn't get on, but judging by the way Nicola's formidable confidence had begun to crumble as soon as her stepfather was evoked, there was a suggestion that the discord went deeper.

'And your mother?' Clarke asked.

'My mother.' The girl sighed. 'My mother is very fragile. She doesn't sleep well . . . I'd rather you didn't trouble her.'

'Of course,' Frost said, placing a comforting hand on the girl's.

'You seem very upset by the manner of Tom Hardy's death and, if I might add, unsettled by any mention of your stepfather. Is there anything more you can tell us that might help with our investigation?'

The girl looked beseechingly into Frost's eyes. She hesitated, fear tripping her up. 'I . . . I . . . don't get on terribly well with my stepfather.'

'Why's that?' he asked.

'For . . . reasons I'd rather not go into, but . . .' the girl stammered, eyes flitting nervously around the café, finally resting on the empty milkshake glass, before saying in a quiet, shaky voice, 'my stepfather was not happy to discover my cousin Samantha was pregnant.'

The change in her demeanour was not lost on Frost. 'Not happy?' he prompted.

'That's all I can say, Sergeant . . . think of it . . . how you will. Now I must go . . .'

The girl had been intentionally ambiguous. Was it to protect herself? He needed time to think; he'd let her go for now. Although . . . 'One final thing. Tom's sister, Emily, has disappeared. Any idea where she might be?'

'In hiding, I'd imagine.' Nicola Parke slid out of the booth and hurriedly smoothed her pleated skirt. She was clearly extremely anxious to leave.

'Why's that?' Clarke asked.

'She's scared.' The girl looked at Frost intensely. 'Wouldn't you be? Good day, I really must go.'

'One sec!' Frost called, reaching inside his mac pocket. 'This was found in your bedroom.' He slid the diary across the café table. Parke glanced at it but did not pick it up. 'You recognize it?'

The girl nodded. 'Samantha's diary.'

'Yes, but there's not much in it.' He picked up the diary and flicked through it. 'The pages have been ripped out.'

'Maybe she didn't like what she wrote?'

'Then why not throw out the whole diary?' Frost raised his eyebrows. 'There's virtually nothing left.'

'Search me.'

'Don't—' He stopped himself. 'We'll be in touch, Miss Parke.'

And the girl was gone, the café door swinging in her wake.

'Jumped-up little tart,' Clarke said, as they stood in the drizzle outside the café. Clarke was unimpressed with Nicola Parke's patronizing lecture on contemporary feminism. She wouldn't last a day in Eagle Lane, she thought scathingly.

'She certainly has spirit,' Frost said, sparking up in the fine rain. 'But that spirit was soon dampened. And whether it's likely to be evil enough to wreak the mayhem we're dealing with, I'm not so sure.'

'I agree,' Clarke conceded. 'I can't see her lugging bodies through the undergrowth. She's tiny.' Clarke retrieved her own cigarettes. 'And we still have no idea why the body was even left on the golf course . . . Too busy tying ourselves up in knots over *how* it got there without a thought as to *why*.'

'That reminds me.' Frost turned to face her. 'Have you still got that Ordnance Survey map?'

'In the car. Why?'

'Father Lowe at St Jude's put me in touch with this bloke Hollis who wrote a book I borrowed. He's something of an expert on local folklore. He says it's thought there used to be an ancient chapel sited on that new part of the golf course. The chapel was built on ley lines. Apparently there was an article about it in the press last year, when planning permission was granted for the work to the golf course.'

'Ley lines?'

'Yes, ancient, invisible "pathways", for want of a better word. These pathways are imbued with supernatural properties – magic energy, and what have you. Think of Stonehenge and druids. It may be a load of old cobblers to you and me, but it's possible that at the ninth hole of the new Denton Golf Club, two such lines cross.' Frost looked at her, the bemusement she felt mirrored in his face. 'Apparently, the point at which ley lines intersect has special significance – a convergence of energy, if you will. Many pagan sites or monuments are built at such points.'

'Bloody hell,' Clarke breathed.

'I know, I'm having trouble with it myself. But we don't have to believe there's anything in it, we just have to accept that others may. I have the map coordinates written down some-where . . .'

'And so the burial ground in the woods itself is not so import-ant, but this site, now a golf course, is?'

'Seems so,' Frost said, his hair now matted with rain. 'If a sacrifice was carried out then it's likely this would be the spot.'

'But our girls were playing by the tumulus – the candle wax corroborates this.'

'I know. Something doesn't add up.' Frost stared at the station as another trainload made their way out into the wet Denton streets, joining the Saturday-morning shopping crowd. A week ago today Samantha Ellis went to London never to return to Denton alive, Clarke thought.

'Did you see how the girl lost her pluck at the mention of her stepfather?' Frost said suddenly. 'She looked almost petrified. I thought it odd. You'd expect a girl in her position to be scared – two dead friends, and one missing – but she held it together perfectly until her stepfather was mentioned. She was trying to help, I could sense it. But she was too frightened.'

'I did think she seemed a bit jittery . . . and what was all that about Ellis's pregnancy?'

'I think I've worked it out,' Frost said gravely. 'Maybe Michael Hartley-Jones was sleeping with his niece.'

Clarke turned to him in surprise. 'You think so?'

'Well, what else do you think she was trying to say?'

Clarke cupped her hands over a cigarette, shielding it from the rain as Frost fumbled with his Zippo. He continued, 'And I don't think it stops there. Samantha Ellis was dating Tom Hardy. If she really was involved with Hartley-Jones, then maybe *he* killed the boy. Out of perverse jealousy, or something. And maybe he did it in a way that would throw suspicion on his stepdaughter and the rest of her friends in a "let that be a lesson to you all" type of way. Remember how little Nicola froze when she learned the manner of Hardy's murder?'

Clarke was wide-eyed.

'Think about it, how the Five Bells would be seen by the outside world, the same way we saw them; as a cult dabbling with witchcraft who had carried out some ritual sacrifice. Perceptions can be dangerously misleading . . .'

Clarke nodded. 'But Jack, you're forgetting that the Hartley-Joneses weren't in Denton when Tom Hardy was killed. They were a 100 miles away on the South Coast.'

'A technicality.' He shrugged. 'Come on.' He tapped her on the behind. 'I have a plan, but let's get out of the rain first.' They made for the car.

Saturday (2)

Frost didn't have to wait long. He flicked his cigarette end out on to the pavement, wound the Cortina window up rapidly, and slid down into the seat. They were parked within sight of number 7 Forest View. He had banked on Michael Hartley-Jones leaving the house at some point – he wasn't the stay-at-home type.

Now he watched the man shut the door behind him and stride towards the dark-green Land-Rover on the drive. Wonder where you're off to, chum, thought Frost. To calm your nerves by blasting a few pheasants out of the sky? Hartley-Jones was in a Barbour, flat cap and wellies, and he had what Frost took to be a shotgun in a case under his arm. Clarke could confirm that later. She was stationed around the corner on the main road, Union Street, ready to follow in the unmarked Escort. Frost wanted to keep tabs on Hartley-Jones; he thought he might do a bunk if things got too much. He had to play it carefully, until he had a case against the man bang to rights; the last thing he wanted was him blabbing to Mullett, and the super going off on one again.

The energy boost he'd derived from the morning's freshen-up at Clarke's and the subsequent lead from interviewing the Parke girl had started to fade. Even so, sitting behind the wheel of the car, he still felt perky. Perky and together enough to allow his domestic situation a moment's thought. He'd not been in touch with his mother-in-law or wife since Wednesday night. It wasn't that he'd forgotten, or hadn't been concerned, it was just that he was never near a phone when he had a moment. There again, this morning at Clarke's, had he given it a moment's thought? The shameful answer, he realized, was no. A sharp twinge of guilt pushed that thought aside. Once he was done here, there was a call box on the Bath Road.

He looked at his watch. 12.15. He'd give it another few minutes, just to be sure Hartley-Jones had gone, and so as not to arouse suspicion. He now felt convinced that Hartley-Jones was the killer, and that he must have come back from the spot where the couple were allegedly staying over the bank holiday and murdered the boy. He'd find out through the wife. Frost didn't think her complicit, but thought she might unwittingly give her husband away. Forensics had discovered a wealth of prescriptions for sleeping pills and valium made out for Vera Hartley-Jones, corroborating her daughter's story that the woman had trouble sleeping, but would Hartley-Jones really have had time to perpetrate such a complex murder? How long did it take to rip a boy open? Ten minutes? But what about the body? Did he drop off the remains in a dustbin and hammer it back down to the South Coast? If the boy was killed on Friday, how come the body wasn't discovered until Wednesday? Frost got out of the Cortina. The course hadn't been open and the boy wasn't discovered until the groundsman did his final sweep.

'Afternoon, Mrs Hartley-Jones.' Frost smiled from the doorstep.

'My husband is not in,' was the nervous reply. Frost couldn't quite equate this timid creature to one of the rebellious original Five Bells.

'Not to worry,' he replied gently. 'It was you I really wanted to see. I just wanted to put your mind at rest. May I?' He moved to cross the threshold.

'Oh, I suppose so.' She stepped aside to let him through. 'Cup of tea?'

'Lovely. Nicola about?'

'No, she's out too, I'm afraid.' Frost pulled out a stool from the breakfast bar while Vera Hartley-Jones flicked the kettle on. 'She'd barely got back before she rushed out again. Gone to catch up with friends. All this business is terrible for the youngsters.' The woman was visibly uncomfortable and unsure of what to do with herself.

'Yes, it must have been a trying time for you all,' Frost said, as though picking up the thread of a proper conversation. 'There you were, looking forward to a nice weekend away, and no sooner have you gone than all this happens.' He raised his hands as if a minor inconvenience had occurred, such as the weather breaking, and not two dead teenagers.

'Yes.' She sighed, pouring the tea. 'It seems an age ago, but it was only just over a week ago that Michael was picking the car up from the garage ready for our trip, and I felt so happy at the prospect of going away.'

'What was wrong with the car?' said Frost casually, biting into a chocolate digestive.

'Oh, nothing. Michael always insists on getting the car serviced before any long drive. I haven't driven in years.' She smiled wanly. 'Michael charges about in the Land-Rover most of the time, for shoots and so forth. The Audi only comes out for special occasions.'

'Oh, really? So you've not used it much since the trip to the coast, then?' Frost slurped on his tea.

'We haven't used it at all.'

'Really? That reminds me, I need to get my old rust-bucket serviced. Where does Michael go?'

'Why, the Eagle Lane Garage, next door to your police station.'

Frost had him; the odometer on the car would provide the answer. The garage would have a record of the mileage from the recent service; if the miles clocked up since then were significantly more than Denton to Poole and back, then Hartley-Jones would have some serious explaining to do. Frost would have to move quickly and impound the Audi; who knows what else they might find in the vehicle.

'So, let me just run through your trip once more. You left on Friday afternoon for the South Coast. Where was it exactly?'

'We didn't go directly to Poole, we stopped at the Trust House Forte hotel, just outside Reading, to visit my brother, Norris. He's been ever so poorly.'

Frost pulled out his notebook and pen. 'Reading? Nice this time of year. And not too far away.' Everything was slotting into place. Reading was certainly feasible as far as a furtive trip home was concerned. One thing remained a mystery, though.

'One final question if I may, Mrs Hartley-Jones. My colleague DS Waters was convinced you had a number of large candles on the premises. They seem to have vanished. I was curious about what you used them for.'

'They're altar candles,' she said, sipping her tea. 'I'm on the church committee and the vicar lets me have a few every year when we go away.'

'I'm sorry, I don't follow. When you go away?'

'The caravan site in Poole has very unpredictable electricity. The big church ones last for ages. Michael puts them in the boot of the car, and if we don't use them I bring them back and return them to the church.'

Bingo, thought Frost. That explained the wax on Hardy's face. He didn't get it from a bizarre satanic ritual in the woods; Hartley-Jones had the body in the boot of the car, where it must have come into contact with the candles. It also explained why the SOCOs couldn't find them on their subsequent visit. She'd taken them back to the church.

Superintendent Mullett thoughtfully sipped his coffee on the patio. What a week, he mused. Although it was just after midday he still had the residue of a hangover from the previous evening's gala dinner. Eyeing his wife through the kitchen window a sense of normality returned to him; he smiled weakly at her before noticing she was mouthing the word 'phone'.

Closing the door to his study he picked up the telephone receiver lying on the mahogany desk. 'Mullett here.'

'Sir, I have him.' It was Frost.

'You have *who*?'

'Michael Hartley-Jones for the murder of Tom Hardy.'

Mullett stared intensely at the aquarium before him, the words not registering. 'I'm sorry, what did you say?'

'Hartley-Jones is the killer—'

'Are you mad? Michael was on the South Coast. What about the girls? Witchcraft and so forth?'

'No, that's what we were meant to think, that it was all the kids. But it was Hartley-Jones. I can prove it with the mileage on the car.'

Mullett's head was reeling. Deep down he had had an uneasy feeling all along, but nothing he could quite put his finger on. If this was serious, he needed to distance himself from his erstwhile friend as soon as possible.

'I'm on my way in. Don't do a thing until I get there.'

*   *   *

'What did he say?' Clarke asked.

'Mr Mullett is on his way in.' Frost frowned and scratched the back of his head.

That wasn't good, she thought. 'On a Saturday? Sounds like you've filled him with confidence, then . . .'

'Sod this,' Frost said, exasperated, chucking down his pen. 'Why do we have to wait? Let's nick Hartley-Jones now. I'll ring the *Echo* and tell Sandy . . .'

'The *Echo*? Can't you wait five minutes, Jack? The super will be here in five minutes. What exactly did he say?' She knew Frost was banking on Emily Hardy reappearing as soon as an arrest for her brother's killer was announced, but she sensed panic creeping in, which meant he wasn't so sure the girl was in hiding; rather, he was afraid she was in danger.

'He didn't say much.' Frost flicked through the Rolodex. 'Every minute counts for the Hardys. Every second that little girl goes unaccounted for . . .'

'What *did* Mullett say, Jack?' Clarke persisted, her finger on the telephone cradle.

'Do nothing.' Frost sighed.

'If Emily Hardy is safe, a couple of minutes won't make any difference.' She tried to pacify him, but his doubts were infectious.

'I doubt the girl's mother would appreciate you saying that. What if she's sleeping rough? Anything could be happening to her.' Frost reached for his cigarettes, and turned his full attention to Clarke. Until this moment he'd barely registered it was her in front of him. 'Now, tell me, where did Mr Hartley-Jones go in his Land-Rover? Some farm out near Rimmington or Two Bridges, no doubt, for a spot of shooting.'

'Not as far as that. He parked in the overflow car park used on match days at the bottom of Foundling Street.'

'Can't imagine there's much to shoot down there, except perhaps the odd footballer.' He shrugged. 'After the season they've been having, though, it might be an idea to have a few pot-shots at the back four. Wake them up a bit.'

'What do you mean?' Clarke asked. 'Shoot what? He was off to the game. Denton are at home today.'

'Not a chance,' Frost said, sharply. 'Not his scene at all. Besides, he's dressed up to go decimating the wildlife. Wellies, Barbour and twelve-gauge.'

'Sounds like a different man altogether,' Clarke said. 'He was wearing a denim jacket, footy scarf and trainers when I saw him get out of the car.'

'Eh?' Frost stood up from behind the desk. 'Why would he do that? Unless—'

'He was going somewhere he shouldn't . . . or at least where he didn't wish to be seen.' She suddenly realized what had happened. God, she'd messed up.

'Or going to see someone he shouldn't. Someone he's holding captive. Someone who's been missing for the best part of a week. And what better way to lose yourself in a crowd – pretend to the wife you're off with your cronies to bag a few pheasants, kitted out in full shooting garb, then slip off the Barbour and mingle with the hundreds heading for the afternoon match.'

Clarke nodded as it all became clear.

'What else is round there?' Frost asked.

'Nothing much,' Clarke replied. 'Football stadium on one side, and the old mill on the abandoned industrial estate on the other. The canal runs along to the south.'

'Did you see which way he went?'

'There were people everywhere. I was stuck in the car, and I assumed he'd gone to the match. Sorry, Jack.'

'Get on to Control,' Frost said urgently, looking at his watch. 'Get all available area cars down to the old industrial estate and seal off the Piper Road exit. If he's on the estate we can net him – but we'll have to move quickly, before the match is over, or we'll lose him.'

'And if he's not there?' Clarke asked.

'Then he's at the match, although I doubt it, and we'll pick him up at home after a chat with the super. Ah, boys, how did you get on with the Everetts?' Clarke turned to see Simms and Waters behind her. Waters started to speak but Frost cut him off. 'No, tell me en route, we've not got time now. Simms, take Clarke and head for Oildrum Lane off Piper Street, towards the industrial estate. We'll meet you in the middle. She'll fill you in. Go, off!'

Simms looked at Waters in disbelief. 'Is no one interested in . . . ?' But it was too late, Frost was halfway down the corridor.

Saturday (3)

Desk Sergeant Bill Wells looked up from the *Sun*'s racing pages. Only minutes previously Frost and Waters had hurtled out of the front door; now DCs Clarke and Simms followed suit.

Frost had mouthed 'not a word' as he'd hurriedly exited the building, which usually meant 'you've not seen me'. That could indicate only one thing – the divisional commander was expected. Wells shuddered. On a *Saturday*? Most unusual.

From what he could make out from Ridley on Control, a siege was planned on the old industrial estate by the canal. The estate had augured bad tidings for many years now; originally it had been occupied by the cotton mill, which had once been the heart of Denton; this had closed shortly after the Second World War, and since then a number of business ventures had started up on the site. None had lasted. The most recent attempt was to convert the old building itself into flats, but the construction company had gone bust when the recession started to bite last year.

'Wells.'

'Super.' Wells looked up, surprised to have his thoughts actuated so soon, and fumbled to turn the wireless down, although Superintendent Mullett marched straight past the front desk and turned not left towards his own office, but down the corridor towards CID. Wells amused himself by trying to guess how soon it would be before the super returned; he was moving at some pace, so his money was on less than a minute.

'Where on earth is everyone?'

Forty seconds.

'It's Saturday, sir.'

'I know what day of the week it is, Sergeant. Where the hell is Frost? I said I'd be here directly.'

'He left in a bit of a hurry.'

'And where are the rest of them? I thought we were on the verge of a breakthrough?' He appeared exasperated. Wells said nothing. 'How can there be nobody here? And why is the back door wide open?' He paced the lobby, troubled.

'The builders are in, sir,' Wells suggested, 'to sort out the problems with your rear entrance.'

'I beg your pardon?' The station commander stepped up to the desk.

'The back door, sir. It's going to have to come off.'

'This really is the limit,' Mullett huffed. 'Get me Frost, immediately. In the meantime I shall deal with the tradesmen.'

Wells wondered whether he ought to tell him that they had the housebreaking suspect, Everett, in the cells. Surely that would lift his spirits? It was too late, though. Mullett had already stormed off back down the corridor to the rear of the building.

As he reached for the telephone, which had been mercifully quiet all morning, it rang.

'Sergeant Wells.'

'Speaking.'

'It's Miller. PC Miller. Is Sergeant Frost about? I meant to call him earlier but I was desperate for a kip.'

'He's out on a call,' Wells said, 'but no doubt he'll be back later today.'

'Let him know I called, will you?'

What would Jack want with that reprobate Miller? Terrible attitude, that lad. Then he remembered Miller had been seconded on surveillance duty in the centre of Denton . . .

The roar of the crowd carried on the breeze from the stadium half a mile away and reached the two men who were standing in front of a chicken-wire gate. Waters clocked a shabby BEWARE OF THE DOG sign hanging off the fencing. He doubted there was still a security guard in place.

'What's the plan?' Waters asked, regarding Frost dubiously.

'There isn't one,' Frost said nonchalantly. 'I'll go and poke around inside while you wait here.'

'Wouldn't it be better if we both went in?'

'Nah, I need you here to keep a look-out. And to keep in contact with Simms and Clarke on Oildrum Lane.' He reached inside the car's glove box. 'We can keep in touch with these.'

'Christ, where'd you get those, the War Museum?' Waters said, wiping what could best be described as 'matter' off a walkie-talkie. 'Wouldn't we be better off with a plastic cup and a bit of string?'

'Maybe,' Frost said, frowning and thumping his handset on the roof of the car. It burst into life. 'There, you see, it works. Seen better days, I'll grant you . . . Go easy on the batteries, they may be low on juice, so we'll keep usage down to a minimum.'

'If you're sure.'

'Of course I'm sure. Look, somebody's helpfully left the gate open.' He nudged it and it gave easily. Behind it was a cluster of vacant Portakabins, and beyond that the towering, derelict cotton mill.

'OK, well, keep it on. And give me a shout in five minutes,' Waters said reluctantly. He didn't feel happy about this. Frost looked dog-tired, and although he was an experienced officer and an intelligent guy, Waters couldn't help but feel concerned for him. 'Are you sure it's safe in there? I mean, the structure and that . . .'

But Frost was already halfway across the concrete wasteland.

Simms twiddled with the car radio.

'I checked with Control. We should be able to pick up Frost's frequency,' he said reassuringly.

Clarke was standing outside the car, peering through binoculars; at what, she wasn't sure. It was an old Victorian building with not a sign of life. A panda car pulled up beside them. It all seemed a bit excessive, and surely if Hartley-Jones caught sight of uniform he'd panic? And then what?

'Sorted,' Simms said, leaning out of the Escort. 'Waters says Frost has just gone in.'

'Good,' she said, uncertainly.

Simms got out and stood next to her. 'Don't worry, I'm sure he'll be fine,' he said, unconvincingly. 'You're as jittery as Waters.' He lit a cigarette. 'Hartley-Jones isn't armed, is he? I know Frost saw him leave with a shotgun, but he wasn't carrying anything when you saw him park up, was he?'

Clarke felt a rasp of panic in her throat. She wasn't sure. Having seen Hartley-Jones leave his vehicle she'd assumed he'd gone to the match and hadn't paid attention to what, if anything, he was carrying. It was only when she'd arrived back at the station and the possibility arose that he probably wasn't heading anywhere near the match that she'd realized her slip-up.

'What's up? You don't look sure.' He frowned at her.

'I don't know.' She turned to look at Simms. 'I don't know whether he was armed or not – I can't be certain . . .'

'Jesus Christ.' Simms dived back in the car for the radio handset.

Clarke scoured the building again with the binoculars. It wasn't her fault, she told herself. Hartley-Jones may well have a concealed weapon on him anyway; he was suspected of murder after all! Bloody Jack, always charging off without thinking . . .

Frost looked up. The timber ceiling creaked again. Somebody was moving around on the next level. The floorboards groaned repeatedly in the same place, indicating that someone was pacing back and forth overhead. He switched off the walkie-talkie and retraced his steps to the front entrance of the mill where the main staircase was situated.

Once he'd reached the first floor he made his way gingerly across the atrium, careful to avoid the plentiful debris of Coke cans, campfire remains and loose masonry. One wrong step could alert his quarry to his presence. Directly in front of him were rows of industrial skeletons, machinery that over the years had gradually been stripped bare. To the left were the overseers' offices. A sudden noise that sounded like a chair being scraped or dragged came from within one of them. All were glass-fronted, except, from what Frost could make out, the centre one, which was panelled, and he could see that they were linked by adjoining doors. As carefully as he could, he edged towards the office next to the panelled one.

As he drew closer he heard voices – no, *a* voice, a deep, mellifluous voice. Frost stood motionless outside the door, barely breathing, listening intently.

'I'm afraid, my flower, there's no time. No time left for us at all.'

Frost collected his thoughts. He stood pressed to the door that led to the panelled office, gripping the handle. He had no doubt that it was Michael Hartley-Jones waxing lyrical on the other side.

'We will never bloom.'

Suicide: is he talking about suicide? Frost decided he had no choice. He gently opened the door.

'Damn.' Waters tossed the radio on to the passenger seat. Simms had just told him that Hartley-Jones might be armed. Of course he might be armed. He tried the walkie-talkie. Nothing, which was fair enough, really. If Frost was creeping around in there, he would hardly want that antique relic crackling away. I should have insisted on going in with him, he thought. He gazed at the building. Dark clouds had moved in from the south, giving the Victorian edifice an air of foreboding. 'Damn,' he repeated, slamming the car door shut and making for the mill.

He hadn't seen which entrance Frost had chosen. The grand front vestibule struck Waters as too open; he reckoned the rear was the safer option. A side door was open. He entered and stood stock-still for a moment, assessing his surroundings. The building was silent. He quickly ascertained that nothing was happening on the vast, open-plan ground floor and stealthily made his way up to the first floor by the back stairs.

As Frost entered, Hartley-Jones looked up, startled. He stood behind a chair, to which was tied a girl of about fourteen. She was gagged and very distressed.

'Afternoon,' Frost said with half a smile.

'Ah, the tenacious Inspector Frost,' remarked Hartley-Jones with uncanny composure, strikingly at odds with the words Frost had heard through the door.

'Detective Sergeant,' Frost corrected. 'The rank of inspector as yet eludes me.'

'I'm sure it's only a matter of time, *Jack*; Mullett is forever apologizing for your . . . how should one put it . . . ?' Hartley-Jones placed the tip of what Frost took to be a fisherman's knife quizzically on his chin. '. . . pig-headed blundering?' He smiled.

'To the extent that he's worried he might just have to promote you. Stanley, bless him – you should have seen his face on the golf course when the boy was discovered. My, it was worth it for that alone!'

'So, you admit killing poor Tom Hardy?'

Frost then spotted the 12-gauge standing prominently in the corner of the room. Hartley-Jones noticed Frost's gaze, but continued, 'And we don't want that, do we?' He flicked the knife between thumb and index finger, upending it so the point rested on the girl's cranium.

Frost couldn't look at the girl; he knew the terror in her eyes would distract him. 'I think that unlikely, Mr Hartley-Jones. Or can I call you Michael?'

'Mr Hartley-Jones to you. Familiarity from the working classes is not something I like to encourage.' He sighed. 'But I'm glad you've turned up. A change of plan has come to mind. There was I growing maudlin, feeling troubled that things just . . . weren't going my way.' He looked at Frost for corroboration. 'But then you – shabby, unconventional Jack Frost – blunder in. And suddenly things aren't looking so bad.' Hartley-Jones straightened himself and stood erect, without releasing the pressure on the knife.

'Not going so bad? You're in it up to your neck. I know all about what you've been up to. You treated Emily here and her friends like your own personal harem. A bunch of schoolgirls! You got one of them pregnant, you bloody pervert.'

Hartley-Jones convulsed with laughter. 'Idiot! You don't understand it at all. The girls and I had such a precious bond. They worshipped me! Little Gail and Sarah, lovely Emily here, naughty Samantha . . . even Nicola, until she began to get wilful. And then Samantha started *screwing* Tom Hardy.' Emily winced. 'That's when it really fell apart. It was *he* who impregnated her, the filthy little piece of scum! Not me.'

'Well, it's all over now,' said Frost, 'and there's nothing to be gained from terrorizing young Emily, so why don't you pack away the knife and come quietly.'

'Oh I don't think so.' Hartley-Jones smiled. 'Everything that's been said will stay between these four walls. Precious Emily here would never breathe a word.' He stroked the quivering girl's chin. 'So now, Detective Frost, you have a choice.'

'A choice?' Frost felt for his cigarettes. As he did so he caught sight of the handle of the door to the next office, behind Hartley-Jones, slowly moving downwards.

'Yes. You or the girl. You see, *you're* the problem, aren't you? You disappear, and we can all carry on as before. Myself, Gail, Sarah, little Emily here . . .'

'Nothing's as it was before! Emily knows you sadistically murdered her brother. And the motive is even more twisted than we thought. The poor hapless lad was a goner the second he asked her out. You couldn't stand one of your girls being touched by anyone but yourself . . . sick bastard.' Frost was having difficulty maintaining his composure. He was fighting every instinct to rush the man and send him tumbling to the ground.

'Very good, Sergeant. Too good. And that's why you must sacrifice yourself now.'

'Yes, sacrifice, a pertinent choice of word. Exactly how you wanted the Hardy boy's murder to appear – as a ritualistic killing that could implicate your stepdaughter and her friends; the so-called School of the Five Bells. No one would suspect you, not even your stepdaughter. Tom Hardy arrived at your house on Friday night, came in, unusually, and like a well brought-up boy took off his shoes. You knew he was likely to escort Samantha there. You waited for him to leave and offered him a lift. Then you killed him. Heaven knows why you had to go so far. Wouldn't a stern warning have been enough?'

'Ahh, Sergeant, you still haven't grasped the dynamics of the situation. The girls seem to think they don't need their Uncle

Michael quite so much now they're growing older. But what if the outside world believed them all to be evil, sadistic witches and they were ostracized by society, and I alone understood their predicament? And that is why I took so much trouble. Aside from that, I'm impressed with your detective work. I think Mullett does you a disservice. So how exactly did you find out about the School of the Five Bells?'

'A tattoo. At Samantha's post-mortem.'

'Poor Samantha. Yes, and the other two were on the same train. Now, you can't hold me responsible for that one. I wouldn't have harmed a hair on her head.'

'Then why hurt Emily? Hand her over to me, and we'll do a plea bargain for diminished responsibility – driven insane with jealousy.'

'What sort of fool do you take me for? They'll throw away the key. No, this one here made the mistake of telling Nicola she had read Samantha's diary. You've met Nicola, have you? A fiery one that one. She's innocent, though. She tried to warn me. The diary had things in it one would rather didn't get out. And as you knew about the Five Bells it would only be a matter of time until you got to Emily, having already hauled the other two in. If only Samantha hadn't been such a loose cannon, I could have kept it all under control without it coming to this. Come, Mr Frost, time marches on. What's it to be?'

'The agony of choice.' Frost played with a cigarette but couldn't light it – he feared the girl might choke, as she seemed to be having trouble breathing through the gag. 'But the building is surrounded. You'll never get away with it.'

'Very funny,' Hartley-Jones snorted. 'You've never worked with anyone in your career. You're a loner. A maverick. Mullett told me that too. But the problem with being alone is that there's nobody to look out for you when you overstep the mark. No, Mr Frost, I'd like to be out of here by full-time. Your decision, please? Suicide? The maverick detective ends it all; a failing marriage proved too much? Yes, I know about that too. The story would be wholly convincing, I'm sure you'll agree. "He took his own life, with a shotgun in a disused warehouse."'

'How do I know you'll let her live?'

'You don't. But you have no alternative. Turn round, please, face the corner.' Frost turned round and took a pace forward. Hartley-Jones followed him. Frost felt sure he could overpower the bigger man as long as he got the right hold. He braced himself ready to turn and pounce. The question was, where was the knife? As the killer moved in behind him, near enough for Frost to smell his cologne, and the cold steel barrel of the shotgun was held against his neck, there was a sudden creak as the door in the opposite corner flew open. The gun was swiftly retracted. Frost spun round to grab the man's arm and caught a familiar face rushing in.

Clarke distinctly heard the blast. As the pigeons rose in a cloud of alarm from the roof of the building, her heart almost stopped.

'Shotgun,' Simms said flatly across the roof of the Escort. The constable from the area car was at Clarke's side. 'Gunfire, ma'am.' He stood awaiting instructions.

Saturday (4)

'He's dead, sir,' said Frost in a matter-of-fact tone.

'Dead?' Mullett said, amazed. 'Well, I'm staggered. How?'

'He took his own life.' Frost paused. 'Well, sort of.'

'*Sort of?* Can you be more specific?' Mullett fiddled nervously with the ivory letter opener.

'There was a tussle, and Mr Hartley-Jones shot himself in the chest. I think his original plan *was* to shoot himself, but when I turned up he thought he might be able to go on living if I were out of the way.' Frost gestured his innocence. 'And I may well have been, if it wasn't for DS Waters here.'

'Well, what a relief,' Mullett said, not really sure what he meant. He scrutinized Waters, who sat looking comfortably unruffled. Frost himself looked positively spruce and betrayed no signs of having recently wrestled for his life. He got up, moved to the window and tweaked the blinds. It was probably for the best, he mused. No awkward questions on his close association with a murderer to answer. Who'd have thought it; he'd known Michael Hartley-Jones for twenty years or more.

Mrs M had always thought him odd and prone to depression, but a murderer? Heavens, this really didn't bear close scrutiny. Best buried and forgotten. 'And the girl?' Mullett finally asked.

'Fine, if a little traumatized.'

'Hmm . . .'

'The girl, Emily, had read Samantha Ellis's diary, in which she wrote about Hartley-Jones and falling pregnant, though she was unsure who the father . . .'

'Jolly good, jolly good, well done. I'll read the rest in your report.' Mullett had more pressing issues. There had been an offer already on his house. 'But in future, be so good as to let me know what your movements are. If I make the effort to come in on a Saturday, at least have the decency to leave a note or tell the desk sergeant.'

Frost was speechless.

'Now, moving on, why do you have my estate agent in the cells?'

'Ah yes. Mr Everett is suspected of . . .'

'Yes, I know. He's involved in some very important business.'

'What . . . selling houses?' Waters said, who'd remained quiet until now.

Mullett ignored him. 'Now, about the question of bail.'

'Bail!' Frost spluttered. 'He's a bloody murderer!'

'Oh, come now, Jack,' Mullett soothed. 'You don't really think he murdered a chimney sweep, do you? He's a regional manager of one of the country's most prestigious estate agents.'

Frost pursed his lips, visibly rattled. 'And members of the golf club don't go around gutting teenage boys and laying them out on the course?'

Only now did it occur to Mullett that Hartley-Jones had been there on Wednesday, proudly witnessing the discovery of his own crime. He gave an involuntary shudder. 'What proof do you have? Circumstantial evidence? OK, so the sweep may have called round at the Everetts', but where's your motive?'

'The times all match. The man was killed on Tuesday afternoon, the same time he visited the Everetts. And the video recorders in the van are the ones that were stolen in the burglaries.'

'Maybe the *sweep* is the thief?'

'Oh, do me a favour!' Frost blustered in disbelief. 'Everett is even allergic to animals, which would explain why he killed the Hartley-Joneses' cat. I don't know how or why he killed the sweep, but, believe me, he did!'

'I spoke to the wife,' Waters said calmly. 'She said there are still birds in the chimney. Jack reckons the sweep was interrupted in his work; maybe he'd just started on the Everetts' chimney and for some reason Everett didn't like it.'

Mullett scratched his moustache irritably.

'So you're saying that Mr Everett returns home, discovers his chimney, is, what, being *violated*? And so he hacks the man to death.' Mullett leaned back in his chair, glaring at Frost, his eyebrows reaching his thinning brow in incredulity.

Frost bolted out of the chair, causing Waters to jump. 'Bleedin' hell, yes, maybe it was exactly that! Perhaps Everett was hiding stuff up there!' He sucked rapidly on a cigarette as though hoping for an appearance on *Record Breakers*.

'What, video recorders?' Mullett scoffed, taken aback by Frost's outburst.

Waters interceded. 'The lady of the house did ask whether the chimney sweep was a thief, having read about the video recorders. She said something was missing.'

'What?' asked Mullett and Frost.

'An antique.'

'What sort of antique?' Frost prompted.

'A salmon gaff,' Waters replied.

'Can estate agents be "prestigious"?' Waters smiled as they stood outside Mullett's office. He'd heard that Frost and Mullett didn't get on, but it had taken until the end of a very long week to appreciate the true level of that misunderstanding. The pair clearly had absolutely no tolerance of each other's opinions. 'I thought they were all a bunch of sharks wheeling around in flash motors.'

'You kept that quiet,' Frost said, 'about the salmon gaff.'

'We hadn't had a moment to talk,' Waters said. 'And anyway, there's no hurry – we have him in a cell.'

'You know what a gaff is, I presume?'

'Not until the lady told me. A poacher's hook.'

'Not dissimilar to a butcher's hook. When inserted into, say, a man's jaw for instance, the wound would be just as fatal.' Frost had a glint in his tired eyes. 'First let's call Regal Estates for a chat with Everett's staff. Then we'll have a word with our pals at Rimmington Division – check out their unsolved house break-ins; Regal has a sister office there.'

Everett sat in the bare interview room with a stoic, silent PC for company. He'd read somewhere that if an officer was present *inside* the room it was an indication that the police thought the detainee a suicide risk. Well, it was an option, but he was no quitter; the odds were upped, yes, but he wasn't done yet. The police were unsure when the van was left at the sauna, but according to the paper, the current theory was that it was dumped on Thursday morning, just before Baskin discovered it. This put Everett out of the picture – he was doing the school run on Thursday morning, as witnessed by dozens of other parents: the perfect alibi.

Of course, he'd actually left the van on Wednesday afternoon, but the sauna had been shut all day and Baskin had taken the afternoon off, so nobody was there to notice it.

The door went, and in came the sandy-haired detective, Mr Frost. He looked fresher than on previous sightings and Everett thought he detected a spring in his step, which was a little unsettling. His tall black sidekick followed him in, shutting the door behind him.

'Cigarette?'

Everett took one from the proffered pack.

'Now, let's work this through,' Frost said, scraping back the chair opposite. 'And,' he continued, fixing Everett with a steely gaze, 'you let me know if we have any of this wrong.'

Everett sat back and listened to a catalogue of robberies that had occurred within the Denton and Rimmington areas over the last two years, all of which were jobs he'd done. It seemed he had been clumsy. The black detective had noticed that the window he'd smashed at Forest View had not been the obvious pane to break, being a stretch from the latch. On another occasion, a cottage window outside Rimmington was the only sign of a forced entry, but it was physically impossible to reach the latch through it. Thus the police had rumbled him; all the broken windows were decoys. Keys were evidently being used. The plods had turned up the fact that all the properties had had a change of ownership within the last two years, and that Regal had handled the sales.

The sandy-haired one, Frost, relayed this information without smugness or arrogance, and said that if Everett had not been mugged, the police would probably have been none the wiser; a fact that he'd rather have not known. It was bloody unfair to be caught out by bad luck and not their detection.

'Our sweep, Ken Smith, was also unlucky,' Frost said. 'His misfortune of being in the wrong place at the wrong time cost him his life. But don't worry, I'm going to do my damnedest to make sure you forgo the best of yours. I've met your sort before; bored with the cushy day job and turning to crime for kicks. It makes me sick.'

Everett swallowed hard and said, 'It wasn't me – I didn't kill him . . . I was at the school on Thursday morning dropping off the kids when the body was discovered.'

The two policemen exchanged glances, causing Everett to feel an involuntary rumbling in the bowels.

'Thursday morning?' Frost said. 'Who cares where you were Thursday morning.'

'But I read in the press . . .'

'You don't want to believe what you read in the press,' Frost said seriously. 'We know you drove across town on Wednesday between three and four in the afternoon.'

Everett started to protest.

'Ahh. Ahh,' Frost cautioned. 'You gave some fictitious appointment to your staff, which sadly for you just doesn't ring true.'

'Why?' Everett said eventually.

'It rained on Wednesday afternoon, the first time it rained in Denton for some days.' After an interval of silence, Frost said, 'You made one fatal mistake.'

Everett looked mystified.

'You left the wipers on. When you turned the engine off, they were halfway across the windscreen.' Frost smiled.

Clarke was glad the BMX gang had been caught. Not for her own sake; the wound she'd sustained on Monday was a distant memory. Frost had given the nod to uniform to pick up four boys, with the understanding that Wakely junior would be treated favourably. It was going to be messy and tiresome to resolve; given the age of the boys, Social Services would be involved, and the case would drag on for months, but at least the streets would be safer.

With the demise of Michael Hartley-Jones, Superintendent Mullett, who'd just left Eagle Lane for the rest of the weekend, no longer had any interest in the robbery cases, so Clarke was unlikely to have to testify. This was a great relief, as what she would have said she had no idea, having failed to recognize her attackers.

The morning had been an eventful one, and she pondered

how she'd left things with Frost. She felt daft sitting around the office on Saturday afternoon – essentially waiting for Jack to finish. Her purse was out on her desk and the strip of the Silk Cut pack with Danny's number was poking out of the top. She'd decided to tear it up.

'Right, that's me done.' Simms stretched back in his chair. 'It's been a week and a half, this one. What you up to now?' He smiled. 'Fancy a beer?'

Despite being at a loose end she felt reluctant to join him. 'Got a few things to do.'

'OK, well, I'm meeting some friends in the Bull. Nice beer garden. Perfect afternoon for it.' She feigned a smile; the Bull was rough, and not her pub of choice. He got up to go. He really wasn't a bad lad. 'Well, if you have a change of heart, you know where I am.' Was he hitting on her? Kim Myles told her he'd just dumped Liz Smith, Mullett's secretary, as soon as he found out she was Martin Wakely's cousin.

'Yeah, OK, maybe. See ya.'

'Aha.' Frost entered the room, patting Simms on the shoulder as he left. He looked pleased with himself. 'Got him sussed.' He grinned.

'Well done,' Clarke said. 'I wish we could say the same for that pervert this morning.'

'How do you mean?' He flopped down opposite her in Simms's chair and bashed the fan on.

'Well, do any of us have *him* sussed? What sort of man seduces teenage girls and disembowels their boyfriends?'

'Well, clearly, mates of Hornrim Harry,' Frost surmised.

'Jack, it really isn't a joking matter. I mean, why go to all that trouble? And what did he do with the boy's heart? Did he kill him out of revenge for getting the Ellis girl pregnant, or was he a psychopath?'

'He was crazy, that's all we can be sure of. Who can tell what was going on in his mind? I guess the inspiration for the witch-craft thing came from his wife and her daughter. He clearly meant to implicate the girls, but what he hoped to achieve by that was anyone's guess. Maybe scare them into submission? He obviously hated the fact they were growing up and he was losing his power over them. They started to realize they could stand up against this filthy pervert and were turning against him, and the revival of the School of the Five Bells was their weapon.'

'Weapon?' said Clarke. 'How do you mean?'

'Their little secret society united them, which gave them strength, and excluded everyone else – specifically men. Well, is it any wonder they hated men, with the likes of him pawing them? Unfortunately, he jumped at the chance to teach them a lesson. All he needed was for the good folks of Denton to believe that a bunch of feisty girls with a grievance against men were in actual fact a gang of evil, murderous witches. Not so difficult, as it turned out.'

'And Samantha Ellis?'

'That we'll never know for sure. Probably suicide: I don't think we can pin it on her friends just because they lied to us. I accept they may have been frightened. Maybe Ellis *did* go to London on her own. She probably wasn't in the mood for pop concerts.'

A thought flashed through Clarke's mind that perhaps the girl had gone to London to try and get an abortion. Why did she think that? Was it because she herself was now a week late? The hair on the back of her neck suddenly prickled. No, surely not, she must have miscalculated.

'Hey, what's the matter?' Frost said. 'You've suddenly gone very pale.'

'No, no, nothing, everything's fine. What are you doing now?'

'Waiting for John to get back from Denton General. He's up there with poor Mrs Hartley-Jones, thoughtful young man that he is. That reminds me, I must check the original Five Bells file . . .'

The words 'What about this morning, does it mean anything?' were on Clarke's lips, but instead she looked out of the window and thought what a beautiful day, I want some of that. She pulled out her hair clips, shaking her hair free, chucked her purse in her bag, and left the office for the Bull.

'Come on, let's clear off and have a pint. I've had enough for one week. Just need to make one final call.' Frost closed the tatty file from 1962. He hadn't really taken anything in, his mind was on Sue Clarke, the way she had gaily skipped off half an hour ago, full of life. He shouldn't have gone round to her place this morning. Or should he? He didn't really know. Tiredness gnawed at his every bone. He had to call his mother-in-law, Beryl Simpson. Time to put his foot down – Mary was coming home. He reached for the receiver.

'Miller's here. He wanted to explain things,' Waters said, rousing him from his reverie. Frost pulled back from the phone and on to the pack of Rothmans.

'Oh, spoke to you, did he? What did he have to say for himself?'

'He apologized profusely. He said it was pure jealousy, nothing to do with race. He reckons he's had a crush on Kim for years. They were at Hendon together.'

'She is a cracker, all right,' Frost admitted, yawning.

'He's waiting outside.'

'Sergeant Frost.' PC Miller nodded. Frost didn't recognize Miller out of uniform. The constable removed his cheap shades to reveal tired, puffy eyes.

'Yes, son?' The man looked nervously over his shoulder at Waters, who stood behind him. 'You've nothing to fear from DS Waters now, have you?'

Miller shifted uneasily on his feet. 'The stake-out. You had me watching the Pink Toothbrush.'

Frost rubbed his weary eyes; the shampoo he'd been made to use this morning had irritated them. He never used the stuff usually. 'Yes, yes, *and*? Unsavoury goings-on as Hornrim Harry wished for?'

'Yeah, there was that, all right, as the superintendent anticipated but—'

'Really? Good work, son. You put it all down in a report and we can present it to Hornrim Harry on Monday. It's been a week and a half, this one.' He yawned, patted Miller on the shoulder and made to leave. 'And now it's time for a pint.' He smiled at Waters.

'Wait a second,' Miller said. 'It's not so much what happened at the Toothbrush. More a question of *who* . . .' His eyes darted nervously between Frost and Waters.

Frost's interest was aroused. 'Sit down, I'm all ears. Sergeant Waters, push the door to.'

Miller pulled up a chair, and lit a cigarette.

'Well,' he said fixing Frost with a look, 'unless I'm very much mistaken, I saw Assistant Chief Constable Winslow leave the Toothbrush with a young lady in his Granada.'

'Bleedin' hell,' Frost exclaimed softly, rocking back on his chair. 'How sure are you?'

'It was him, all right,' Miller said confidently.

'Right, this is going to need some careful handling. You get yourself down the boozer with John – kiss and make up, buy him a beer, settle up for the tyres, and then some. Understood?'

Miller nodded and got up. Waters held the door, allowing Miller out first, then said to Frost, 'Don't be long, Jack. You could do with one yourself.'

Frost waved him out, and pulled out his pocket diary. He wasn't convinced by Miller, but that could wait . . . What on earth was Winslow doing? Frost had nothing against the ACC;

he seldom came into contact with him, and thought him pleasant enough when he did. Frost's old partner DI Williams had always rated him, and had said Winslow had respect for Frost and it was Mullett who stood in the way of his promotion. And what would Superintendent Mullett have to say? This could be interesting. Frost laughed to himself, thumbing the diary for his in-laws' number, not for the first time today.

The Simpsons' phone rang half a dozen times, before a male voice answered.

'George, it's William,' Frost said to Mary's father. He thought this was odd – the old man never usually answered the phone.

'William, we wondered when you might call,' Simpson said, allowing the rebuke to hang in the air between them.

Frost swallowed hard. Something was wrong.

'George, I'm after Mary – I want her to come home . . .' Although he realized as the words left his lips it was too late.

'Mary's very ill, William.' The voice at the other end was quivering. 'It's cancer . . .'

The week flashed before him in an instant – lying to Sue Clarke that Mary was ill; Mary asleep in the chair; the pain – not tiredness – in Beryl Simpson's eyes; this morning, lying with Sue . . .

'How long?' Frost forced the words out. He felt his head begin to spin.

'Six months. They've given Mary six months to live.'

Acknowledgements

Thanks to Sarah Adams, Sarah Neal, John Gurbutt, Elisabeth Merriman, Kate Samano, Bill Scott-Kerr, Phil Patterson.

James Henry is the pen name of James Gurbutt, who has long been a fan of the original R. D. Wingfield books and the subsequent TV series. He worked for several years as an accountant before moving into publishing at Random House. In 2009 he set up Corsair, a literary imprint for Constable & Robinson, Wingfield's original publisher. He lives in Essex.

After a successful career writing for radio, R. D. Wingfield turned his attention to fiction, creating the character Jack Frost. He published six novels featuring Frost. The series has been adapted for television as the perennially popular *A Touch of Frost*, starring David Jason. R. D. Wingfield died in 2007.

'James Henry has captured my father's style superbly. Fans and newcomers alike will not be disappointed.'

Philip Wingfield, son of the late R. D. Wingfield